2084

THE END OF DAYS

DEREK BEAUGARDE

Corkerhill Press

Published in 2016 by Corkerhill Press

ISBN Paperback: 978-0-9935551-0-7
ebook: 978-0-9935551-1-4

A CIP catalogue copy of this book can be found in the British Library and the National Library of Scotland.

Published with the help of Indie Authors World

ACKNOWLEDGEMENTS

The author wishes to acknowledge the assistance of Indie Authors World in the publishing of this book. The author also wishes to thank his editor Gillian McGee for her ardent endeavours, friends John Steele and Robin Dale for the inclusion of their names within the book, fellow alumni Sir Dirk Bogarde for the pseudonym and Allan Glen's School for the superb education. The author wishes to ascertain that this is a work of fiction and that any relation to any persons living or dead is purely coincidental.

*'Then they gathered the kings together to the place
that in Hebrew is called Armageddon'*
Revelation 16:16 (New International Version © 2010)

BOOK 1 - GENESIS

CHAPTER 1

Earthdate 13:35 Wednesday January 1, 2081 Central Standard Time - CST

In the beginning it was just about the sex. But now, out here in the dark silence of space, there are times when a man gets to thinking really clear. As Jack sat alone before his flickering monitors he felt the wave of love for Peggy Sue as sharp as a winter's day in the Blue Ridge Mountains after a fresh fall of snow. The crackle abruptly broke his pleasant musings.

"Mars Galactica 3, this is Houston calling, do you copy?"

The operator at NASA HQ waited through the obligatory moments of radio silence as his voice winged its way across the solar system to the small United Nations Joint Space Station orbiting 26 miles above the surface of Mars. He heard the distinctive return crackle then the reply came back with remarkable clarity through the Earth 2 Mars Satellite Network, known as the E2MSN.

"Houston this is MGal3 calling. Ah'm reading you loud and clear. Izzat you Lex, ya washed-up radio ham? Happy New Year, ya old fart. It's Jack Crossan here, copy?"

As he waited for the reply from Lex Kosloff back down on Earth, Commander John "Jack" Crossan rubbed the dirty stubble on his chin and glanced out of the porthole to his right just as the first glint of the far distant sun rose on the Martian horizon. It always looked so much smaller than the big yellow-red sun which rose on a lovely bright Earth morning. Jack's tour of duty on MGal3 was coming to an end. In four months he would be back on his beautiful and peaceful farm just outside Lexington, Virginia with his loving second wife Peggy Sue and their two young sons Milner and Jack Junior. He was subconsciously smacking his lips at the thought of making love with Peggy Sue and breathing in the fresh farm air, when Lex broke in over the radio waves.

"A Happy New Year to you, too, Jack. I ain't touched a drop of the good stuff yet, but I'm going to have a blowout when I get home tonight. What's your daily status report MGal3, copy?"

Again, after the long pause Jack replied.

"Same old same old, Lex, nothing much changes up here above Mars. Had a minor glitch with the mainframe computer about ten hours ago but the tech boys down in the bowels managed to sort it PDQ. Seemed to think some hacking bastards back on 3R were trying to patch in through the E2MSN. Techs seem to think it was a pretty amateurish effort. Not much else to report. The next 'ice shift' ain't due back up for another 27 hours yet, so things are pretty darn quiet. I'm hitting the sack in about an hour when Xi Xhu Pan comes up on the bridge to relieve me. Do you copy, Lex?"

As Jack waited through the radio silence his thoughts drifted back over his report relayed down to Lex Kosloff. 3R was the common space jargon for planet Earth, because it was the third rock from the Sun. The 'ice shift' was a regular freight space shuttle from the Martian North Pole Base where ice and dry ice was continually 'mined' to provide the precious water and carbon dioxide needed to maintain the various small Martian bases and the three functioning Martian space stations. They were named MGal2, 3 and 4. Mars Galactica 1, nicknamed Magellan, had been decommissioned in late 2077, although it was still maintaining its orbit above Mars. Magellan was so old it had originally been manufactured from large functional sections of the International Space Station which orbited Earth in the early 21st century. Its last crew just called it the "Rust Bucket".

A few moments later, Lex crackled back over the radio waves, snapping Jack back from his musings.

"Copy you, Jack. I'll let you get off the line and get the head down. Have a good sleep and don't have nightmares - over and out."

Jack was oblivious to the fact that Lex's thoughts had drifted off to a 16-year-old bottle of Lagavulin Scotch whisky. Lex fully intended to celebrate the New Year with the aqua vitae when he got back home to his place out in the south-west suburbs of Houston.

"Okay, Lex. MGal3 here is signing off - over and out."

Jack tapped the button on his touch screen pad and the radio static went dead silent.

*

GENESIS

"Fuck me – we're in!"

"You're kidding?"

Gary Mackintosh stared at the computer screen in front of him with a mixture of awe and total incredulity. He had half believed that he could hack into NASA's mainframe system but the other half of his ego told him that he was just playing at it. After last night's Hogmanay celebrations in the centre of Edinburgh, where Gary and his best mate Ewan Sinclair had really tied it on, he had no idea how he could possibly have managed it in the first place. They had only had about two hours sleep when they had started to hack in about nine o'clock this morning. The idea for the hack had started during their drinking celebrations and had ended up as their New Year Resolution. It had been snowing all day so there was a good incentive to stay in, knock back some fizzy Irn Bru as a hangover cure, and keep on at the hack.

"Ah'm not kidding – we are defin-totally fuckin' in there, man!"

Gary growled just a bit too loudly, reminding himself of that whisky-soaked hangover still there in the recesses of his throbbing skull. He gulped down a soothing throat full of Irn Bru and awaited Ewan's response.

"You don't mean NASA's effing main frame?"

Ewan, unlike his Glaswegian mate, could not bear swearing when speaking. The son of a Wee Free Minister, he had been strictly raised by his parents on the idyllic island of Islay, off Western Scotland. Ewan had gone on to study mathematics, physics and cosmic sciences at Oxford University, ending up with a First and an accent reminiscent of a Highland aristocrat. Gary sounded much more down-to-earth and still retained his guttural Glaswegian accent. He had studied computing science at Glasgow University in his home city and he had also gained a distinguished First.

"Not only NASA, my good friend Ewan – we are also patched right through to the E2MSN!"

"E2MSN – what the hell's that, Gary!?"

"Ah mean the E2MSN no fuckin' less! The Earth to Mars Satellite Network! Fact, the bastards up there on Mars cottoned onto us a right good few hours ago. You were dozing at the time. We were nearly in the back door. But they put a lock on us and patched us back out the system. But they left a side door key lying there right in front of us and at this moment they have no idea that we are connected into the whole fuckin' shebang. NASA HQ – E2MSN – the whole friggin' lot! I'm telling ye Ewan, you want to know anything that is going on in the whole fuckin' solar system it is right there in front of us!"

"Fuck me, Gary!"

Gary's head swivelled round sharply from the computer screen.

"Ewan Sinclair - that's the first time ah've ever heard you swear since ah met ye!"

*

<u>Earthdate 22:41 Tuesday January 21, 2081 Israel Standard Time - IST</u>

A dog-tired Ari Schenkler drained his third cold plastic coffee. He was fighting off sleep as he prepared to make some fine-tuning adjustments to the Nimrod Star Hunter 2 telescope. Ari was sitting at his touch screen keypad in his laboratory office at INSACC, the Israeli National Space Administration and Cosmology Center, in Tel Aviv. The Nimrod SH2 was orbiting in deep solar space almost half way between Earth and Mars and the data from the largest and most powerful telescope ever constructed by man was relayed back to Tel Aviv via the NASA E2MSN system.

Ari was always thankful for that 'special relationship' which had existed with America since the modern State of Israel was founded in 1947. In his view the co-operation between the two countries helped Israel found the ISA, Israeli Space Agency, in 1988. It was mainly limited to small satellite launches and later the development of TAUVEX, Tel Aviv University Ultra-Violet Experiment, in Ari's home city of Tel Aviv. From the experiences gained out of the TAUVEX ultra-violet telescope project and also with Israel's development into manned space missions the ISA expanded in 2039 into INSACC with three main divisions. These were manned-space shuttles serving both Moon and Mars bases, satellite and space station production and their cosmology division, of which, the Nimrod Star Hunter 2 telescope commanded the largest slice of the cosmology budget.

In an effort to keep his mind alert, Ari stole a brief distraction with a glance at his brand new iTab80. It gave him paid access to more than 30 online tabloids from around the globe on a 24/7 basis. His favourite 'Bloid' was the New York Times and his iTab80 was presently set on the continuously updating NYT front page. The bold headline screamed at him – "WEST AWAITS RESPONSE FROM LEAGUE OF ISLAM" – and a fearful thought flashed through his mind.

"There's gonna be big trouble ahead for Israel."

Ari read on through the article.

Israel has taken a step closer towards war in the Middle East following continuing rising tensions between Western powers and the LOIN.

The League of Islamic Nations (the LOIN) was formed in 2033 when the pro-Islamic nations stormed out of the United Nations in response to a failure to agree on a series of UN Resolutions and legislative dictates. This had followed the many years of unresolved conflict and nuclear proliferation in the Middle East since '9/11' almost eighty years before in 2001. The LOIN HQ in Tehran was built and administered on a similar model to the UN Security Council in New York. It consisted mainly of Iran, Iraq, Pakistan, Afghanistan and Indonesia, and many other Islamic states. Ironically, since the LOIN's inception there had remained an uneasy peace in the Middle East for almost 50 years, mainly due to US/UN diplomacy and the fact that Israel's tactical nuclear arsenal and Weapons of Mass Destruction had far outpaced that of the poorer Iran - Iraq Alliance's nuclear and WOMD capacity. However, following recent massed Islamic military training maneouvres in north-eastern Iraq and Israeli protests to the UN Security Council, tensions were mounting between the West and the LOIN states. Israel had just recently raised its alert level to 'IMMINENT' and effectively put itself on a war footing.

In fact, Ari, still only 28, had been served mobilisation papers which meant he could be called back into the Israeli Military Reserve practically at a moment's notice. Although, for the time being, the Israeli Knesset still valued his proficiency as the country's most highly respected astronomer and astrophysicist. For the past few distracted moments, given the enormous salary he was paid, which was part-funded by the Yanks, Ari had been transfixed by the disturbing headlines on his iTab80. He closed his eyes and shook his head vigorously, psychologically readjusting himself back to the paid task in hand. Ari chastised himself.

"Concentrate Ari! Right, what are the new vectors for tonight's eye in the sky?"

Ari punched on the touch-screen and pulled up the new coordinates. His project on the Nimrod SH2 was to scan an area of deep space focusing on super-galaxies over 45 million Light Years from Earth, searching for terrestrial-type planets, mainly ones with high carbon-oxygen structures which could possibly be life-bearing. Although planet hunting in other star systems had begun early in the 21st century, relatively little progress had been made in this field of astrophysics. Ari started to type in the new figures from the list on the screen in front of him. He was on the last set of numbers when his mind again wandered back momentarily to the Bloid news report.

"Those bloody Arab bastards. They'll destroy us all!"

As Ari entered the vectors into the computer a CGI of the Nimrod telescope flashed up on the screen and he watched it swivel into position. Up in solar space the actual telescope received its computed instructions and its solar panels generated the small micro-thrusters needed to reposition Nimrod. Once fixed in position the telescope began transmitting the deep space pictures back to the closest satellite on the E2MSN and back through the network to INSACC's main frame and, of course, also sharing the data with NASA HQ's main frame. Ari called up a rerun of the CGI. It always gave him pleasure to know that watching the little computer generated imaging video demonstrated the power that he had to shift a huge man-made object deep in space. He felt like some little godlike creature situated on Earth with the power to shift the heavens. Yeah, *right*, he thought to himself. The CGI was running and rerunning itself on the screen in front of him. Ari thought that something did not look quite right. He could tell from experience that the pitch and angle of the telescope's transmission looked all wrong. He recalled the numbers he had punched in.

"Scheissen!"

He realised that the last set of vectors he had entered had been transposed. He quickly corrected the figures. Up in space Nimrod repositioned itself and was soon sending the exploratory pictures from its required deep space transmission. Ari noted down the start and end times that Nimrod had been transmitting incorrectly and, with a keen eye for detail, was able to compute in his mind where Nimrod had been incorrectly focused. About 2 minutes and 11 seconds of shots taken from Nimrod was basically wasted footage and of no real interest to the project or the wider planet-hunting community within the US/Israeli astrophysics network. He guessed that he had just cost the Yanks a few tens of thousands of dollars and the Space Center's director, Yosep Goldenheim, would probably chew his ear off about it. Goldenheim would probably threaten to send him back to the army sooner rather than later. But Ari knew he was worth too much to the project at the moment for that to happen.

"Better send an APB to let the guys know they should ignore that piece of crap. Jesus, be lucky if it sends anything back further than the Belt!"

Ari drew a picture in his mind's eye. The Kuiper Belt was that dark remote region furthest out in the solar system. It was a conglomeration of billions of small objects of ice, rock and comets with irregular orbits around the Sun and included Pluto, which had long been declassified as a planet.

*

GENESIS

Jill Geeson rushed into her office at the London Times precariously weighed down with her laptop satchel, an oversized handbag, miscellaneous folders and the obligatory Grande double-shot Starbucks coffee. The tube train from her flat in Kew was extremely late due to a broken rail at Ealing Broadway. The London Underground was nearly 250 years old and, by God, this morning it felt like it to Jill. In fact, the way her shitty life was at present Jill felt more like 250 than the 27 that was the Scots-born journalist's actual age. I think I'll suggest an investigative piece to the Ed about the decrepit state of the Tube, Jill thought as she arrived at her workstation. She was just about to offload all her bags and other accoutrements on to her desk when a shrill sharp voice sounded behind her and Jill almost jumped out of her skin.

"Jill!"

The Starbucks jumped out of Jill's hand, hit the desk at an oblique angle, which popped the plastic top off and the Grande coffee sloshed out all over the desktop and spilled over on to the grey carpeted floor. The continuation of this morning's disasters welled up inside Jill and the feral cry from her was almost one of complete despair.

"Oh, shit! That's all ah need!"

Jill swivelled around sharply to face the dropped jaw and widened eyes of her trainee reporter Ruthie Venters bulging out from her huge spectacles. Ruthie was quite old fashioned. Very few people in the 2080s wore spectacles due to the huge advances in laser eye treatments. Her dress sense was also that of early 21st century frumpiness. Christ, thought Jill, who wears jeans nowadays? Ruthie was apologetic and cowed when she spoke.

"Oops. Er, sorry Jill. It's just – um – Ed's meeting started over 15 minutes ago. He's been asking where you – er – are."

"Ah know, ah know, Ruthie. Tube's a bucking mess again this morning!"

It crossed her mind that she would have to stop using that awful word 'bucking'. Jill grabbed her eTab100 for her notes at the meeting, waving back at Ruthie as she hurried out the workstation.

"Sorry, Ruthie, can you clean up that mess for me. Please? Ah gotta go or Buckley's gonna bucking have me for breakfast…!"

As Jill rushed down the corridor to Senior Investigative Editor William J Buckley's office her thoughts raced over the shitty morning that she had had so far and how it just seemed to be a reflection of how her whole life was at present. Everything had been so different just a short ten months ago. Jill had been an up and coming investigative journalist at the Glasgow Herald when the job came up in the London Times. She had just won the prestigious Scottish Journalist of the Year award, particularly for her explosive exposé on the 'sex, lies and videotape' scandal involving the seriously aged Scottish First Minister and the gorgeous young Chinese Attaché. Buckley and his News Editor were like putty in Jill's hands and she literally breezed through the interview and into the job at the Times. Jill's promotion was perceived in the British journalistic community as being a particularly meteoric rise. She moved down to an overpriced little flat near Kew Station. Soon after Jill met the handsome, ambitious property dealer Khan al Ahmed at a summer press party on one of the slick floating club-restaurants on the Thames. Khan moved in with her and life, sex and her job had been going just fantastically. However, in the last few weeks things had cooled down between her and Khan. Jill had been working long hours on a story about a sex trafficking cartel operating through the Dover – Calais ferry routes. Khan had been away most of the time up in Manchester working on a potentially huge property deal. They had hardly spent any time together. Then two days ago Jill had received that strange lovey-dovey text message from Khan. It was not the kind of thing that he normally sent her. The text had plagued her since she read it, but she had not raised it with him - yet. Khan was due back from Manchester tonight and she needed to broach the subject with him.

Jill arrived at the glass door of the office which was marked '*William J Buckley – Senior Investigative Editor*' and she sheepishly pushed it open. Six heads swung round to glower at her and totally out of character Jill blushed slightly as she made her apologies.

"Sorry, Buck, the bloody Tube was frazzled again. I was actually thinking that I could do a piece on it..."

Buck Buckley cut her short and jabbed his finger at an empty seat.

"Oh, sit the fuck down, Jill!"

As she did so her ruddy-faced boss continued his rant towards the whole editorial gathering.

"Anyone else late this morning because the Tube was frazzled...? No!? Didn't fucking think so? So – Jill - can we get on with this morning's fucking agenda? Lot's to do. Can we just get on with it?"

"Yes, Buck - ah'm sorry Buck."

That 'bucking' word flitted across her mind again as Jill snaked herself into the empty chair, feeling all eyes still burning on her. Everyone else basked in the triumphalism of making it to the meeting on time. Christ Almighty, Jill thought to herself, Khan is going to feel her wrath tonight. As her favourite Scottish poet Robert Burns had penned 300 years ago, *"nursing her wrath to keep it warm"*. The thought then crossed her mind on the name of that decades old Star Wars movie that she watched as a wee girl back in Glasgow. What was it called? Oh, yes - *'The Wrath of Khan'*. A crooked little half-suppressed smile crossed her lips.

"Geeson? Are you at this fucking meeting or what? Do you find something funny?"

"No, Ed."

"Look, Jill, we need to have a talk sometime this week, yeah…?"

Jill nodded lamely in agreement knowing she would face another bollocking from Buckley.

"Now, everyone, can we get back to business?"

*

<u>Earthdate: Wednesday 09:37 January 22, 2081 GMT</u>

Dr Marcie Bloom Venters stood impatiently in the corridor outside her genetics lab at London's St Bartholemew's Hospital, known as Bart's to all and sundry, with her mobile pressed to her ear. She kept glancing at her watch and thinking to herself, I really don't need this. On the other end of the line was her daughter Ruthie who was calling from her office phone at the London Times. Marcie could detect that Ruthie was near to tears.

"She treats me like some sort of paid servant, Mom. I don't think I can take much more of it."

"Who do you mean, Ruthie? Is it that Jill?"

"Uh, huh - I've just finished mopping up coffee from all over her desk. Sometimes I feel that she never gives me a proper job to do."

Marcie, under pressure to get off the phone, reverted to the New York Jewish momma that she was and became singularly unhelpful to her daughter.

"Well, Ruthie, you know papa and I wanted you to become a doctor like us and - grandpapa before you…"

Ruthie cut her mother short.

"Aw, momma – I don't need this. You know I always wanted to be a journalist -"

"I know Ruthie, but you had the brains to do better."

"Momma, you're not helping me. Look, I'll talk to you at home tonight, okay?"

"Okay, baby, I'm sorry. I gotta go. I'm due at a presentation in five and I've gotta grab my notes. See you tonight?"

Marcie hung up first. She felt a small pang of guilt clench her stomach and she told herself that she would make it up to Ruthie tonight. Marcie would cook her daughter a nice Yiddish meal and show a real interest in her new career in journalism. But Marcie's father, Dr Ezra Bloom, the Nobel Prize winning geneticist, would be turning in his grave in Brooklyn's B'nai Jeshurun Jewish Cemetery to know his only granddaughter Ruth Bloom Venters left as a straight-A student from high school and decided not to enter medicine. Marcie shot into her office. She grabbed her papers and the memory stick containing her presentation on the 'Techniques and Advantages of Super-storage of Human Procreative DNA'. She went at a gallop down the corridor frantically checking her watch as she ran. Two minutes! Fortunately, the small auditorium that had been set aside for her talk was on the same floor as her lab. A little thought niggled at the back of her mind. Her administrative boss Dr Angela Mortimer had implored her to try and keep the presentation low key.

"Please, Marcie, don't give the gutter press a headline."

Marcie literally crashed through the swing doors. The small audience of doctors, clinicians and journalists, which had been lazily chatting together, had their attention drawn to her by the hasty entrance and swiftly fell silent.

"Good morning, ladies and gentlemen. Just give me a moment to get set up and then we can get started…"

Marcie tailed off the end of her sentence as she set out her papers and inserted the memory stick into the auditorium's computer. As she loaded up the presentation on the large screen the small hum of chatter rose again from the audience and she looked up towards the auditorium. More journalists than medicine men, she thought, they'll be looking for that controversial headline as usual. Don't give them the headline, she warned herself. Marcie finally had her presentation ready to go and she dimmed the lights.

"Okay, then! Good morning everyone again…"

The audience fell silent and all eyes were on her.

"…My name, as most of you will know, is Dr Marcie Bloom Venters. As most of you also know, I'm originally from New York City and I studied for my doctorate in genetic sciences at Harvard Medical School. For the last three years I have held the post of Collegiate Professor of Clinical Genetics at Bart's specializing in fertility and embryology. I am here this morning to deliver my presentation to you on the 'Techniques and Advantages of the Super-storage of Procreative DNA'. In particular, I will discuss the mass storage of human stem cells, male sperm, female eggs and fertilized embryos. I realise that this might be a very controversial subject, as I can see from the swollen ranks of the men and women of the press."

A small ripple of subdued laughter drifted out from the dimness of the auditorium. Marcie always liked to inject a little humour into her presentations. It was a good way to engage the audience and check they were still awake in what could be a dry and technically complex subject matter. She pressed on into the presentation and demonstrated her sublime knowledge of the subject. Marcie drew the audience into the scientific world of human DNA. The geneticist outlined the growing problem of infertility across the globe, which in some of the Western developed countries was approaching 1 in 3 men and 1 in 4 women. In some developed countries, such as the UK, serious genetic abnormalities in embryos and foetuses were as high as 1 in 30. Marcie explained that although many of the causes of the high instances of infertility and abnormality which had emerged in the late 21st century had still not been fully identified it was generally accepted that the causes were in the main man-made. The causation elements were not really the area that Marcie was dealing with, although she retained a strong concerned interest in the outcomes of the investigations into that sector of genetics. The area she felt needed development and funding was for a vast network of storage facilities across the globe, a superstore of human DNA, which had screening facilities to check for the purity levels of fertility of sperm and eggs and the screening out and removal of DNA with genetic defects, disease and abnormalities. The advantages, she argued, would be, in the short term, to help the growing army of couples who currently had fertility problems to tap into a vast storage bank of DNA to enable them to conceive and, in the long term, to progress towards the eradication of certain diseases and abnormalities, providing humanity with a future purification process for its gene store. Marcie discussed the funding issues allied to setting up this network and outlined the key centres around the world where she envisaged a DNA network being sited. There would be three in the UK, ten across Europe, twelve each in the USA, India and Russia, twenty in China and various others to be sited in Japan, Africa, Central and South America and Australasia. A key disadvantage to the system, in Marcie's opinion, was that it was foreseen that the League of Islamic Nations would not participate in this genetic undertaking and, in fact, would be positively excluded from the network. As a scientist Marcie explained that in some ways the DNA superstore network would be politicised by this exclusion.

Marcie finalised her presentation by summarising all her key points and then prepared to open up the auditorium for questioning. She took a gulp from the bottle of water she had brought with her and raised the lighting in the room. As her audience came into focus out of the diminishing gloom she felt a little quiver of nerves and a small knot tied itself in her stomach. Marcie was a good presenter but this was the part that made her most uncomfortable, particularly in having to deal with those bloody journalists. They always twisted her conclusions by quoting them out of context. The question flashed across her mind as to why Ruthie had discarded a medical career to becoming one of those bloody journalists.

"Well then, I hope that you all found that enthralling? Can I throw the room open to any questions?"

There was the usual awkward silence, but it was only momentary.

"Dr Venters. Dr Broinn Mulholland, I'm attached to the Boston Center for Genetic Sciences. As you can tell from the accent I'm Oirish, but it doesn't make me a bad person!"

Again a ripple of light laughter flowed out from the audience and the little knot in Marcie's stomach eased.

"Dr Venters, I was privileged to have studied many years ago under your distinguished father Dr Bloom and can I say that the work that you have carried on in the science of genetics is a credit to your father's memory."

"Thank you, Dr Mulholland. You are very kind to mention my father."

"Dr Venters. I believe that your proposals are highly laudable, particularly given the current state of infertility and gene pool defectiveness. Why, even in the State of Massachusetts where I'm based, the forecasts for infertility in men alone are worse than even those that you described in your own presentation. My concern is how do we pull this network of DNA superstores together?"

Marcie took a sip from her bottle of water, taking time to digest Broinn Mulholland's question.

"Dr Mulholland, I am very well acquainted with the excellent work that the Boston Center does in the furtherance of human genetics. In fact, I have visited it on numerous occasions, although I do not think that we personally have met each other…?"

Mulholland shook his head to agree in the negative that they had indeed not met.

"…In fact, Broinn, the Boston Center is actually earmarked to be upgraded to be one of the 20 DNA superstore centres in the USA. I should clarify that I believe the 20 centres actually cover North America, i.e., USA and Canada."

"That is also my understanding, Dr Venters, but again how do we pull this all together?"

"Well, I have to state that there is still a lot of detail to be sorted out in this area. It will be a huge undertaking to administer. But, in principle, the idea is to run it from a new administration centred in New York under the auspices of the UN. The proposal is to call it the United Nations Organisation for Human Genetic Sciences. All the databanks of human DNA materials will be administered by this new UN department and the computer systems required in maintaining this network will be controlled by this department. It probably does not fully answer your question, Dr Mulholland, as there is much work still to be ironed out. Will that suffice at present?"

"Yes, thank you, Dr Venters."

Marcie awaited the next question much more relaxed and confident.

"Dr Venters. Cordelia Sommers, Daily Telegraph. You talk about this being a worldwide network and imply that it is something that will serve the whole of humanity. But would you not agree that in actuality this is just another wedge being stuck in between the UN, who you say are going to run this, and the LOIN, who are actually being excluded from it?"

"Ms Sommers, is it? Yes. Well, Ms Sommers, I am not a politician, I am a scientist. And as a scientist my ethos, as was that of my father before me, has always been to work for the good of all humanity. At present the politics and the ethics of the Mullahs running the League of Islamic Nations has precluded them from entering into any agreement to be part of this DNA network. It was proposed to them and they declined, but it is not part of my job to encourage the League to join this network. I am satisfied that four-fifths of the world's population will be genetically protected if this network is put in place. I only hope that in time diplomacy will prevail over the many issues that divide the UN and the LOIN and that the League will one day become a part of the integrated DNA network."

Marcie fielded a few more questions which tended to be more of a technical nature on the ability to superstore DNA, the technicalities of mass screening to separate the "good DNA from the bad" as one questioner put it, the programming and storage of all the data on a UN supercomputer and some further clarification on where centres would be sited. Marcie dealt with these with ease and she was feeling pretty upbeat as she eyed the clock on the auditorium wall behind her audience. It was time to wind up the presentation. In fact, she had run over time a little.

"Okay, ladies and gentlemen, I see that I have kept you a bit longer than booked and your stomachs will be beginning to grumble. I can take one final question before you all rush off to lunch - anyone else?"

"Dr Venters. Mahmoud El Kharroubi, journalist for Al Jazirah. Don't you think this whole concept of a vast network of human DNA, only, as the questioner before called it – good DNA – is something straight out of a Frankenstein horror movie?"

That knot in the stomach quickly returned. She thought whether she should even grace the questioner with an answer, but Marcie felt compelled to defend her work.

"Mr El Kharroubi. I realise that many people around the world will hold ethical, political and religious views which will make them disagree vehemently with the type of work that I and many of my colleagues in genetics are conducting around the world today."

The journalist tried to interject with a 'but'. Marcie raised her hand and stopped him in his tracks. Marcie continued.

"But, nothing, Mr El Kharroubi - I am not the Frankenstein's monster that you may have your readers believe. Many parts of the world are facing a genetic crisis. Right now males and females are being born infertile in their droves. Babies are increasingly being born with inherited defects and diseases. Now, we can guess at the reasons for this crisis. We may think we know what the reasons actually are. But until we do, we need to find a method of retaining pure DNA across the world until we can eradicate the causes of mounting infertility and abnormality…"

Mahmoud El Kharroubi decided that he was not going to be cut short again and seized on a word in Marcie's unfinished answer to his question.

"Yes, Dr Venters, that is the word you geneticists strive for, isn't it!? Pure - pure DNA - genetic purity - the Aryan Race! That is the kind of pureness that the Nazis strove for back in the early 20th century. The kind of work that Dr Josef Mengele did for his beloved Adolf Hitler, would you not agree?"

The auditorium fell into a deathly silence shocked at El Kharroubi's rude and undignified outburst but also awaiting an answer from Marcie. The answer surged out like the pyroclastic flow from a huge volcanic eruption destroying everything in its path.

"MR EL KHARROUBI. I AM A JEW! For you to compare me and my work with that Nazi butcher Mengele – der Todesengel - is a total and complete insult to me. I cannot and I will not give you the satisfaction of an answer! Good day, ladies and gentlemen!"

Marcie grabbed her notes furiously and crashed out of the auditorium as quickly as she had entered it. There was a very small ripple of applause, which the now long gone geneticist failed to hear, mainly from the clinicians, but the remainder of the audience sat stunned at the conclusion of the presentation. Eventually everyone began to either leave for lunch, return to work or to go to other meetings. As they all milled about waiting to exit through the swing doors that Marcie had crashed through, Mahmoud El Kharroubi surreptitiously slipped Marcie's memory stick from the computer and into his pocket. He thought to himself, maybe it's not that controversial, but what the hell, might as well take it for background material. Back in her lab office Marcie sat slumped and beaten behind her desk. She thought resignedly - well, the gutter press got their headline!

CHAPTER 2

"**H**ere comes the Big Baby, Jack!"

Jack Crossan caught the message from Xi Xhu Pan on his intercom and a broad smile cracked his craggy unshaven face. He jumped off his cramped bunk that gave him constant backache in his tiny galley and flipped back a quick reply.

"Ah'm comin' up to the bridge, Xi Xhu."

Jack calculated that the shuttle was about 4 hours early as he half-scurried, half-floated through the low gravity of the decks of MGal3 on his way up to the bridge. He was guessing that it must have gotten blown along on some favourable solar winds as it was more often or not later than its normal scheduled arrival. A few of the other crew members that he passed gave the Commander the thumbs up. One or two to signify that Jack was soon to be on his way back home to Earth and one or two others to show that they too would be joining him. Within a couple of minutes he hauled himself through the open hatch door and into the bridge. Jack wheeled himself into the empty seat beside Xi Xhu Pan, who was Watch Commander that evening. Xi Xhu pointed Jack to the viewing porthole. Xi Xhu knew that there were more detailed views of the arrival on the bridge monitors but he knew Jack would want to see the actual ship arriving – the real deal. Xi Xhu directed Jack's gaze by wagging his index finger and exclaiming.

"Thar she blows!"

The huge space shuttle Oceanus, which was not at first sight unlike a giant whale, cruised slowly in at docking speed towards the space station after a 14 week journey from Alpha Base, 56 million miles away in Earth orbit. Oceanus was to remain above Mars for a week to refuel, change crew and unload and reload supplies. It would then be making the longer 15 week return journey home to Earth, clocking up an additional million miles, due to the variable orbits of the two planets around the Sun. It was also forecast that the solar winds would be against the spaceship on its return journey. Jack stretched out his arms as if to give the 'Big Baby', as it was affectionately known, a huge hug and shouted out to Xi Xhu.

"Peggy Sue, honey, ah'm a-comin' home!"

Xi Xhu tried to bring Jack back to the task in hand.

"You want to bring her in, Yank?"

"Hey, Xi, you're Watch Commander, you bring her in. And ah've told ya before – I ain't no Yankee dog – ah'm a good ole Southern Johnny Reb!"

Before Xi Xhu could begin the docking preparations, Jack leaned over and wrapped his arms playfully around the Beijing-born astronaut in a tight bear hug. At the same time the first crackle of communication from the Docking Engineer on the bridge of Oceanus echoed from the radio.

"Oceanus calling - ready for docking instructions - MGal3 respond, copy?"

Xi Xhu wriggled out of his Commander's grasp.

"Jack, let go of me! We're not all heading back to Earth…"

The puzzled Oceanus engineer responded to Xi Xhu's comment.

"Oceanus here – copy that instruction again?"

Jack laughed and started to float out of his chair with a playful goodbye wave and added.

"Oops, sorry Xi – better leave you to get on with it. I got my bags to pack anyhow!"

Xi Xhu Pan gave Jack a quick silent friendly jerk of his middle finger then he turned back to the bridge console to carry out the tricky docking procedure for Oceanus.

At the same time back in Houston Control Center, Lex Kosloff was in touch with his 'oppo' on the bridge of the Oceanus, both men ensuring that the docking manoeuvres were carried out to plan. Lex was exhausted and desperate to get his shift finished on time at 'zero two hundred hours' in about twenty five minutes. He had cursed when he had heard from Oceanus that their arrival status was to be four hours earlier than scheduled, which meant it was going to be smack bang at the end of his nine hour shift. Any delay would mean that he would be into overtime, as it was deemed too risky changing controllers during the complex docking stage. Lex radioed the engineer on Oceanus.

"This is Houston to Oceanus. What is your current dock position - copy?"

As he waited for the response Lex rubbed the day old stubble on his chin and then smacked his face vigorously as he sat at his station in NASA HQ.

Jimmy Soderline sitting next to Lex's station looked over at Kosloff and thought that his workmate had been looking pretty rough lately. Soderline questioned Lex sympathetically.

"You okay, Lex?"

"Yeah, no sweat, Jimmy - I just need a good night's sleep. These night shifts lately have been doing my head in."

"I know what you mean. At least we're back on days in a couple of weeks. How's the Big Baby doing anyway?"

"Ah'm just waiting to hear from them."

Lex turned back to his monitors as he still awaited the Oceanus response. What he did not share with Jimmy Soderline was he was not only exhausted from his long night shifts. Lex desperately needed a drink. Since New Year he had been hitting the Scotch hard – really hard. When he arrived home at his place at 1938 Robindale Drive over in south west Houston on New Year's Day, after his radio communication with Jack Crossan, he had been in a pretty good mood. Lex was looking forward to celebrating the special day with his gorgeous wife Marna and, of course, some smoky peaty Lagavulin. Lex's thoughts were interrupted with the distinct crackle.

"This is Oceanus to Houston – Verne Andriessen here Lex. Able to report that the docking grabs on MGal3 are extended and we should be on them in two minutes our time. Copy?"

Lex responded sluggishly.

"Houston to Oceanus - copy that Verne. Let me know when Oceanus is hooked up to MGal3. Do you copy?"

As he reviewed his monitor Lex noted all the indicators looked good from Oceanus. He let his thoughts drift back to New Year. When he had arrived home at Robindale Drive the place was neat and tidy and Marna had obviously been very busy making it nice for Hogmanay. The previous year 2080 had not been great between Lex and Marna, mainly because of his frequent drinking. He had promised his resolution for 2081 would be to get on top of it. However, he did tell her the previous night that he would only have one or two drams of Lagavulin. Just to celebrate. After all, it was New Year. As soon as Lex walked in to the living room he saw the small note neatly folded and placed in the centre of the black glass coffee table. Lex opened it and read it as if viewing some awful disaster unfolding on live 3DTV.

> *Lex,*
>
> *I can't take any more. I can't cope with your drinking. You're just killing me. I have gone back to my parents' place up in Dallas. I need*

time to think things out. You really need to get help.

Marna

Lex had collapsed onto the sofa completely crestfallen, Marna's note fluttered down to the wooden floor and slipped slowly under the sofa. He knew things had been bad lately but he just did not expect to lose his wife. He looked over at the drinks cabinet and the bottle of single malt was practically screaming at him. He did not just have one or two that night. Lex crashed out on the whole bottle. Next day, with his head in a real fog, Lex had tried calling Marna up in Dallas, but her father fiercely rebuked him and told him that his daughter did not want to hear from Lex until he had dried out - completely dried out. Lex yelled down the phone at her dad.

"I'm no alcoholic, ya know!"

Since the call to Dallas, Lex had been hitting the bottle almost daily. As yet it had not affected his work at Houston Control, but he thought that it was only a matter of time before he was caught in one of the random drugs and alcohol tests. However, he told himself he was still going to need a couple of softeners when he got home after tonight's shift, just to take the edge off. Just then Verne, the engineer on Oceanus, radioed back.

"Oceanus to Houston - docking procedure safely completed, Lex. The Big Baby is in bed for the night. This is Oceanus signing off - over and out."

"Houston to Oceanus - Lex here - Houston copies that - over and out."

He noted the time. 01:55. Lex tapped his touch screen and switched over to call his supervisor, Irene DuPré, who was stationed a couple of rows behind him.

"Hi, Irene - did you catch that on the Oceanus? The Big Baby docked safely at 01:55 CST."

"Yeah, Lex – that was a good job."

"Okay for me to sign off at zero two hundred as scheduled?"

"No probs, Lex – oh, yeah - before ya shoot off? Ah just wanna remind you that we're scheduled in for your Performance Appraisal on Friday 7th next week, okay?"

Lex groaned deep inside but replied as upbeat as he could muster, then lied to Irene.

"Yep, eh, good for me on the 7th – um, it's in the diary."

"Good, 'cos there's an issue that I want to run by you then. Okay, g'night, Lex. You get off home."

Lex thought that sounded ominous but Irene switched the call off on her monitor before Lex could reply, or that was the impression that Lex got.

There is an issue that Irene wants to run by me? It rung in Lex's ear and buzzed in his brain. She must have cottoned on to his drinking. How? Maybe Jimmy suspected that he had been on the sauce or smelt it on him. Nah! Lex thought that it must be something else. He tried to convince himself to stop worrying but right then he felt a small tremor in his right hand. Suddenly, he felt a gentle elbow in his arm and he looked round a bit too sharply at Jimmy. Soderline laughed at Lex.

"Hey, man, you goin' home or what?"

Lex nodded his head wearily. He started powering down his monitors as there was no relief post for his station tonight. He grabbed his stuff, tapped Jimmy lightly on the shoulder and made his way back to the locker room. He thought Irene looked rather grimly at him as he passed up near her station. She gave him a cursory wave acknowledging his departure. As he took his bag out of his locker, Lex groaned, God, I'm gonna need that drink when I get home.

*

Earthdate: 13:21 Sunday February 2, 2081 GMT

Gary Mackintosh and Ewan Sinclair sat with their double espressos in Chuck's iCafé just off the Royal Mile in the heart of Edinburgh. Ewan was daydreaming as he surveyed the scene outside the large picture window, looking out at the buildings which were still much the same as they were over 300 years ago. The street had been pedestrianised many years ago and because it was such a freezing cold winter's Sunday afternoon there were only a few people walking outside the café. In fact, there had been a sprinkling of snow which added to help erase any signs of 21st century modernity. Ewan thought to himself with a wry smile that he would not be surprised to see Rabbie Burns or Deacon Brodie walk in for a 'wee café latte or twa'. Gary was otherwise deeply engrossed on his laptop, which had voice activation response built in. However, because they were in a public place, albeit the café was practically empty, Gary was operating the laptop with touch screen commands with the voice activation switched off. In fact, there were actually only two others in the café. A waitress called Michelle was reading behind the counter and an old well-known drunken ex-soldier called Buster had come in out of the cold for a sly kip. Gary and Ewan had been in the café for about an hour with nothing much said between them. Ewan was now feeling bored and beginning to perceive that nothing was being achieved with Gary faffing about on his computer.

"C'mon, Gary, give that effing NASA thing up and let's head down the Mile for a couple of pints."

"Och, will ye just gimme a minute, Ewan? Ah think ah might just be on to something here."

Ewan groaned loudly and the girl behind the counter looked up from her digital gossip magazine. Michelle quickly scanned the café for some sign of customer movement, but there was none. The old drunk was still blissfully asleep. Michelle yawned and went back to reading her celebrity gossip. Ewan whispered in Gary's ear.

"You've been farting around with that E2MSN system for over a week and the best that you've come up with is some pretty boring pictures of Mars and a couple of ship's manifests for the space shuttle Oceanus. Come on, Gary, let's just leave it alone. We'll end up getting extradited to the US on hacking charges and for what – nothing!"

Gary did not even look up and Ewan snapped in exasperation.

"Oh, for God's sake, Gaz - look, I'm heading off down to Brodie's Bar for a drink. Are you coming?"

Ewan pushed his cheap metal café chair back with a slight screech on the tiled floor which extracted a tutting rebuke from Michelle for interrupting her gossip read again. He started to push himself up when Gary raised his palm to stop him from leaving, swivelling his laptop round to face Ewan.

"Mars and manifests? Mars and manifests is it? Well, just take a fuckin' look at that then!"

Diffidently, Ewan sat down and looked at the screen as indicated by his friend's wagging finger pointing triumphantly at the webpage. Ewan seemed unimpressed with Gary's apparent revelation.

"It's an email. So what – I've seen an effing email before."

Gary raised his eyebrows slowly, looked up and gave a slight shrug. He then answered in mocking repetition.

"It's – an - email. Just - a - fuckin' - email. Seen – one - ah - them – before – huuuuh?"

Gary hesitated for effect and then stabbed his finger at the screen.

"Just read the fuckin' thing!"

Ewan began reading and slowly it dawned on him that this was certainly a bit more interesting than a few bland photos of canyons and craters on Mars or the Oceanus crew and passenger list for next week's return trip to Earth. As he read the email his left eyebrow arched higher and higher and Gary's smile kept getting broader and broader.

From: arischenkler@insacc.is
Cc: yosepfgoldenheim@insacc.is
Bcc: Internal Nimrod SH2 Contact List – Top Secret
Subject: Nimrod SH2 scanning error
Date: 23:32 January 21, 2081 IST

To all concerned,

I have to report that I incorrectly entered the wrong vectors for this evening's scan for the Nimrod SH2 at 22:51:21 IST and this was not corrected until 22:53:32 IST. Please ignore this 2' 11" of footage as the SH2 was not directed to the planned position within super-galaxy M-KON543 for this evening's programmed terrestrial planet-hunting scan. Note that the SH2 was correctly repositioned at 22:53:32 IST.

I realise that the SH2 budget is extremely tight and that this was potentially a costly error and I apologize profusely for this mistake,

Ari Schenkler,

Senior Astrophysicist,

Israeli National Space & Cosmology Center, Tel Aviv

Ewan looked over the laptop at his friend who had now stretched out his arms with the palms thrust upwards. Gary prompted Ewan.

"Well?"

"Interesting - someone's going to get his arse kicked for that then?"

"Too right he is, Ewan. But just think what ye're wee friend down in London could do with that info?"

He looked blankly at Gary.

"My friend in London - who do you - ?"

Before Gary interrupted him, Ewan's eyes were already beginning to gape widely as it dawned on him who Gary was talking about.

"Jill – Gary, don't say you mean Jill Geeson?"

"Yeah, that wee cracker of a journalist at the Times that you used to go out with. She would pay big money to see that email."

Ewan's voice was beginning to rise and become slightly shriller, causing Michelle to shake her head a little. Those two were always arguing in here, she thought.

"No way, Gary - for Christ sake, she wouldn't be able to touch it with a barge pole. That's a leaked document from a top secret Israeli – NASA communiqué. We'd all get thrown in Guantanamo and get hung by the Katangans!"

"Look, calm down, calm down, Ewan. Nobody's goin' on their holidays to Cuba here. There's ways to handle this properly. What we do is speak to Jill –"

"No, Gary!"

"Just listen for a minute, will ye?"

Ewan nodded and fell huffily silent with his arms crossed tightly. Gary continued explaining.

"As I said, what we do is speak to Jill. Do a wee bit of negotiating with her. Let her know what we have, which gives her the heads up on it – i.e., the fuckin' exclusive. Then we release it to one or two of the major Web Leaks sites to publish it simultaneously and at the same time Jill gets the scoop on it in before the online tabloids get a sniff. Bingo, we get paid!"

Ewan remained unconvinced.

"Yeah, well, I mean to say – it's not exactly a major exclusive. I admit it is a fairly large blunder by this Ari guy. But what's your headline. Astronomer puts telescope to blind eye! I mean, c'mon Gaz, big wow!"

Gary dismissed this with a flurry of his hands quickly crossing over each other.

"Naw, naw, Ewan, ye're missing the point. Your pal Jill can make more capital out of this than that. Here we have an Israeli scientist in cahoots with the Yanks, sitting on the doorstep of the League of Islam, or whatever they're called – "

"The League of Islamic Nations or just call it the LOIN."

"Right, Ewan, right. So as ah said, Israeli scientist – doorstep – LOIN. What does he do? He accidentally punches in a few wrong numbers and makes a complete arse of it. Okay?"

Ewan was still puzzled and looked quizzically at Gary who was now in top gear with his idea to make a little bit of cash.

"Here's the story. Put your friend Ari in a US backed Israeli Nuclear Defence Establishment. Hear me out here, Ewan. Poor old Ari is sitting twiddling with his tadger while he just happens to be inadvertently punching in a few wrong numbers. What happens next?"

Ewan groaned once more his head going into his hands.

"Yeah, Gary, what happens?"

"Poor old Ari only goes and fires 4 or 5 nukes at Iran and Iraq. He gives the old LOIN the chop. Get it, Ewan, the loin chop, ha, ha, ha!"

Ewan shook his head as Gary continued to laugh at his own joke.

"Look, Gary, I don't think this is enough for Jill to make anything of."

"Course it is. She'll make mincemeat of a story like this. Just think what she can say. If the Yanks can't trust the Israelis with a fuckin' telescope, how are they gonna trust the Yids with a whole fuckin' nuclear arsenal!"

"I need to think about this, Gaz. There might be something there for Jill and the Leaks sites but I still need time to think it through a bit. I mean there might be more capital in it if I could actually see the two minutes and eleven seconds of bum footage. See what our pal Ari actually did record. But -?"

"But – but what?"

"Well we don't actually have those shots from the Nimrod, do we?"

"Who doesn't actually have the shots?"

"Don't tell me?"

Gary gloated triumphantly.

"Yep, good old helpful Ari tagged a hyperlink of the spoiled footage to his email. Given that the rest of his colleagues are more interested in Mekong 123 or whatever you call it, you might actually be the only person on the planet who actually wants to see it."

Ewan was now excited about Gary's find.

"Can you download it on to a memory stick for me? And don't do anything about Jill until I've looked at it!"

"Consider it done, old pal. Still want that pint down at Brodie's?"

"I thought you'd never ask. And by the way, Gary, it's M-KON543 and it's one of the largest galaxies ever found by man. It would blow us all away just to imagine its size even in comparison to our own galaxy. It could eat the Milky Way for breakfast and still feel hungry."

CHAPTER 3

It was unusually warm outside for an early Monday morning in February and Tel Aviv was already hitting 25 Celsius and rising. The air-con unit in the meeting room was frazzled again. Everyone in the room baked and cursed the global warming which had remained unchecked throughout the 21st century. Although, the early-century predictions on global temperature rise, sea levels and natural disasters had proven to be recklessly wild forecasts. The end of the world was not nigh, but it was certainly a scorcher today. Ari wondered about bringing the zip down on his already open-necked top by another few inches. He thought against it as he had been ribbed mercilessly before by the women about his inordinately bushy and hairy chest putting them off their coffee and biscuits. Ari just had to put up with the trickles of sweat running down the inside of his top. Yosep Goldenheim, who also looked hot and bothered, snappily called the 10 o'clock 4-weekly staff meeting to order.

"Right, guys, everyone got a coffee? Let's get the meeting brought to order as I want to try and get finished by 10:40. I have a meeting right after with the Director. I can tell you all that budget constraints and efficiency savings are going to be high on the agenda there."

Efficiency savings! That meant jobs on the line and everyone straightened up or fiddled purposefully with their ePads, except Yosep, who still liked to take notes with pen and paper. Yosep Goldenheim was out of the old school. Or as his staff joked behind his back – out of the Ark! Yosep waved his pen around the room to draw everyone to his attention.

"Right you've all got your agendas in front of you. First up, we have the planned NASA delegation from the States visiting us on the 10th. That's next week so I want to know that the presentation is well in hand. Ari? You are leading the presentation team. What is the latest update on that?"

Ari gave a couple of taps on his ePad to try and project an air of purposefulness to the others, but it was really just to give him a few seconds to compose his thoughts.

"Um, yeah, Joe, uh, I am leading that team to prepare the presentation to our NASA colleagues on the 2082 Project Plan for the, uh, Nimrod Space-Hunter 2 project. As most of you know my team is composed of, um, myself as team leader and Jerzy Winklowicz, Assistant Senior Astrophysicist SH2 project. Jerzy, who you all know, of course, is with me today."

Ari curved his palm towards his left-hand side to introduce his blond curly-headed Nazarene assistant who nodded and smiled coyly to everyone present. Ari continued uninterrupted by Yosep.

"Also on the team are Assistant Astrophysicists Rebecca Menachim and Noam Rebbetzin. So we have an excellent team on the case. I believe that NASA will be sending their Project Director and four astrophysicists and with you, Yosep, and my team of four, it will be a like-for-like forum?"

Goldenheim corrected Ari.

"Nearly right, Schenkler - looks like our Center Director will also be sitting in this time. As I've mentioned budgets are going to be way up there and we need to have them nailed down tight for this presentation. The finance boys are telling me that the initial forecast for the Financial Year to the end of March on SH2 is looking to overshoot by 6%. You've probably heard that too, Ari?"

Ari thought to himself whether it was getting warmer in the room or was it just him. Why someone cannot fix the damn air-con is beyond me, he thought.

"Um, I haven't seen those figures officially yet, Yosep. But, yes, a little birdie did run that one by me. But Jerzy is on top of the financials for the presentation and we're just about there on that one. Is that right, Jerzy?"

Jerzy, also now feeling the increasing heat in the quietly expectant room, ran his finger along the inside of his top, loosening his collar.

"Ah - definitely so – um – ah - yep, Ari - I reckon that the budget slides are, eh, say 95% nailed down so far –"

Goldenheim thumped his right fist down, his pen shooting up into the air and rattling across the meeting room table. He waved agitatedly for someone to toss the pen back as he growled at Ari.

"For God's sake, Ari, I don't want to hear that we're 95% of the way on this thing! We need to be 110% screwed down or these NASA guys'll toast us. Know what I'm saying?"

Ari gulped and thought, not again. Goldenheim had gone through the roof with him last week when he had read Ari's email 'to all concerned' regarding the 2 minutes and 11 seconds of wasted footage sent back from the Nimrod. He had threatened to get Ari's National Service papers sent through from the Israeli Army HQ in Jerusalem if there were any more screw ups. Ari swallowed nervously again.

"Yes, Yosep."

Yosep Goldenheim raved on as one of the girls in the room tossed him back his pen and Ari could feel the suppression of sniggers from the others at the meeting. Goldenheim pressed on with the agenda.

"We've got 9 days till the Yanks get here from Houston and we need to be on the ball with this whole Nimrod presentation. Budgets, project plan, timelines, the whole deal. We've got to be right on the money with this one. Are we clear on that?"

Ari and Jerzy both nodded. Ari spoke on. He was trying to sound as confident as possible, but the sweat trickles on his brow betrayed his confidence.

"I – we, my team and I - plan to have the draft presentation finalised by the 4th and we've scheduled in a run through with you on the, eh, 6th. I guarantee you that it will be 110% specked by then. So, hopefully, we'll just be discussing tidy ups round the edges for the actual meeting with the NASA boys on the 9th. How does that sound, Yosep?"

Goldenheim replied as he exaggeratedly looked at his wristwatch and then he made his pitch.

"Not bad. But here's the deal. I'm putting money on it that the Director's going to tell me in about 25 – 30 minutes time that we are going to have to trim the 2082 SH2 budget by another 5 to 6%. You are going to have to build options into the presentation to the Yanks next week for savings to that effect."

Strike one. Ari was angry at this bombshell curve ball and he blasted back at his boss.

"Aw, come on, Yosep! We've been at this thing for weeks now. It's unrealistic to trim the budget by up to 6% and have those figures ready for next week's meeting with the Yanks. I don't think we can do it. What do you think Jerzy?"

Unfortunately for Ari, Jerzy only managed a half-hearted shrug before Goldenheim fired back with his next wildly swinging pitch.

"Look here, Schenkler! Maybe if you hadn't screwed up the Nimrod's positioning the other week – then - just maybe - we wouldn't be looking at a 5 – 6% cut in the first place!"

Strike two. All eyes were fixed on Ari and he flushed with anger.

"That's not fair, Yosep. You know fine well that error, for which I have already apologized to you in person, did not represent anything like a 6% overshoot on the SH2 budget. There are good reasons for the overspending – "

"Good reasons, my ass, Ari. There has been a sloppiness that has crept into the SH2 project over the last fiscal year and it needs to be sharpened up. I want those 5 and 6% options built into the draft presentation for next week."

Ari stepped up to the plate for his last swing at the bat.

"You want those 5 and 6% options, Yosep? I thought you said it was the Director who was expected to request the options?"

Strike three. Goldenheim blew a gasket, but in a controlled wave of anger through gritted teeth.

"Look, Schenkler, just get the job done as I ask or go and pick up your army papers. It's up to you?"

Ari just nodded numbly and sat bowed. He was hardly listening as his boss carried on with the meeting.

"Right, everyone, that took a bit longer than I had hoped so let's get back to the agenda. Okay, next up is staffing levels. In the last month our headcount has dropped by three. Joachim Levy has retired early on health grounds and I'm sure we all wish him well. Aaron Halevi and Shifra Ben Haim have both been called up to do their honourable duty for the defence of our beloved State…"

Ari thought that Yosep Goldenheim was putting just a bit too much emphasis on his phrasing of 'honourable duty for the defence of our beloved State' and guessed it was just another dig at him. Ari quickly scanned the rest of the short agenda on his ePad, saw that there was nothing else that he would be strongly involved in and he more or less switched off for the rest of the meeting. Goldenheim went on to argue the case for only filling one of the three posts vacated due to the Center's budget constraints. Ari could not care less at this moment whether Goldenheim filled any of the vacancies.

*

Earthdate: 20:15 Monday February 3, 2081 GMT

Jill had only been home at her small studio flat in Kew for about five minutes. The working week had started badly again and the underground train home from Victoria had been late again. She was starving and exhausted and she had literally thrown everything down and collapsed onto her sofa in the open plan studio flat. Buckley had been on her case since the disastrous editorial meeting 11 days ago. After the meeting Buckley had her in his own office and told her that he felt that her work lately had become slipshod and sloppy. Jill tried to deny that Buckley's assertion was actually the case and that she always gave him and the Times 100% commitment.

"C'mon, Jill, I've been in the paper business for thirty odd years now. Who are you trying to kid?"

Buckley still called it the 'paper business' even though the presses had stopped rolling years ago and the public read their daily news on the online 'Bloids'. God, thought Jill, he's so bloody old hat, but she admitted, he was pretty damn perceptive.

"Look, Buck, I'm really sorry. You're right. I have probably taken my eye off the ball a little bit lately…"

Buckley listened. Here it comes, he thought to himself, as he let Jill carry on.

"…You see, I'm, uh, kinda havin' some personal problems at home at the moment. But I'm on it, boss – totally gonna get it sorted out."

"Well, I'm not going to pry, Jill. But it better get sorted and PDQ. As you know, Jill, I'm not one for carrying any liabilities on my team. I've a mountain of investigative work and a pile of it is heading your way. Are you up for it?"

Inside, Jill's stomach churned. In fact, she felt strangely like vomiting but she suppressed the feeling of rising bile. Until she straightened things out with Khan the last thing she needed was a mountain of stressful investigations and deadlines. Jill had broached the subject of the lovey-dovey text signed to 'A' with Khan and he had put it down to a simple typo. He had obviously meant to type a 'J' but he had done it in a hurry between meetings. He pleaded with her to believe that it was not a misdirected text meant for some other girl. Jill knew deep down it sounded pretty lame. It was just not the type of text he would normally send her in the first place. Half-heartedly she told Khan that she would accept it was a mistake and that night he made love to her gently and passionately. As Khan lay sleeping beside her a little niggling doubt kept Jill from getting to sleep right away. Now Buckley was putting the pressure on her to get down to some hard-knuckled journalism. Subconsciously, she chided herself. For God's sake Jill, you're a bloody investigative reporter – that's what you do for a living.

"No, uh, I mean, yes, Buck, totally. I'm totally buckin' up for it!"

Buckley arched his eyebrow suspiciously. Jill groaned inside. She knew that careless word would slip out one day. God, half his staff used it behind his back.

"Are you taking the piss, Jill?"

"No, sorry, boss. It just slipped out."

"Well don't! Oh, yeah. Before you go, Jill - another small favour to ask?"

"Yes, Buck."

"I want you to delegate more reporting work to the new trainee. You know - Ruthie Venters? The girl I assigned to you before Christmas. I would like a bit less of Ruthie running about getting you coffees and photocopies, if you please? I'm a big golfing buddy of her father - Dr Rolf Venters – he's a top gyno in Harley Street. Told him I would keep an eye on his baby babushka. So I want to see her being stretched a bit more, okay?"

That had been over a week ago and Buckley was as good as his word. The mountain of work had duly arrived on Jill's desk and since then she had been madly running around the south east of England on the various investigations into known drug barons, organised gangs and the odd shady MP or three. She had been putting in far too many hours and missing too many lunch breaks. The only good thing that had come out of it, Jill thought, as she sat slumped exhaustedly on her sofa, was that Ruthie had actually turned out to be a real find. The girl was a workaholic and had the instinctive bloodhound's nose for sleuthing out a top-notch story. Ruthie reminded her of the Jill she used to be not that long ago. The Jill she fully intended to be again. Just then her mobile rang shrilly and she stuck it to her ear, still half-numb with hunger and tiredness. She could not even bring herself to speak and she just listened for the caller to break the silence. He spoke in a whisper.

"Hi, it's me. I've been meaning to call you…"

His voice was so low and muffled that she could not tell who it was, although she was sure the voice was familiar.

"Sorry, can you speak up a bit?"

He spoke just a fraction louder this time and Jill could hear the other muffled voices in the background.

"It's me, it's Khan. I'm still at this latest meeting in Manchester. We're just taking a short coffee break. I can't speak for long –"

"It's bloody late for a meeting, Khan. I thought you were coming back tonight?"

"I can't, Jill. This property deal is busting my balls up here. But, I think I've just about got it cracked –"

Jill's fraught nerves made her feel irritable and snappy and she also felt a little nauseous again. In fact, she was beginning to worry that there was something medically amiss with her body lately. But then, she told herself, it all comes back to that niggling bloody text message from Khan.

"What do mean you can't come home tonight? You promised you'd be back!"

Khan tried hard not to raise his voice. The other guys in the room who had been chatting over coffee were starting to pay attention to the rising irritation in his voice.

"Jill, baby, this is a twenty million pound deal and it has been hanging in the balance for weeks. I'm getting real close to closing this one down –"

Jill lost her temper and snapped down the phone at him.

"I'll tell you what's hanging in the balance, Khan! You're wanderlust cock and our bloody relationship – that's what! You're going to be staying with that fuckin' bitch you've got up there, aren't you?"

Khan gritted his teeth and hissed back.

"God, Jill, I've already told you there's no-one else. It's only you – only you, love. Look, they're calling me back to the table. I've got to go, my sweet baby. I'll phone you tomorrow…"

Khan quickly finished the call before Jill could respond. He crossed back over to where the meeting table was across the room and sat down with the others who had now finished their coffees and had been waiting for him. The six men were all of various Middle Eastern origins, like Khan, who was himself a Muslim Kuwaiti-born Arab. His Jordanian friend spoke first.

"She is beginning to be a problem, Khan, my friend –"

"Look, Mahmoud, I can handle it. She doesn't suspect a thing about what our Group is doing. She only thinks I'm screwing around."

Mahmoud El Kharroubi, the Al Jazirah journalist, who had known Khan al Ahmed since their university days in Cairo, wagged his finger at his old comrade.

"Yes, but, in the name of Allah, you *are* screwing around, my friend!"

Khan snapped his arms out with his palms spread open in a revelatory motion to the whole Group. This was the only name that they had agreed to go by when meeting, but secretly they were part of the wider Brotherhood of Jihad. Although, what Khan blurted out was no great revelation. The Group all knew what he was involved in as it was related to the Group's mission.

"That is not the same thing as Jill! I am doing that with the other woman for the cause of Islam. Aisha al-Gazari is our portal to the path we seek to follow in order to help our brothers in the LOIN to destroy the infidel scum."

One of the others, a bearded thuggish swarthy-looking man, known only to the group as the Palestinian, spat an oath back at Khan.

"That bloody white journalist is the infidel scum!"

Khan jumped out his chair knocking it reeling backwards and clenched a fist at the scowling Palestinian.

"Take that back, you bastard! I have feelings for that girl –"

The Palestinian also made a half-hearted threat to rise from his seat but Mahmoud El Kharroubi stood slowly and upraised pacifying outstretched arms to each of the two men glowering darkly at each other.

"Brothers – brothers - Allah *will* be gratified to see that we are spending the cause fighting each other - rather than directing all our venom at our enemies in the West. Please, sit my brother Khan?"

Khan slowly pulled his chair back in to the table and sat down again throwing an apologetic gesture with his slightly raised palm across to the Palestinian. The Palestinian gave a slight nod in grudged acceptance. El Kharroubi continued.

"Khan – you have got to accept, my brother, that this arousal of Jill Geeson's suspicions, albeit somewhat misdirected, is dangerous for our Mission here in the UK."

Khan made to interject but Mahmoud stopped him with a quick raise of his hand.

"Listen, Khan, I am a journalist by trade, so I know what I'm talking about. Jill - she is an investigative journalist. If she really wanted to, how long do you think it would take her to find out things about you, find out things about our Group? I have made discreet enquiries myself. I admit behind your back, my brother, for which I apologize. My journalist friends tell me that she is like a ferret in a rabbit warren. She will dig and dig until she sinks her teeth into the jugular of a story that she is pursuing. She would not necessarily be looking for us, but inadvertently she could stumble across us. And then –"

Khan looked aghast at El Kharroubi and stuttered over his words.

"And – then – wha – at!"

Mahmoud did not get a chance to answer. The Palestinian answered for him in a low and deadly hiss.

"And then she would have to be eliminated!"

Back in her small kitchen the microwave oven pinged too loudly in readiness. Jill had been crying since Khan had hung up on her and by now her head was throbbing mercilessly. She went over and slipped the piping hot TV dinner onto a plate. As she peeled back the pierced film on top of the carton a blast of boiling steam burnt her fingers. Jill cried out in pain. She reacted instantly by picking up the plate and smashing the dinner into the kitchen sink. She burst into tears again, sobbing over the sink. Then she vomited. Oh God, Jill thought, what is up with me? Just then her mobile rang and she grabbed it, still half-sobbing into the mouthpiece.

"Khan, you bastard -"

A startled voice spoke back to her.

"Jill?"

"Sorry, eh, who is this?"

"It's Ewan Sinclair, Jill."

"Oh, fuck off, Ewan! Not now -"

Jill hung up on her fellow Scottish ex and switched her mobile off. She could not face any more calls tonight.

*

Across London, in their more upmarket townhouse in Chelsea, practically in über-posh West Kensington, the Venters family had begun to clear up the dishes after a satisfying dinner of homemade kosher ground beef meatloaf in puff pastry, spiced red cabbage and mashed potatoes. Ruthie's father Rolf had an important paper for an upcoming gynaecological conference in Paris to work through and he needed some peace and quiet time. So Ruthie and her mother Marcie took everything through to the stylishly outfitted designer kitchen to load up the computerised dishwasher and generally tidy up.

"Mmm! Momma, that meal was just so delicious."

Marcie gave Ruthie a warm motherly hug.

"Thank you, bubba. I knew you would like me to make your old Grandma Bloom's favourite recipe."

They continued to busy about the kitchen clearing up.

"So, Ruthie, you say things are better at work these last few days?"

Ruthie gushed happily.

"Oh, Momma, it's been fantastic! Jill has been pushing some great work my way and I've been working real hard on some juicy stories. Of course, I can't tell you about them – sworn to secrecy and all that - until they hit the press. Jill has even promised I'll get a by-line on a couple of the smaller articles."

Marcie ruffled her daughter's long dark glossy black hair and gazed lovingly into Ruthie's brown liquid excited eyes.

"That is fantastic. You seem to be so much happier about it. I'm sorry again, Ruthie, for rubbing you up the wrong way about your new career. Little bubba's gotta find her own path in life and you are doing it really well. I'm so proud of you!"

Ruthie hugged her mother back and exhaled a little shriek of excitement.

"Thanks, Momma. You and papa have been so great and I just want to make you proud. Funny thing is, I'm not sure what changed things with Jill. Although, I believe from one of the other girls in the office that Jill probably got a bit of a rollicking from Mr Buckley."

Marcie hesitated, not wanting to spoil the moment.

"We-ell –"

Ruthie looked quizzically at her mother.

"Well what, Mom?"

"Well, er, maybe I asked your papa to have a quiet little word with your boss, Mr Buckley. They were playing golf last Saturday and I just said, Rolf..."

"Aw, Momma - I want to do this myself!"

"Look, what you gonna do, huh? You gonna push the rock to the top of the mountain all by yourself? Sometimes you need a little hand, baby."

"Okay, Mom, but you've got to let me go my own way from now on."

Marcie tweaked her daughter's nose playfully.

"Sure, baby."

They had finished loading the dishwasher and clearing up the worktops and Ruthie turned to head up to her room to chill out. Marcie called her back.

"Ruthie, have you seen my red-coloured memory stick lying about anywhere?"

"Nope - sorry, Momma - I'll look out for it though."

Damn, thought Marcie, I haven't seen that darn thing since that God awful presentation.

CHAPTER 4

<u>Earthdate: 08:36 Wednesday February 5, 2081 GMT</u>

Ewan Sinclair and Gary Mackintosh walked briskly out of Kings Cross Station and along Euston Road, both of them nervously glancing around. They should not have been so nervous. However, their fear was primal and instinctive. Gary had assured Ewan that their hacking incursion into the E2MSN network, as far as he could possibly ascertain, remained completely undetected by NASA HQ. Furthermore, Gary, using his consummate computing skills had set up his hack through more than a dozen computers spread across the globe, totally unknown and unseen by their computer owners, with a level of encryption that would take Alan Turing weeks to crack, never mind the NASA boys. If NASA cottoned on to them they would be more likely to think the hackers were in Lagos or Lima than in London. Ewan just prayed Gary was right.

Only a few minutes ago, they had alighted from the 5.30am red-eye Superliner train from Edinburgh Waverley, which had cruised down the newly upgraded East Coast High Speed Line in just under three hours. Four hundred miles and only five minutes late. They walked on past St Pancras Station and the British Library and continued towards Euston Station. The two friends did not speak as they nervously walked along clutching their satchels, which they had slung over their shoulders. Instead they surveyed the peak hour traffic building up in central London as they strode purposefully along. Traffic was mainly electric powered buses, trucks, vans and black taxis at street level and, above the tall buildings, streams of air-cars zooming purposefully towards their place of work. Now and then they were curious to see the odd old petrol-driven or hybrid car running along Euston Road. Most of them were actually collector's classics, almost too expensive to run these days. By about 2040 the price of oil had become so prohibitive that by then almost all new vehicles were fitted with super-efficient electric engines. This also had the effect of strangling the Middle East's most powerful, and in particular the LOIN's, most powerful economic weapon –

crude oil. The dramatic fall in the demand for crude had also paradoxically helped to contribute to the long uneasy peace between the LOIN and the West. Basically, this had led to the stranglehold of the OPEC cartel totally collapsing and vastly diminishing the economic muscle of Iran and Iraq. This brought about the demise of the internal combustion engine and the end of the suffocating rise in surface-level traffic. The traffic jams had almost brought the great Western cities to a state of virtual gridlock. It also led to the invention of the air-car in 2052 and the subsequent development of the sky-level traffic flows.

Ewan turned his thoughts to their impending meeting as he tried to keep up with Gary's quickening pace. Gary was excited, even in his nervousness, because he was planning the upcoming financial negotiation in his head. If truth be told he was actually planning how he was going to spend the cash. On the other hand, Ewan was apprehensive. He was trying to formulate the right words to put to Jill. Especially after the way she cut him off on the phone a few nights ago. Fortunately for Ewan, Jill had returned his call the following day and apologised for her outburst. She told Ewan that she thought it had been her boyfriend Khan calling her back. Ewan did not question Jill further, but he had thought that maybe she and Khan were going through a bad patch. Ewan wondered if there was still a half chance of him and Jill getting back together. They had enjoyed a short fling together when Jill was still working at the Glasgow Herald, although she had finished their relationship just before she got the job at the Times in London. Ewan had only met Khan al Ahmed once, at a party when Jill had invited him down from Edinburgh to her flat-warming at Kew. From the initial invite Ewan had misconstrued that he and Jill might have a chance of getting back together. When he arrived at the party, Jill immediately introduced Khan and Ewan took an instant and abiding dislike to the Arab. However, Ewan had to admit that Jill, with her long-blond hair, sparkling blue eyes and classic Nordic features, and Khan, tall, dark and swarthy with a powerfully-framed physique, looked a striking and handsome couple. Ewan thought he could never compete with someone like Khan and he told himself that getting back with Jill was a forlorn hope.

Ewan and Gary arrived just outside Euston Station. Gary pointed to the large three-storey block that had been built on the square in front of the station terminal building called the Euston iCafé.

"Is that the place, Ewan?"

"Yes, she said to meet her on the first floor."

They entered the huge iCafé which was extremely busy already, even at this early hour, and they scaled the stairs to the first floor. Jill was busy checking her inbox on her laptop, so she did not see the Scottish duo enter the first floor café. Gary spotted her first and he dug his elbow into Ewan's side and indicated where she was sitting with a knowing nod of his head. Gary whispered an aside to his friend.

"Pssst! There's Jill over there. By the way, she still looks absolutely fuckin' gorgeous. How did you manage to let her get away?"

"Och, leave it out, Gary!"

Ewan and Gary sidled through the busy tables, trying hard not to accidentally knock coffee cups over onto the dozens of users' laptops and iTabs as they squeezed past. Jill, who had by then spotted them, stood up and gave them a hesitant wave. Ewan smiled back and thought that she did indeed still look drop-dead gorgeous, but she also had a tired strained look on her face. They all said their hellos and Jill gave Ewan a kiss on the side of his mouth. He knew it was just a platonic greeting from an old friend but the kiss sent a pang of emotion shooting straight to his heart. How did he manage to let her get away? Gary went up to the counter to order black coffees for him and Ewan and a fresh latte for Jill. Jill and Ewan sat and exchanged pleasantries while they waited.

"It's good to see you, Ewan. It's been a while. I'm really sorry I swore at you the other night. As I said – I thought you were Khan. We'd been having a tiff on the phone."

"No worries, Jill. Just glad you phoned me back."

"So what're you doing with yourself, then? Are you the big-shot astronomer now?"

Ewan's eyes dropped momentarily to his lap.

"No! I'm nothing like that. The jobs market in the UK for a recently graduated Doctor in Astronomy and Astrophysics is totally zip at the moment. I'm doing some part-time paid research work in Space Science on a post-grad basis at Edinburgh Uni. But, I'm afraid to say it's mainly casual work in the World's End pub that's keeping the wolf from the door. Look at you, though - you're looking great, Jill -"

"I dunno, Ewan – I've been feeling like shit recently."

"You and Khan…?"

Ewan stopped himself and let the question hang. Jill shook her head.

"No, no. Well, not just that. Ach, you know what London's like. It's just so much more stressful than Glasgow or Edinburgh. Y'know – the job, relationships, traffic, even the bloody trains have been doin' my nut in lately."

Gary arrived back with the coffees and he set them down on the table.

"Ah've no' interrupted a wee tête-à-tête, have ah?"

Ewan groaned to the heavens.

"Aw, Christ sake, Gaz. Sit down and zip it!"

Jill smiled genuinely amused. She had never fancied Gary Mackintosh, even when they were at Glasgow High School together, but he always knew how to lighten even the most serious of situations. Jill sipped her latte savouring the creamy coffee flavour, then spoke.

"Right, boys, what is the pressing matter that has brought you down to London to see me – one that you couldn't talk about on the blower?"

Gary held up his palm and stopped the conversation with some of his usual toilet humour. "Gentlemen be seated and let the matter drop. Before we start – first things first…"

Gary put his upraised index finger to his lips to indicate that he required silence. Jill was amused but slightly confused by this cloak and dagger performance. He took out his laptop from his satchel and hooked it up to the café's power socket and Wi-Fi internet connection. He gave a voice activation command to the computer.

"Run - Prog - Blood - Hound –"

Jill was now completely bamboozled.

"What are you on about Gary?"

Gary suspended his palm in the air momentarily.

"Hold on. Wait a wee sec. Right, that's it operational. I've just activated a piece of software that is scanning the immediate area for any electronic bugging devices that might be listening in. If it detects any then it just fuckin' blocks out the reception and garbles anything that we might say to each other. Ta, da!"

Jill shot a quizzical glance at Ewan.

"Ewan, what in hell's name's goin' on here?"

Ewan looked nervously around the room but Gary butted in first.

"Eh, before Ewan does his spiel, Jill, ah just want to say that we did not just rattle down to London for a birl on the London Eye and catch up wi' old friends. What you are about to hear is priceless. In fact, Jill, ah take that back – what you are about to hear has its price, if you know what ah mean?"

"Look, guys, I'm in the press business so don't try and teach your granny to suck eggs. If you have a genuine story then I am prepared to discuss a price with my boss. The final say lies with him."

Although, fat chance of a big pay out, Jill thought. Buckley was as tight as a duck's arse when it came to paying for any story never mind an exclusive.

Ewan spoke up at last.

"Gary, let me tell Jill what we have come down for, okay?"

"Okay – but, Jill – you get nothin' for nothin'!"

Ewan waved his hand agitatedly for Gary to shut up.

"Jill, we're here to see you because something has come into our hands - information - which has potentially global ramifications. And I'm talking global, Jill –"

"I'm listening…"

"Well, the first thing that came into our possession was an email from a high-ranking Israeli astrophysicist. He is working on a joint US – Israeli deep space astronomy project…"

"Do you mean Nimrod?"

"You've heard of it?"

"Boys, what kind a journalist do you think I am - a buckin' Mickey Mouse one?"

"Sorry, Jill - yes, it is the Nimrod Star Hunter 2 programme. Well, for some unknown reason this guy in Tel Aviv punched in some erroneous digits and he sent the telescope spinning to view the wrong part of space. Shall we say inner-space rather than deep-space? A very costly budget mistake on his part…"

Jill looked at Ewan contemplatively.

"Do you have the email?"

Gary interrupted again.

"Course we do – but that comes along with the money!"

Ewan was irritated.

"Gary, let me do the talking. We can trust Jill totally on this. As Gary said, we do have the email. I wasn't so sure if there was enough collateral in the email for you to make a story out of it. However, Gary's view is that - because the Yanks are so intertwined with the Israelis, not just on this SH2 project, but economically, politically and defensively – then if a screw-up like this could happen on this guy's watch, who's to say the same thing couldn't happen in some Israeli Nuclear bunker? What with the Israelis sitting nuke to nuke across the fence from the LOIN and the US having played it softly-softly all these years to maintain the peace in the Middle East? You know what I'm saying or is that just a load of old tosh?"

Jill pursed her lips thoughtfully and looked at Gary.

"No, not really, I think Gary's got a point. There are the bones of a story in there…"

Gary was triumphant.

"See, ah told ye Ewan!"

Jill continued.

"But Ewan, you said that was just the first thing?"

Gary nudged Ewan excitedly. He also quickly glanced at his monitor. The Bloodhound programme still showed all clear.

"Tell her, Ewan. Tell, Jill!"

Ewan bent down and pulled out some papers from his satchel, which was placed on the floor beside his seat. He glanced around furtively. Everyone around seemed engrossed on their laptops. Ewan pushed the papers in front of Jill and she could see that they were what looked like grainy large black photographs. Jill could not make anything much of the pictures and gave another puzzled look towards the boys.

"You'll need to help me out here, guys. Is this our global story?"

Gary gave Ewan an excited prod to gee things up a bit. Ewan spoke slowly and deliberately.

"Jill, this is a set of still photos taken from the Nimrod SH2 during the two or so minutes when it was misdirected by our pal in Tel Aviv. I have studied the footage about a million times in the last few days and from what I have interpreted I am fairly excited –"

Jill looked down at what just looked like a mass of black on the photos.

"Fairly excited, Ewan, I thought we had a world exclusive on our hands?"

Gary gushed in.

"Jill, Ewan is more than fairly excited. He is abso – fuckin'- lutely over the bloody Moon about this! For Christ sake, tell her, Ewan?"

Ewan continued, still the deliberating scientist, slow and deadpan, but inside his heart was pounding with the adrenalin surges shooting through his body.

"To be honest, the two minutes eleven seconds of footage was rather on the short side to allow me to compute a complete calculation and because the SH2 was supposed to be looking way into deep space the focus wasn't super-perfect. However, let's look at this first shot…?"

Ewan directed them to the topmost photograph by pointing his finger.

"Right, Jill, what the Israeli scientist captured was a shot of an area in the solar system known as the Kuiper Belt, the co-ordinates identifying its location are printed on the bottom left of the photo."

"Okay, I see that, Ewan."

"What I have done to the photos is effectively black out any objects further away than the Kuiper belt, i.e., I have removed all distant stars and galaxies.

Right, well, look just above the co-ordinates. Can you see anything of any significance?"

Jill peered at the almost totally black photograph with some difficulty.

"All I can see is a little white speck."

"Good, Jill. Well that little white speck is actually Pluto. It used to be classed as a planet in the solar system when it was first discovered, but we really just class it as one of the larger asteroids or dwarf planets in the Kuiper Belt. Other dwarf planets there include Haumea and Makemake, although they are not within this photo's range. The Kuiper Belt, otherwise known as the Edgeworth-Kuiper Belt is basically a ring of debris, mainly hundreds of thousands of orbiting ice particles, which forms the outer ring of our own solar system. Close inspection of the photos show some of these ice particles."

Jill screwed her eyes tightly and squinted at the photographs.

"Hmmm. Maybe to your eyes but I can hardly make out anything. Anyway, so the photos show Pluto in the Kuiper Belt. So what? That's hardly earth-shattering..."

Ewan drew an imaginary circle with his finger over the photo.

"Look again, Jill. Look at the top right. See anything there?"

Jill looked hard for a few seconds and then it dawned on her.

"Oh, yeah - looks like a little white dash. Is that it?"

Gary blurted out in excitement.

"My God, she's got it Ewan."

Jill looked at Ewan as she struggled to see the significance. She was beginning to get a little agitated as she felt that this was all developing a little sluggishly as the sort of global exclusive Ewan had made it out to be on the phone. She caught a quick glance at the time on her laptop. 09:15. Jill was due to meet Ruthie down at Tilbury Docks at 10:30. They had an important interview with a notorious East End gangster, Alfie 'Dinky' Budge, who was willing to spill the beans on his crime-lord boss, Nesto Petrianni. Alfie, well-known in the underworld as a hit man got his nom-de-plum for his preference to, as he called it, 'dink' his targets with his old .357 Magnum fitted with an ultra-modern silencer. That interview was beginning to look much more important than her current one and time was now starting to run out for Jill.

"Ewan, look I know this must be important to you, but I've got another vital meeting to get to and my time is running out."

Ewan showed more urgency in his pace of speech.

"Okay, Jill, I'll make this fast. That little white dash, as you called it, is actually a brand new comet. As far as I can tell its composition is rock and ice. For some unknown reason it has just recently been sucked into the solar system from who knows where. It is currently passing its way through the Kuiper Belt."

Jill was now showing a bit more interest.

"Mmm, now that is more like it. So not only did your Israeli muck up his co-ordinates but in doing so he actually stumbled onto something new and he doesn't even know it?"

"You've got it in one, Jill."

"So what have you called this new heavenly body - the Sinclair-Mackintosh Comet?"

Before he had stopped to think Ewan replied.

"No - Schenkler's Comet –"

Gary dug Ewan painfully in the ribs.

"Too much info, Ewan –"

As Ewan rubbed his sore spot Jill came back at them.

"Look, guys, if there is a story in this, which I am now happier that there is, then I need to know everything. Okay? So who is Schenkler? Let me guess – he is your Israeli friend…?"

"Well, Jill, Gary and I thought – well, in a way Schenkler was the first to discover the comet. We thought we would give him his place. Look I know you're pressed for time, but there's more to it. Have you got a couple more minutes?"

"Go on, Ewan, you've got me hooked now."

"Okay, so we have definitely found a new comet. Using Schenkler's limited piece of footage I have been able to construct a computer simulation model of the comet and its trajectory. As I've said its core is composed mainly of rock and ice. The core is roughly one and half times the size of Pluto – 1.515 actually, so it is quite sizeable. It has a tail of ice particles extending in towards the Sun's gravitational pull, something in the order of one and a half to two million kilometres from its core. Here's the thing – using the model, which as I've said is only based on Schenkler's limited photographic data, I have computed this comet is going to pass Earth spectacularly closely in late May 2084. It will shine even brighter than the Moon in the night sky!"

Jill, ever the optimistic journalist, hit back with the 64,000 dollar question.

"Is there any chance this thing could hit Earth?"

"I would certainly need a lot more data than 2 minutes. But on my computer model the parameters of proximity of the comet's core to Earth in 2084 are going to be between 3.8 million kilometres away and 1.5 million kilometres as a closest approximation. So it does not look like it will collide with Earth – but it will be spectacularly close. There is also a more than good probability that the planet will suffer some pretty extensive collateral damage as we are going to be pretty close to the tip of the comet's tail. Earth's gravity is likely to attract some pretty hefty meteor showers probably starting around mid-February 2084."

Jill picked up the photos, her ice-blue eyes now sparkling with excitement. She was already dreaming up the banner headlines – SCOTS ASTROLOGER DISCOVERS NEW COMET – NEAR MISS WITH PLANET EARTH IN 2084!

"Well, why didn't you tell me that in the first place? I think we really do have a story now, don't we? Look, I really need to go. But I'll put this past my boss – and, yes, Gary – I will talk money with him. In the meantime you guys put everything you've got together and I'll be in touch by mobile – no later than the day after tomorrow. One last question though? How did you come by all this info? Was it a reliable source within the field of space science that passed this data on to you?"

Ewan and Gary looked at each other, then Gary slowly raised his hand as if asking Jill for permission to speak.

"I, eh, guess that's where ah come in, Jill…"

Jill's journalistic nose informed her immediately to the situation.

"Oh, don't tell me – not hacking?"

"Ah'm afraid so."

"Who have you hacked, Gary?"

"NASA…"

Jill jumped up angrily.

"Sorry guys! I can't touch it. My boss would crucify me –"

Gary stood up and placed calming hands on Jill's shoulder to make her sit down again.

"Just listen for one sec. We have a plan, Jill. We know you can't go straight to press with a hacked story - especially one from NASA. What we do is give you all the stuff as an exclusive to your online Bloid. You have the presses ready to roll, so to speak. When you are ready we release the info to three or four of the political leak websites. You know, like WikiLeaks, WWWLeaks,

GoogLeaks and so on. When they put Schenkler's stuff online you hit the iTabs the same day with breaking news. You get the fuckin' scoop before the rest of the Bloids. Do we have a plan, Jill?"

"It could work. Okay, let's run with it. But seriously, I really have got to shoot –"

Jill hurriedly packed up her things and made to rush off out the iCafé. She managed a parting shot to Gary.

"I thought that NASA's systems had been made impregnable since the hacking incursions decades ago?"

"Jill, nothin's fuckin' impregnable!"

CHAPTER 5

<u>Earthdate: 20:12 Thursday February 6, 2081 CST</u>

Jack Crossan lay uncomfortably on his bunk in his cabin reading a trashy well-thumbed sci-fi novel from the ship's library that had certainly done the rounds with the numerous crews on Oceanus. The vessel had made its departure launch 26 hours ago from MGal3 without a hitch. Mars was now just a small red ball in the vast blackness of space and Earth remained a tiny flickering blue dot way ahead of her. Science fiction was not really his bag and the book was failing to hold Jack's attention. He yawned widely and laid his head back on the bolster behind him. He succumbed to the creeping tiredness and grab some shut-eye as his shift as Watch Commander was not due to start for another two hours. None of the returning astronauts who had been working on the stations on or above Mars were exempt from duty on the Oceanus. Basically they were all replenishing the crew from Oceanus who were now detailed to work on or above the Red Planet. Jack had his planned rotas scheduled all the way back to Alpha Base, the main space station orbiting planet Earth. The 'good ole 3R', thought Jack. The only passengers going home on Oceanus were the ice-miners and the engineering and maintenance staff from the various Mars bases. Mars, mainly due to its hostile environment, as yet was still some way off being truly colonised by humans just for the sake of living and working there. In some ways the astronauts had it easier because the four month journey between Mars and Earth was slow time. At least the astronauts had work to perform to help make time pass quicker. The miners, engineers and maintenance staff tended to spend their time boozing, gambling and invariably fighting. Some astronauts were detailed to act part-time as space marshals to ensure that civil order was maintained on board, although Jack was glad that was not part of his rota.

Jack's mind's eye drifted back to his Virginian dairy farm near Lexington. Peggy Sue would be getting Milner and Jack Junior settled for going to bed soon. Milner was ten and young Jack was almost seven. Jack would miss his youngest son's birthday, which was a long-standing occupational hazard for any astronaut. Peggy Sue would also be in bed early tonight as she had to get up at 5.30am to organise the milking of their prize Jerseys. Jack looked forward to those more mundane farming duties ahead of him, but he was gratified that it would be a good deal warmer than Peggy Sue's shift tomorrow. A great wave of emotion washed over Jack as he lay with his eyes closed. His love for his second wife Peggy Sue had become so deep-rooted lately, particularly on this last four months' tour of duty on MGal3. It had not always been so.

Jack had been born John Alexander Crossan in one of the large 'trailer trash' parks just outside Lexington, Virginia in 2029 on what was deemed the wrong side of the tracks, although, in reality, there was no longer a railroad track in the immediate vicinity. Jack's upbringing was fairly erratic. Both his parents squandered what little spare welfare they received on drugs and alcohol. They spent little quality time bringing up Jack, who in turn, spent a great deal of his formative years cleaning up his parents' mess. In one vivid memory, five-year-old Jack was in his trailer bunk with a high fever and he lay there tossing and turning in sweat and pain. Suddenly, he woke up and there in front of him stood a shadowy figure with his arm outstretched. He jumped out of bed and rushed past the figure and straight into his parents' bedroom crying in anguish.

"Mom - Mom! Pop! Come quick! There's a man in ma room with a gun –"

His parents both lay sprawled on their bed shit-faced on crack coke. Only his father Andy could muster a muted response.

"Jo-ohn – muss be a bad dr-eam. Go back ta be-ed son…"

He looked down in helpless dismay at his parents for a few moments and then he very slowly crept back and peered cautiously into his room. The man with the gun had gone. Was he real or was he just a dream like Andy had stammered in his drug-fuelled stupor. Young Jack got back into bed and slept off the fever. Jack grew up fast despite his parents. He was extremely intelligent and a real battler, a thirsty fighter for knowledge and understanding. His ambition was to get into the US Air Force when he graduated from school. If Jack was truthful his real deep-seeded ambition was one day to become an astronaut on the NASA space program, but he was realistic enough to set his achievable goals on a more down to Earth target. Once an obnoxious teacher had spat in Jack's face that 'trailer-trash don't get to go to Mars' but he was gutsy enough to convince himself that 'one day I'll get jets'. Jack was always fascinated by space travel but his early burning desire to become an astronaut arose from a strange incident that occurred when Jack was aged six. Jack had been playing alone not far from the family trailer in a patch of allotments nicknamed 'the Gardens of Gethsemane', although it was colloquially corrupted to 'Geth's Gardens'. It was not unusual for Jack to be playing alone. The other kids tended to avoid playing with Jack, mainly because their parents called Jack's parents 'alkies' and 'druggies'. He was not bullied as such by the other kids as he was not afraid to beat the crap out of someone twice his age. Jack was happy as a loner and just as happy feeding his fertile imagination by himself. That day as usual Jack played happily just outside the green-painted picket fence of old Jimmy Reid's tidy little garden lot. Jimmy, known as Uncle Jimmy to everyone, had been a railroad engineer before the tracks in Lexington had been all torn up and they pensioned off old Jimmy. At that particular moment old Jimmy had not been working in amongst his potatoes, tomatoes and pumpkin rows and Jack amused himself. He had been running wildly in circles burning off his youthful energy– a little spaceman orbiting some far distant planet light years from Earth. But he had to stop in front of the green picket fence to catch his breath. Puffing hard to replenish his oxygen tanks, Jack grabbed hold of the painted railing of the fence with both hands. He was now a rocket back on the launch pad at Cape Canaveral on the clear blue Florida coast. Jack prepared for lift-off and began the launch sequence countdown.

"Five – four – three – two – one - Houston Control - we have lift-off!"

Jack squeezed his hands tightly on the wooden rail of the picket fence and concentrated with all his might on the lift-off, imagining his feet to be the huge booster rockets of his 'Santa Maria Super-shuttle'. Suddenly he felt his two feet start to rise off the ground, which at first startled him, but he continued to concentrate. Soon Jack was levitating, still holding on to the picket fence, his body floating completely level in the air above the grassy ground below his body. He cried out excitedly.

"Ah'm floatin' - ah'm floatin' in space!"

This immediately broke his concentration and his body came quickly back down to grassy Earth. Jack held on to the fence and tried to repeat the levitation but nothing happened. He was wondering if he had imagined what had just occurred or whether he had just been dreaming, when he heard footsteps behind him. Jack looked round to see the tiny frame of kindly old bald-headed Jimmy Reid striding down the path towards him. Jack and Jimmy got on famously and the boy often helped him in the small garden lot where he could talk easily with the old man. Jack ran up to his old gardener friend.

"Uncle Jimmy – did ya see me? Ah was floatin' in space –"

"Whassat you said, Jacky boy?"

"Over there at your fence – ah was just floatin' up in the air!"

"Ah dunno 'bout that, Jack? Heard tell that long time ago there wez an ole canal came right through this area. Filled in hunners a' years back - maybe ya wez jest floatin' on the ghost of that there ole canal, ma little Jacko?"

The old man laughed and ruffled Jack's dark mop of hair.

"But ah definitely was floatin', Uncle Jimmy!"

"Okay, Jacky boy, but you an' ah's got tomatoes ta pick for Missus Reid's dinner table. So we best get workin' at that pickin' –"

Jack's excellent grades at Lexington High earned him a scholarship to Cal Tech where he studied for a degree in Aviation and Avionics. Of course, his parents both missed his graduation, even if they could have afforded the flight from Virginia to California. His father Andy had been arrested on a drugs misdemeanour and was being held in the County Jail for the umpteenth time. His mother Annabel was so out of her face on crack that she would not have been able to state where either of the two men in her life were at that particular time. In 2058, Jack got a place on the flight programme at Quantico back in Virginia and graduated top of his class. His father Andy, who by that time was doing better in a private rehabilitation programme in Lexington funded from Jack's salary, made it to the flight school graduation. Sadly, Annabel had died of a drugs overdose the previous year. Andy looked about twenty years older than the mid-fifties that he actually was, but Jack felt that he showed a new spirit and resolution of character that the young Jack had never seen before. It struck Jack that his father, who had been miserably broken by his own parents in his youth, demonstrated some of the genetic traits that Jack had to muster as he grew up through his torrid adolescence. Jack could see where his fighting spirit came from now and he was pleased to recognise that. After the graduation and parade of the newly qualified pilots Andy came up to his son, sporting the new suit, badly ill-fitting, that Jack had paid for. Andy's chest was just bursting with pride and the tears were welling up on the rims of his bloodshot eyes. He spoke chokingly to his son in his slow Virginian drawl.

"Son, ah don't have the words really. What ah would like to say to you? Ah jest don't quite know. Ah'm jest real proud of ya. Never thought ah'd see ma son in one a them swanky U-S-A-F duds. Ah only wished that your mom could see ya today, son…"

Andy's voice finally cracked and the tears streamed down his face. Jack's tears were flowing freely too and the father and son hugged each other like they had never hugged before. They were never quite as close again as they were that day on the parade ground at Quantico, but Andy never slipped back to the sordid addictive life-style that he had led since he was that wild teenager with the big chip on his shoulder. After Quantico Jack went to 'get jets' flying on the F-69 ultra-stealth fighter programme based at Andrews Air Force base in Maryland and again his intelligence and air prowess saw him rise to 'Top Gun' in the F-69 fighter squadron. He had tours with the squadron in the Persian Gulf, Japan and the South China Seas before returning to Maryland in the spring of 2063. It was that year at a club in the New Holiday Inn in Silver Springs, a few miles from Andrews, that he met Maria Conchita Gonzales. Maria was a gorgeous fiery-tempered flame-haired Tex-Mex, who also worked as an auxiliary on the base at Andrews, although they had never met each other before. They immediately became lovers and within months Jack had asked her to marry him. One day in the locker room at Andrews he told his best friend and wing man, Vance Mulcahey, a Princeton graduate, that he was marrying Maria. Vance was taken aback and implored Jack to rethink.

"Jeez, man, Maria's a great lay, Jack. But, for Christ sake, she's only a base cleaner. With your film star looks you could have any one of the rich debs up in DC if you wanted!"

Jack had to admit to himself that his looks had attracted scores of beauties into bed over the years, but this time it felt different. Vance was his most trusted wing man and the closest of friends but Jack, with a slam of his locker door, snapped back angrily.

"Ah love Maria, Vance! Don't matter what she is or where she comes from. If you ever saw the trailer park ah came from, you might a thought twice about havin' *me* as a friend!"

"Sorry, Jack – I was totally out of order there. Congratulations, Big Bro', hope I'm gonna be best man? You need a good wing man on your wedding day!"

After the wedding Jack and Maria bought a small neat bungalow in Silver Springs and both continued to work at their jobs on Andrews. They both talked about wanting to raise a big family and it was only a few months after their marriage when Maria fell pregnant. They were delighted but it turned out to be a nerve-wracking pregnancy. Maria had collapsed and she was diagnosed a month into her second trimester with a previously undetected small hole in her heart. The doctors at the base hospital determined that she would require an operation, but it was too risky to carry it out while Maria was carrying her unborn child. It was touch and go, but Maria gave birth to bouncing baby Isabella Annabel Maria Crossan on 26 May 2064 in the maternity suite at Andrews Air Force Medical Center. Nine months later she was back at the Center for her heart operation. Jack had left Isabella with her grandfather Andy, who had journeyed up from Lexington, and he spent three long nerve-jangling hours in the waiting room before the base chief surgeon came in head lowered and looking serious and drawn. Jack's heart sank.

"Is she...?"

"Don't worry, Mr Crossan, she's fine, but, ah –"

"But – but what, doc?"

"Well, the keyhole surgery has revealed that Maria suffered additional damage to the small tear in her heart during her pregnancy and when giving birth. We have, however, been able to repair it quite successfully."

"So she's gonna be fine, Doctor?"

"Maria's gonna be up and around in a week or so and she'll go on to live a long happy life. But, one thing, Mr Crossan –"

"Call me Jack."

"Jack – the thing is this. Maria's heart is never gonna be 100 per cent again. The pregnancy has taken a lot out her and the heart has been severely weakened. I am going to advise her – and I'm telling *you* – it will be too risky for Maria to have another child."

"But Doctor, she's Catholic. She won't take the pill –"

"Then, Jack, it's up to you. From now on it's either the male contraceptive or else –"

The surgeon indicated what he meant by motioning two fingers as snipping scissors towards Jack's private parts. When Maria got home she looked so much healthier than she had been in a long time and Jack, Maria and baby Isabella knuckled down to enjoying family life. For a while things were going great. Jack went back to the F-69s and Maria gave up her job at Andrews to bring up Isabella. Maria would not hear of Jack going on the male pill and also that Jack was not going for any snip. Secretly, Jack was pleased about that part. It would have been a dent to his machismo and he did not fancy being a member of the "I Only Fire Blanks Club". Maria stated adamantly, that as a Catholic, she would only be happy with the rhythm method of contraception.

"If it was good enough for my parents, then it is just as good for me also!"

"Jesus, Maria, your parents ended up with nine kids!"

"Yeah, well I'm gonna do it right. We'll have plans and charts and we'll stick to them, okay, big Jack?"

"Okay, Maria Conchita, you are the boss!"

In mid-September 2066 Jack arrived home one night laden down with a magnum of champagne, a huge box of chocolates and an even bigger bouquet of flowers. Maria squealed with delight and little Isabella, already in her baby-grow pyjamas, clapped her hands excitedly. Jack had already had a couple of Jack Daniels and he was feeling elated.

"Jack, darling, what's the occasion?"

"Maria Conchita Crossan - you're dearly beloved husband has only gone and gotten the Big One!"

Maria screamed so loud that Isabella started crying with fright.

"Eeeeh! You got Air Force One?"

"Ah sure did, honey bunch. John Crossan, pilot to the President of the U-Ni-Ted States of America, at your service, ma'am!"

After Isabella was put to bed, they celebrated into the night, finishing the champagne and Jack helped himself to a few more bourbons. By the time they were in bed Jack was pretty tipsy and full-on horny. Jack snuggled up to Maria and kissed her neck.

"C'mon, baby, big Jack needs his momma –"

"Oh, no, Jack – we are way off the charts tonight. You know it's too darn risky."

"Big Jack promises his Maria that he'll jump off the train before it hits the buffers. Ba-by, Jacky needs his Maria Conchita?"

"You better jump off that damn train okay or ah'm gonna kill you Jack!"

Three weeks later Maria, in tears, gave him the news that she was pregnant again. Jack was profusely apologetic. He knew he had crossed the line and had put Maria's life in jeopardy.

"Maria, I'm so sorry. Ah was so drunk that night ah just couldn't stop myself. Look, baby, the best thing to do is go for a termination."

Maria swiftly crossed herself and stared at Jack in horror.

"Jack Crossan, you horny bastard, don't you swear at me. *Madre Dio!* My parents and my priest would kill me if they even thought that I would contemplate an abortion. No, Jack, the baby is ours. I want my baby."

Over the next few weeks Jack tried to talk to Maria into the abortion. She would not even hear of it and Jack worried himself sick over Maria's health. Maria on the other hand bloomed magnificently as each trimester passed. The doctors were delighted at her progress but they advised that Maria should take it easy during the pregnancy, including no alcohol and little sex. As far as Maria was concerned that meant no sex, nothing, nada! Jack, now flying in Air Force One squadron, was at lunch one day at the base canteen with his old wing man, Vance Mulcahey, who was now 'Top Gun' on the F-69s.

"So how's Maria's pregnancy doing, Jack."

"Oh, ah guess she's doin' fine, Vance."

"You sound a bit disgruntled there, Big Bro'? You okay?"

"Man, ah'm just friggin' gaggin' for it Vance. Maria won't let me near her till the baby's born."

Vance put his arm around his old friend's shoulder.

"What you and I need to do is to get our old F-6-9 buddies together and have a real good ole blow-out up there in DC. What do ya say, Jack?"

"Good idea - so long as we're only talkin' drinks here, Vance?"

"It's the only thang on ma mind, Jacky boy! Although we both know what 'F' and '69' really stands for!"

The eleven Old Boys of the F-69 squadron were having a grand old night out up in downtown Washington. It could not have been any better for Jack. Maria had flown down to San Antonio, Texas with Isabella because her grandmother was very ill in hospital. So it had not been a problem for Jack when Vance and the other guys suggested staying over at the InterContinental in DC. The cash and the drinks were flowing. They had started with a bar meal of Buffalo wings and burgers washed down with jugs of Bud in Georgetown. Then they all jumped into three yellow electri-cabs and headed back to hit a couple of clubs on the edge of Foggy Bottom, where the eleven guys all started knocking back shots dropped in Jack Daniels and Coke. To finish the night they all staggered on to one of the Potomac's water-taxis and sailed leisurely down to get into one of the exclusive clubs in upmarket Alexandria. As they floated past the infamous Watergate building, Jack's eyes were swimming as he looked on to the swirling Potomac, inky black in the darkness and interspersed with dancing eels of light.

"Man, great idea, Vance. I so needed a blow-out like tonight."

Vance was actually avoiding looking at the swirling river. The dancing eels of light were making him nauseous.

"Jeez, Jack, ah'm to-tally wrecked, Big Bro'. Ah think ah go back to Inn-Con-nen-nen-al-"

"Vance, you're as drunk as a monkey, man. How d'ya end up like that?"

When the boat arrived at the pier at Alexandria, most of the guys realised that enough was enough and that they had drunk their fill. They argued for heading back to the InterContinental and finishing the evening with a night-cap. Jack was certainly not finished with his night out.

"Aw, come on guys. This is the first big night out ah've had since ma daughter was born. Who's up for paintin' Alexandria red?"

It certainly would not be Vance. He was already being held up between two of his buddies. The heads were all beginning to shake except one, Dan Kowalski.

"I'm still game if you are, Jack."

"That's ma boy, Dan the Man!"

The pair ended up drinking in The Fish Market, Alexandria's most exclusive night club, which catered for guests who liked their R & B music, mainly from the late-20th century and expertly mixed by the world-famous techno-jock DJ Steeley from "Steel-town" Pittsburgh, Pennsylvania. Jack spotted her drinking alone at the other end of the bar. She looked mesmerisingly stunning, but Jack reminded himself that most women began to look stunning after the amount of alcohol that he had consumed. She spotted him and smiled, subconsciously signalling to him by gently rocking her glass on the bar to signify that her drink was requiring replenishment. Jack turned to Dan. He was already chatting up a very pretty black girl in a stunning and clinging red dress who worked up at the Pentagon. Jack indicated with a nod of his head towards the other girl at the end of the bar, who was in an equally slinky little black number.

"Dan, you okay here? Ah has a friend down there lookin' mighty thirsty."

"Ah'm doin' great, Jacky boy. I'll see ya at breakfast in the mornin'. Good huntin'!"

Jack never made it back to the InterContinental that evening. Instead he woke up in a strange bed in a small apartment across the river in Anacostia, his head bursting with the worst hangover ever. She walked into the bedroom wearing only a very short skimpy Japanese silk dressing gown and carrying a tray arranged with a light breakfast of grits, eggs over easy, biscuits, grape jelly, orange juice and coffee.

"Morning, Jack."

Jack rubbed his forehead and glanced at her through his fingers. She was still beautiful, even in this semi-sober state, he thought. She had long dark auburn hair and legs up to her armpits. Just the way I like them, Jack thought.

"Hi, eh, have we been introduced, ma'am?"

"Many times, Jack. Why you were introducing yourself to me all night long."

"Oh, God, that's what I feared. Look – ah – look - ah don't even know your name."

"Ah'm Peggy Sue Milner from Birmingham, Alabama - at yore service, sir."

"Look – ah – Peggy Sue. Ah don't think you're gonna be surprised to hear that ah am a married man."

"Don't worry, you told me that last night before we even made love. Ya were a proper gen-nel-man, so ya were."

"So where do we go from here, Peggy Sue?"

"Let's jest start with breakfast, Jack."

That night had been the launch pad for a torrid affair between Jack and Peggy Sue. He saw Peggy Sue each time he was up at the Pentagon in Washington for briefings on the scheduled plans for Air Force One flights over the coming weeks and months. The sex was amazing, but every time Jack looked at Maria's ever expanding abdomen he flagellated himself with the guilt he felt. One night he even pleaded with Maria to make love with him but she was adamant that they should not take any risks.

"*Madre de dios,* Jack. Can you not keep it tucked away for a few more weeks? It won't be long my darling."

Another night while in bed in Anacostia with Peggy Sue, he had a nightmare, which had caused him to wake up in a blinding fear-laden sweat. In the dream his drugged up mother Annabel came up to him and Peggy Sue while they stood outside a multiplex, which they had recently gone to in Washington Center. Annabel was like a spitting cobra swirling in front of them.

"John Crossan. Get back to your wife. Get back to your wife, you devil!"

But Peggy Sue was like his drug. He was addicted to the adrenalin rushes every time he knew that he was going to see her, have those wild sexual encounters with her. He never thought of it as truly making love with Peggy Sue. In his mind he had reserved that for Maria. Then one afternoon in a restaurant in Anacostia Peggy Sue exploded the life that he thought he had under control like the flash of a supernova. She whispered across the table.

"I'm pregnant, Jack."

"Oh, God, no, Peggy Sue - how could you? You said you were always careful on the pill?"

"Ah was, Jack. But you see - ah love you. Ah loved you when ah first saw you in Alexandria –"

"No, Peggy Sue, this can't be. Ah love my wife, Maria."

"Ah know you do, honey. But that's why ah wanted to get pregnant. If ah can't have you to myself then ah want to have something that is a piece of the two of us –"

Jack blurted out loudly in a mixture of anger and confusion, which turned the heads of some of the other diners seated in the eatery. He felt his life was being sucked into a black hole. Its gravity was so powerful that he was not going to escape its fatal attraction. A strange feeling crept over him. He felt the presence of the man in the room with the gun and this time his finger was on the trigger.

"Christ sake, Peggy Sue, Maria's pregnant too!"

Peggy Sue showed genuine surprise. Jack had never let on.

"Oh!"

"Peggy Sue, you gotta get rid of it?"

"No way, Jack. Ah want this baby desperately an' ah am Catholic."

The black hole's pull was getting stronger and stronger. The man's finger on the trigger was just itching to put a bullet in Jack's head.

"You're Catholic - God - not you too, Peggy Sue?"

When Jack got home to Silver Springs that same night he had thought through what he needed to do. He loved Maria and Isabella so much that come what may, Jack had decided to come clean. He told Maria about his affair with Peggy Sue and that she had deliberately allowed herself to become pregnant. Maria went ballistic. The only Mexican words that he picked up from the tirade of abuse that she spat out at him were Madre de dios! Mother of God, he thought, what have I done? It was like he felt the bullet exploding in his brain. A couple of days later, despite Jack's protestations, Maria, heavily pregnant, packed some things and took Isabella on the plane down to San Antonio to stay with her parents. Although he tried many times he knew after each call to Maria that she was finished with him and he knew that he only had his super-ego self to blame. Peggy Sue begged him to move up to Anacostia. She had determined the sex of the baby she was carrying and told Jack he was going to have a son. Peggy Sue told him that she would be expecting Jack to accept paternity over the child, which he knew he could not and did not want to argue against.

"Jack, he'll be called Milner Crossan – a piece of me and a piece of you."

Jack did not move to Anacostia but threw himself into his work on Air Force One. Fortunately for Jack, but less so for the cause of world peace, some dangerous flashpoints had arisen in the Middle East and also on the Pakistan / Indian frontier causing tensions to rise between the UN and the LOIN. The US President realised that the fragile peace, which had existed for a number of decades now, was under threat and he and the UN General Secretary embarked on a whistle-stop round of diplomacy on Air Force One across Europe, the Middle East, China and the Indian subcontinent. It did not take the President long to pacify the Mullahs but at least it provided Jack with some breathing space. He still yearned to have Maria, Isabella and the imminently arriving new baby back in Silver Springs. In late May 2067 Jack got a call from one of Maria's sisters in San Antonio. Maria had given birth to a healthy baby son, which Maria had named Xavier Gonzales Crossan after her father Xavier Gonzales. Jack was allowed to go down to San Antonio for Xavier's christening. Maria's parents blanked out Jack but Maria's brothers and sisters were politely pleasant to him. Xavier was a beautiful boy. He had Jack's look about his face but he had the fiery auburn hair from his mother – and her Mexican temper too. Xavier screamed throughout the Christening Mass in San Antonio's San Fernando Roman Catholic cathedral. Maria was polite enough to speak with Jack after the service in the Gonzales' backyard where the christening party was for Xavier. Jack saw the bloom of her pregnancy had gone and she looked sickly, sad and pallid-looking.

"Maria, I'm asking you one last time. For the sake of your health, if not for me. Please come back to Maryland with me?"

"I can't, Jack. You have broken my heart. I'm suing you for a divorce."

Three months later in August 2067 Jack got the call to say that Maria had been found as if asleep beside Xavier. She had died of a heart attack in her sleep. Maria's parents requested that he stay away from the funeral in San Antonio. They could not bear him to be at their beautiful Maria's burial. On the day of the funeral Jack sat for hours in an electri-bus shelter at Silver Springs Metro Station weeping uncontrollably for Maria. Maria's parents filed a petition in San Antonio County Court for custody of Isabella and Xavier. Jack phoned Xavier Senior and told him for their sake and Maria's memory that he would not drag them through the courts. Xavier told Jack that he would never see Isabella and Xavier Junior again if he signed the papers.

"Just get the damn papers to me, Xavier, and I'll sign them."

One rainy night in October 2067 he arrived back home to Silver Springs on his Harley Davidson air-bike from a briefing at the Pentagon to find a yellow electri-cab sitting on the street outside his house. He watched as Peggy Sue got out carrying a well-wrapped bundle. She walked hesitantly over to him through the increasingly heavy rain and stretched the bundle towards him. The rain poured down their faces like tears of the past washing away their sins.

"Jack, this is your son Milner."

Jack looked at the boy and he thought, well this is one son I *can* see and I better not mess it up this time .

"Jack, ah heard from Dan Kowalski about Maria. Ah – am – so – so - sorry. Ah don't know what else to say?"

Maybe Jack could escape the pull of the black hole. Maybe the man might just take his finger off the trigger, just maybe.

"You'd better come in out the rain, Peggy Sue."

Jack and Peggy Sue married in a registry office in DC in June 2068 and Vance Mulcahey was Jack's 'wing man' for a second time. Peggy Sue truly loved Jack and Jack tried his best to reciprocate. She was patient with him and somehow she knew within her heart that she needed to give her 'fly boy' the time and the space to really get to know her and hopefully, in time, to be able to love her back. In some ways that is what Jack did – take the time and the space. In 2070, with the development and growth of the joint UN outreach to the Red Planet now in full swing, Jack was accepted on to the NASA space programme. At last he was the genuine Southern Boy astronaut from Virginia that he had dreamed of being. During his astronautic training period at Cape Canaveral, with the big money rolling in, he and Peggy Sue bought the small dairy farm down in Lexington. The Southern Boy was home again but this time he was on the right side of the tracks. Peggy Sue showed a great flair for managing the farm when Jack was working at the Cape and she found no problem in overseeing the two dairymen that they employed. On 5 February 2073, just months before his first trip out to Mars as a junior astronaut on the brand new Oceanus, Jack Junior was born. It was round about that time that Jack began to feel something more than friendship and companionship with Peggy Sue. Although, now eight years later, he still had not gotten around to telling her yet that he loved her. Suddenly, his intercom crackled to life.

"Jack, zis is da vifteen minoots call for you up on da Bridge. Okay, Jack?"

The sound of the rough-spoken Russian cosmonaut Viktor Tomazschenko startled Jack back to the here and now in his bunk, making him drop the trashy book on the floor. He pressed the button beside his left ear and spoke into the microphone.

"Thanks, Viktor, roger that and out."

CHAPTER 6

She looked nervously at the brass engraved plate on the door in front of her which read:-

ANGELA K. MORTIMER

SENIOR EXECUTIVE OFFICER

HUMAN FERTILISATION & EMBRYOLOGY DEPARTMENT

Angela Mortimer had been on holiday for a week with her partner in Dubai. Marcie hated these pen-pushing managers within the NHS that she had to kow-tow down to in terms of departmental policy, resources, planning and finances. She was a doctor and felt much more comfortable in the field of medical matters and scientific laboratory work than having to deal with budgets and policies and responsibility statements and performance reviews. God, they bored the pants off her. Marcie was at her happiest when she worked among her Petri dishes and ultra-zoom electron microscopes. However, Angela was now back sporting a tan and Marcie needed to tell her boss about the issue that had been worrying her over the last few days. She tapped the door quietly, somehow, hoping that the flights from Dubai had been disrupted.

"Come in!"

No such luck on the flights, thought Marcie. She slowly stuck her head around Angela Mortimer's door.

"Dr Venters, come in, come in. Sit down. I was hoping to see you this morning…"

As Marcie sat down in front of her boss she thought she had detected an air of sarcasm from Angela, but then these administrative managers always came across to Marcie that way. She noted Angela had indeed picked up a deep brown tan from the Gulf trip or that there was also a hint of fake spray-on tan. Marcie also noted with surprise that Angela had what looked incongruously like a newspaper in front of her. Two things struck Marcie about the oddity of the situation. Firstly, after a week's holiday she would have expected to see Angela catching up with the backlog of paperwork in her in tray, but, even stranger, it had been years since Marcie had actually seen a printed newspaper. Everyone in the UK read the Bloids on their iTabs nowadays!

"Did you have a great holiday, Angela? Dubai, wasn't it?"

Angela flashed angry black eyes at Marcie as she spun the newspaper around to face the geneticist.

"It is a bloody distant memory now, Dr Venters! I happened to pick this little souvenir up in Dubai –"

Marcie had been so taken aback by Angela's immediate outburst that the printed words just seemed to swirl before her eyes. She thought she recognised some of it as being printed in Arabic, but she stumbled to say anything cogent.

"What? I don't un-der-sta-and, Angela?"

Angela Mortimer stabbed her beautifully manicured bright red-polished index finger viciously on to the newspaper, hissing low at Marcie between her clenched laser-whitened teeth.

"Well, please allow me to explain, Dr Venters. This is an English-language copy of last week's Al Jazirah newspaper. Unfortunately, many of our poor Arab Muslim cousins cannot afford to purchase expensive iTabs to digest their daily news -"

Marcie knew that Angela was having a dig at her knowing she was Jewish but she gritted her teeth and said nothing in reply.

"- I just happened to buy it for some light reading on the beach in front of the 6 Star Burj Al Arab Hotel, where I was trying to enjoy my holiday. Of course, the first thing I see on the front page is this poisonous article by some journalist called, eh – El Kharroubi - berating St Bart's and the presentation you gave last week! He has compared my department to some sort of 21st Century Auschwitz and that you are the Todesengel of St Bartholemew's! What in hell happened when I wasn't here?"

"Angela, that man was extremely rude to me in front of many of my fellow professionals!"

"Professional - you call yourself professional! I have made enquiries this morning and from what I hear you stormed out of that presentation. If you had been professional you would have stayed and headed off this Kharroubi fellow with reason and logic."

Marcie felt the anger rising within her, the rims of her eyes forcing back tears.

"You want me to reason and logic with that Arab? I could not. He compared me with that beast Mengele. My forebears were butchered at the hands of that perverse Nazi bastard. No way would I try and reason with that!"

"Okay, okay, Marcie, let's both calm down. Sometimes I think that is your problem. In the lab you are focussed and emotionless. But take you out of your comfort zone and, well, sometimes you become erratic and emotional."

Marcie sucked in a deep breath to calm herself.

"I am always emotional about my work. And like you – I am a woman -"

"Agreed, Marcie, I am a woman. But I try to keep my emotions for when I am outside my work. I just ask that you also try to do the same. Let us just hope that this Al Jazirah thing just dies away quietly. Now what had you come to see me about?"

Marcie swallowed hard and thought that her next staement was not going to help matters.

"Well, you see, Angela, the thing is this – I have misplaced my memory stick. The one I was using at the presentation. I cannot find it anywhere -"

"Do you not have a copy of the presentation on your main computer?"

"Yes, but –"

Angela cut Marcie off.

"Well what's the problem? It's just a small stationery item. Just indent the stores for a new one!"

"I've already done that. It's not that –"

Angela was getting frustrated and agitated again. She thought to herself, Venters thinks I'm some sort of stationery clerk.

"Well, Dr Venters, what exactly is the problem?"

Marcie swallowed even harder this time.

"It's just that, em, you see, Angela – my workload on this Superstore DNA project has been such that I have been doing a lot of work at home lately –"

I'm now the Payroll Manager, Angela thought and interrupted again with her bitter sarcastic tone.

"And I commend you for that, Dr Venters. As you know your management contract does not allow for overtime payments. Any additional work is taken into consideration at the time of your Performance Appraisal –"

Marcie snapped back.

"Oh, for God's sake, Angela, I'm not talking about money here! There was more than just the presentation on that memory stick!"

Marcie could almost see her boss's mind whirr into gear and a dawning realisation come into Angela Mortimer's widening eyes. Angela's tan / fake tan went several shades paler than when Marcie first entered her office.

"What *was* on that stick?"

"Just about everything vital to the development of the project was on it. The list of proposed sites worldwide, detailed plans for the extensions required on site, laboratory design and layout - DNA collection and screening processes – need I go on?"

"Dr Venters, I don't believe this. What the hell did I come back from holiday for? This has put your job on the line – my fucking job on the line. If that info fell into the wrong hands – Web Leaks, Christian Pro-Life groups, heaven forbid, terrorists even –"

"Oh, wait a minute, Angela, you're taking it a bit too far –"

"I'll take it too far alright – where's the last time you saw that memory stick?"

Marcie thought hard.

"I'm not sure? I think it may still have been in the auditorium computer when I rushed out of the presentation."

"Oh, it just keeps getting better –"

Angela snatched up her phone and pretended to talk to her secretary next door.

"Hi, Julia - Angela here - can you please book me on the next flight back to Dubai? Better still, can you send up hospital security and send me off to the nearest bloody nut farm!"

Angela crashed the phone back down on the receiver and slapped her head into her hands. Marcie just stood and watched and perversely thought who was the one being emotional at work now? Angela raised her head and spoke slowly and deliberately.

"We may never get that data back but we are going to try. However, I do not want you crashing about like a bull in a china shop and inadvertently raising someone's misguided interest in this matter. What you are going to do is give my secretary Julia the list of everyone who was present at your wonderful little show and she will write to all of them with an innocuous little request for the tiny unimportant little stick's return. Is that clear?"

Marcie felt drained and was in no mood to argue.

"Yes - absolutely clear."

Angela Mortimer lowered her head and waved Marcie out.

"Can you go now, Dr Venters, I badly need a strong coffee."

*

In the Times central London office, Jill Geeson and Ruthie Venters were sitting at Jill's workstation. Both girls were in upbeat moods, especially Jill. Two things had lifted her spirits. Firstly, Buckley said he was reasonably interested in the 'Schenkler comet' story, so long as her source's information was rock solid. Secondly, she and Khan had spoken again on the phone and had agreed to have a cooling off period of separation. The only thing Khan had requested was that he could pick up a few clothes and things from the flat at Kew. Jill agreed, but asked him to get his stuff while she was out at work as she could not face another confrontation at this point in time. Khan had agreed, saying that it suited him that way and that he would be in touch in a couple of weeks. Jill and Ruthie were doing a final run-through on the interview with Alfie 'Dinky' Budge down at Tilbury Docks. After Jill had rushed away from Ewan and Gary she managed to get on the Tube and it was running fine, but when she changed on to the London Overground railway it was badly screwed up by a broken down train at Purfleet. By the time that Jill had arrived at the derelict warehouses just off the run-down area at Ferry Road she found Ruthie standing waiting there on her own. Dinky Budge had long gone. Jill felt sick to her stomach and disconsolate, because Alfie, knowing of Jill's high-profile standing within the field of investigative journalism, had stated that he was only prepared to speak to Jill and Jill alone. She apologised to Ruthie for screwing it up. Ruthie just replied as calm as a cucumber.

"Don't worry, Jill. I just told him that I was Jill Geeson. Alfie didn't even ask for any identification and he obviously doesn't know you from Adam – or is that Eve – or Ruthie for that matter -."

Ruthie, smiling broadly, held up her tiny micro-recorder and a Manila folder.

"Dinky sang like a budgie and I think we've got a great exposé in this little thing here. He confirmed that the quarter mill is in his Swiss account and that he will be flying out for an extended holiday to 'don't ask no questions and I'll tell you no lies' land, wherever that is? So when the story on his boss Nesto Petrianni's dirty deeds hits the front page - Alfie will be nowhere to be seen. He has also provided an extensive dossier full of papers and invoices and disks full of incriminating evidence that the police are just going to love to get their hands on. Voila!"

Jill smiled a huge smile of relief.

"God, Ruthie, ta loads for covering my arse!"

"Look, Jill, I'm just so pleased to be in the game now and you've helped me get there big-time. As far as Buckley is concerned it *was* Jill Geeson that conducted the interview -"

Ruthie switched her polite upstate New York accent and tried to imitate Jill's Glaswegian accent.

"Ah even tried tae use that hellish Glesga accent o' yours, Jill."

Jill laughed out loud.

"Oh please tell me ah don't sound anythin' like that!"

So now Jill and Ruthie were sitting in the Times office putting the Dinky Budge exposé to bed for tomorrow's front page. Jill had allowed Ruthie a lot of leeway on the writing up of the piece and she was really impressed with Ruthie's gutsy determined journalistic style. Jill had agreed that the article would show both their names in the by-line and Ruthie was over the Moon. Jill was keen to put it to bed by lunchtime as she had planned to meet Ewan and Gary back at the Euston iCafé at 2 o'clock, although she now also knew that she could trust Ruthie to iron out any last minute changes. Jill's mobile rang and she saw it was Ewan's photo on the screen.

"Hi, Ewan -"

Ewan hesitated.

"Um, hi, Jill –"

Jill could not make him out very well as it was very noisy in the background.

"What's that noise? Is that the train?"

"No, Jill, it's a helijet. Gary and I have just taken off from Edinburgh Helipad. But –"

"Okay, Ewan, we still on for two then -?"

"Look, Jill, the thing is this – something new has come up. We are actually heading for -"

The helijet must have been taking off as Jill could not make out what Ewan said.

"Ewan, you cut out there. Where are you going?"

"Islay, Jill –"

"Islay - what the hell's there? What about our meeting, Ewan? Ah've gone out on a limb with Buckley on this 'cos you're a friend!"

"I know, Jill, I really appreciate that. But I'm following up a new lead on the comet. Gary and I just need another couple of days –"

Jill was mildly irritated, but Ruthie had put her in such a good mood, that she laughed and joked back to Ewan.

"Okay, Ewan, but don't come back to me unless your news from Islay is earth-shattering!"

"I'll do my best, Jill. Speak later."

*

Earthdate: 12:35 Friday February 7, 2081 IST

Rebecca Menachim answered the ringing phone on the Nimrod SH2 2082 Project Team monitor. Yosep Goldenheim's shaven-headed face appeared on the screen. He barked through his goatee beard in his usual Billy Goat Gruff manner.

"Rebecca! Is Ari there or has he gone out to lunch?"

Rebecca, a feisty Kibbutzim-raised single Sabra, who had already done two years National Service in the Israeli Army before studying for her astrophysics degree, had no fear of Goldenheim's bullying techniques.

"Lunch, Mr Goldenheim! We're too busy for lunches down here. Ari is right here - working hard as we speak with Jerzy and Noam on those budget saving options."

Goldenheim softened his harsh tone with Rebecca. Goldenheim's attitude at work had not been helped by his recent long-running and bitter divorce after 19 years marriage. Yosep had a secret admiration for Rebecca, but she was 14 years younger than him and as yet he had not plucked up the courage to reveal his attraction to her.

"That's, eh, great to hear you're all hard at it, Rebecca. Could I have a quick word with Ari, please?"

Ari was already standing at the monitor and Rebecca moved back out of range of the web cam to let Ari speak. Making sure Goldenheim could not see her, she signalled to Ari by sticking her tongue out and pretending to make herself sick by thrusting two fingers towards her open mouth. She knew Goldenheim fancied her and secretly Rebecca had hidden reciprocal feelings for her boss. Ari waved at her to cut out her playacting in case Goldenheim spotted it.

"Yes, Yosep - is everything okay?"

"Ari, how's the NASA presentation going?"

Ari replied with an air of confidence.

"I think we are making good progress. We're just about there on the 5% savings option and we have brainstormed some ideas to work up to the preferred six. It'll be tight but I've a great team and I am sure that we can pull it off, Yosep."

"Great, Ari, that's really good news. Look, tell you what – I've worked you up a bit of breathing space on this thing. The NASA team have put back the meeting until the 17th. Is that good for you?"

Ari flashed a quick glance at the calendar.

"Yosep - that really would be a life-saver. I think we could kick this one into touch with an extra week. Thanks for fixing it up for us."

"No problem. Tell the truth, Ari, it was the NASA boys who asked for the postponement. Apparently, something more important has come up at their end."

"Well, Yosep, they're doing us a big favour."

"Okay, leave me to reschedule the meeting room, etcetera. Oh, and Ari? Get your team the hell down to the Yoezer Wine Bar right now and have a good long lunch. In fact, it's Friday afternoon. Don't bother coming back until Monday. Oh, and Ari – you can tell my PA, Golda - the bill goes on *my* expense account. Okay?"

Ari was surprised and delighted by Goldenheim's unexpected gesture.

"Thanks. Much appreciated, boss."

Ari ended the call on the monitor and turned around to face Jerzy, Noam and Rebecca, all smiling broadly back at him. The four of them simultaneously raised their arms triumphantly and cheered so loudly that Ari would not have been surprised if Goldenheim could hear them in his office two floors above them.

*

<u>Earthdate: 15:28 Friday February 7, 2081 CST</u>

Lex Kosloff slowly opened his matted and bleary eyes. At first he was unsure exactly where he was. He slowly realised that he was in his own semi-darkened living room at Robindale Drive. The blinds were half shut and sitting wildly askew. Lex slowly looked around through his stinging bloodshot eyes as he lay prostrate on his crumpled sofa. The living room was like a disaster zone. It looked to him as though he must have trashed the place in a drunken tantrum. He tried to work out what day it was and what had happened recently, but nothing was registering. Lex took a deep breath and pushed his creaking body painfully up and stumbled off the sofa. His head spinning nauseously, Lex crashed awkwardly against the drink-stained coffee table, knocking a half empty coffee cup and an almost finished cheap bottle of rye on to the wooden floor. He grimaced at the cold coffee spilling across the already messed up floor, but he took some gratification from the fact that the rye still had the metal cap screwed on. He caressed his pounding head and told himself that there was still a shot or two left for later. Lex weaved gingerly through the messed up room and powered up his monitor and used the touch screen to turn on his 50" Total Surround 3DTV. A live game of American football blasted out at him and he groaned painfully as the sound pounded his mashed-up brain like the gloves of a heavyweight boxer. He quickly dragged the volume down and turned over to CNN 24/7 news channel and squinted at the date and time on the bottom right of the TV.

15:33 Feb 7, CST

Kosloff shook his befuddled head and looked again as he sunk back onto his favourite black leather recliner in front of the huge 3D screen. He spoke aloud to himself.

"Nah - that can't be right? February 7?"

As he put his head in his hands to think, the TV seemed to want to talk back to him, although Lex was not paying the slightest bit of attention.

"In breaking news – recently inaugurated President Josh Trueman gave a speech in the last hour in Chicago stating that he would be fighting tooth and nail to get his highly controversial Defense of the Nation Bill through Congress next week. This is despite an expected resolute battle from the minority Republican opposition. The key thrust of the Bill will be to divert $500 billion dollars over the next 5 years from the NASA space program and plow most but not all of the money into strengthening the US Defense Budget. It is expected that financial savings of some $30 billion dollars will also be made in the proposals. In his speech, President Trueman argued that recent tensions in the Middle East and the worrying military and nuclear build-up by the LOIN meant extra funding needed to be sourced to resolutely defend the interests and security of the US and its UN allies. Stating that he regretted having to drastically cut the space program. This included areas, such as, expansion of the US colonisation of Mars, modernisation of the E2MSN satellite network and joint funding in terrestrial planet-hunting programs, mainly on the Nimrod SH2 project. To provide an immediate reaction to the President Trueman's speech we have waiting in our Washington studio Democratic Senator for Connecticut - Pip Rapland. Good afternoon Senator Rapland…"

The CNN 24/7 anchorman droned on in the background but Lex remained oblivious to what would normally have been disconcerting news of genuine interest to the NASA Controller. However, Lex was in no fit state to worry about President Trueman's speech or the implications that it might have on his future. He was too busy raking around in his alcohol-befuddled brain to remember where the last three days had disappeared to. He forced his memory banks to rewind back those three lost days. Back to Tuesday which was the fourth. Kosloff remembered that on the previous day, the Monday, he had been rostered 'off monitor' in Houston Control, which usually meant slow time spent on training, going over policies and procedures or boring team meetings. Lex had known it was going to be an 'easy' day and over the weekend he had pretty well drowned his sorrows over Marna in the seedy bars down on Hyde Park and Crocker, Houston's infamous red-light district. However, he had forgotten his boss Irene DuPré had called a team meeting for the Controllers who were 'off monitor'. At that meeting on the Monday afternoon, Lex, still slightly hung-over, had the feeling that Irene kept banging on about the Performance Appraisals on the seventh. He kept telling himself that it was no problem, Irene was not out to get him personally. On the Monday night into Tuesday he lay in bed tossing and turning and he could not get to sleep. He dare not take a drink to help him because he was back on the monitor all day Tuesday. Lex was communicating with the crew on the Alpha Base international space station and they were doing a critical and dangerous maintenance job on the outside hull and he needed to be 100% sober. When his alarm went off at six on the Tuesday morning he reckoned that he had probably had two hours in total of nightmare-ridden sleep. Lex made a move to get out of bed and suddenly his stomach was gripped by shock waves of uncontrollable fear and anxiety. He began sweating profusely and his muscles were shaking violently and going into nervous spasms. In his fear and confusion he spoke aloud to himself.

"Oh my God – what's up with me?"

Lex lay on the bed trying to control the anxiety attack but the spasms and the nausea kept flowing over him in cold rhythmic terrifying waves. As a senior and experienced Controller at Houston for 15 years he had never been out of control like this before. He kept glancing at the clock as time moved slowly, but still too quickly for Lex. He wanted time to stand still. 06.30. 07.00. 07.15.

07.15!

Jesus, he thought, Irene usually gets in to her station at 07.25 or 07.30. Lex bolted out of bed and switched on his monitor, disabled his web cam, and rang the station number at Houston Control. As the number rang his heart was beating wildly and his legs were shaking with fear as he stood naked in his cold bedroom. The number connected at Houston and Lex spoke first, weakly and croakily.

"He-ello, Irene?"

"No, it's Jimmy Soderline here. Irene ain't on the station yet. That you, Lex? God, man, ya sound terrible…"

Lex, a wave of relief relaxing his tension, laid the croaking on even thicker for Jimmy.

"Gaaawd - hi, Jim - man, woke up this mornin'. Ah'm dyin' with that flu – feel terrible –"

"Hell, Lex, ya sound awful. Glad ya didn't bring that thing in here today!"

Lex threw in a coughing fit for good measure, but he knew Irene would be arriving any minute and it was time for a sharp exit.

"Ah'm just goin' back to bed, Jimmy, an' ah'll phone the doctor later. Make an appointment. Can you tell Irene ah should be back in a day or two with a bit of luck?"

"Hey! No sweat, Lex. Ya take care now."

Lex had quickly ended the call on his monitor for fear of Irene's arrival at work and he felt his stomach and leg muscles immediately relax. He had jumped back into bed and he slept until late into the Tuesday afternoon. Okay, that much I do remember, but what next, he asked himself. Lex strained to dig deep into his subconscious. Some vague memories floated in and out from the back of his mind. On the Tuesday evening after he had eaten a light omelette washed down with a Coors Light, which was about the only thing he could face, he took an electri-cab down to his local watering hole – Tiggy's Bar. What happened there? He started hitting the shots and something had gotten him real sore. What was it? He could not quite remember, maybe someone bumped into him at the bar. Who knows? Lex seemed to remember a scuffle and – oh, yeah – he remembered the barkeep barring him from coming back to Tiggy's. Maybe a cab home again? He must have, because Lex now remembered waking up on his sofa on the Wednesday morning. Yeah, that would be the fifth. He had stumbled into the toilet for a piss and noted that there was vomit on the floor. When he looked in the mirror he looked like shit and he had a small bruise under his left eye. Okay, he thought, so what happened on the fifth. He had told Jimmy Soderline that he would see a doctor. His doctor was still in Houston Center. Lex and Marna had not gotten around to changing doctors when they moved out to the new suburb of Robindale following his promotion two years ago. After breakfast – well, just a strong sweet coffee - and cleaning the toilet up a bit he jumped on the new MetroXpress line from Robindale Station heading for Center Station. He told himself that he should have tried to ring for an appointment but that he would just take his chances when he got to the Houston City Medical Center. Lex tried to remember what happened next. Oh, yeah, he had dozed off when the train arrived at Center and the electronic train announcement had startled him.

"You have now arrived at Houston Center Station. Please mind the doors when leaving the train?"

He just sat and did not move. Lex felt the waves of anxiety well up again in the pit of his stomach and he froze in his seat as other commuters entered and exited the train. The train doors closed and the waves eased and subsided. He needed to get a drink to calm his nerves. Yeah, he remembered, get a drink and that will help. From his seat he looked up at the station plan pasted above the train windows. Where to go? Where does this train go? He remembered spotting Avondale Station further up the line. That's it, he told himself. Avondale was where he had been at the weekend. He could walk from there into the red light district on Hyde Park and Crocker. Once in one of the seedy bars on Crocker with a few bourbons in him all the tension would begin to disappear. He could remember being in quite a few bars on Wednesday, but now things were getting pretty hazy. What else? There was something else gnawing at his memory. What was it? Nope, it ain't coming. Then it struck him. That was it – on the Wednesday afternoon he had picked up a hooker. Truth be told, he was so out of it the hooker had picked him up. Lex had a vague memory of being back in her grubby untidy little apartment, then the two of them naked. Had he managed it? Lex could not remember. Did she have a name? Yeah, she called her self something. What was it - Cutie – Cupie - Kitten? Oh, he just could not remember. God, he thought, why would it really matter? So, Thursday sixth then, what about that? Thursday was a complete and total blank and now here he was sitting in a dreadful state on his recliner on Friday. A wave of fear gripped his stomach again and he looked at the time again on the CNN channel.

16:27 Feb 7, CST

The Performance Appraisal! It was today and Lex had not even phoned Irene and she would be finishing work for the weekend in half an hour. God, she'll kill me, He thought, I'm gonna have to phone her and give her some bullshit excuse. The fear tightened its grip again on his throat and gut. I can't call her, he argued with himself, I gotta or my job is down the John. He plucked up the nerve and rang her number on his computer. Irene picked up immediately. Had she been waiting all day for his call?

"Irene DuPré."

Lex choked and spluttered.

"I-rene - Lex here – so-orry ah ain't called in. Ah got a real, uh, bad bout ah flu."

Lex coughed violently.

"Kosloff – as far as ah'm concerned, you've got the fuckin' man flu!"

Lex was taken completely aback. Irene was not going to be pulling any punches.

"No-o-o-o, I-rene, ah –"

"What did your doctor say then, Kosloff?"

"Ah – ah – ah ain't been out a bed in th-ree days, boss."

"Bullshit, Lex! Ah know exactly what you're problem is, Kosloff, but ah ain't prepared to say it over the phone and you get me hauled up for discrimination. But when you get back here we are going to thrash this out at you're appraisal. Got that?"

"Ye-es..."

"Now you either get back into Control fit and rarin' to go next week or you better get an official doctor's note sent in here Monday. Else consider yourself under suspension. Catch ma drift, Lex?"

Lex did not get to answer as Irene crashed him off at her end before he could respond. He felt sick. In fact he did not just feel sick – he rushed to the bathroom and threw up violently in the toilet bowl. Lex told himself that this was the worst week of his whole life. As he ran his head under the cold faucet to try and knock some sense back into his battered brain he told himself that things just could not get any worse. As he turned the running faucet off he thought he could hear the doorbell ringing. Lex thought to himself, God couldn't possibly throw anything else at him, could he?

CHAPTER 7

<u>Earthdate: 17:10 Saturday February 8, 2081 GMT</u>

The five men had arrived just after two o'clock on the Isle of Skye by means of a plush upmarket Mercedes 7-seater air-car. Dick Threlfall, the English owner of the Ardvasar Hotel, had stood with nervy expectation outside the large flaky-white painted old building set 50 yards back from the rocky seaweed-strewn shore, watching as the large vehicle slowly came into view. The air-car had gracefully whizzed through the misty sodden air over the silver sands of Morar, past the fishing port of Mallaig and directly across the white-headed choppy grey waves of the Sound of Sleat, which separated Skye from the mainland.

Dick was extremely grateful to see the men arriving because business had been really slack this winter. In fact, if business did not start picking up he was on the point of trying to sell up and return back to his home county of Yorkshire. He had helped them unpack the mountain of expensive climbing gear in the boot of the air-car. They had everything needed for winter climbing in the arduous and treacherous Cuillin Mountains about 20 miles north of the Point of Sleat from where the hotel was situated. Rucksacks, electrically-heated mountain gear, ropes, ice-picks and crampons. Absolutely everything, Dick thought, they must have spent a fortune on it all and everything looked brand new. He was glad he had charged them over the odds because they were the only guests staying at the Ardvasar tonight and Dick badly needed their flash cash. The man who had made the booking went especially out of his way to introduce himself and his four climbing companions and they all shook hands vigorously with Dick.

"Good day to you Mr Threlfall. My name is Mahmoud El Kharroubi, UK correspondent for Al Jazirah. These are my four friends also staying at your – eh – beautiful hotel. They are Mr Khan al Ahmed - Mr Mossab Mohammad - Mr Akbar Ali Mohammad - and Mr Hassan Ben Ali."

It was now ten past five and four of the men sat in the snug by the restaurant bar. Dick and his Slovak bar tender Oliç, a student at Sabhal Mór Ostaig Gaelic University a mile up the road from Ardvasar, began to bring out their evening meals from the kitchen. Dick looked around the otherwise empty restaurant for the fifth man.

"I'm sorry gentleman – but is your friend, um, Mr Kharroubi not joining you just now."

Khan, who was pretty unimpressed with his surroundings, although he did not show it to Threlfall, flashed a huge laser-white smile at the hotelier.

"Mr Mahmoud El Kharroubi is just outside having a cigarette – I know, dirty habit these days – and Mr Mahmoud El Kharroubi is also making a call on his mobile, Mr Threlfall. I believe that he was having some difficulty with a signal within your lovely establishment. If you leave his meal on the table please, I will call Mr Mahmoud El Kharroubi inside in a minute."

Dick and Oliç laid the meals down and the hotel owner thought to himself that there would not be much chance of forgetting these dark-skinned men and their oft-mentioned names. Before Khan went outside to call El Kharroubi back in he scanned his eyes around the restaurant where they sat. Lovely establishment, Khan had thought to himself. By Allah, he thought, it was more like being caught in some sort of a time warp. The painted ceilings were low and oppressive. The once-white paint was now brown interspersed with heavy dark oaken beams. The walls were covered with a heavy dark red wallpaper that added to the claustrophobia of the deserted restaurant. The small tables were made of heavy dark stained wood, matched by the tiny stools surrounding them. In the snug where the Group were placed, a mainly yellow tartan covered seat stretched along the wall facing the bar and continued to the small dark wooden bar. Threlfall added a few more stools to allow the five men to sit with each other, eat and talk together. Tacky prints of Scottish uniformed soldiers of bygone eras and the odd cheap picture of Bonnie Prince Charlie were dimly lit by low energy light bulbs with burnt-brown shades. The carpet was a dark blue and black tartan which looked as though it had been trodden on for decades and was heavily ingrained with dirt. Hassan Ben Ali, who had started eating his Mallaig fish and chips, which they had all ordered, saw Khan looking about and spoke out.

"In the name of Allah, what made Mahmoud pick this dump?"

Khan shrugged and replied indifferently.

"Look, Hassan, we don't need a five-star hotel. What we need is something just like this. It is quiet, so we will stand out and be remembered and it needs to be as far from London as we can make it –"

Hassan grumbled back.

"Yeah, well I'm the one stuck in a small dingy single room on the back of the ground floor. It is freezing, damp and smells horribly musty. Allah save me, I'd rather spend the night in an Israeli prison cell."

"Okay, let me call Mahmoud back in for his fish and chips and I'll to speak to the owner later about moving you."

Hassan went back to his meal along with the silent Mohammad brothers and Khan went outside to call Mahmoud. The Jordanian journalist had just finished stubbing his cigarette out on the now darkened road separating the hotel from the rough grassy patch sloping down to the rocky shoreline, which could only just be made out in the diminishing light. Khan looked across the Sound and he could see the twinkling lights of little Mallaig hemmed in by dark foreboding mountains on three sides. Khan waved El Kharroubi over, signalling with an imaginary knife and fork motion that his meal was ready. Mahmoud strode across the darkening deserted road to the low restaurant doorway and Khan addressed him.

"Did you speak with the Palestinian, Mahmoud?"

"Yes, he is in place. I have also confirmed the go-ahead with Brother Suleiman –"

El Kharroubi put his hand on Khan's shoulder and guided the Kuwaiti into the restaurant. They joined Hassan and the Mohammads and everyone ate in silence. Although, the restaurant was empty apart from their table, next door in the bar room it was filled with raucous, drunken locals who had, according to Dick Threlfall, been watching a now-finished Scottish football match on 3DTV. The manager had called it the Old Firm game but that meant nothing to the Group. Suddenly, their silent eating was disturbed as two drunks staggered in from the adjoining corridor which linked the restaurant, toilets and bar. The taller fat local, known as Aldo, wore a blue football top and the smaller skinny local, known as Paddy, had ginger hair and wore a top with green and white hoops. The larger drunkard Aldo spoke to the Group first.

"Haw! Haw! What's this then, Paddy?"

The five men looked up startled by the two drunks precariously holding each other up with their arms extended. Aldo, the fat drunk in the blue top with an enormous beer-belly hanging over his belt slurred again in an almost unintelligible Scottish accent.

"Any chance o' wan o' yer chips?"

Khan, who was sitting closest to the inebriates, spread his palm out towards his plate and replied.

"Please, my friends. Do help yourself. I have had too much to eat anyway."

Aldo and Paddy lunged towards the table, grabbed a few chips from Khan's plate and guzzled them down noisily with rude beer-sodden burps in between. Paddy ventured to engage the Group in conversation.

"Ah take it ye huv aw met the manager Dick? We call him Richard at Home and Dick at Work."

The two pals guffawed generously to each other as the other five men sat bemused. Paddy continued with his one-sided conversation.

"By the way, ah hope ye don't mind me askin'? Ah thought ah detected a wee bit o' an accent there. No offence an' that - but are you guys aw Pakis?"

Khan continued to be the mildly irritated spokesman for the Group.

"No, actually - we are all Arabs, my friends –"

Aldo's face immediately became illuminated with drunken jocularity.

"Arabs - haw, Paddy boy, these guys are aw Dundee United supporters. Haw, haw, haw!"

Paddy made a mock sneering gesture into nowhere specifically.

"Tangerine bastards – sorry, man, we don't mean anything by you guys. Mean tae say – ah'm a fuckin' Celtic man masel' and big Aldo here supports the Teddy Berrs. But we're ra best o' friends an' that, y'know? We are aw fur Wurld Peace. Issat right, Aldo?"

"Too true, wee Paddy boy, Wurld Peace – that's oor goal!"

The Group all glanced sideways at each other in bewilderment. They had no idea what Aldo and Paddy were talking about. Mahmoud made an almost imperceptible sideways gesture with his black brooding hawkish eyes for Khan to get rid of them. Khan pulled something from his pocket and handed it over to Paddy and the eyes of the two drunks lit up immediately at the £50 note.

"Allah has blessed us with a little spare cash today. Take it and buy your friends through there a drink on us, okay?"

"Brilliant, man - a fifty spot - what aboot that, Aldo?"

Aldo and Paddy pumped Khan's hands and waved goodbye to the others in the Group. They staggered off in each other's grasp shouting for world peace and laughing at their good fortune. Dick Threlfall slunk out from behind the bar and moved towards the Group. He looked down at the plates and all were empty except for Khan's. Threlfall broke the momentary silence.

"Please accept my apologies for the state of the locals. Have you all finished, gentlemen? Did you enjoy your meals?"

Khan could not face any more from the plate after Aldo and Paddy's grubby hands had been all over it. He answered for the Group, lying about the food.

"We are all finished, thank you very much - the fish was delicious."

Threlfall started gathering up the plates and then stopped momentarily as a thought had just crossed his mind.

"Oh! By the way gentlemen - I've just listened to the weather forecast for tomorrow, Sunday – and a blizzard is meant to hit Skye. It will be very tricky climbing in the Cuillins."

Mahmoud El Kharroubi raised his arms to heaven and put on a false smile.

"Allah be praised! You have just given us our alibi, Mr Threlfall."

"Alibi?"

"I don't really mean alibi, Mr Threlfall. I mean excuse – an excuse for not going up those blasted mountains. What we will do instead is sit in your wonderful lounge all day tomorrow and drink coffee and play cards. Maybe you will join us?"

Threlfall thought it peculiar that these men had travelled all this way bringing the best of kit and were put off their climb so easily. Instead they intended staying in and spending money in his hotel and that was fine by him.

"I'd be delighted, gentlemen."

Khan groaned inside at the thought of being stuck in a snowstorm in this dingy hole, but he bit his lip, then spoke.

"One last thing Mr Threlfall – Dick - my friend Hassan Ben Ali is uncomfortable in the single room you have placed him in. We would be happy to pay for a third double room if you could move him, please?"

Threlfall could not believe his luck. More money!

"Certainly - I will have you moved to a good sized double on the first floor, Mr Ben Ali. I'll put you in room 101."

*

Earthdate: 19:25 Saturday February 8, 2081 GMT

Jill unlocked the door of her flat in Kew and pushed it open. She picked up what little mail there was and entered. Mostly flyers for local junk food shops and quotes for air-car insurance that she did not require. There was one letter and she knew immediately it was Khan's business account bank statement from the London branch of the Royal Bank of Kuwait. No-one nowadays wanted paper statements with everything available online. However, Khan said he was old fashioned when it came to money. Jill threw the mail on the breakfast bar along with her keys and bag and flopped down wearily on her sofa. Saturday had been a good day off and Jill was also looking forward to tomorrow's day of rest.

In the morning she had taken her sports gear and went to nearby Kew Gardens to run with the local Kew Crew Jogging Club to burn off a few calories. After showering and changing back at her flat she caught the train into London's Hyde Park and met Ruthie Venters. Khan had bought two tickets weeks ago before the trial separation for an open-air concert. It was the revival World Tour of the late-20th century rock group Queen's "We Will Rock You!" Khan had left the tickets and told Jill just to use them with a friend. She asked Ruthie as a thank you for saving her on the Dinky Budge story and Ruthie was delighted to go along with her. Initially, Hyde Park was pretty chilly in the open air, but with the large open-air heaters and the crowd's banging enthusiasm, the girls were soon warmed up. After the concert they went to a nearby McDonalds and giggled like two teenagers when they ordered two Happy Meals and giant chocolate shakes. They even had the audacity to take the free kiddie toy - a plastic model of the spacecraft Oceanus. It had been a great day but Jill was just glad to be home again. She had already promised herself a long lie in bed on Sunday morning. Jill caught a glance across at the breakfast bar and saw Khan's bank statement poking over the edge of the counter. She had never opened his private mail before but the envelope niggled at her. Jill thought, if I just sneaked a quick look there might be the odd meal out or a clandestine hotel booking that would confirm that Khan had been as unfaithful as she had been accusing him of being. She couldn't, she scolded herself. Then she jumped up and grabbed up the white windowed-envelope marked the Royal Bank of Kuwait. The clear window was addressed:-

Mr K Al Ahmed

Flat 7/2

45 Kew Gardens Path

Kew

Greater London

6SW 10XX

Jill lifted her keys and used one to roughly zip open the letter and she pulled out the statement. She scanned over the statement and the transactions certainly looked like any that a normal property dealer might transact. Nothing seemed out of the ordinary. Then her eye caught the very last transaction on the second page, which read:-

03 Feb 81 Bank transfer credit

Money In £20,000,250.00

Balance £20,155,375.76

A horrible wave of guilt swept over Jill and the nauseous feeling returned. Oh shit, Khan, I'm so sorry, she thought, you were telling the truth about that 20 million pound deal after all. She asked herself what she should do. The shock of seeing the figure on the statement brought back the day's weariness and it made Jill lie down on the sofa. She quickly fell into a fitful sleep full of guilt-laden dreams. It was much later when she awoke. The clock on the wall told Jill it was now almost nine forty at night. She felt a bit peckish as it had now been many hours since the long-digested McDonalds. She thought that she would treat her stomach to something sugary to sooth her pangs of guilt and hunger. Jill spoke aloud to herself.

"Strong sweet coffee - hot chocolate fudge cake and whipped cream. That should do the trick."

While awaiting the frozen chocolate cake to defrost in the microwave and also for the kettle to boil for her coffee, she wandered aimlessly over to look out at the darkness from her seventh floor Art Deco curving picture window. Jill looked out over towards the upmarket townhouses of Richmond and down towards even posher Windsor and Eton. She could just see part of the tastefully floodlit Windsor Castle, the magnificent stately seat of Great Britain's ruling monarch, Queen Elizabeth III. Although the Head of State role was only that of a figure-head in Britain, Elizabeth had been on the throne now for almost 15 years and she was extremely well-respected by her people. Jill thought back to the time she and Khan had been introduced to Queen Elizabeth and her husband Prince Regent David at a Windsor garden party. As Jill continued to admire the view of the night down to the castle, suddenly her microwave switched off with a loud *Ping!* The ringing sound startled Jill. Then, what seemed a split second later, Jill's head started backwards in fright as she equally suddenly saw a blinding flash high in the sky. Jill watched in horror as a huge ball of flame streaked Earthwards not that far from Windsor Castle. It was quickly followed by a large violent explosion on the ground in Windsor town centre and a huge plume of fire and smoke mushroomed into the air. Jill could not believe her eyes and blurted out in alarm.

"What in hell's name was that?"

As she watched the flames licking up menacingly into the night sky over Windsor, Jill scrabbled around in her mind to think of an explanation for what had just occurred. She rewound back to the recent interview with Ewan. A meteorite, she thought! Surely not – she seemed to remember that Ewan had said **Earth's gravity is likely to attract some pretty hefty meteor showers probably starting around mid-February 2084.** Jill did not know what the explosion was, but she knew that she had to find out. Thoughts of chocolate cake and long lies in bed on Sunday were quickly forgotten and she was instantly into professional journalist mode. She quickly donned her heavy winter jacket, grabbed her mobile and her mini-video camera and stuffed them in her deep jacket pockets. Jill started scrimmaging about in the messy cabinet drawer below her wall-mounted 3DTV, while keeping one eye out of her picture window. The fire was still burning although a little less fiercely as she spoke aloud in frustration.

"Khan, please don't have taken them?"

Then she found them – the keys to Khan's Honda air-bike. In the distance she began to hear the muffled sounds of police, fire and ambulance sirens wailing, muted by the triple-glazed windows. Jill could see the floodlights of a police helijet reaching out as it zoomed over the roof of her apartment building heading towards Windsor.

"Shit, ah better get a move on before the place is crawling with TV and journalists! This is tomorrow's big story –"

*

Earthdate: 23:30 February 8, 2081 CST

A groggy-looking Lex Kosloff was politely escorted into the Houston PD interview room and he was asked to take a seat. To Lex's present thinking his life had been transformed into a complete blur for the second time in the same week since he answered the ringing doorbell. That had been when he pulled back the door to be confronted by Houston PD's finest, two burly plain-clothes detectives flashing their silver badges at him. The senior cop addressed him gruffly.

"Alexander Kosloff?"

"Yes -?"

"May we come in? We would like to question you about an incident which took place a couple of days ago in Dallas?"

If the policemen had said anything else on his doorstep that Friday evening then Lex had not heard it. He just thought – Dallas? Marna? Oh,

God, no – something's happened to Marna. Lex's already weak legs from the constant days of drinking and vomiting completely buckled under him and he passed out in front of the two cops. He had spent Friday night mostly in and out of consciousness and all of Saturday recovering in some nondescript hospital in Houston stuck on an IV drip, wired up to the hilt with various monitors beeping and whirring incessantly at his bedside. Only three hours ago the doctors had told the police that Lex was sufficiently recovered from shock and a mild case of alcohol poisoning. His stomach had been pumped. Again they asked Lex politely if he minded answering a few questions down at the 3rd Precinct. Lex agreed and asked if his wife was okay, but he was told that all questions would be handled at the station. Now here he was just after a half hour to midnight on Saturday night sitting facing the two detectives who had arrived at his home the previous evening. Lex looked behind them at the blackened mirror-glass and reckoned he would be being further scrutinised by the cops' superiors. The larger broad-shouldered white detective poured Lex a glass of water and then broke the ice.

"Can you confirm that you are Alexander Kosloff of 1938 Robindale Drive, Houston, Texas?"

"Ye-es, but can ah just -?"

"I realise you have many questions, Mr Kosloff, but for now can you just answer our questions, okay?"

Lex nodded numbly and the broad cop who sounded like a politely-spoken Northerner, maybe New England, continued with his questioning.

"Mr Kosloff, I take it you do not have any objections to being recorded for the purpose of this interview?"

Lex shook his head dumbly. Neither cop made any move to start any recording equipment so he assumed that the recording had already begun. He could feel his body shake with small uncontrollable tremors and a thin sheen of cold sweat came in waves across his chest and back.

"Now, Mr Kosloff – can you tell us where you were on Thursday afternoon, February 6?"

Lex looked blankly at the two cops and his tongue felt swollen in his mouth and his throat constricted. He sat there struck dumb. The slimmer black cop named Detective Madsen then spoke.

"Are yah exercising yah right to remain silent, Mr Kosloff?"

Madsen was a Texan like Lex.

"No-o-o…"

"Well, can yah answer Detective Magruder's question? Where were yah Thursday afternoon -?"

"Ah g-guess ah was at home in R-Robindale…"

Magruder allowed his voice to rise just a little with a hint of sarcasm.

"You guess that you were at home on Thursday? Why is that, Mr Kosloff?"

"You see – ah – ah got real bad drunk Wednesday an' ah must a slept it off all day Thursday - an' a just came to at home on Friday. Look, d-detectives, what is this all about? Have ah done somethin' wrong?"

Magruder continued the questioning. Madsen remained silent with his arms tightly crossed. Magruder, his eyes tightening, leaned across the table a little menacingly towards Lex.

"Is there any chance that you could have been up in Dallas on Thursday? You could easily have flown there and back in a few hours?"

Lex racked his brain, but Thursday remained a blank.

"Ah sure don't think ah was in Dallas? Is this about Marna – is Marna okay?"

The detectives ignored the question for now making Kosloff feel sick with worry. Madsen uncrossed his arms and continued with the questions.

"Marna, now she is yah wife, right?"

"Yeah…"

"What's she doin' up in Dallas for anyways?"

"We were, uh, havin' some difficulties. She went to stay with her folks for a bit."

Magruder stepped back in.

"From what we have heard Marna's been in Dallas with her parents since New Year. Quite some difficulties is it not, Mr Kosloff?"

"Marna thought ah, um, ah was drinkin' too much. She needed some time away but ah have pleaded with her to come back –"

Magruder jumped on Lex's last statement with some more menace.

"So you pleaded with Marna to return and she refused! That must have made you mad, Mr Kosloff?"

"N-n-no - ah've been real down 'bout it – suppose ah've had one or two too many to try an' drown ma sorrows. B-b-but ah could n-never get mad with Marna. Ah love ma wife!"

Madsen changed the subject.

"Mr Kosloff, do you own a gun?"

Lex's stomach turned a cartwheel, the cold sweats and shakes returned and his mind went into overdrive. Marna – Dallas – gun – what in hell is going on here?

"A g-gun?"

"Yeah, Lex, do yah own a gun. Y'know – a little pointy thing – fires bullets!"

"Of course ah do – everyone in H-Houston owns a gun."

"Do yah know the make?"

Lex did not know too much about handguns – he hated the things - and he toiled to think where all this questioning was leading to, but it gave him a terrible feeling in the pit of his churning gut.

"Ah - ah believe it's an ole Walther, but ah couldn't tell ya anything else about it. Ah ain't seen it in years –"

Magruder took over – the constant changing of detectives was starting to make Lex's head spin.

"Where do you keep your gun?"

"At home – last time ah seen it was in the drawer of ma bedside locker. It should still be there as far as ah know."

"Would you be happy to take us to your home and show us the gun - and while we are there do you have any objection to us looking around?"

Lex looked at the two cops in complete bewilderment. He had never before in all his life been in trouble with the police. He screamed at himself to remember what happened on Thursday. Remember! It's important, Lex! Remember!

"Y-yeah – ah mean n-no. Ah mean ah can show you if ya like…"

Madsen stood up swiftly, slapped his thigh loudly and barked at Lex with mock gusto.

"Well, Lex, no sense in losin' time over it. We all might as well do it now!"

Magruder signalled to the mirror-glass behind him that the interview was ended.

CHAPTER 8

<u>Earthdate: 06:54 Sunday February 9, 2081 GMT</u>

It was still dark outside her big picture window. Jill yawned painfully wide and gave an aching stretch of her weary arms, which caused various bones and joints to crack and pop as she leaned back from her laptop. She had been up working all night down at the crash site at Windsor. She had been interviewing, videoing, and generally gathering as much information for her piece as was possible in the timescales. Jill had also excitedly phoned Buckley, who was still up and watching the breaking news unfold on the BBC 24/7 news channel, in order to get him to hold her the Bloid home page. Buckley could not believe his luck that one of his own journalists was the first reporter on site, even beating the TV crews in their helijets. Jill had arrived back at her flat in a heavy shower of sleety rain on Khan's air-bike about 3.30am. After reheating the chocolate cake, which she was not sure would be safe to eat, and grabbing a cup of hot sweet black coffee to keep her awake, Jill got straight down to writing up her article, which was now almost finished and ready to transmit straight to Buckley for final edit. She glanced up at the clock for the umpteenth time that morning knowing the pressure was on her to get the article into the Times. Nearly seven o'clock. Buckley needed it for seven fifteen to give him forty five minutes to add his editorial and then it would be published at eight on the London Times online *'Bloid'* in the home page *'Sunday Times Breaking News'* section. On the seven minute air-bike flight from Kew to Windsor Jill had thought that if this was one of Ewan's meteorite strikes then it would be a huge public interest story and a real precursor to the Times printing the exclusive on the new 'Schenkler Comet'. When she arrived at Windsor she found the fireball's impact had exploded on the main street right in front of Windsor Castle and even part of the castle was on fire, although it did not look too serious. A secondary fire there was being dealt with by one of the four fire crews already on site. One of the other three crews tended a clothes shop which was burning fiercely and the other two crews were fighting the main cause of the fire on the street. The police had more or less cordoned off the whole area and Jill was kept well back in an area which was beginning to be quickly populated by arriving journalists and TV media crews. A huge crowd had also gathered around the blue and white taped cordon. Mainly Saturday night revellers and local residents. It had quickly become apparent to Jill that this was no meteorite strike. She could clearly discern from the burning wreckage being doused with two powerful jets of water that this was actually a large air-vehicle on fire. Her subsequent enquiries, interviews and the police and fire chief press releases soon revealed that the story was even bigger than a meteor crashing down to Earth. Jill began to read over her column on her laptop for the last time before final transmission to Buckley.

PRINCE OF WALES DEAD:
HEIR TO THRONE DIES IN AIR-CAR TERROR
By Jill Geeson, Senior Investigative Reporter, London Times, Feb 9

Today the country is in mourning following the tragic death of His Royal Highness, Edward, the Prince of Wales, who was killed in a horrific crash in front of Windsor Castle last night. Fire crews and other emergency services fought in vain in an attempt to save the heir to the throne and his aides from the burning wreckage of the Royal air-limousine at around 9.50pm. Six people died and 23 people were badly injured in the carnage that is still smouldering this morning. Not for the first time in its long and eventful history Windsor Castle is burning today amid the wreckage.

Along with Prince Edward, 24, it is believed that the driver of the air-limo, the Prince's Royal Protection Officer and his Press Aide-de-camp, along with two pedestrian passers-by were among the dead. Police and national security have launched an investigation into the cause of the incident and senior officers have refused to confirm reports of the sound of an explosion going off before the crash.

It is believed the Prince was returning to Windsor following a private dinner at the Ritz Hotel in Paris. The police have not formally released the names of the other occupants of the limo, but two of the victims have been named locally as Harry Poll, 47, the Prince's chauffeur, and Aisha al-Gazari, 25, his Press Aide. Their Royal Highnesses Queen Elizabeth and David, Prince Regent are reportedly 'deeply shocked and distressed' at the sad loss of their oldest son and heir. A Buckingham Palace spokesman told the Times that Her Majesty has expressed her condolences to the families of all the victims of this tragedy.

Queen Elizabeth III is expected to make a further statement on the events later today. An eye-witness to last night's disaster described the scene prior to the limo exploding front of Windsor Castle, describing it "like a huge fireball appearing in the night sky followed by a burning streak of fire like some terrible meteorite crashing to Earth!" One of the first to arrive at the scene of the crash, resident Ernest Postlethwaite, a 43 year old part-time St John's Ambulance paramedic, described scenes of terror and carnage.

Mr Postlethwaite stated, "The vehicle exploded onto the street about 150 yards from where I was walking home with my wife. I immediately ran towards the air-limo and tried to rescue any occupants, however, the fierce heat from the flames kept beating me back. There was nothing anyone could do to save them. I suspected the car may have carried members of the Royal Household, but I am totally shocked and saddened to learn that I had failed to save the Prince of Wales. I am heart-broken for Her Majesty Queen Elizabeth."

The cause of the crash is unknown and the Metropolitan Police, the Berkshire Fire Division and the Royal Protection Squad have crash investigation teams on site working on site throughout the night. The area has been cordoned off in a four-block radius and the limo is now covered by a protective tent. The police have refused to confirm eye-witness reports which claim the sound of the initial explosion was 'like a huge bomb going off in the air'.

The senior investigating officers at the scene, Chief Superintendent Mike Hollingsworth, supported by Chief Fire Officer Rob Lang, held a press conference for media representatives from around the globe crammed into the narrow Windsor street at 5am this morning. CS Hollingsworth stated,"At the present time the Metropolitan Police, supported by the Berkshire Fire Division and the RPS, are currently investigating the events leading up to the terrible tragedy, which occurred here in the main street of Windsor at around 21.51 local time on Saturday 8th February 2081 - and which has led to the awful and sudden death of His Royal Highness Edward, the Prince of Wales. Along with the regrettable loss of the Prince and heir to the throne, three members of the Royal Household and two members of the public also died".

"To date, 23 members of the public have been reported with serious injuries and have been taken to the Royal Berkshire Hospital for

treatment to their wounds. It has been reported to me by the receiving hospital that seven are critical and nine are seriously wounded but that none of those at the Royal Berkshire is in a life-threatening condition. The investigation into the cause of the tragedy remains at a very early stage at this time and all possible eventualities are being investigated."

"The crash investigation teams will consider all factors such as an air crash, bird strike or failure of a technical nature to the Royal vehicle. However, it is believed that the vehicle was travelling along recognised air lanes and had not collided with any building or other ground-based structure. Furthermore, media speculation that the crash was as a result of a terrorist attack on the Royal Household is extremely premature."

Hollingsworth added, "No internet traffic has indicated a rise in the threat levels leading to a possible terrorist atrocity nor are there any terrorist cells or organisations known to be actively operating on these shores. However, currently the investigation has not established direct causation for the Royal air-limo crash. Therefore, terrorism has not been ruled out amongst all the other various factors under investigation."

"Due to the ongoing and lasting peace that has existed globally for almost fifty years there has not been a serious terrorist attack on mainland Britain in that time. No known serious terrorist threat to Britain's shores has been reported to or currently is being investigated by the National Security Services at this time."

In a tragic twist of fate, the incident is reminiscent of Her Majesty's own predecessor Queen Elizabeth II's 'annus horribilus' 90 years ago, when she suffered the loss of her daughter-in-law Diana Princess of Wales in a car crash in the Alma Tunnel in Paris and a fire in Windsor Castle that same year. Queen Elizabeth III is expected to make a brief statement on TV later in the afternoon to the British public and the world's media following an updated press conference by the police. The Queen will express her sympathy and condolences to all who lost their lives in this terrible tragedy and also to give some initial outline details as to the arrangements for Prince Edward's State funeral, which is fully expected to take place later this week pending a post-mortem.

Jill was now satisfied with her finished article. She attached it to a covering email, which she had ready with the photos she had taken at the scene attached, and sent it to Buck Buckley at 07:14. Jill knew that he would open it immediately. Within five minutes after Buckley had speed-read the article he emailed back. *'Fantastic work, J. Made couple of small but minor changes. Off to get my editorial finished for 8, BB.'*

Jill looked out her window past Richmond in the lightening but heavy grey and cloudy Berkshire sky. Sleet was falling again and she could still make out a pall of black smoke rising ominously over Windsor. Police and TV helijets buzzed around the billowing smoke like angry wasps round their smashed and invaded nest. Jill had had enough for one night. Exhilarated but by now completely exhausted she closed the black-out blinds of her bedroom and climbed into bed. Sunday *was* after all going to be her day of rest.

*

Earthdate: 11:05 Sunday February 9, 2081 GMT

Ewan sat dreaming away during the service in the small whitewashed Round Church. It was prominently situated at the top of the hill on the road south leading out of Bowmore. The road bent around the church and headed off down to the Mull of Oa and Port Ellen, the Isle of Islay's southern port and now on the major European tourist marina network built by the Swedish multinational ROMANCE (Ranulf Olafsen Marine and Nautical Corporate Enterprises). It was said by the highly superstitious islanders that the Round Church had been built in the Victorian era to a circular design in order that *'the Devil cannae hide in the corner'.* Ewan sat in the long dark wooden pew a couple of rows back from the pulpit beside his parents. His father was the 71 year-old Reverend Dr John Archibald Lewis Sinclair MD, retired minister of the Free Church of Scotland, and his mother was Jessie McAffer Campbell, 10 years younger than her white-haired husband. The Round Church was actually a part of the Established Church of Scotland. Ewan had rejected his father's stricter sect in his mid-teens, mainly because most of his Boy's Brigade friends belonged to the Round Church and he wanted to follow them. It had taken his parents many anguished years after his father retired from the **'Wee Frees'** to come to worship here in Bowmore. Even before his retirement the Reverend John-Archie's congregation had all but collapsed and when he finally left at 65 the Free Church Assembly in Stornoway decided that the church in Port Ellen was no longer viable. Ewan knew that even the established Church was struggling on this once strongly religious isle off the Scottish mainland, which faced the Mull of Kintyre to the east and Northern Ireland to the south. Islay was no different to the rest of the world when it came to religion. It was a globally dying art.

Christianity, whether Catholicism or Protestantism, Judaism, Hinduism and all the other major religions. They were all being deserted in their droves. Even the strictly controlled Islamic religions headed up by the pseudo-legal, political and religious leaders of the imams and the Mullahs had required a relaxation of many of the stricter Shariah laws of the Qur'an. They had been under pressure over the last fifty years by increasingly restless Muslim populations crying out for greater freedom and prosperity. In the 2080s there was basically only One True God – and the One True God was Money! Money was now the root of all good. The peoples of the world prayed for Money, they worshipped *It*, they slaved their guts out for It, they gambled excessively for It and they bowed before the altar of It.

Ewan tried to drown out the minister rambling through his sermon. He thought it was something to do with Noah, the Ark, the Great Flood followed by something about the Second Coming and the Day of Judgment. He thought that the minister was trying unsuccessfully to fit this entire Biblical catastrophic panoply loosely around the catastrophic events unfolding on this morning's news. Ewan just slipped back into his dream-world. Ewan thought to himself that Gary Mackintosh was a case in point. Ewan had asked Gary to come along to the church in Bowmore. They had been sitting at breakfast at his parents' little cottage in the hamlet of Dunyveg on the sea loch just off the Ardbeg road, past the distillery village of Lagavulin, where Ewan was raised 25 years ago on the family farmstead of Surnaig. Gary laughingly dismissed Ewan's invite to church on the basis that he had his own gods to worship that morning.

"Fuck off, Ewan. Ah'm not even an agnostic. Ah'm a total aetheist, man! Anyway - ah've got money markets opening in the Middle East ah need to work on, while you're away buyin' in to your God. Ah might just make a killin' while the rest of the world watches the Greek Tragedy at Windsor Castle, he, he!"

Gary was indeed a case in point. Ewan did not know exactly what Gary did for a living. He was not employed by any corporation as far as Ewan knew. Gary seemed to work for himself as a self-made online computer expert. He was probably into buying and selling on the world stocks, currencies, commodities and futures markets, but Ewan had never been too sure. When pressed on his sources of income Gary just joked that he was '*something huge in pork bellies*'. Ewan did not even know what pork bellies were. But he did know or at least suspected that Gary worshipped *It* – the Great God Money. The minister, who by now had finished his sermon, came down from the pulpit to the front of the altar and he had called the congregation to prayer. Ewan had earlier counted a meagre total of twenty five heads including himself and his parents. Ewan bowed and clasped his hands together and prayed aloud with the congregation.

"Our Father, Who art in Heaven, Hallowed be thy Name, Thy Kingdom come, Thy will be done, On Earth as it is in Heaven, Forgive our Debts..."

Ewan strayed back into his subconscious and thought back on all that had brought him to be here in this church on this particular day back on Islay. Ewan was born the youngest of four children on 5 January 2056 in the Maternity Wing of the South Glasgow University Hospital in Govan, Glasgow and he was brought up by his parents in Lagavulin village on Islay. His father John Archibald Sinclair was the practising minister at the Free Church in Port Ellen. When John-Archie was a wilder, rebellious young 18 year-old he had signed up against his parents' wishes into the British Army and he served as a Private with the 2nd Battalion the Royal Regiment of Scotland in the Second Afghan Conflict during 2029-31. John-Archie had been based in the Nad e-Ali district in southern Afghanistan at New Camp Bastion, nicknamed the *'Nou Camp'* after Barcelona's famous football ground. The fighting between the British troops and the resurgent Taliban rebels was extremely fierce and particularly dirty. In later life John-Archie never really talked about his army experiences but in one sermon at Port Ellen he did talk a little about what had brought him on the path to Jesus. It had been a quiet Sunday morning at the *Nou Camp* not long after church service had finished. Only a trickle of soldiers had bothered to go along and John-Archie was not one of them. He had pretty much fallen away from the faith of his Islay forefathers. John-Archie and a few of his mates, including his best friend, Somerset-born Sammy Crossan, were sitting in the compound playing cards and gambling at Stud Poker. They were all bare-chested with just their shorts and underpants on, their dog-tags glinting brightly in the fierce July Afghan sun, which they had become inured to. Suddenly, without warning they all heard a great whoosh and someone yelled a fearful cry.

"Incoming! Mortars - !"

Soldiers flung their bodies low on the sandy compound or dived for cover as a huge crump of an explosion rocked the *Nou Camp*. Suddenly soldiers on guard duty were in battle positions on the battlements and pouring huge amounts of live ammo out into the rocky desert in the general direction from where the mortar had been fired from. Some return fire of little magnitude came back from the rocky outcrop and a Sergeant on the parapet pumping his automatic for all it was worth screamed at the top of his voice.

"Enemy engaged! Enemy engaged - Taliban - twelve o'clock!"

Other troops quickly ran to assist the Sergeant and a brief fire-fight ensued. Two Taliban fighters with old semi-automatics about 150 yards south of **Nou Camp** jumped out of their rocky hiding place.

"La ilaha illallah! La ilaha illallah!"

'No God but Allah' they cried in their last breaths as they were mown down in a hail of British lead and the fire-fight was over almost as quickly as it started. The two Taliban were happy now in Heaven with Allah as martyrs to the cause of Islam. John-Archie had been knocked unconscious by the force of the mortar blast and he knew nothing about the fire-fight. He had only been out for a couple of minutes and when he slowly came around, the camp was in chaos, with soldiers and medics running about all over the place. He winced as a pain shot from his left arm to his brain and as he lay in the sand he slowly turned his head in a foggy daze and saw that a large gash ran down the inside of his forearm. John-Archie thought that he must have been caught by a piece of shrapnel and the wound was covered in sand and running freely with warm sticky blood. He squeezed his right hand tightly above the wound to stem the flow of blood and called for help.

"Medic – I need a medic!"

A voice close by answered him immediately with urgency in his tone.

"We're here, son – we're busy right now! We'll get to you in a minute -!"

John-Archie thought as he lay there, bastards have obviously put me down as a non-urgent. He turned his head dizzily to his right and eventually saw in his swimming eyesight two army medics working on a wounded soldier, whose bare body seemed to be half outside of the smouldering blackened crater where the missile had exploded. Poor bastard's taken a direct, he thought. Then his focus came back a bit clearer and his adrenaline started pumping, bringing him back into full consciousness.

"Oh - God - no - SA-A-A-MMY!!"

His best friend Sammy Crossan had taken the full force of the impact. Ignoring his own injury, John-Archie quickly scrambled across the sand towards his friend being tended as best as the medics could, but Sammy's injuries looked really grim.

"Sammy! Sammy!"

One of the medics, an English doctor, pushed at John-Archie's bare chest.

"Stay back, Jock! We need to help this soldier –"

"I-it's my friend Sammy –"

"What's his name, Jock?"

"Private Sammy Crossan. Will he be…?"

John-Archie stared down at his friend's unconscious and battered body. As his eyes shifted down towards the crater where Sammy's legs should have been, John-Archie could see there were none. He felt his left arm wince in pain and he turned away and threw up violently on the hot burning sand. Then he heard a whisper, just the faintest of whispers.

"John-Archie…?"

He turned back and saw that Sammy had wearily opened his eyes and was looking up at him. The English doctor who was putting an adrenaline shot into Sammy's chest shouted above the mayhem that was going on round about the tragic little scene at the crater.

"Stretcher - can we get a stretcher over here now!?"

The quiet intelligent young 19 year-old from Somerset raised a shredded arm to hold on to the screaming medic and he spoke quite clearly and calmly.

"It's okay, doctor – where I'm going I don't need any stretcher…"

The doctor seemed to comprehend the finality of Sammy's statement and it only took a split-second more for it to sink in for John-Archie. He slid in beside Sammy's body and this time neither of the medics made any move to stop him. He cradled Sammy's head and great salty tears welled up in his eyes blinding him with the sun belting off the sand. He spoke gently to his dying friend. John-Archie had never actually seen anyone die before.

"It is fine Sammy, you're gonna be okay. The doctor's are gonna fix you up…"

"N-o-o, Jock, I do-don't think so…"

The medics were looking at each other. They knew the futility of Sammy's situation and they were on the verge of deciding whether to move off to other serious casualties nearby. John-Archie raised his head to the heavens as he cradled Sammy and a deep-throated feral cry welled up in his gullet.

"God! You bastard! How could you?"

Sammy clung to John-Archie's right arm and a warm calm smile came over his pained and bloodied face.

"No, no, John-Archie. It is okay – he's here –"

John-Archie looked at his friend in bewilderment.

"Who's here, Sammy?"

"Jesus – Jesus is here for me…"

John-Archie's throat constricted tightly and he suddenly felt freezing cold on that blazing hot Afghan Sunday. He felt fear grip him tightly and when he tried to speak nothing would come out of his mouth. Sammy spoke instead.

"He's asking if it's okay –"

"If wha-at's o-kay, Sa-mmy?"

"Jesus wants me to go with him. Is it okay?"

John-Archie looked pleadingly to the English medic. The tears were streaming down his face. The medic gave a simple nod and the Scot turned back to look deep into his friend's eyes. Deeper than he had ever looked into a man's eyes before or since. He saw Sammy's soul staring back deep into his own and a great wave of awe and love touched the pair for the first and last time. John-Archie cried desperately as he answered Sammy.

"It's okay Sammy. It's okay."

Sammy closed his weary eyes and slipped into oblivion. The medics let John-Archie weep for a moment over his friend and then the English doctor stayed to tend his shrapnel-torn arm. He sat numbly allowing the doctor to clean and dress his wound as Sammy's body lay dead beside him. He looked at Sammy lying there peacefully and suddenly he felt a warm calming feeling flow through his whole body. It was a feeling like nothing he had ever felt in his life but he knew exactly what it was. Yes, Sammy – Jesus is here. John-Archie left the army soon after Sammy Crossan's death and went home to Scotland to study for his Master in Divinity at Glasgow University.

A tear trickled down Ewan's cheek as he looked at his father sitting on the pew beside him. The minister began his prayer of intercession and Ewan slipped back into his musings. When Ewan was five he went to the Primary School in Port Ellen which had been built on the shore of lovely Kilnaughton Bay near the Port Ellen Maltings, which supplied the malted barley to the various distilleries that had made Islay world-famous for its heavy peaty Scotch whiskies, including Lagavulin. It was while he was eleven and in his last year at primary school that Ewan developed his love for all things cosmic. His teacher Mrs Hunter had given the class a PowerPoint presentation on the Royal Astronomical Society's (RAS) controversial proposal to site a new observatory containing one of the world's largest reflecting telescopes at the Mull of Oa. The Mull of Oa is the highest point at 131 metres above sea level on the Oa peninsula the most southerly point on Islay sitting on the western side of Kilnaughton Bay and to the east of Lochindaal. The proposal was to install the 11.2 metre reflecting telescope named CORSAIR (controlled optimal resolution single aperture integrated reflector) by the year 2069 in a purpose built observatory on the Mull of Oa. The telescope would be of similar design to the huge 10.4 metre reflecting telescope, the Gran Telescopia Canarias (GTC) which was sited 2,267 metres above sea level in an extinct volcano on La Palma in the Canary Islands. The GTC had been a very difficult and expensive build due to the inaccessibility of the location. The RAS were able to propose the more accessible Mull of Oa site for their new telescope on the basis that the promontory was still one which was relatively pollution-free, with mostly good clean air that was required to operate CORSAIR successfully. In addition technological developments in single-aperture reflector manufacture and advanced computer generated control allowed both for CORSAIR to be built larger than the GTC and operate at a much lower level. Ewan, who had been fascinated by space since his earliest childhood memories, was absolutely captivated by Mrs Hunter's presentation, although he could see the rest of the class were bored by it. When the teacher asked for any comments Ewan was the only hand that shot up in the air. He answered with supreme confidence.

"Mrs Hunter. I'm going to be an astronomer when I leave school."

There was a ripple of laughter around the class and Ewan scowled indignantly at everyone. Most of the boys had aspirations to work up at the Maltings or in the distilleries and most of the girls wanted shop jobs in Glasgow or Edinburgh. Mrs Hunter held up her hand to stop the laughter and looked straight into Ewan's excited brown eyes.

"And I believe that you will be an astronomer, Ewan Sinclair, if you put your mind to it."

However, Ewan was about the only person on Islay who was excited about the CORSAIR project. The insular islanders were in uproar over the proposals and hundreds of objections to the planning application were lodged with Argyll and Bute Council. The main thrust of the islander's objections was two-fold. Firstly, the Mull of Oa was an area of outstanding natural beauty and also a Site of Special Scientific Interest (SSSI). The deserted promontory was home to various protected sea birds and rare plants, flowers and grasses, which the objectors argued would be disturbed or even destroyed by the huge building project. They argued that it would be a giant blot on a landscape that was practically unchanged since the Ice Age, *'a great white pimple on God's own soil'*. The second objection was that the proposal necessitated the relocation of the old American Monument, which would require being moved 200 metres to the west of where it was originally built after the First World War. The monument had been erected *'sacred to* the immortal memory' of American soldiers and sailors who had perished in the sinking of the transport ships Tuscania and Otranto by German submarines in 1918. Again the objectors argued that moving the American Monument would be like desecrating a war grave. There was even a large body of objections from the US, especially descendants of servicemen who had perished in the sinking of the two vessels. Despite the objections the local authority unanimously passed the planning application and in February 2068 work began on the Oa peninsula in earnest. Ewan was captivated by the project build as he played football in the playground at breaks or when he was on the sandy beach of Kilnaughton Bay. He would watch the huge 50 tonners, which had just rolled off the specially commissioned ferries from the pier at Port Ellen, thunder past taking building materials up the Oa. Or be fascinated by the brand-new helijets and some older style helicopters freight in more specialist and technical materiel. A large part of the Mull had been fenced off to keep people out for safety and security, but Ewan loved nothing better than to cycle up the Oa at the weekend and watch the 'white pimple' taking shape. The security guards were forever shaking their fists and yelled at him.

"Get oot o' here ye bloody wee scamp!"

Ewan took great pleasure at shouting back as he free-wheeled back down the hill.

"I'm going to work there one day!"

The security guards just laughed at him as he cycled off each time with a flea in his ear. The second important event in that same last year of primary school for Ewan was that his teacher Mrs Hunter had selected two boys and two girls in the class to sit the entrance exam for the prestigious Glasgow High School. Ewan was one of the boys. Ewan's mother Jessie was against this because her **'baby'** would be away in Glasgow during the school year. John-Archie argued Ewan's case.

"For goodness sake, woman, it's not as if the boy is going to outer space! He's only going to Glasgow and it is only 45 minutes away on the new helijet service from the Machair. I've spoken with Margaret and she and Jim have agreed Ewan can have their spare room. They're practically round the corner from the school where they are in Anderston. And anyway the boy hasn't even passed the exam so who knows whether he'll get in or not?"

After buckets of tears from Jessie and pleading from Ewan she relented and Ewan sat the exam in late March. Jessie had an unmarried cousin Bella McAffer who was also very maternalistic and sympathetic to the cause. Bella comforted Jessie with optimistic thoughts of failure.

"We'll let Ewan sit the exam then. We could be lucky Jessie and he'll not be getting in to the Glasgow High School."

Although the competition for places at Glasgow High was fierce Ewan passed with flying colours, as did shrewd Mrs Hunter's other three applicants from Port Ellen Primary. The results had come through with only two weeks to go until the summer holidays and Mrs Hunter asked the two boys and two girls to stand up at their desks in class.

"Peter McEachern, Ewan Sinclair, Elizabeth MacFie and Mhairi Gillespie have all been accepted for places at the Glasgow High School. It is a great honour for Port Ellen Primary to have had all four sit the exam and all four pass with such distinction. I would like to say to all four of you – children, I am proud of your wonderful achievement. Class please show your appreciation?"

Ewan's chest swelled to bursting as the whole class burst into a raucous round of applause and cheering. A week before First Year was to begin Ewan had settled into his sister Margaret and husband Jim's spacious apartment in the large Edwardian-façade terrace on the corner of Cleveland Street and Kent Road in the Anderston district of Glasgow. It faced the magnificent Victorian edifice, the Mitchell Library, which Ewan would spend many hours of study and research in. Margaret was the oldest of the four Sinclair children and she was 13 years older than Ewan. She and Jim did not have any children and it did not look like they would ever have any. Jim was one of the growing ranks of infertile males spreading around the globe like a virus with no finite causation as yet identified. That week before school started was like a holiday in the big city for the wee Islay boy. Margaret and Jim took him to Pollok Estate and the Burrell Collection, Kelvingrove Art Gallery, the Riverside Transport Museum on the north side of the River Clyde and Ewan's favourite. It was the Glasgow Science Centre on the opposite side of the river from the Transport Museum. Anything to do with space in that museum and Margaret would end up having to drag Ewan onwards. The impressive blond-sandstone Glasgow High School was situated on the other side of the bridge which crossed over the M8 motorway, on Elmbank Street in the Blythswood district. Rev John-Archie and Jessie had come to stay in Glasgow and to support Ewan through his first week at the High School. Although Margaret's flat was big she only had the one spare room, which Ewan was using and his parents booked into the nearby Glasgow Hilton to make a holiday of it. On the Monday morning John-Archie and Jessie came over to Margaret's for breakfast and to see their **'big boy'** get into his smart new dark blue uniform with the High School crest emblazoned proudly on the jacket pocket. After breakfast and tearful hugs from his father and sister, Ewan walked the short distance from Cleveland Street to Elmbank Street with his mother Jessie beside him. They walked quietly and watched the rush-hour traffic go by. The electri-cars, trucks and taxis clogging up the M8 trying to get into the city and also above them the build-up of air-car traffic in the lower air lanes and helijets in the upper lanes. As they turned off Bath Street into Elmbank Street they could see the hordes of parents and children streaming into the school gates. Jessie put her arm around Ewan's shoulder and reassured him.

"I'm awful proud of you son. Remember to always push yourself to achieve your goals. If you work hard then you can play hard."

"Okay, mum - thanks."

The first week went past in a blur of timetables, new teachers, new friends and the new concept to Ewan of moving from one subject to another. By the end of the week when his parents were due to return home to Lagavulin, Ewan was absolutely exhausted at school. His parents were driving back in John-Archie's new Honda Xe electri-car and then catching the huge CalMac catamaran super-ferry which skimmed between the pier at Kennacraig on West Loch Tarbert and Port Ellen Ferry Terminal on Islay. It departed Kennacraig at 7pm, the last crossing on the Friday night during the summer timetable and they were ready to leave from Margaret's more or less as soon as Ewan came home. Ewan came into the flat at 4.25pm and saw his parents standing beside their packed bags and saying their last goodbyes to Margaret. Jessie turned round to look at her drained and emotionally charged son biting his lip and she tried to remain upbeat.

"Here's my big boy. Well, how was your first week at the big school?"

Ewan just grabbed his mother's waist and clung onto her sobbing his heart out. He was not actually quite sure what was making him cry so dejectedly, because the High School was everything that he had hoped it would be. Jessie asked him optimistically if he would rather go back to Bowmore Academy instead. However, Ewan was insistent.

"No, I love my school. I don't know why I'm crying."

After that first emotional week Ewan settled right in to the High School routine and he excelled in all his subjects and especially Physics, Mathematics and Computer Science. In his third year Ewan chose to be streamed into the science subjects and it was in his new Maths and Computing classes that he met Gary Mackintosh and they became firm friends, although they were two completely different personalities. Although Ewan did not know it at the time Jill Geeson was in the year below him at Glasgow High, although she chose to be streamed in English Lit subjects rather than science. It was a few years later after they had all graduated that Gary introduced Ewan to Jill at a party. They had become lovers for just short of a year when Jill up and took the job at the London Times. Ewan was more heartbroken at losing Jill than he would admit, even to Gary. After the High School Ewan became the first Sinclair to get a place at Oxford University reading in physics, applied mathematics and cosmic sciences. In his third year at Oxford he required to take a placement and, of course, Ewan chose to work at the Royal Observatory on the Mull of Oa back at home on Islay. By that time his parents had sold the larger farmstead at Surnaig and moved to the small house at Dunyveg on the other side of the sea lochan at Lagavulin. Ewan preferred to be in his own place so he rented a flat on Frederick Crescent near the pier at Port Ellen. During the week he worked and researched up at the observatory and at the weekends he took a job with CalMac on the super-ferries which ran between Port Ellen and Kennacraig and also between Port Ellen – Port Askaig and up north to Oban. Although his parents were still part funding him they joked that the ferry job helped 'keep him afloat'. Up on the Oa Ewan became an expert on the huge CORSAIR telescope and the astrophysicists who worked there were enormously impressed at his deft handling of the huge reflector. Ewan graduated with a First in Astrophysics from Oxford and again his parents were enormously proud of him.

"And now we'll sing the Benediction..."

The sound of an off-key note on the organ startled Ewan back to the present in the Round Church. John-Archie nudged him to stand and sing as the minister and the two elders on duty walked up the aisle to the front door, which looked down the hill to the old Bowmore distillery buildings and the cold grey February waters of dark Lochindaal.

"Praise God from whom all blessings flow, Praise him all creatures here below, Praise him above ye Heavenly host, Praise Father, Son and Holy Ghost."

CHAPTER 9

She looked at the small packet lying on the breakfast bar like it was some sort of deadly toxic chemical, totally untouchable. Jill had tossed it on there just over an hour ago when she had come back to her flat and now she could not bring herself to pick it up again. She had slept in bed until about 1 o'clock on the Sunday afternoon. She then dragged herself into the kitchen still feeling groggy and nauseous. Jill told herself that she had knocked her body clock's biorhythms out of synch lately and last night's reporting in Windsor had made things worse. She would go to the local Boots the Chemist in Richmond and ask them for something to help. She was also ravenous, after having eaten only the McDonalds Happy Meal and the chocolate fudge cake yesterday, and so she made herself a huge toasted BLT with three slices of brown bread. She wolfed it all down with two large mugs of Nescafe instant and exclaimed aloud to herself.

"God - ah needed that. Ah was starving!"

Jill went on to her laptop and connected to the Times on Sunday website. Her article was right there in bold Technicolor emblazoned on the Bloid home page alongside dramatic photographs of the tragedy at Windsor. She noted with satisfaction that Buckley had even used two of the dozen or so photos that she had emailed to him. Jill read her piece with satisfaction and particularly reviewed it to see what Bill Buckley might have changed in her original transcript.

"Buckin' never made a change at all!"

Jill read Buckley's editorial and she had to hand it to her experienced boss, it was sharp and incisive as per usual. She hoped one day in time she would be in the boss's shoes and she could write as effortlessly as William J Buckley. Her thoughts went back to last night's awful and historic tragedy and she turned from the impersonal professional journalist's article that she had written, to the personal and emotional feelings that now welled up inside her. She had not known Prince Edward well. She had been introduced briefly to him at the same Windsor garden party that she had taken Khan to, the one where she had also met Queen Elizabeth and Prince David. Having shaken the hand of someone who had just last night been blown to Kingdom Come sent a creeping shiver up her spine. Again she had not known Aisha al-Gazari too well either, but they had spoken for a few fleeting moments at the garden party. They talked press speak together and exchanged business cards. Once a few months later Aisha had phoned Jill at the Times with a question but Jill could only refer Aisha on to the Times' Royal Correspondent for an answer. There had been unsubstantiated rumours in press circles that Edward, the world's most eligible bachelor, and Aisha, the gorgeous dark smouldering daughter of a minor Saudi Royal, were lovers, but that had certainly been well suppressed within British press circles. No doubt, Jill thought, it will be alleged on the home pages of Das Bild, Paris Match and Le Monde within the next day or two as they try to maintain the momentum of the tragic story. She switched on the BBC to catch up with the latest news and a sickly feeling arose in her stomach making her chide herself.

"For goodness sake. Ah thought you were havin' the day off and here you are still working!"

It was now a quarter past one and the BBC anchorman looked grim.

"In breaking news on last night's tragedy at Windsor we are going straight to the Metropolitan Police HQ where Superintendent, sorry, Chief Superintendent Mike Hollingsworth is about to give a statement to the waiting world media –"

The programme immediately switched over to the Met Office headquarters and Hollingsworth looked even grimmer than the anchorman as he stood in front of an array of microphones. He waited momentarily as dozens of press photographers flashed again and again to get their press pictures and then he spoke slowly and deliberately. Jill sat glued to the box.

"As I intimated at Windsor last night at the scene of the most indescribable horror, I am now in a position to release a further statement on the ongoing and as yet incomplete investigation into the tragedy –"

Hollingsworth took a deep inhalation and steadied himself. The world was waiting with bated breath and this was *his* fifteen minutes of fame.

"Our initial investigations have led us to determine that the crash of the Royal air-limousine outside Windsor Castle last evening, which has resulted in the deaths of six persons, including His Royal Highness,

Edward, Prince of Wales, was as the result of a remotely-triggered explosive device..."

Jill gaped at the TV. Hollingsworth was interrupted by an audible gasp from the media surrounding him and the flashing cameras went ballistic. Journalists started screaming out questions and they had to be quietened by the Met's Press Officer sitting beside Hollingsworth.

"Quiet! Quiet please! Chief Superintendent Hollingsworth will not be taking any questions at this time. Please allow him to finish his statement –"

The hubbub slowly settled and Hollingsworth continued.

"As I said a minute ago, and I will reiterate, the crash was as a result of an explosive device and in consequence, I have stepped up the investigation to that of a deliberate and callous act of serious criminal terrorism, which has resulted in the assassination and cold calculated murder of the following persons. I am now in a position to formally name all six. They are His Royal Highness, Edward, Prince of Wales, Royal Protection Officer Ernest Victor Clark, 41, of Crawley, Surrey, Royal Chauffeur Harold Cresswell Poll, 47, of Reading, Berkshire, Royal Press Aide-de-camp Aisha al-Gazari, 26, a Saudi national of West Kensington, London, Maud Beatrice Hepplestone, 73, of Windsor, Berkshire and Jonathan Vernon Meechan, 16, a pupil at Eton School and of Salisbury in Wiltshire. Our condolences and sympathies are extended to the Royal Family and to all the families and friends of all six victims who were so cruelly murdered last night."

Hollingsworth paused for dramatic effect before continuing.

"As you will all be fully aware it is almost fifty years since a terrorist atrocity, certainly of this magnitude, has taken place on mainland Britain. I can assure you that the British Police and the National Security Services have not been complacent over that extended period of peace on these shores and that we have remained vigilant at all times. However, at present, although we have had no information on the radar screen, so to speak, we now have to assume that a terrorist or terrorist cell is operating in this country at present. Our current assumption is that this dastardly crime is too complex to have been carried out by one individual working alone and therefore, we believe that we are currently hunting for an extremely adept and cunning group of terrorists. It is our aim to bring these desperate and cowardly criminals to justice and we will leave no stone unturned to meet that

aim. At this time I do not intend to make any further comment except to say that it is still hoped that Her Royal Majesty, Queen Elizabeth will address the nation from Buckingham Palace at 3 o'clock. That is all, thank you!"

Hollingsworth marched off camera to a roar of unanswered questions and flashing cameras. Jill had sat in front of her 3DTV completely mesmerised and she wondered who was covering it for the Times on Sunday. Probably the Royal Correspondent or the Senior Crime Reporter, but the way she was feeling herself at that moment she was glad they had not phoned her to 'get her arse' down to the Met Office. Then Jill thought, a terrorist assassination in Britain after 50 years! Who? Why? She felt like picking up the phone and asking Khan if he had seen the news. Had he seen that the poor girl Aisha they had met at Windsor was dead too? But the way she was feeling at that very moment she resisted calling him. Jill was feeling so fragile that she felt that she would break down emotionally on the phone and she did not want to show Khan any weakness. By the time Queen Elizabeth came on TV to make her address to the nation, Jill was feeling so groggy and poorly she was finding it difficult to listen and take it all in. Jill was still able to marvel at how stoic and stiff upper lipped these Royals managed to project themselves, even in their worst tragedies. It was like they were born to act out life in a Shakespearian Tragedy. Jill groaned at the TV.

"Christ sake, Lizzie, break down, girl - you've just lost your oldest son!"

Jill could not take any more. She had to go down to Boots and get something or she would not be fit for work on Monday. She slipped on her winter jacket, grabbed the keys and left Queen Elizabeth speaking to her empty studio flat. Jill zipped down on Khan's air-bike and headed for Richmond High Street. In the air above Kew on the bike Jill suddenly had a brainstorm! Surely not, she questioned herself. In the empty Boots shop, the women behind the pharmacy counter were glued to the Queen's address and one of them was sobbing pitifully in a Cockney accent to her colleagues.

"I'd just die if I had lost me o-oldest son. Can't think how Her M-Majesty can put hersel' up there like that – bloomin' marvellous!?"

Jill knew that the women would be annoyed at being interrupted so she quickly asked for the packet and zipped back to Kew. And now here she was at quarter past six looking at the blue and white printed packet and asking of herself, will she, won't she? Thirty minutes later she stared numbly down at the white plastic strip with the cheap USB cable plugged into her laptop.

She then dared herself to look at the monitor. She looked up and gasped in shock as she read the bold type.

"*CONGRATULATIONS! YOU ARE POSITIVE!*"

*

The Group sat crowded together in Room 101 on the first floor of the Ardvasar Hotel on Skye, the room that Dick Threlfall had moved Hassan Ben Ali into from the cramped damp single room downstairs. As Mahmoud had planned, they had earlier spent the snow-filled day in the hotel lounge keeping Threlfall and the Slovakian barman Oliç as involved with them as much as they possibly could. The Group spent the alibi money like it was going out of fashion and Threlfall would never forget such unbounded generosity. Maybe business was picking up after all, Threlfall thought. The Mohammad brothers sat on the end of the lumpy creaky old double bed, Hassan and Mahmoud each sat in small uncomfortable wooden chairs and Khan, who looked pensive and slightly detached from the others, sat perched like a hawk on the narrow wooden window sill. He could not see it behind him, but the snow, which had fallen all day on Skye was still falling lazily and heavily. Mahmoud reached into a white carrier bag and pulled out a presentation box containing a bottle of 16 year-old Talisker malt whisky and held it high above his head like some great victorious trophy being held aloft in triumph.

"Allahu akbar!"

Mahmoud gave the cry '*Allah is the Greatest*' but he was careful not to raise his voice too loudly for fear of arousing the suspicions of any unlikely infidel who happened to be in the vicinity of Hassan's room. Hassan and the Mohammads responded in amusement at having to mute their cheers.

"Allahu akbar! Allahu akbar!"

Mahmoud noted out of the corner of his eye that Khan had remained sulkily silent as he sat aloof on the window sill, his dark eyes watching through hawkish slits.

"Khan, my brother, tonight we drink a toast to the success of our mission. Our Palestinian brother is now in hiding at a safe house in the north of England. Allah is pleased, our Brothers of Jihad are pleased and I have been told that Brother Suleiman is proud of our great achievement for the cause of Islam and our great God Allah –"

Mahmoud, who had bought the Talisker from Threlfall's bar at an exorbitant price, started pouring whiskies into five glasses from the bar that he had borrowed from Oliç, making sure that Oliç received a memorable

£20 tip for his trouble. Khan, who was obviously uptight, vented his spleen at Mahmoud.

"So, brother, we drink the infidel poison in the name of Allah? You know it is forbidden under Shariah law!"

The youngest member of the group Mossab Mohammad half rose off the bed and tried to calm the rising tension in the heavily claustrophobic room.

"Khan – surely Allah will allow us this one little indiscretion…?"

Khan let out a bitter sardonic laugh which forced Mossab to sit slowly back onto his perch on the bed. Khan spoke with a sharp hiss.

"Yes – Allah will allow us just one little indiscretion. Does Allah forget that we have been involved in the deaths of six human beings, my brother - Mossab!?"

Mahmoud jumped in between Khan and Mossab who were glaring at each other with black bitter hate-filled stares. Mahmoud spoke with assertive pacification.

"Khan! Enough! We are all *mujihadeen – al-jihad fi sabil Allah!* We celebrate because we have won a great victory last night in the name of our blessed God over the *infidel* scum!"

Mahmoud El Kharroubi, although sounding to the others like a man rising to anger, knew exactly what he was saying. He suspected what was eating at Khan's black heart and he intended to shake it out of him. Khan rose easily to Mahmoud's bait. Khan struck back with rising venom in his hissing voice.

"Yes, my brother – Mahmoud. Please can you pour me a Scotch to celebrate striking at the heart of the infidel scum? I would like that. Of course, Aisha was not infidel scum, was she -?"

Mahmoud raised his palms towards his Kuwaiti friend in a placatory motion.

"Khan, my friend, Aisha is now a martyr sitting at the right hand of Allah."

Khan sprung like a striking hooded cobra from the window sill spitting poisonous venom at El Kharroubi who jerked back his head and shoulders at Khan's verbal assault.

"AISHA WAS NOT MEANT TO BE IN THE CAR! I'm going to kill that Palestinian bastard -!!"

Hassan intervened with a puzzled look on his face.

"- But, Khan, your white girl? Jill -?"

Khan swivelled his cobra-hooded stare around to Hassan.

"Are you all so naïve? Jill Geeson was a front – a means to an end! I loved my beautiful Aisha and when I get that bastard from Gaza, I'll…"

"ENOUGH – KHAN!"

Mahmoud El Kharroubi finally exerted his authority over the Group and the two men glowered at each other with a deep dark blackness in their eyes. Mahmoud did not flinch as he continued to speak with a steady control in his voice.

"The Palestinian is not to blame. It is I who ensured that Aisha would be in the car."

A terrible silence filled the crowded room. Khan visibly paled with disbelief. His best friend had betrayed him and he felt a steely coldness like a stiletto stabbing his broken heart.

"Ma-ah-moud…?"

"Yes, Khan, it was I and our masters in the Brotherhood of Jihad who took this terrible decision."

Mahmoud gulped hard as he continued with his dark revelation.

"We felt that Aisha knew too much and that she would be a danger to the greater cause of Islam if she lived. She had to be sacrificed, my brother –"

The silence was palpable, throat-constricting. Khan slumped back on the window sill, his darkened soul in another place. Time had seemingly stopped in the room and Mahmoud El Kharroubi knew he had to break the suffocating silence.

"Well, my friends, are we going to have that drink before we show our faces again to Dicky al-Threlfall and have our dinner in his esteemed infidel presence?"

Khan sprang off the window sill again and barged his way past the others crowded around the bed. He spat out venomously at the rest of the Group.

"You know where you can stick your drink! I will see you all at dinner for the sake of the cause! Meanwhile – I am going out for some air that I can *actually* breathe - !!"

Khan sprinted downstairs, past a surprised Oliç who was setting up the Group's table for their evening meal in the snug area, and the Kuwaiti ran outside into the snow. Oliç thought that the Arab must be desperate for a cigarette. The snow had eased down to a mere few flakes but the ground was well covered with up to 10 centimetres of an unspoiled white virginal blanket. Khan sprung over the low snow-covered dry-stone dyke and ploughed downhill through the thick snow, past some placid red shaggy-haired Highland cattle that looked almost sympathetically at him as he trudged by. When he reached the dark slippery seaweed-covered rocks on the shoreline he knew he could go no further. Khan stood shivering in the freezing cold night and looked across the Sound of Sleat to the twinkling fairy lights of Mallaig. The lights looked big and watery in his eyes and he wept silently for his lost love Aisha.

*

Earthdate: 20:45 Sunday February 9, 2081 GMT

"Ewan Sinclair – I hope that you and Gary are not going out on the drink on the Sabbath?"

Ewan and Gary had obviously been getting their gear ready to go out for the evening and Ewan did not want to give too much away to his mother Jessie. Before he had thought what he was saying to his 'Wee Free' mother and committee member on the Lord's Day Observance Society, Ewan knew immediately that he had blurted out a fatal reply. It would have been better to have said that he and Gary were actually going to the pub.

"No, mother, we are just going for a run in the car round to Portnahaven with Uncle Duncan…"

Ewan winced and knew right away from his mother's darkening scowl that he had said completely the wrong thing.

"Don't mention that man's name in my house, especially not on the Lord's Day!"

"Oh, mother - !"

Jessie Sinclair raised a warning palm to Ewan.

"No – don't utter another word, Ewan Sinclair!"

John-Archie, who had been sitting blissfully beside their original old-fashioned peat fire trying to read his Bible, looked up and tried to pacify the stormy flickering flames being fanned between his wife and his son.

"Jessie, give the boy a break. He has always got on well with his uncle, ah…"

John-Archie refrained from using the name.

"…and anyway he has never done any bad to this family."

As far as Jessie was concerned John-Archie might as well have poured oil onto those flickering flames.

"No, John-Archie, he has not – but the Jezebel witch that he is married to certainly has, God forgive me for saying that on the Sabbath!"

As the room fell into a chilly silent atmosphere, Gary looked at the three pensive family members and wondered what the hell that was all about. Ewan certainly knew, as he and Gary sat ready in silence for his Uncle Duncan McNeilage to arrive in his electri-car and pick them up. The trouble had begun long before Ewan was born, in fact, it actually happened about two years after Jessie McCaffer Campbell had married John-Archie Sinclair and even before they had borne any of their four children. It was while Jessie and John-Archie were staying in their small 'single-end' tenement on Byres Road in Partick near to Glasgow University where John-Archie was studying for his Doctorate in Divinity. Jessie had been one of five children born in Lagavulin to father John Angus Campbell, known as Iain-Angi Mhór, and mother Shonaig McCaffer. The others were the oldest son Alex, who lived in Glasgow and youngest daughter Mary, who lived in Bowmore. There had also been two other sons. Iain Campbell who had been killed on active duty in the Second Afghan Conflict in Nad e-Ali serving with the 4th Battalion the Royal Regiment of Scotland. John-Archie had known young Iain Campbell well and had attended his memorial service at the Nou Camp. Another son William McCaffer Campbell had died shortly after birth in the Glasgow University Hospital in Glasgow with a congenital defect of his male reproductive organs and he had been buried at Kilnaughton Cemetery. In the same grave as his brother Iain was later to be buried in. Jessie's father Iain-Angi Mhór had died before she met and married John-Archie, but Jessie's mother Shonaig had still lived in Lagavulin. A year after Jessie married John-Archie in the chapel at Glasgow University her sister Mary met and married Portnahaven man Duncan McNeilage. Mary and Duncan were married in the Round Church in Bowmore. Jessie was bridesmaid and John-Archie was the best man. Later that evening, Mary and Duncan prepared to leave on their honeymoon to Nice in the French Riviera from the riotously happy wedding reception in Portnahaven Village Hall - riotous due to the fact that Duncan's father had laid on a welcome 'free bar' for the thirsty island guests and they were freely partaking of the 'water of life'! Before the happy couple jumped into the waiting electri-taxi, Mary pulled Jessie aside and they happily hugged each other tightly. Mary looked into her big sister's teary eyes and joyfully wept.

"You're my best sister and you'll always be my best friend!"

Jessie shouted laughingly after them as the cab drove off from the waving guests.

"I'm your only sister, Mary, always will be! And don't you ever forget that!"

Jessie and John-Archie continued to live in Partick in Glasgow, Mary and Duncan moved down south to live in Blackpool in England and Alex lived in Pollok on the south side of Glasgow. A year later, their mother Shonaig McCaffer Campbell died intestate after a short battle with cancer and Alex took the reins and stated that as the only surviving son he would arrange all the funeral details and the winding up of their mother's tiny estate, which in financial terms did not amount to a great deal of money. A week after their mother had been buried in the family plot at Kilnaughton beside her husband and two sons, Alex drove over from Pollok to Partick to discuss the financial affairs with Jessie. Mary and Duncan were back down in Blackpool by that time. Alex laid out the details to Jessie.

"I've a cheque here for you and John-Archie to cover your travel costs to Islay and I've also sent cheques to Mary and Duncan and the other relatives who had to make the trip over to mother's funeral."

Jessie could not remember the last time that she had actually seen a cheque as the banking world by that time was 99% electronic and online based. However, their mother on Islay still liked old-fashioned paper banking.

"Now as you know, Jessie, mother did not have a will. She never liked those 'bloody leeching lawyers' as she would call them. After settling the funeral expenses, I think there is only going to be about six thousand left in mother's account. Not a lot these days!"

"My goodness, Ally, is that all there is left?"

"I'm afraid so Jessie. I've made enquiries through a pal of mine and he says that if we get the lawyers into it there will be virtually nothing left to split. What I propose if you agree, is to settle up with the bank on Islay and split the six thousand equally three ways between you, me and Mary? What do you think?"

"That sounds okay? Does Mary agree to that?"

"Och, Jess, you know me and Mary have never got on for years. For goodness sake, she never even invited me to her wedding. Look if you trust me to do the right thing then just you tell Mary what we've agreed to –"

"Of course I trust you, Ally."

Jessie and Alex had always been close but her fiery short-tempered red-haired sister Mary had fallen out badly with Ally about five years ago. She would never tell Jessie what it was all about. When Jessie phoned Mary in Blackpool the next day she was more than a bit hesitant about Mary's reaction. Jessie had heard Mary's sharp tongue before but never like this.

"You've agreed to let that bastard brother of mine do this thing, Jessie? I swear on the fresh soil of my mother's grave and God forgive me, Jessie, but I hope the two of you choke on the money!!"

"For pity's sake, Mary, Ally says that there will be no money left if we bring in the lawyers…"

"I don't give a damn if the bloody lawyers get the whole rotten stinking six thousand. I wouldn't trust Ally as far as I could throw him, so you get back on to that shitey bastard brother of ours and you tell him to get a lawyer and do this thing properly!"

Mary then cut Jessie off. Jessie repeatedly tried ringing Alex in Pollok but his phone did not even go on to voicemail and she began to feel a rising sense of dread. John-Archie tried to calm Jessie down.

"Look, Jessie, if the six thousand means that much to Mary and Ally then let them fight over it. We don't need it so much that it is worth falling out about –"

Jessie remained adamant as she replied.

"No John-Archie. Apart from my mother's wedding ring and her old photo album, I have nothing else to remember my mother by –"

"Jessie, it is the memories of our parents that we should treasure the most."

"I'm entitled to my mother's money as much as Mary and Ally - I am going to have my share!"

Another two days passed and then Jessie decided to phone Ally's brother-in-law Bobby who also lived in Pollok and asked if he had heard from Alex. Bobby sounded quite taken aback.

"Surely you know Jessie? Alex and Betty have immigrated out to New Zealand – they've been planning it for months now."

Jessie felt sick to the base of her stomach. How could she possibly tell Mary that she had been right all along and that their deceitful little brother had run off with their mother's money? Jessie thought that Mary would go totally ape, but instead when she phoned and explained what Alex had done, all she heard was an icy silence before the phone went dead. That same evening Jessie received an email from Mary. She printed if off and thrust it into John-Archie's hand.

"Well, read that then. It has all come down to this –"

John-Archie read the note with a sorry heart.

Dear Jessie, I find it hard to express how much I hate you and that thieving bastard who is no brother of mine. You are nothing but a harlot and a witch for consorting with the Devil himself, and I hope that you both rot in Hell. Mary McNeilage.

John-Archie spoke to Jessie sympathetically seeking reconciliation.

"Oh, Jessie, Mary's heart is filled with a black rage. She cannot mean those terrible words. Destroy that blasted thing and we'll find a way to make the peace."

Jessie grabbed the note out of her husband's hand her eyes burning fiercely.

"No, John-Archie! This piece of bile is going into my treasure box beside my mother's ring. As long as it lies there Mary McNeilage is no Campbell and she is no sister of mine. And that is my final word!"

Gary who broke the silence as he spotted the lights outside, bringing Ewan's thoughts back to the present.

"That looks like a car has just arrived, Ewan."

Ewan hurriedly grabbed his bag in an effort to escape the frosty atmosphere at home.

"Right, Gary, get the gear and let's get out of here."

Ewan and Gary trudged down the path over the crunchy thin layer of snow to meet Ewan's Uncle Duncan who was standing beside his big electric Land Rover Eco 4x4. Ewan sensed the twitching curtain behind him as he greeted the big warm friendly man before him.

"Ciamar a tha thu, a Dhonnchaidh!"

"Tha mi gu math, Eóghann!"

Gary butted into this private greeting between uncle and nephew.

"Hey! Hey! Can we aw get back to a language that God himself would understand?"

As Duncan pumped Gary's hand he laughed at the Glaswegian.

"You'll be Gary then? I'm Ewan's big Uncle Duncan – and by the way the *Gàidhlig* **is** the language of God."

Ewan had been standing checking the night sky. He had been praying that the earlier light February snow would be blown out to sea and his prayers had been answered. The black inky Islay sky was as clean and as clear as he could have hoped for. He could clearly discern the billions of stars of the Milky Way swathed silkily across the firmament. The God of all religions had been with him and Gary tonight in more ways than one. As Gary and Duncan chatted lightly beside him he scanned about him. He looked across the inlet to Surnaig, panning round to the floodlit whitewashed distillery buildings with the giant black-painted lettering *LAGAVULIN* painted on the white wall. He then gazed down to the bottom of the little Dunyveg road past his parents' house and saw the ancient black shattered stump of Dunyveg Castle silhouetted against the shimmering ink-filled sea. His mother told him the tale as a wee boy in Lagavulin of his ancestor, the son of an Irish clan chief, Caffer og McCaffer who escaped Cromwell's forces in Ulster over four hundred years ago and brought his men in boats over to Dunyveg. In the *Gàidhlig 'cath bharr'* (pronounced ca-far) means *'from the battle'* and the McCaffers were the shield bearers of the McDonalds of Dunyveg who were eventually ousted from Islay by the Campbells. Duncan McNeilage gave Ewan a nudge to bring him back to the present.

"Hey! Dream boy – are we doin' this thing tonight or what?"

The three men all jumped into the Land Rover and Duncan turned the smooth silent-running 4x4 and drove it purposefully down through Lagavulin, past the distillery at Laphraoig and on south to Port Ellen. They went past the modern European ROMANCE marina with the huge white yachts swaying and clinking in the swell and on down past the well-lit buildings of the Maltings, which ran a 24/7 operation to produce the malted barley for the unending whisky production and to fill the inexhaustible coffers of the Great God Money. At the end of Kilnaughton Bay the road passed the cemeteries and Ewan could see a low eerie mist roll in off the sea and over the darkened gravestones, but he thought that would not be any problem up on the Mull of Oa. Duncan lowered the gears as the Land Rover began the climb up onto the great large promontory that was the Oa peninsula. The snow was heavier here but the climb up through the Cragabus farmlands presented no problems for his powerful car. They had all been pretty silent since leaving Dunyveg but Duncan broke the impasse.

"I hope you know what you're doing, Ewan – and I trust that you are ready for what's up there?"

"I hope so, Uncle Duncan."

Ewan looked back from the front passenger seat to the gear on the back seat beside Gary and it made Ewan swallow hard as some acid rose into his throat. On top of Gary's satchel containing his laptop and computing equipment there lay a pile of clear elasticated face-masks and two sterilised blue plastic hooded coveralls, the type used by police forensic scientists. When Ewan had phoned his Uncle Duncan about the possibility of getting into CORSAIR for a couple of hours on the Sunday night, he did not really have a firm plan as to how he could possibly pull it off. The Royal Observatory on the Oa was manned almost every night in the year and the astronomy staff knew Ewan well. However, he did not know how he could possibly convince them, without the proper authority that he needed to use the telescope for two hours for his own research. Duncan McNeilage provided the stroke of luck, in conjunction with tonight's clear dark sky that gave Ewan the perfect opportunity.

After their marriage Duncan and Mary had lived in Blackpool for many years and Duncan worked as a big copper in the Lancashire Constabulary. When Duncan inherited his parents' cottage in Portnahaven, he took early retirement from the police force and moved back to Islay. As luck would have it the Security Officer's position at CORSAIR had become vacant and Duncan was easily the best candidate and he got the job, which was a real 'cushy number'. Although there had been a great deal of local objection at the start of the controversial Observatory's life on Oa, it actually blended into the environment extremely well and also enhanced the tourist attraction of the Oa itself. Duncan had an easy life keeping CORSAIR safe and secure. After passing Risabus farmstead they reached the new single track road sign posted *'HM Royal Observatory, Mull of Oa'*. Ewan was pleased to see that the 5 centimetres of snow ahead covering the road was pure white and unblemished. Not another car or person had been up here tonight and, of course, Ewan knew why. CORSAIR was his to use as he pleased and Duncan had agreed to let him in on condition that he did not tell him what he was up to.

"Well, Ewan, just so long as it's not illegal – I am an ex-cop you know."

Ewan told his uncle a little white lie, maybe not as pure as the driven snow ahead.

"No, no, Uncle Duncan, it's all above board!"

In two minutes Duncan had crunched the Land Rover up to his private car park spot next to the great white-domed building sitting only 20 yards or so from the sheer cliff edges of the Mull. It was like some Arabian mosque which had been mystically transported to Islay on a huge white Aladdin's magic carpet. The three men got out of the Land Rover and all stared misty-eyed out to the glassy sea over four hundred feet below them. City boy Gary marvelled at the sight of the dark brooding cliffs which looked as if they had been sheared off in ancient times by some great all-powerful giant. He put his arm around Ewan's shoulder and Gary felt a pulse of electricity race to his heart.

"My God, Ewan, what a magnificent view!"

"It is truly magical, Gary, I love it up here."

Duncan McNeilage interrupted the star-crossed lovers' sight-seeing.

"I can assure you that where you two are going, you'll certainly not love it! Right, the pair of you get stripped and into those plastic suits and masks and I'll open up."

Duncan's boots crunched over the frozen snow as he took out his key pass to open up the Observatory for Ewan and Gary. The two boys stripped down shivering in the freezing night air to their underpants and donned the coveralls and masks. Gary lifted all his computer equipment and the two of them followed Duncan over to the atrium of the Observatory. Duncan had already used the security key to open the door.

"In you go and don't ask me to follow you. You know where everything is Ewan better than your old uncle. I'll sit in the car and have a doss till you've finished."

Gary was first to catch the smell before they had even entered the front door.

"Oh, fuckin' hell, Duncan - that would give ya the boke!"

"Ah did tell you it was going to be bad. The sewage pipe outlet down the hill there to the septic tank is totally frozen – apparently, the bloody contractors put in the wrong type of piping. The staff toilets are totally blocked up to the gunnels and the place will need to be fumigated before they can open it up again for business…"

Ewan and Gary peered gingerly inside trying desperately to hold their breaths. Duncan gave them a gentle nudge in the back.

"Now don't be scared boys! In ye go – and mind, Ewan, not a minute more than two hours. My head's on the chopping block here and I was getting pelters from your Auntie Mary for allowing this."

Ewan and Gary entered CORSAIR looking like two aliens from outer space entering new and uncharted territory. The smell of rotten excrement was absolutely horrendous and the two boys almost immediately started gagging and retching and baulking up bile. Ewan was beginning to think that he had not been so lucky tonight after all. He choked towards Gary who was in two minds whether to turn back.

"I'll get the canopy doors open. The fresh air might help a bit, Gary."

Gary looked up at the huge and magnificent looking reflector telescope with bated breath for more than one good reason.

"How long is it gonna take to position the telescope and get ma computer hooked into the download, Ewan?"

"About twenty minutes…"

"Well, thank fuck for that, 'cos we're outta here in twenty minutes!"

"No, Gary, - oh, Christ, that smell – no, we need the full two hours for me to be able to do my computations."

"Yeah, well ah have a plan –"

Gary reached into his satchel with a grin on his face half-hidden by the clear mask. He pulled out a huge home-rigged piece of USB cable which must have been at least 50 metres long.

"Once you've set everything up, Ewan, we're outta here and we'll do the download sittin' in the fuckin' Land Rover."

"Gary, Einstein would have been proud of you!"

CHAPTER 10

The incessant clanking of steel cell doors kept Lex Kosloff awake. His head was spinning and his hands were trembling badly. Lex had not touched alcohol since last Wednesday, or was it Thursday, and his body was beginning to rebel. His mind was also reeling at the speed of descent with which his life had so spectacularly crashed in the last few days. Detective Magruder's words just kept thumping away in his brain over and over again.

"Alexander Kosloff. I am arresting you on suspicion of the murder in the first degree of your wife Marna Nilstrom Kosloff at or around 14.30 on Thursday February 6, 2081 in Fair Park, Dallas. You are not obliged to say anything, Mr Kosloff. You have the right to remain silent…"

Over and over again - Magruder kept on accusing him of – of murdering his beautiful wife Marna. Lex's brain was exploding and he screamed out from his cell in the 3rd Precinct in Houston.

"N-O-O-O-O!!"

Another prisoner trying to sleep shouted down the corridor.

"Will ya shut the fuck up?"

For the last few hours Lex had been lying on the hard bunk and he had been trying to go over events again and again. He tried to make some sense out of it all. Did he kill Marna? Could he kill her? It just did not make any sense to him at all. He loved Marna and he had wanted her back. So what could have possessed him to kill his wife? He had to admit all the circumstantial evidence that Magruder and Madsen had presented, both to Lex and his lawyer looked damning. His lawyer Leo Cagliari felt that until Lex could think clearer and had some straight answers, then Lex should keep his mouth shut.

"At this time Detectives Magruder and Madsen, my client is pleading the Fifth –"

Lex almost drifted off in his cell and then there was another steely clank. The other prisoner down the corridor lost his rag again.

"Oh, for Christ sake – what's a guy gotta do ta get some sleep in this shit-hole?"

Lex forced his thoughts back over the events and the evidence against him. He had agreed to let Magruder and Madsen have a look over his Robindale home. Lex felt that he had nothing to hide. He arrived home in a black and white driven by two uniformed Houston PD officers and the two detectives followed in an unmarked police car. Lex reminded himself again that he had nothing to hide. But when he opened his front door he was sorely embarrassed at the state of his living room. It had been trashed a hell of a lot worse than he remembered. Madsen was first to comment.

"Jeez, Kosloff, that's some mess there. Ya must have a real bad temper, Lex?"

Lex stuttered back.

"Ah-ah c-can't remember wh- what ha-happened here. It's j-just not like me –"

The Houston PD detectives made him sit on his black recliner while they had a look around his trashed home. It was not too long before the black detective Madsen pulled up the small sheet of paper from under the sofa. He read it quickly, showed it to Magruder, and then he questioned Lex.

"What's this, Lex?"

Kosloff looked at it slightly bewildered.

"It's a note Marna wrote me when she left to go to Dallas –"

Madsen read it again and then he glared at Lex.

"It's pretty damning stuff here, Kosloff? *Lex….you're killing me!* Does that mean what ah think it means?"

Lex was indignant at the detective's accusation as he watched Madsen bag the letter.

"That letter doesn't mean nothin', officer - Marna was angry at me and it's all just talk –"

Magruder interrupted Lex.

"Okay, Lex, you said you kept a gun – an old Walther handgun. Can you show us it?"

Lex took Magruder through to the bedroom, which was in an equally trashed-up state and he went over to his bedside locker. He rummaged about in the untidy drawer and became increasingly agitated.

"S-sorry officer – ah-ah can't seem to find it?"

Magruder called Madsen into the bedroom and Lex looked around to see the black detective holding up a second clear evidence bag. Magruder pointed to the bag.

"Mr Kosloff, does this Walther handgun look familiar? Ah may add that we have already checked the registration details."

Lex agreed that it was almost certainly his missing Walther. Magruder spoke slowly and clearly.

"Mr Kosloff, ah have to inform you that this gun was found in bushes in Fair Park, Dallas, no more than twenty yards away from the body of your brutally murdered wife. Tests show that she was shot three times with this handgun. Do you have anything to say about that?"

Lex was struck dumb. He slumped down on the bed. After the officers had concluded their initial search they advised Lex that they were taking him back to the station for further questioning and advised him to call his lawyer, Leo Cagliari. Cagliari had spoken with his client prior to facing Magruder and Madsen again.

"Look, Lex, at the present time, it sure doesn't look too good for you. The letter and the gun are pretty damning evidence. Apparently they're gonna show that your prints are on the gun too, but considerin' it's your gun we can argue that ain't no surprise. They're also gonna argue you don't have an alibi for the day and time of the murder and that you could easily have flown, or less likely, driven up to Dallas and then shot Marna."

"Yeah, Leo, but what about the black pro' that ah was with in Avondale on the Wednesday. We gotta find her, maybe she can vouch for me on the Thursday –"

"Well, do ya have a name?"

Lex looked blankly at Cagliari.

"Ah – ah can't remember, but ah must a paid her…"

Cagliari looked back at Lex pensively.

"Yeah, well that's the thing, Lex. The cops have examined your bank accounts and on the Wednesday you withdrew two hundred bucks cash from an ATM in Avondale…"

"That's great, Leo, that would be money for drinks and to pay for the black chick!"

Leo did not seem to be as optimistic as Lex.

"You see, Lex. On the Thursday morning the cops state that you further withdrew one thousand dollars cash from your account at an ATM in George Bush Airport. Enough to pay for a cheap return flight. They are still checking through flight records and CCTV at all Houston and Dallas – Fort Worth Airports to see if you show up. All in all Lex, it looks pretty bad for you and when we go in to that interview room, ah'm havin' you plead the Fifth meantime. That means ya keep your mouth shut!"

*

<u>Earthdate: 08.50 Monday February 10, 2081 GMT</u>

Mahmoud El Kharroubi walked into the buzzing Al Jazirah press office and hurried straight to his work station and powered up his desktop laptop. A head popped up over the top of the sound-proof baffle from the next work station. Mahmoud looked quizzically at fellow journalist Reema Ben Achara who was smiling down broadly at him.

"By the beard of Allah, Mahmoud - you certainly picked a fine weekend to go mountain-climbing in Skye. All hell has been let loose down here while you've been up in Scotland –"

Irritated by Reema's interruption Mahmoud replied sarcastically.

"Yes, Reema, they do have television in Scotland you know. I saw it all on TV. I would have come back to cover the terrible event but we were snowed in at the Ardvasar Hotel. It was so bad we could not even go out climbing. So, all in all, it was a wasted weekend and it looks like I may even have missed the biggest story of the decade!"

"You know, of course, Mahmoud that you are going to get blamed for it!"

Mahmoud stabbed a dark look at Reema – did she know something? He slapped his palm on his chest and stuttered.

"Me–e–e!"

"Well, not you personally, Mahmoud – I mean you, me, all the Muslims. You wait and see, we'll all get blamed for the bombing –"

"I know what you mean, Reema. A bomb goes off in Europe or in the USA and all of a sudden they are running around looking for Islamic extremists everywhere. No-one thinks of the IRA or ETA any more – just us Muslims. Look, I've a pile of emails that I haven't caught up on because I was away. Do you mind, Reema?"

The Group had only just arrived back in Manchester at around 6.45am that morning. Although Khan had reluctantly joined them at dinner the previous evening he was still dark and brooding with a seething anger kept just below the surface. Mahmoud could not placate his Kuwaiti friend and Khan just sat eating and watching them all with his black hawkish eyes. After dinner and while Threlfall and Oliç were tied up through in the much busier bar, Khan turned to Mahmoud and spoke with a low determined voice.

"I need to get out of this stinking hole, Mahmoud. I want to go back to Manchester. Now!"

It was still only nine o'clock on Sunday evening and they were booked in until Monday morning. Mahmoud needed to be diplomatic but he needed to keep the Group tightly knit and Khan kept on a short leash. Mahmoud tried to reach out to him.

"Khan, my brother, none of us is particularly enjoying it here. Are we – my brothers?"

Hassan and the Mohammads shook their heads to indicate they were all in agreement. Khan started to tug at the leash.

"Well, Mahmoud, let us get to hell out of here?"

"Khan, you know that the plan is for us to stay here until Monday and make ourselves conspicuous and unforgettable. If we leave tonight we make ourselves look suspicious and arouse the interest of the infidel security services. We leave in the morning as we planned, as you planned?"

Undeterred in his anger, Khan snarled back.

"Well, Mahmoud - I don't remember planning to get Aisha killed –"

Mahmoud saw the hooded cobra rising again in Khan and he knew that he needed to find some palatable compromise.

"Khan, this is not the time for us to fight about Aisha. Look, what if you settle the rooms and pay the bill with Threlfall tonight and you tell him that we need to start out before breakfast? We'll leave at three thirty and be back in Manchester in three hours. How does that sound?"

Khan hesitated for a moment and thought to himself. The time to fight about Aisha may come again one day soon, my friend Mahmoud. Khan grunted in grudging accord.

"If that is your best offer, Mahmoud, then for the Group's sake - I'll take it."

Khan settled the bill with Threlfall including the breakfasts that they would be doing without and then the five men all stayed in the bedrooms until they had to leave. Hassan agreed to swap with Khan for the double room 101 that he had enjoyed on his own and Hassan joined Mahmoud until half past three. They all travelled back in the dark in the Mercedes, taking the fastest air lanes straight down to Manchester. The plan was for the Group to split up six separate ways, including the Palestinian who had triggered the bomb, for two to three weeks and for them all to lie low until then. Mahmoud was glad that Khan would get a cooling off period and he hoped that he would come to recognise that Aisha's sacrifice was for the best. After they all split, Mahmoud picked up his own air-car in Manchester and flew the relatively short distance to Bradford, to the northern office of Al Jazirah, where he now sat looking through his emails. Plenty of email traffic to look at from the Middle East offices on the bombing, ahem, the mission, Mahmoud thought. He saw one email address he did not recognise and opened it out of interest, actually more out of lazy disinterest. Probably junk mail, he thought.

From: juliaorourke@stbarts.nhs.gov.uk

To: mahmoudelkharroubi@aljazirah.co.uk

Cc: St Barts Internal List

Date: 15.55 Feb 7, 2081

Subject: Recent presentation on super-storage of Human DNA

Dear attendee,

Many thanks for your recent attendance at the presentation given by Dr Marcie Venters on the techniques and applications for the super-storage of Human DNA at St Bart's Hospital on Wed. January 22, 2081. As St Bart's is always looking for ways to improve its communication techniques to its customers in the field of medicine and within the media, we would ask if you could reply to this email address with any relevant comments that you may wish to make regarding this presentation. Your opinions will help us to improve the presentation skills of our staff in the future. In addition, a memory stick containing Dr Venters' presentation went missing around the time of her presentation. If you come across it would you be so kind as to return it to my office. My tel. no. is 0207 999 5555 extn. 335.

Yours Sincerely,

Julia O'Rourke

Personal Assistant (Angela K Mortimer)

Mahmoud thought that it might be nice to vent his spleen at the woman he called the 'Todesengel' but he thought that he better not cause any friction in the current security climate. The Group needed to keep their heads down below the parapet. He still had loads of other emails to get through and he did not need this one. He was just about to press 'Delete' when it struck him. Memory stick! By Allah, I had forgotten all about that. He reached down into the bottom of his case and fumbled around. No, maybe it has gone? No wait – here it is. He pulled it out and glanced surreptitiously around the office. Everyone was either too busy to bother with him or away at their various editorial meetings. Mahmoud had fifteen minutes before his first morning meeting so he thought he would just have another quick browse at the Jew doctor's sickening presentation.

*

A couple of hours later that same morning Jill and Ruthie stood facing each other in the ladies' restroom on the 8th floor of the Times office. Buckley had been mightily pleased with Jill and the other Times staff who had worked hard to get a great story out about the tragic, historic and horrendous events at Windsor. But, Buckley demanded that the whole team needed to knuckle down because the Times was going to have to be filled with each day's developing events on this momentous story.

"Ruthie, you're covering everything that goes for a shit out of the Palace, right up to Thursday's State Funeral for Prince Edward. Can you handle it?"

Ruthie was elated. She was entering into the big leagues now. Ruthie exclaimed a bit too enthusiastically.

"Yes, Buck!"

Buckley turned to Jill and stabbed a finger at her.

"You're on the investigation side of the bomb plot. I want you to crawl all over Hollingsworth and every blue-arsed copper who has something to say about it. And I want you to turn over every stinking stone and unearth each and every snivelling snitch and grass that you know. I want the Times to be the first paper to print the name of the bastard organisation that carried out this atrocity. Okay, Jill?"

"What about the Schenkler thing?"

Buckley threw his notes down hard on his desk.

"Fuck the Schenkler thing! That's next week's news if it ever gets that far. This week we're only interested in Her Majesty and any fucking terrorists. Are we on board with that, Jill?"

"Absolutely, boss."

Ruthie gave another tissue to Jill from the cheap scented box on the restroom wash counter. Jill wept sorely just as another girl from the Finance department stepped in, but just as quickly stepped back out again when she saw the floods of tears.

"Oh, God, Ruthie – this pregnancy thing has got me so fucked up, ah cannae think straight!"

Ruthie gently touched the back of Jill's hand.

"How do you feel about it, Jill, are you happy?"

125

"Ah don't know what to think, Ruthie. Ah phoned ma mum in Glasgow last night. She's over the bloody moon about it. Always wanted to be a granny, she said. But ah don't know how ah feel."

Ruth probed Jill a bit further.

"Do you want this baby?"

"No – ah mean, yes, maybe – och, ah don't know, Ruthie. Khan has got me all messed up at the moment. First off ah tossed him out 'cos ah thought he was screwing around - then it looks like ah might have been wrong about that. And now here ah am carrying his baby – our baby…"

Jill hesitated and looked at Ruthie with liquid-filled bloodshot eyes but Ruthie saw something begin to sparkle in those reddened teary orbs. Ruthie smiled and indicated with her beckoning palms.

"A-a-and?"

Jill collapsed into Ruthie's arms.

"Of course ah bloody well want this baby. Oh, Ruthie ah'm just so happy and excited…"

Ruthie held Jill at arms length and the young girl spoke in a serious and matronly tone to her new Glaswegian friend.

"Well there is a lot to think about, Jill…"

"You're right, Ruthie. Buckley's gonna have us working up to the hilt this week on this Windsor story. So ah better start thinking about that and park the baby for the present…"

Ruthie scoffed with a huge smile on her face.

"Sod that Buckley - who's talking about him? You need to think about getting your *ultra* and your *amnio!*"

"Oh, yeah, ah forgot about them, Ruthie."

The 'amnio' was the legally obligatory amniocentesis procedure in which a small amount of the amniotic fluid surrounding the baby in the womb is removed to detect whether or not a foetus has inherited a chromosomal disorder, such as Downs syndrome. In 2066 the Liberal Democrat and Labour coalition government came under pressure to act on the rising numbers of genetic disorders and human infertility. They passed the highly controversial Abortion Amendment Act 2066, which was vehemently opposed by the Conservative opposition and Christian, Muslim and other Pro-Life groups. The Act made it law for all pregnant women in the UK to have an ultrasound scan at 12 weeks and again at 15 weeks. Women also required to give blood samples and take an amniocentesis test, also at the 15 week stage. Women would then have to receive a counselling session on the test results, although this was only to provide the women with choice and no woman was legally required to abort their foetus. However, Jill would certainly need to take the tests.

"The thing is this, Ruthie – ah would hardly trust ma doctor's centre to prescribe me an aspirin, never mind take an amnio from me!"

Ruthie thought for a moment and then had a brainwave.

"Tell ya what, Jill – this is right up my mom's street. She's a brill doc at Bart's – I'll ask her for a big favour."

Jill looked in the mirror and started tidying up her smudged mascara.

"That's great, Ruthie. Look we better get back to work before Buckley sends out a search party!"

The girl from the Finance department popped her head in gingerly to check if it was now safe for her to pee.

CHAPTER 11

Earthdate: 10:28 Thursday February 13, 2081 GMT

The butler in 10 Downing Street poured tea into the china cups for the two men, quietly and efficiently. They hardly noticed his presence. The butler backed out of the understated study and left Prime Minister John Ralston and US President Joshua Spengler Trueman to enjoy their morning tea and biscuits and to continue their meeting in private. Ralston spoke first.

"It's a damned rotten business this, Josh!"

The large imposing black ex-5 Star General US Army from Birmingham, Alabama was in total agreement with his British counterpart.

"Too fuckin' right it is, John! Taking down Prince Eddie is real bad. Ah really liked that young guy. Ma fear is that this is the start of a resurgence in global terrorism, the likes a' which we ain't seen in fifty years. An' ah ain't standin' for it on ma watch!"

"Nor on mine, Josh, but it appears to be here and right now. And the British police and Security Services have drawn a blank so far as to the perpetrators of this bloody atrocity."

Trueman empathised with the Prime Minister.

"It's the same ma side a' the Pond, John. CIA and Homeland Security ain't turned up diddly squat. But ma money's still on the LOIN. It just smells like Islamic extremism to me. That's why ah think that we fire a shot across Suleiman's bow!"

Ralston nodded his agreement.

"Shall we make the call then, Josh?"

Trueman nodded and Ralston patched through to his secretary to connect the secure line to Tehran. They sipped at their tea quietly in nervous anticipation. It was only a moment or two before the distinctive deep voice of the Iranian President and Secretary-General of the LOIN, Mullah Abdullah Suleiman came through clearly and confidently. Suleiman, a Cambridge graduate, spoke perfect English with the softest of accents.

"Good morning, Prime Minister Ralston."

"Good morning, President Suleiman. I also have President Josh Trueman here beside me this morning."

Trueman was never one for standing on ceremony.

"Yeah, Josh here Abdullah. How are y'all doing?"

"Mmmm, for an old man I am doing very well. Allah has blessed me in mind, in body and in spirit. And Prime Minister Ralston and yourself President Trueman? I trust that your God has smiled also on you both?"

Trueman looked over at Ralston who nodded for the US President to continue.

"Well, as you know, Abdullah, John and ah are due at Westminster Abbey at one o'clock for his, ah, His Royal Highness, Prince Edward's funeral –"

There was a slight pause before Suleiman replied.

"Yes, my friend, a dreadful business. I apologise to you Prime Minister Ralston that due to pressing commitments I am unable to attend His Highness's sad funeral this afternoon. I trust my Vice-President Mullah Ahmed Rahman has arrived to represent the great Islamic Republic of Iran?"

Ralston nodded again to Trueman, who continued to speak.

"Yep, Abdullah, John says that Vice-President Rahman is in London and we thank you for his presence. What ah would like ta run by you, Abdullah, is if your guys have heard anything at all about who might be behind this terrible atrocity at Windsor?"

Again Suleiman paused before replying.

"Josh, my friend, I hope that is not a veiled accusation against Iran or the LOIN?"

Trueman tapped his nose at Ralston then lied.

"Ah ain't accusing anybody of anything, Abdullah. As you well know there has existed a sort a' Pax Romana in the world for the last fifty odd years. And John and ah would like to, uh, try and keep it that way. Ah trust that you want that too, Abdullah?"

Mullah Abdullah Suleiman sounded mildly irritated.

"President Trueman, it is my belief that it was the foresight of the previous Islamic leaders – my predecessors - in walking out of the UN and creating the strength of Islam within the LOIN that actually contributed to this Pax Romana, as you call it. As you both well know, the beloved Qu'ran urges all of its followers to seek the path of peace…"

Trueman interrupted Suleiman.

"And Prime Minister Ralston and ah would commend that path is taken by all the followers of Allah, including yourself Abdullah. All ah would like to say, my friend, is that the governments of Great Britain and the United States will leave no stone unturned to find out who *is* behind this barbaric terrorism. And when we do…"

Ralston shook his head vigorously and held up his palm at Trueman in restraint. Suleiman interjected during the slight impasse becoming more irritated.

"…and what exactly will you do, President Trueman?"

John Ralston interjected instead.

"We will bring all the perpetrators to justice, President Suleiman. All that President Trueman and I seek is for the continuation of world peace to exist between all the nations in the UN and the LOIN. I trust that is your own aspiration?"

Suleiman's voice suddenly changed and he now sounded like a venomous viper ready to strike.

"Of course, Prime Minister Ralston - I will always follow the path of my great and beloved Allah in striving for the true peace and justice deserved of all his Islamic peoples. Now I must go and allow you both to prepare to *grieve* - for your dead Prince. Good day, gentlemen."

The line went dead and Ralston and Trueman looked at each other with pained expressions.

"Goddamit, John, that was a fuckin' veiled threat if ever ah heard one!"

"Yes, Josh, I believe that Suleiman may have been inferring that a holy *jihad* is in the offing. My impression was that he was not just telling us to grieve for the Prince today, but also to grieve for what is to come in the future!"

*

Earthdate: 11:48 Thursday February 13, 2081 GMT

As Gary sat glued to the small 3DTV in his flat, he thought that it really should have been a Black Friday. Instead it was a Thursday the 13th rather than a Friday the 13th. In twelve minutes time the State Funeral procession of His Royal Highness, Edward, Prince of Wales was about to begin and the cameras were already rolling. The sombre British commentator on the BBC advised the hundreds of millions of viewers sitting mesmerised that *'the eyes of the world are watching this terrible moment'*. Gary glanced over at Ewan, who was busily poring over notes and diagrams and CGI models on his computer screen. Gary thought, well not *all* the eyes of the world are watching.

"Jeez, Ewan, gonna give that a bloody rest for five minutes. Are you not gonna watch the funeral on TV?"

Ewan looked up momentarily, more at the TV than at Gary.

"Sorry, Gary, but I need to work on this. It's important and I want to have it ready to take down to Jill on Saturday afternoon."

Jill had phoned Ewan on the Monday after the death of Prince Edward and Aisha al-Gazari to say that her boss Bill Buckley had put his whole team onto the bombing and funeral reportage and that she would have to put the *Schenkler* story off at least until the Saturday. The plan was for Ewan and Gary to catch the Edinburgh train down to London on Saturday morning and then come over to Jill's flat in Kew in the afternoon. Ewan had told Jill that this idea suited him, because he needed to work on some more in-depth research on the comet. Gary had become increasingly fed up with Ewan's inordinate obsession with the blasted comet. Gary gave a loud harrumph to signal his disapproval and went back to watching the funeral on TV and growled at Ewan.

"Och, suit yerself, Ewan."

The BBC camera panned in on a Welch Guardsman, a soldier of Prince Edward's own regiment. The guardsman was dressed in his smart funereal black and grey uniform and he was wearing the traditional tall black Busby. He was standing to attention and holding the reins of Prince Edward's huge white Arabian charger *Churchill*. The horse looked nervy and restless as it waited to lead the awful procession from the gates of St James's Palace. Great plumes of frosty air shot out from its nostrils as it tugged on the reins. Behind the unmounted horse, there stood the four senior male princes of the Royal House of Windsor. They were trying desperately hard not to look frozen as they stood in the courtyard on the bitterly cold February morning: David, the Prince Regent, in his full blue-grey RAF Air Marshall-in-Chief's uniform, Georgie, the young Duke of York, and now the new heir to the throne, his younger brother William, Earl of Sussex, and the Queen's cousin the Duke of Kent, in his dark-blue naval uniform. Behind the four princes, stood four very patient and glistening black stallions, mounted with four Welch Guards. They were dressed in tight black and grey gun carriage drivers' uniforms.

An awful thought went through Gary's mind that they reminded him of the Four Horsemen of the Apocalypse, those harbingers of doom foretelling the end of the world. The four black horses were hitched and reined to the old World War I gun carriage which was mounted with the Prince of Wales's coffin, wrapped in the Union Jack, with his Colonel-in-Chief's cap for the Welch Guards lying atop the flag. Behind the gun carriage sat the bullet-proof electri-limousines, which would carry Queen Elizabeth III and the other royal and military dignitaries. The procession would be completed by a troop of immaculate red-jacketed Horse Guards also in Busbys followed by grey-coated bandsmen, then massed soldiers, sailors and airmen representing the Armed Services. Down at Westminster Big Ben solemnly boomed out twelve o'clock. Wispy ghostly freezing fog blew up off the River Thames and swirled up towards St James's Palace. The armed bands began to play the blood-chilling chords of Frederic Chopin's **Marche Funebre**. The BBC commentator lowered his voice to a respectful whisper.

"And now with head bowed the Prince's great white charger Churchill is slowly led out of the gates of St James's Palace. It will lead the funeral procession and the coffin of His Royal Highness, Prince Edward of Wales: down Pall Mall, past Trafalgar Square, along Whitehall and into Parliament Street. The funeral procession will then turn into Victoria Street where it will arrive at the Prince's final resting place at Westminster Abbey..."

Gary sat riveted to the TV broadcast. He was not really a Royalist supporter at heart, but it was one of those terrible moments in history that people felt compelled to watch. Those terrible moments when human beings can place themselves in time and space and would state, *"I remember where I was when President Kennedy was shot....when Princess Diana died."*

"That's the procession started, Ewan."

"I've got one eye on it, Gary. Now will you leave me alone please?"

Gary fell into a silent huff as he watched the long procession pace forward to Chopin's slow metre. He thought drearily to himself, God, I've spent half my life leaving you alone, Ewan. Gary remembered that other moment in his own history when he first met Ewan Sinclair, the lad from Lagavulin, Islay. Gary's upbringing had been much different to that of the red-haired son of a Wee Free Minister from the rural island community. Gary was born on 25 February 2056, over a month after Ewan, also in the Maternity Wing of the South Glasgow University Hospital. Gary was raised in the deprived housing estate of Castlemilk in the south east suburbs of the city. Gary had been brought up by his parents, Frank and Annie Mackintosh, to practise in the Roman Catholic faith, but Gary could never see the point of religion. He rejected the faith to the eternal dismay of his mother, who was a devout Catholic. Instead Gary grew up worshipping his own two gods -

the Computer and Money. He soon found out at an early age that he was adept at the altar of both his gods. He learned computing pretty quickly and started to get into the gaming circuit. A professional online gaming circuit had emerged about twenty years before he was born and huge amounts of money could be made. Of course, it was illegal for children under sixteen to enter the circuit but talented players could always find a way in. Gary, who was only nine when he started, created a clone, an avatar of his older self, on the circuit and started playing on the small stakes local online sessions. By the time he was eleven he had graduated to the big international gamers' leagues and although he had sometimes lost big stakes in the beginning, he soon found that he was competing with the Big Boys. The money started rolling in to his various online and offshore bank accounts. In his last year at primary school, Gary asked his father Frank, a moderately paid council worker, if he could sit the bursary examination for Glasgow High School as his teacher had recommended that he give it a try. The bursary only covered the first three years and fees were required from parents for the last three years. Frank looked at Gary reticently.

"Ye can sit it if ye want, son, but ye'll have tae go back tae St Margaret Mary's Secondary after the three years. Ah cannae afford to pay the fees once the bursary is up."

Gary looked earnestly back at his father Frank.

"Don't worry, dad, ah'll pay the fees myself."

Frank Mackintosh roared with laughter at Gary. However, when that time came, Gary stumped up the fees to the amazement of his parents. Annie told her son that it was a gift from God and that she would light a candle at Mass for him. Gary just laughed and said that it was a gift from gaming. In his first year at Glasgow High, Gary had been fascinated by the economics class and he showed a keen interest in the laws of supply and demand and stocks and shares. He became much less interested in pitting his wits against gamers hooked on winning money through playing soccer, sorcery and death and destruction games online. Gary found a whole new world of international stock markets, which were quite amenable to accepting Gary's avatar so long as he was putting up the money. He slid seamlessly from the gaming circuits and started investing heavily in stocks, shares, investments and commodities and the money kept rolling in. It was at the start of Gary's second year at Glasgow High and this new guy had marched right up to the empty desk beside Gary, as he sat alone in the maths class.

"Hi, I'm Ewan Sinclair – mind if I sit here?"

Gary did not mind at all, because he was a bit of a loner, the computer geek that most of the other boys just ignored. It was the start of a great new friendship and the two boys were like limpets at school, stuck to each other like glue, helping each other with their studies. Gary hated chemistry and physics and he relied on Ewan to help him with his homework. Ewan tapped into Gary's obvious adeptness at computer science. Together they made a great team and they became the closest of friends. However, for Gary, it was never close enough. Gary began to realise that he was gay. He loved Ewan the moment that he had sat beside him in class, he still did. Gary felt destined never to reveal his love for Ewan, because Ewan was as straight as they came. Gary discovered he was fairly popular with many of the girls at school, probably because they tapped into his sexuality. He presented no threat to the girls and he seemed to be able to tap into their femininity. Gary seemed to be Ewan's conduit to getting all the good-looking girls and Ewan made the most of it. It was actually Gary who had known Jill Geeson from school and again he would later be the one to introduce her to Ewan. Gary always thought that the pair were the real deal and he ended up being the shoulder to cry on when Jill eventually split from Ewan. Gary thought Ewan was probably still in love with her. Maybe even the **Schenkler** story had become so important to Ewan because he saw that it was a pathway back to Jill, now apparently single again following her split from Khan. For Gary the story was just about making more of his beloved Money and even then he knew that he did not really need it. God, if only Ewan knew his online portfolio had a balance of around 30 million Euro in stocks and shares. If Gary could not love Ewan then he could devote his life to his Money. How sad, he thought. Then, as Gary watched the sombre procession on TV, slow tears trickled involuntarily down his cheeks. Ewan just happened to look across from his work momentarily.

"Are you crying, Gary Mackintosh? I thought you didn't give a toss for royalty?"

"Why don't you fuck off, Ewan!"

*

At the Times office Jill and Ruthie were also watching the funeral procession. It had now reached the Cenotaph, which stood like a great white granite sentinel halfway along Whitehall. Jill had been trying unsuccessfully to contact Khan on the phone. She wanted to tell him that she was pregnant and she believed Khan that the £20 million property deal was genuine. Jill was going to ask Khan if he wanted to make another go of it and come back to Kew. She also knew Khan had a lot of contacts in the Arab and Muslim communities around Britain and he might be able to give her some sort of lead into information on the terrorists. If indeed the terrorists were of Middle Eastern or Islamic origin, which was a dangerous assumption to make at this point in time. Jill had found that even the police were struggling to get any sort of lead. The cops' insiders and Jill's 'snitches and grasses' had heard nothing on the underworld grapevine. Ruthie had even managed somehow miraculously to get in touch with Dinky Budge, wherever in the world he was, but even he had not heard a cheep. Although, Dinky Budge warned Ruthie not to try and find him again. He said that it was too dangerous for both of them. Ruthie was preparing to type up her main story on the Prince's funeral, while she simultaneously watched it proceed on video feed on the corner of her laptop. She began to type her first draft and an emotional lump welled up in her throat. Ruthie asked herself, why do we Americans get all mushy over royalty? The BBC commentator's voice came across the airwaves in deep hushed tones.

"Today, it is as if the world has stopped. Stopped to hold its collective breath and to shed a universal tear..."

*

Earthdate: 16:30 Thursday February 13, 2081 GMT

Two hours after the TV broadcast had ended Gary was sitting staring at Ewan in a state of awe and love. Ewan was aware that Gary was in awe of him, but he was oblivious to his love. However, Ewan was not in awe of himself at this moment in time. He was wracked with self-doubt about what he had actually achieved this afternoon while Gary had watched the sombre events unfold on TV.

"I don't know, Gary, what if all this is just a pile of mince?"

"But if you're right, Ewan, Jill gets the story to end all stories –"

Ewan shook his head dubiously.

"We can't take this thing to Jill now - just on my say so. We are going to need someone else to corroborate this. It's too big to be wrong, Gary!"

"Well, what about yer mates up at CORSAIR? Get it to them to have a wee look at it –"

"Jesus Christ, Gary, if they find out that we were up there without authority, they'll probably get us thrown in jail!"

Gary nodded in agreement.

"Aye, yer probably right."

The two of them sat silently mulling over the problem when Gary came up with a suggestion.

"Ah've got it! Why don't we get yer pal Schenkler to look at it? Ah mean to say, he's got the Nimrod telescope to play with that found the comet in the first place –"

"Gary, please tell me you're kidding. Schenkler would have the whole of NASA down on top of us before we could say boo to a goose!"

Gary gave a wry smile and a raise of his eyebrow.

"Not if Schenkler thought we *were* NASA –"

Ewan made to interrupt and Gary raised his palm to stop him.

"Naw, Ewan, you've done your bit, but this is where ah come in. We have access to Schenkler's email, right? On it we have his NASA contacts and in turn they have their NASA contacts and their NASA contacts, et cetera. Ah dig around in the E2MSN and find a NASA guy who Schenkler is unlikely to know. Now hear me out here! We send Ari an email from this guy saying that he has picked up the Nimrod footage and kicked it around a bit. The NASA guy says that he has researched it further and what we do is send your stuff attached to Ari's email. We then ask Schenkler to independently verify your results as a matter of urgency."

Ewan looked at Gary unconvincingly.

"But - what if Schenkler twigs what we're up to - and what about NASA? Won't they know what's going on?"

"Ewan! It's Gary boy yer talkin' to. Ah'll have this NASA guy's email cloned so well that if he ever saw it – which he won't – he'd swear on the Holy Bible that he had actually sent it to Ari Schenkler himself!"

"Gary Mackintosh, I could kiss you!"

Gary grimaced inside and he wished that Ewan would do just that.

*

Earthdate: 18:55 Thursday February 13, 2081 IST

Ari was in big trouble. His wife Ava had booked a table for eight o'clock at the Yoezer Wine Bar on his recommendation after he and his team had dined there on Goldenheim's expense account lunch. But here he was just before seven still tidying up in the office at INSACC. To be fair, it had actually been a very productive day. In the afternoon, Ari and his project team had gone through the final dry run of the 2082 Nimrod SH2 presentation in front of the Center Director and his boss Yosep Goldenheim and it had actually been received really well. In fact, it went much better than Ari had expected. The team's options for the 5% and 6% budget cuts held up well under intense scrutiny, considering the short timescales that Ari's team had been given. The Project Director and Goldenheim had only requested some minor adjustments and Ari and Jerzy had worked late to finish the final presentation. Jerzy, who had gone home just ten minutes ago, had been happy to stay on with Ari to get the job finished. Jerzy knew Ari was on the night-shift Friday night on Nimrod and it would have meant the two of them coming in over the weekend as the NASA team would be arriving on the following Monday. Ari had a weekend sea-fishing trip booked off the coast at Joppa and Jerzy had a family wedding to attend in Nazareth. It suited both men to work late tonight and get things finished. Well it did suit until Ari realized that he was starting to run late for his date with his wife. He scolded himself aloud in the empty office.

"Time I was out of here!"

Ari started packing his briefcase with his laptop and papers to work on Sunday night before his big presentation the following day. He made to shut down his desktop monitor when it *pinged!* An email had just arrived in his inbox marked *URGENT.* He could see it was from someone in NASA. Another glance at the marching clock made him speak aloud again.

"I'll look at you tomorrow night –"

Ari bent over to boot down his machine and something made him stop. What if it is some last minute request from NASA about Monday's meeting, he asked himself? What if I need to see Yosep about it tomorrow? He opened the email, which was from someone in NASA he did not know of and he quickly scanned through it.

From: Beth O'Donnell, NASA HQ – Classified
To: arischenkler@insacc.is
Date: 10:57 Feb 13, 2081 CST
Subject: Investigation of Nimrod SH2 scanning error

Ari's heart sank. Someone in NASA was just about to give him another roasting about the money wasted as a result of his error. He quickly looked at the wall clock but could not resist reading on.

Dear Ari,

I am responding to your email of Jan 21 2081 regarding your instruction to ignore the 2' 11" of incorrect footage taken by Nimrod SH2 telescope that same evening. As a matter of routine this was passed to my office and in researching the Nimrod film, I have discovered that it actually contains material of important interest. I have conducted further more extensive research on this data and I would like to have your valued opinion on it. I need your results ASAP, no later than Saturday morning Houston time. Please find attached files containing your original footage, a further 110 minutes of footage gathered subsequently, a CGI model and my research notes, calculations and conclusions. I look forward to hearing from you on Saturday.

Beth O'Donnell, NASA.

Ari could not believe it. The two minutes and eleven seconds from Nimrod had actually turned out to be of value after all. Wait until Yosep Goldenheim hears about this. Ari's cell phone rang shrilly in the empty room making him jump out of his skin. It was his irate wife Ava.

"Ari Schenkler! Where in God's name are you? You should have been home already!"

Ari slapped his forehead. Ari you dumb schmuck!

"Ava, darling – Jerzy and I had to work late to finish the big presentation for Monday…"

Ava showed a blatant disregard for the big presentation.

"Are we going to Yoezer's tonight or not, Ari?"

Ari had to think quickly.

"Look, Ava, tell you what. You jump in the electri-car and drive up to Yoezer's. You'll find it at Ish-Habira Street, near the old Clock's Square in Jaffa. I have a clean top in my locker here. I'll do a quick wash and brush-up and then grab a cab and meet you there. I'll phone the wine bar and tell them that we will be five or ten minutes late. How does that sound?"

Ari could tell that it did not sound too great at all to Mrs Ava Schenkler.

"Oh, you bloody scientists – full of logic, but no common sense. You better be there, Ari, or else…!"

Ava cut him off. Ari thought to himself that he better leave the email until tomorrow night's shift back at INSACC and that he had also better get cracking down to Yoezer's.

CHAPTER 12

The six men sat around the small table. Five of them looked perplexed because they were not actually meant to be there. Not for at least another two weeks. They were at a safe house in Leicester but most of them did not feel that safe. Khan al Ahmed who spoke first certainly did not.

"Why in Allah's name have you called us together so soon, Mahmoud? Even Jill has been trying to reach me and I have been avoiding her calls."

Hassan was in general agreement with Khan.

"Khan is right, Mahmoud. The police and Security Services are crawling all over the place at present. It is dangerous for us to be together like this –"

The Mohammad brothers also mumbled their dubious agreement. Mahmoud tried to placate the agitated Group.

"Brothers! Brothers! Please stay calm. Brother Suleiman has spoken with me and the infidel leaders have talked with him and he is sure that they are still fishing around in the dark."

Khan was still unsatisfied.

"Even more reason to stay apart until the heat cools down. This is the second time you have changed our plans without consulting the Group – first Aisha, now this!"

Mahmoud remained calm.

"As your leader, Khan, sometimes I need to make the difficult decisions. The reason that I have called you all together today is that something new and very important has come to light."

The Palestinian, the one in the Group who was nameless and had remained quietly sinister in the background, spoke with his usual low hiss.

"I pray to Allah it is a new mission, brother Mahmoud. Let us strike at the infidel cur while he still lies on the ground bleeding!"

Mahmoud nodded to the Palestinian in agreement and he related to the Group about his luck in coming across all of Dr Marcie Venters' plans for the development of the DNA superstores at the various sites within existing

Western medical facilities. He had discussed his ideas with President Suleiman and the esteemed Mullah was in full agreement with them. Mahmoud's plan would be for three of the Group to be chosen as martyrs to Islam and to carry out suicide bombings on the relatively 'soft' targets identified: St Bartholemew's in London, Harvard Medical Center in Boston and the Toronto University Hospital in Canada. The bombings on the three targets would be carried out simultaneously in early to mid-March. When Mahmoud had finished his presentation, apart from the Palestinian who was grinning horribly, the others sat stunned and pale. Khan was first to express his doubts.

"In the name of Allah, what kind of a devilish plan is this, Mahmoud? We all agreed that one day we would be martyrs for our great Allah, but since when did we begin attacking hospitals?"

Mahmoud could see that the Mohammads and Hassan also looked gravely doubtful, but he remained calm and rational.

"Fertility is becoming one of the great battlegrounds of the late 21st century, Khan. The inability of many of the human races to successfully procreate nowadays has led the West to develop these unethical ideas. If we strike at the heart of the infidels' barbaric and inhumane plans for these DNA superstores - devised by that accursed Jew doctor - then we are following Allah's will."

The Palestinian leaned across the table towards Khan and hissed.

"Well, I for one am in. You can strap a bomb to me right now. Allahu akbar!"

Mahmoud then lifted his hand which was clutching some small items. They all then saw he was holding straws.

"I commend your bravery in Allah's name, my Palestinian brother, but we do this fair and square. I have here three long straws and three short ones. We each pick one – agreed?"

There was a kind of mumbled and dubious assent from the Group. Mahmoud passed his hand around each one. The Mohammad brothers both chose long straws to their relief. The Palestinian chose a short straw to his own delight.

"Allah be praised – give me St Bart's and I will take the Jew doctor to the hereafter with me, Mahmoud!"

Hassan also chose a short straw and he went even paler than before. Mahmoud held out his hand to Khan and they looked each other bitterly in the eye.

"It is you or me, Khan –"

"What if I don't want to choose to die a martyr for this accursed plan, Mahmoud?"

It was the Palestinian who answered.

"Then you had better watch your back, Khan al Ahmed! Better to die a martyr to Allah than to die a traitor to the cause of Islam."

Khan flashed a look of hatred at the Palestinian and then he reached his hand across to Mahmoud. Khan drew the short straw.

*

Jill was fuming. She had been trying to reach Buckley all morning but he had not been around. His News Editor had taken the editorial meeting and he said he did not know where Buckley was. The second-in-command said Buckley would be back later in the morning. Jill had just written the exclusive of the century for Buckley and her 'bucking' Senior Investigative Editor had gone and pulled it from publication. She could not believe it when she checked the Times 'Bloid' this morning. It was not there. She scrambled around on the Leaks websites and *nada* – nothing!

Jill flicked her thoughts back to the weekend, which had turned out to be very eventful. Apart from the fact that she could not get a hold of Khan. Period. His phone was off and he would not return her voicemails. Jill began to suspect that maybe he was screwing around after all. Although, she had to admit to herself that it was her idea to have the cooling off period. But she had been desperate to tell Khan he was going to be a father. Maybe she should leave things for a few more days and then try Khan again. Jill then patted the small bump on her abdomen.

"Ah'm sure that your daddy will be delighted to hear that you're on the way –"

The Saturday afternoon had been like a blur. Ewan and Gary had arrived at the door of her 7th floor flat at Kew about three, after taking the express train down from Edinburgh. She had asked how the journey had been and Ewan answered first.

"The Royal Scot was bang on time –"

Gary interjected.

"Ah beg to differ, Ewan, but I think you will find it is called the Royal Scotsman!"

As the two boys looked quizzically at each other Jill intervened.

"Well, guys, whether it is the Royal Scot or the Royal Scotsman, it seems to run a lot better than the trains do down here in London. Now come on in out of the cold –"

Gary put a finger to his lips and held up his laptop, which had a CGI cartoon of a bloodhound sniffing around the screen. Jill thought, Gary's got his bloody Bloodhound programme running again! Gary indicated for Jill and Ewan to stay at the front door and he went into the flat holding up the detector equipment attached by USB to his laptop. He came back in about three minutes and signalled for them to step out into the ice-cold landing. Jill only had a short-sleeved top on and she shivered out on the landing.

"Jesus, Gary, ah'm freezin' my nuts off out here!"

Gary smiled back.

"Ah'm afraid to tell ye, Jill, but you don't have any nuts! Anyway, Bloodhound has detected a bugging device in your flat…"

Jill was flabbergasted.

"What! Someone's bugging us?"

Ewan was horrified.

"Oh, my God - we've been sussed out, Gary?!"

Gary was circumspect in his reply.

"Calm down, Ewan. They're no onto us yet. Firstly, NASA is unlikely to know that we would come here, are they? And secondly, it is a fairly cheapish bug. You could pick it up in any High Street electrical store. NASA would be much more sophisticated. No, ah'm sorry to say Jill, but someone's bugging *you*!"

"Me-e-e!"

Jill scratched her brain trying to think who would want to bug her. It could be any one of a dozen lowlifes that she had investigated recently. It could be Nesto Petrianni. His case was still to come before the courts and he would be desperate for any information on the whereabouts of Dinky Budge. Then a horrible thought struck Jill. Would Khan try to bug me? But, why would Khan want to do that? She tried to put that thought way out of her mind. Gary had suggested that they go to a local pub and Jill went and grabbed a coat and her bag. They went to the nearby Botanist on the Green. It was busy and noisy and it was showing a live football match, Arsenal versus Manchester United. As they sat down with their drinks around a small table in the corner, Jill looked at Gary just as Manchester United scored the first goal to load groans and muted cheers from the punters.

"Well, ah take it Bloodhound comes first?"

Gary looked back at the noisy crowd watching TV.

"Don't need to, Jill, it's too noisy in here for a successful buggin'."

As they sipped their cold beers, Ewan related his findings to Jill. He began with the original email from Ari Schenkler, the 2' 11" of Nimrod's footage which identified *Schenkler's Comet,* the boys' trip to Islay and the visit to the putrid smelling CORSAIR on the Mull of Oa, right up to his latest findings and conclusions. Apart from having a good laugh at trying to imagine them in their plastic coveralls in the foul-smelling observatory, Jill for the most part sat open-mouthed at Ewan's story. Jill thought that it was too fantastic to believe.

"…And are you positive that this Schenkler guy corroborated all your findings, Ewan?"

"Absolutely, Jill – I wish he hadn't!"

Gary butted in to the conversation.

"Ari worked on it all last night. He emailed his, ahem, NASA colleague this morning before we left Edinburgh."

Gary pointed his elbow at Ewan, Ari's 'NASA colleague'. The three of them discussed how they were best going to handle it. Gary agreed to get all the data passed to the Leaks websites on the Sunday. Jill would prime up Buckley and work on her article to hit the home page of the Times as a world exclusive on the Monday morning, citing the Leaks sites as the main source of their information. Gary warned Jill to be careful.

"Remember, Jill – don't contact Buckley or anyone else from your flat because of the bug."

"Oh, God – ah'd forgotten about that. Can you no get rid of it?"

Gary thought pensively.

"Well, ah'm pretty sure it's no NASA. But just in case it is them playin' cute, ah'd leave it there until after the story breaks. We don't want to alert anyone just now, do we?"

The football match had just finished. Manchester United had held on for a slim 1-0 victory over the Arsenal. The three of them finished their drinks and Ewan and Gary packed up to head back to Kings Cross for the six o'clock train back to Edinburgh. As the two boys were walking away from Jill at Kew Station she shouted after them.

"Oh, guys, ah nearly forgot. Ah think ah can guarantee you a bumper payday for your story."

Ewan looked back and shouted as they walked away.

"Oh, yeah - and what are we going to need the money for?"

Jill looked slightly perplexed at Ewan and Gary disappearing down the underpass at Kew Station – and then Ewan's words dawned on her. Ewan's words still haunted Jill as she sat at her desk.

"…Penny for your thoughts?"

Jill looked around and saw Ruthie standing smiling just outside her workstation. Ruthie looked her usual upbeat self.

"I've spoken with my mom and she has agreed to do your amnio at 15 weeks, Jill."

Jill thought about her baby and a horrible shudder ran through her body. Oh, my poor baby! Imagine bringing a child into such a terrible world.

"Tha-at's great, Ruthie."

"Are you okay, Jill, you look a bit pale?"

"Just morning sickness, ah guess. Actually, ah'm looking for that buckin' gaffer of ours."

Ruthie pointed towards Buckley's office.

"I think he just got back five minutes ago…"

Jill dashed past the stunned Ruthie who thought that maybe she was off to the restroom to be sick. Jill knocked but then crashed straight into William J Buckley's office. He was talking to his News Editor.

"Mr Buckley – ah need a word!"

Buckley nodded for his News Editor to leave the room and indicated for Jill to sit down.

"Jill –"

"Look, Buck, what the fuck is going on here. Ah have just written the story of the fuckin' century and ah then find that you authorised a pull on it. What the hell…!"

"JILL! Shut the fuck up!"

They both sat glaring at each other momentarily and then Buckley spoke back in calming tones to his seething journalist.

"Look, Jill, I have just come back from 10 Downing Street. I have been with the Prime Minister at meetings all morning. Jill, this is fucking huge. Monumental! Ralston has asked us to sit on this until they can assess the situation. You know – release it in a controlled manner. He says that you will still get first exclusive on this thing –"

"…but what about the Leak websites, Buck?"

"Ralston has asked them to sit on it too, but that they will also get their right to publish in time. They all agreed."

Jill looked aghast at Buckley. Instinctively, she put protective hands on her unborn child.

"Oh, God, Buck…!"

"What is it Jill?"

"Ewan's story – it's completely true, isn't it?"

*

The front door of their neat little house on the outskirts of Tel Aviv opened and an unusually chill afternoon wind swept in. Ari walked in looking deeply worried and Ava, his raven-haired Sabra wife immediately looked concerned.

"Ari, what are you doing home so early from work? Was the presentation that bad?"

Ari shut the door and strode across the room to Ava.

"Hold me, Ava, hold me and never let me go!"

The two of them stood hugging and crying. Ava did not even know why she was crying.

"Ava, I don't know why I'm asking this, but I feel it is just important at this particular moment in time –"

"What, Ari?"

"Let's make a baby – right now!"

"But, Ari, I thought that we were going to hold off –"

"No holding off, Ava, now is the time!"

They had made love gently and passionately. Before Ava fell asleep she did remind Ari that she was still on the pill and that this copulation would not result in a baby. She promised Ari that she would come off the pill. Ava had always dreamed of them having a child. Ari could not sleep as they lay on the bed together in the early evening. He could not get this afternoon's meeting out of his head. He had spent all Friday night working on the data that Beth O'Donnell from NASA had sent him. He had actually wondered who Beth O'Donnell was. Ari could not think of ever having met her. After going over the information at least three times he could only draw the same conclusions as O'Donnell. He emailed O'Donnell as agreed early on the Saturday morning. When he had not received a reply by the Monday morning he had made up his mind what he intended to do. At two o'clock on Monday afternoon they all filed through a glass door into the small windowless room, after having finishing their coffees in the INSACC Center Director's office. The five men from NASA's Nimrod team, the Center Director, Yosep Goldenheim, Ari, Jerzy, Rebecca and Noam: they all sat around the table in the room except for Ari who stood by the computerised whiteboard in order to conduct the presentation. The Center Director nodded for Yosep to begin.

"Gentlemen, we have all done our introductions over coffee. Anyway, we are all reasonably well acquainted with each other. As you know - today's presentation - to be conducted by Ari Schenkler - will cover the proposed 2082 Operational and Financial Plan for the Nimrod Space Hunter 2 project. It will concentrate in detail on the options to make significant and effective savings in next year's project. So without further adieu I will hand the presentation over to Ari. Okay, Ari?"

Ari looked around at the men sitting expectantly in the room and he felt his throat constrict. He picked up the glass of water sitting beside the laptop, which had the presentation loaded and ready to roll. He sipped the water to ease his tight nervous throat and then he began, pointing limply at the whiteboard.

"Gentlemen, as you can see the, ah, idea had been to give you the, ah, 2082 project plan presentation today. However, ah…"

He looked at Goldenheim who was looking bewildered at Ari's stumbling start and Yosep had rolled his hand to indicate to Ari to crank up the presentation. Ari had to go for it.

"However, ah, I actually intend to wind things forward a further two years to 2084. In fact, the 28th of May 2084…"

Goldenheim angrily interrupted and looked apologetically at the NASA team.

"Gentlemen, I think that Ari's had a little too much coffee this morning as his presentation has strayed off base –"

The NASA Project Director, Aaron Eckler, held up his hand to stop Goldenheim.

"Yosep, I am prepared to give Ari a little bit of leeway here. Let him continue."

At the same time, Eckler also waved his hand at the glass door and a young woman entered the room and sat down behind Eckler. Goldenheim was now completely lost and bewildered.

"Will someone tell me what the fuck is going on here? Who in hell is this?"

Eckler looked back at his female colleague.

"That is not important for the moment, Yosep. What is important is what Ari wants to say. Please continue Ari?"

Ari gulped in a bucketful of air and blew it out loudly before continuing.

"I need to start with the errant two minutes and eleven seconds of Nimrod footage taken on the 21st of January this year…"

Goldenheim completely lost the plot.

"Oh, for God's sake – is this what this is all about? Some sort of grovelling apology? Ari, we've been through all of this before!"

Eckler was just as angry but with more control in his voice.

"GOLDENHEIM - shut up and just listen, will you!"

Ari was waved on to continue by Eckler.

"…It turns out that the footage contained some of the most important photographs ever taken by mankind. The footage was sent back to me by someone at NASA for my investigation, in conjunction with more detailed footage shot by NASA, a computer generated CGI model and NASA's calculations, report and conclusions. I have examined all the data available and I have come to the same extraordinary conclusions as NASA…"

Eckler looked back quizzically at the woman behind him and she shook her head in the negative. Eckler looked back at Ari.

"Please continue, Ari."

"The footage identifies a brand new comet which has entered the solar system in the same quadrant as Pluto. My guess is that it is debris from an exploded planet or moon from out of the star system Andromeda. I have named this new comet Har Meggido –"

Goldenheim could not help himself from interrupting.

"Har Meggido - the Hill of Meggido? Why?"

Eckler spoke first.

"We've been calling it Messiah 2, Ari!"

Goldenheim's head was spinning.

"MEGIDDO! MESSIAH! Will someone please explain what the hell is going on?"

Ari now spoke with slow control and confidence.

"Well, Yosep, you and I as Jews are not so familiar with the Christian's New Testament, but it is written in their book of Revelations: ***Then they gathered the kings together to the place that in Hebrew is called Armageddon!*** Har Megiddo, as you and I know Yosep, is the Jewish origin of the word Armageddon. I am also guessing, Mr Eckler, that Messiah 2 is a feeble joke for the Second Coming?"

Eckler nodded with a gruesome grin on his face. Ari looked at all the pale faces before him. They are all hoping that I don't say this, he thought, but Pandora was now out of the box.

"On the 28th of May 2084 the Har Meggido, ah, Messiah 2 comet, which is around one and half times the size of Pluto, will make contact with planet Earth in a catastrophic collision."

The room fell into a deathly silence. The astrophysicists all sat quietly trying to calculate the fatal consequences in their heads. Eckler broke the silence with a more mundane down to Earth question than Ari had been expecting.

"Ari, we concur with your findings. We have been working on it for a couple of weeks now. But the NASA data – which colleague did you say you got it from?"

"I don't actually know her as a colleague. On the email she was named Beth O'Donnell."

The woman at the back of the room spoke up.

"I am Beth O'Donnell, Ari. It was not me who sent that data to you…"

Goldenheim was struggling to keep up with events.

"Wha-at does all this mean?"

Eckler spoke in a low sinister growl.

"It means that an impostor is circulating this data in the world-wide community!"

Ava broke gently into Ari's thoughts. She had woken up beside him and she snaked sensuously against his naked body. Ava smiled at Ari and fluttered her teasing eyelashes.

"Do you want to eat now, Ari, or do you want to try again for that baby?"

CHAPTER 13

<u>Earthdate: 20:33 Monday February 17, 2081 CST</u>

Lex felt that his life was in a perpetual state of limbo. First off, the cops had not placed a formal charge on him for the murder of his wife Marna. His lawyer Leo Cagliari had brilliantly and successfully pleaded his case. Although the police had the damning letter written by Marna and they had also found Lex's handgun at the scene of the crime, plus the cash withdrawals from the ATMs, they had not been able to place Lex at the scene of the crime in Dallas. The police had not been able to produce any CCTV evidence showing Lex either leaving Houston or arriving in Dallas. His electri-car onboard computer had shown no significant mileage on the Wednesday or Thursday, the day of Marna's murder. The police had not found any record of Lex hiring a vehicle or booking a flight. Furthermore, Lex had reported to Magruder and Madsen that his bank cards were missing or stolen and the police had traced a couple of transactions in Houston, which took place during the times that Lex was being interviewed down at the 3rd Precinct. Lex was going on the supposition that the black hooker must have taken his cards. However, Cagliari reiterated to Lex that he was still the lead suspect in the homicide case and that they desperately needed to find that prostitute. Cagliari had arranged for a private detective, in conjunction with the Houston PD, to try to find the girl. Lex had agreed with his lawyer and the police to leave his credit cards live in order that they could help track down their new *'owner'*. Lex reckoned that by the time Cutie or Cupie, or whatever she was called, had finished, he would be into a serious overdraft, although he had managed to shift all his real deposits into a non-carded secure savings account. On the basis that the police could not place Kosloff in Dallas or anywhere near it, Cagliari successfully managed to get Lex out on 1 million dollar bail and posted his bail bond. Lex's second problem was his drinking. With the foul murder of his wife, Lex realised that alcohol had indeed become a real issue in his life. One which he now had to deal with. Walking into the meeting hall the other night was just as hard as facing up to the fact that he was never going to see Marna again. He could not remember the last time that he had been as nervous as when he uttered those eight little words.

"Ma name is Lex. Ah am an alcoholic…"

It had been traumatic for Lex. He had a murder rap hanging over him and he had been barred from attending Marna's funeral. Lex desperately wanted a drink. But he had not touched a drop since waking up that Friday morning after the bender in Avondale. His third problem was his job at Houston Control. Lex had phoned to advise Irene DuPré about the ongoing joint police investigation by the Houston and Dallas PDs. The police had already been in touch with her for background reports on Lex. He admitted his other problem to Irene.

"Irene, ah guess ya know ah've got a pretty bad drink problem?"

His boss sounded pretty sympathetic on the telephone.

"Ah had ma concerns, Lex. Ah was gonna discuss it with you –"

"Well, ah've joined AA, Irene. Ah am dealing with it now."

Irene advised him gently that she had no option but to suspend him from work, albeit on full pay, because he was still the subject of the police investigation and a recovering alcoholic. His job at Houston Control required his full attention because of the detailed and complex safety aspects of his role. Irene told him that the cloud of suspicion did not allow Lex to give his job that full attention. She also advised him to use the time off wisely and get on top of his alcoholism. Irene finished the call almost pleadingly.

"Lex! Ah just hope you didn't kill Marna? She was such a great gal."

As Lex sat in the lounge of his now tidied up Robindale Drive house that evening he was hoping over and over again that he had not shot his wife Marna in that park in Dallas. He tried to convince himself that he just did not have it in him to do such a terrible thing. He had wanted Marna back. He did not want her dead. Suddenly, Lex was startled as his doorbell rang shrilly. Lex looked at the wall clock. A quarter to nine. It must be Magruder and Madsen again at this time of night. Maybe they are going to charge me this time, thought Kosloff. Lex opened his front door and it took him a moment to recognise the man that was standing there.

"Lennart?"

It was Marna's uncle. Lennart Nilstrom was the brother of Marna's father Lars. He stood there in the cool evening in a black overcoat, black leather gloves and carrying a small overnight bag. Lennart spoke quite brusquely.

"Well, Lex, ain't ya gonna let me in. Ah'm freezin' ma nuts off out here!"

Lex stood back in surprise and Lennart brushed past him and settled himself into the lounge area. As Lennart took off his overcoat and laid down his bag Lex quizzed him.

"Lennart, what are ya doin' here – ah wasn't expectin' you?"

Lennart sat on Lex's favourite recliner and swivelled around to face him. Lennart appeared calm and relaxed. Lex tried to assess if Lennart was masking his anger towards him over Marna's death.

"My brother Lars asked me to fly down and pick up some of Marna's things, Lex. I believe that there are some jewellery pieces which Marna's mother – Freda - had given her. Freda would like them back. Lars has also asked me to get a copy of Marna's Will –"

Lex stared at Lennart with a perplexed look on his face.

"Why didn't Lars try to call me about this, Lennart?"

Lennart shook his head slowly, but still calmly.

"Look, Lex, Lars is real sore with ya at the moment. He can't rightly talk to ya. We know ya ain't been charged by the cops so far – and, hey, Lex, maybe ya didn't do it. Ah ain't sayin' that ya did. But the way Lars and Freda are lookin' at it, if Marna hadn't left ya and come up ta Dallas, then she would still be alive."

Lex was irritated by Lennart's response.

"So, basically, the way Lars and Freda are lookin' at it, ah'm damned if ah did do it and ah'm also damned if ah didn't!"

Lennart shrugged his shoulders.

"Looks that way, Lex, you'll have ta give them some space – give them a bit a time. Ah do hate ta ask ya – but did ya do it, Lex, ya know - kill Marna?"

Lex bowed his head and shook it slowly.

"To tell ya the truth, Lennart, ah don't rightly know – but ah feel in ma heart that ah just couldn't kill Marna. God, Lennart, ah loved Marna – ah still do. It damn near broke ma heart that ah couldn't be at her funeral."

Lennart stood up and faced Lex.

"Ah don't think it right that ah stay here tonight, Lex. Ah've booked into the Robindale Ramada for the night. So if you're happy to give me the jewellery and a copy of the Will for Lars and Freda, ah can get out a' your hair – or if ya wanna think about it ah could come back in the mornin'?"

"No – no problem, Lennart. Ah'm happy for Freda to get back her jewellery. Ah can also give them a copy of the Will. Ah know it probably don't look good. Ah believe ah am the main beneficiary, although ah think she has left some money to her parents and her sister Ida. The stuff's in the bedroom. If you stick that copier on by my computer, ah'll go an' get it."

Before Lex turned to head for the bedroom he just watched to make sure that Lennart knew how to put on the printer / copier. He could see that Lennart knew what he was doing and he walked towards the bedroom. Absentmindedly, it struck Kosloff that Lennart had not taken off his gloves. In the bedroom he began taking out the various pieces of jewellery to give to Lennart, which had belonged to Marna's mother and grandmother from his wife's jewel box on the antique dresser. He also found Marna's Will in the top drawer of the dresser lying beside his own Will. Lennart had popped his head in the open door.

"That's the copier ready, Lex – have ya got everythin'?"

Lex looked at the open jewel box double-checking for anything that he had missed.

"Ah think so, Lennart."

"Freda specially asked for that antique Victorian diamond necklace, which was a favourite family piece. Have ya got that, Lex?"

Lex scratched his head.

"Jeez, ah forgot that – where the hell did we keep that?"

Lennart still with his head stuck in around the door pointed to the other side of the king-sized bed.

"Try the top drawer of your bedside locker, Lex."

"Oh, yeah, that's right Lennart – wait an' ah'll just get it –"

Lex started walking towards the locker and his mind started swirling. He was troubled about what Lennart just said. Lex frowned and as he spoke he started swivelling his head towards Marna's uncle.

"Lennart, how could ya possibly know that -?"

Lex stared at Lennart, now standing inside the bedroom. Lennart had his gloved right hand raised and he was holding a small modern steel automatic handgun. Paradoxically, Lex was thinking more about his old Walther, which he had kept in that same drawer beside the diamond necklace. A slow dawning was beginning to creep into Lex's mind. He quickly glanced sideways towards the drawer and a dawning came over him.

"Jesus Christ, Lennart, it was you! You killed Marna – but why?"

Lennart waved the gun threateningly at Lex indicating for him to come back into the lounge area. Lex sat down stunned as Lennart continued, still talking quite calmly.

"It's a long sad story, Lex, which we probably don't have time for. You see ah thought that ah had done everythin' right, so that the cops would have ya in the frame for killin' Marna. The note ya left under the sofa there was a gift. Your gun too – ya see Marna had blindly threatened ta kill me. Ah don't really think she meant it but she inadvertently let it slip where your Walther was kept. Ah got in here ta get it – by the way, your security is shit, Lex – and that's when ah seen the family necklace. The black hooker in Avondale – that was possibly not my best idea –"

Lex stuttered manically, trying desperately to keep up with what he was hearing.

"The h-h-hooker – that was y-you -?"

"Ah'm afraid so, Lex. Ah paid her two thousand bucks to get ya so drunk an' drugged so that ya wouldn't remember where, when or what ya had been up ta. But ah'm guessin' she got greedy and took your bank cards – ah'm ah right?"

"The cops think so – they're still investigatin' that, Lennart. Was her name C-Cupie or somethin'…?"

Lennart shook his head, still holding his gun at Lex, but no longer just as calm as before.

"Cupola Dome – what kinda **dumb** name is that! And as for the cops – well if they keep lookin' for that thievin' bitch then she could lead them back to me – and we don't want that, Lex, do we?"

"But if ya k-kill me, Lennart, then it could still lead back ta you."

"Oh, ah ain't gonna kill you, Lex. You are gonna do that yourself – well sorta. Read that -!"

Lennart had pulled out a sheet of paper and handed it to the stunned Kosloff.

"READ IT!"

Lex read the typed words on the sheet.

Dear Marna,

Reading your Will and thinking about all your money for which I killed you has brought all that terrible day in Fair Park back to me. I find that I just cannot go on living with the crushing guilt. I ask Lars and Freda to forgive me for taking you away and I have decided that I want to be beside you my love.

Lex looked up with moistened eyes at Lennart, who waved the gun at the sheet.

"Ah want you ta sign that confession, Lex. Don't worry about havin' ta shoot yourself – ah can manage that for ya. So sign the damn note an' throw it on the floor with the Will and the jewels, Lex, an' ah'll be outta here an' get back down ta Dallas."

A steely resolve welled up inside Lex.

"Ah ain't gonna sign that thing – you murdered ma lovely wife you bastard an' ain't gonna take the fall for it!"

Lennart was now becoming agitated and angry, pointing and stabbing the gun at the seated Kosloff.

"LEX – you sign that fuckin' suicide note or God help me ah'll blow your fuckin' head clean off!"

Lex tossed the unsigned note, the Will and the jewels onto the floor.

"Kill me if ya like you bastard. Ah don't give a shit – ah've been a dead man walkin' for weeks now anyway. Ya might even be doin' me a favour!"

Just as Lex finished speaking the large frightening wail of a siren startled both men. A distorted voice emanated from a megaphone.

"HOUSTON POLICE – EVERYONE INSIDE COME OUT WITH YOUR HANDS UP!!"

Blaring sirens and flashing lights outside the window distracted the fearful looking Nilstrom. Lex jumped out of his seat and lunged at Lennart, grabbing for the gun. A flash and blast came out the gun and Lex collapsed in pain. The last thing that he heard was a crash of metal on wood. A SWAT team had used a battering ram to smash in the door and armed police in body armour flooded into the lounge. Someone in uniform screamed.

"LENNART NILSTROM – PUT DOWN YOUR WEAPON!"

Nilstrom swivelled round and aimed the smoking gun at the SWAT team surrounding him. He was brought down with a bullet to his right shoulder and another in his left thigh.

*

Earthdate: 04:02 Tuesday February 18, 2081 GMT

Prime Minister John Ralston had barely heard Big Ben chime four times as he sat alone and still half-asleep in his private office in 10 Downing Street. He poured himself another cup of strong thick black coffee as he awaited the secure conference call to come through. He had been briefed that it would only be himself, President Josh Trueman, UN Secretary-General Ravinder Gupta-Chaudry and Israeli Prime Minister Moshi Shalomon in conference. His Personal Private Secretary, Julian Farnham-Browne, did not know what the subject matter was about. Only that it was of the utmost importance to national – and global - security. As Ralston sipped the lukewarm coffee he thought the call was most likely to be an update on the Windsor bombing. Maybe the Israelis have discovered a link to Suleiman and the LOIN, he thought, absentmindedly. The monitor in front of him started flashing and he activated the conference call by using the key on the touch screen. The faces of the four men appeared simultaneously on the screen via their webcams. Ralston covered his mouth as he yawned widely.

"Apologies, gentlemen, I was dragged out of my bed at three thirty and I am still trying to waken up. Am I right in guessing that this has something to do with the recent act of terrorism on British soil?"

The US President spoke first.

"Yore way off beam, John - ah only wish it was as mundane as that –"

Ralston shook himself wide awake at President Trueman's statement and interjected with some surprise.

"For God's sake, Josh, British royalty and our subjects being blown to bits on the streets of England is hardly mundane!"

Gupta-Chaudry intervened in mediatory tones.

"John, you must listen to what President Trueman is about to tell you. He is not trying to minimise the Windsor massacre. It was truly terrible, but what you are about to hear is much more terrifying –"

Moshi Shalomon also pitched in.

"Prime Minister, I would advise you that we must all remain quiet and just let Josh speak."

John Ralston had a terrible thought.

"Oh, God, we are not talking about all-out war with the LOIN states here are we?"

Trueman was beginning to get irritated at not being able to make his pitch.

"Fuckin' hell, John, it's nothin' like that – are you gonna let me tell ya or do ya just wanna play Charades?"

"Apologies, Josh, please carry on."

Ralston watched on his webcam as Trueman looked down, probably at his briefing notes, mentally preparing himself for what he was about to say.

"Gentlemen, ah have to discuss with you tonight the gravest matter ever to face mankind. Let me tell you what ah know, which is still sketchy, and then ah can take any questions after ah have spoken. It appears from information gathered by my NASA team and Moshi's guys at INSACC in Tel Aviv that a new comet – apparently they have named it, um, Schenkler HMM2 – has entered the solar system and it is heading our way. Now, as I have said, the info ah'm gettin' is still sketchy – but, ah, it appears from the options being developed on computer models by the astro-guys that there are two key scenarios. Option A is a near miss with the tail of the comet causing widespread destruction across the face of the Earth. Option B – which, gentlemen, is being given a 75% probability rating at present – is a head-on collision with Earth in 2084 and ah am bein' told that it means the total destruction of our planet – completely vaporised apparently. Do you have any questions, gentlemen?"

There was a stunned silence, with each of the leaders experiencing a nauseous knot tighten in their stomachs. Ralston's immediate thoughts were not for mankind at all but for his wife and two children sleeping soundly and safely – or maybe not so safely – upstairs in 10 Downing Street. Finally, he broke the silence.

"My God, Josh, can this be true? I mean to say – what can we do about it?"

"Well, look here, John, as ah've said – things are still very sketchy. Ah was only given this info a short time ago. Obviously, we need to look at the two key scenarios in detail and come up with plans as to how we are gonna tackle them. Jeez, gentlemen - the whole goddam future of mankind has just been bestowed upon us here! But really, our first problem is how to communicate this to our peoples in an orderly manner. Christ, there could be mass panic out there, the whole fuckin' system could break down – mankind could topple like a house of cards – anarchy, war, famine, economic and infrastructural collapse –"

Gupta-Chaudry spoke trying to remain calm although his stomach was churning. All he could think of was how he could get home to India to see his family.

"Josh, when did you say this comet would arrive and when would we be certain whether we would be looking at option A or option B?"

"Um, eh, yeah good question Ravinder – ah believe that that – um, ah don't have the exact date in front of me – but ah think some time towards the end of May 2084 is when this Schenkler thing gets here. As far as the A / B scenario goes, um, my guys tell me they will be 100% certain when this thing passes Jupiter, ah believe sometime late next year. Somethin' to do with the gravitational pull of Jupiter apparently –"

John Ralston fired in a question.

"Josh, to what extent is this information known in the wider community?"

"Well, John, from what we can see there is no ongoing internet traffic on this info and no garble on the wires about it that we have detected. So, apart from our very tight circle and the NASA and Israeli Nimrod teams the world is yet to fully discover all about Schenkler HMM2."

Ralston thought for a moment and then replied.

"If this sensitive information is not out there as yet, then I would suggest a drip feed approach to this in order to do a damage limitation exercise, Josh."

"Exactly – that is what ah had in mind, John. What ah would propose, gentlemen, is that we prepare a joint statement basically on the basis of option A only at this point in time – the near Earth miss option – and that we are preparing contingency plans, etcetera. We also put in motion behind the scenes – planning for the worst-case scenario option B. We keep a close eye on Intel traffic to determine whether the world is waking up to that Armageddon scenario and prepare to put it out world-wide at that time. Ah would also suggest an emergency in-camera session of the Security Council, Ravinder? All agreed -?"

John Ralston, Moshi Shalomon and Ravinder Gupta-Chaudry all agreed and the UN Secretary-General agreed to arrange the Security Council session in New York within the week. The US President began to wind up the call.

"Okay guys, ah'm sure John and Moshi want to get back to bed – so any last questions?"

Ralston spoke.

"You must be joking if you think I'm going to be able to sleep now, Josh! One final question – the name of the comet - Schenkler HMM2 - what is all that about?"

The Israeli Prime Minister answered.

"It is a combination of things, John. The first photographs taken of the comet were done by one of my top astrophysicists at INSACC – Ari Schenkler. Schenkler had called the comet Har Megiddo, thus HM. Har Megiddo is Hebrew for Armageddon. Josh's guys had named it Messiah 2, or the Second Coming, thus M2."

Ralston yawned wearily and gulped.

"I'm sorry I asked, Moshi."

Trueman broke in.

"Ah'm glad ya did, John. It has reminded me to tell ya all somethin' else. Although the photographs were taken by Schenkler, his data was hacked into by someone on your side of the Pond, John. We believe he or she may be in - or certainly acting in - Scotland –"

"Jesus, Josh, I thought you said that this was not out in the wider community?"

"Yeah, sorry, John - ah forgot about that. But this guy is actually an expert in the astro-field and the guy is not peddling the info on the WWW as yet. I'll get my CIA guys to pass on what we have to MI5. We should be able to take him down fairly quickly!"

Ralston was horrified.

"Josh – take him down – you don't mean…!"

Trueman laughed.

"Hell, no, John - from what my guys tell me this guy is too valuable to all of us. We want him over here working on this thing with us!"

CHAPTER 14

<u>Earthdate: 09:47 Friday 21 February, 2081 CST</u>

Irene DuPré noticed the attractive blond walking into the reception area and recognised her straight away. Irene pushed her way through the milling Houston Control staff and the excited family members of the crew and passengers up on the Oceanus. The Oceanus was in excellent reception range of satellite E2MSN-16 orbiting at a range of eleven million miles above Mars. E2MSN-16 was just short of halfway to **Midway Island,** the huge international space station which remained in an almost continuous fixed position between Earth and Mars. Midway was like an enormous floating space-city and it acted as the main hydrogen / oxygen refuelling and refitting station for ships plying between the two planets. In about a month's time Oceanus would stop at Midway for just two days for refuelling, barring any repairs and refits which might delay departure. The stop would also give the crew and passengers some rest and recuperation. Irene managed to catch the eye of the blond who instantly recognised the African-American Senior Controller at Houston. Irene waved her over.

"Peggy Sue – girl, ya just get prettier every time ah see you –"

Peggy Sue Crossan gave Irene a big warm hug and kissed her on the cheek.

"Who are ya kiddin', Irene? Ah've just come off the red-eye from Charlottesville an' ah'm still bushed. Hey, but yore looking pretty damn good too, honey bunch."

Irene led Peggy Sue over to a vacant table and they sat down. She poured iced water from a jug into two small plastic cups. Irene took a quick sip, glanced at the time on her cell phone and then eyed up Peggy Sue, assessing her body language.

"Okay, Peggy Sue, ya'll be goin' into the booth to see Jack in about five minutes. So, girl, how is everything with ya? The boys okay?"

Peggy Sue's eyes dropped away from direct contact with Irene and she blushed guiltily. Irene lifted Peggy's chin back up into her eye-line.

"Right, girl, spit it out – what's up?"

Peggy Sue blurted it out tearfully.

"Oh God, Irene – ah don't know how ta say this – but ah'm leavin' Jack an' the farm up in Lexington. Ah can't take it any more bein' the lonely wife of an astronaut!"

Irene put a comforting arm around Peggy Sue.

"Well, girl, ah didn't see that comin' – ah thought that you an' Jack were rock solid."

"Looks can deceive, Irene. In a way ah kind a duped Jack into marriage when ah got pregnant with Milner. Ya know somethin' – Jack has never ever told me that he loves me. Ah think he still carries a torch for his first wife Maria."

"That don't mean that ya got ta leave him girl –"

Peggy Sue looked at Irene. Her eyes were still reddened and moist.

"Ah've found somebody else, Irene. He's an English RAF fighter pilot. Ya know – somebody who ain't away from Earth every four or five months at a stretch. Ah'm goin' to take the boys ta England in a couple of weeks' time."

Irene took another brief glance at her watch and then stared at Peggy Sue with deep concern etched in her brow.

"You're due in the booth in one minute, Peggy Sue. You can't tell Jack all this. Christ, these guys can go stir crazy up in those big tin cans. If you tell him you're leavin' there's no sayin' what he might do. Ah mean ta say, he is one of the shift Commanders on Oceanus – Jack needs to have his wits in gear at all times. So ya need ta keep it light in there, okay?"

Peggy Sue quickly tidied up her smudged mascara.

"It ain't what ah had planned, Irene – but yore the boss!"

Irene looked over at Video Booth 13 and the green light was on above the glass door. Irene thought to herself, it would be thirteen – unlucky for some!

"Okay, girl, you're in number 13 over there. Jack'll be on screen waiting for you. Remember you only get five minutes so only give him the good news."

Peggy Sue pecked Irene lightly on the cheek and walked over to booth 13, sitting herself down in front of the monitor, which seemed to automatically activate. Jack's face immediately appeared on screen a bit fuzzily in front of her.

"Jack, honey, it is Peggy Sue here – how are ya doin', darlin'?"

Peggy Sue had made the video call many times before. She knew she would have to wait for the delayed response to work its way through the E2MSN. As she waited Peggy Sue thought back on what she had related to Irene. She had met Justin Smythe at the Cape Canaveral Christmas Party in mid-December. It was laid on for employees and also spouses of astronauts every year. Actually, it had been the first time that she had ever taken up the invite, because the boys had always been so young before. Her parents had agreed to drive up from Birmingham to the farm at Lexington. They would baby-sit for Milner and Jack Junior to allow Peggy Sue to stay over at the Cape for one night. Justin had been at Cape Canaveral to receive some training simulations on the new F-155 ISSS fighter bombers. The F-155 was an inner-space super-stealth plane, capable of flying up to ten miles above the Earth's atmosphere. It was the most sophisticated military plane ever devised and the RAF was interested in purchasing the plane. Justin and a few of his RAF mates had introduced themselves to the group of astronauts' wives that Peggy Sue was sitting with. The girls were known as the **Black Widows.** Peggy Sue and Justin had gotten on famously, although they had kept it purely platonic at the Cape party. Justin had contacted Peggy Sue later when she returned to Lexington and their affair had started from then, although they had kept it discreet. Peggy was sure that even the two farmhands, Paddy Maguire and Ricardo Esposito, had no idea about her and Justin. Suddenly, Jack's voice crackled in.

"Peggy Sue, baby, oh my God, ya don't know just how good it is ta see your sweet face. Ya look fantastic, honey. How ya doin'? How are Milner and Jack Junior? Did little Jack have a great birthday party? Tell me everythin' 'cos it's as borin' as hell up here –"

Her eyes flicked guiltily away from the monitor. Tell you everything, Jack, I wish I could, she thought, but Irene has warned me not to.

"Everythin' is fine down here, Jack. Milner had a touch of flu last week but he's okay now. Little Jack's party was a blast. All the local kids came by - even though it had snowed heavy the day before. In fact, it's been a real hard winter. Ain't been no global warmin' in Virginia! The farm is good, Jack – we will soon be calving so we are gonna be real busy. Oh, and Paddy and Ricky told me ta say hi ta ya –"

She felt that she was beginning to struggle for things to say to Jack. Irene had thrown her plan to tell Jack about Justin into disarray. Justin had managed to get an extension to the RAF's assessment project examining the benefits of adding the F-155 to the British Fighter Command. He would take an air-car up from Cape Canaveral and meet Peggy Sue for afternoon lovemaking sessions at a quiet, if somewhat crappy, motel about 10 miles south of Lexington. Only once did he stay overnight at the farm. There had been a really big snowstorm and Peggy Sue told Paddy and Ricardo to take a couple of days off. Milner and Jack Junior were puzzled to meet this strange guy at breakfast. However, her two sons were not antagonistic towards Justin and they wanted to know all about being a fighter pilot. Justin was a divorcee with no kids and he adored the two boys at first sight. It was nearly two weeks ago when Justin had told Peggy Sue that he would have to return to his home base at RAF Lyneham in England by the beginning of March. Justin told Peggy Sue that he loved her. He asked her to come and live with him in Wiltshire and to bring the boys too. Peggy Sue had thought about it and then she agreed to join Justin. Jack came back on.

"Yeah, tell Paddy and Ricky ah said hi too. Tell them ah'm lookin' forward to getting' ma self up ta ma knees in muck again. That's the thing about space – everthin' is so goddam clean an' sterile. Although, ah don't know if ya know it but they do have an experimental cattle station down on Mars. Apparently, they've built gigantic super-glass pods where they're growin' grass successfully and tryin' ta rear cattle. Anyway, nuff about Mars, tell me more about ma lovely 3R!"

Peggy Sue glanced at the clock counter on the top right-hand of the monitor. Four minutes fifteen seconds.

"Jack, our five minutes is nearly up. We're gonna get cut off soon. So ah'm gonna send your kisses to Milner and Jack Junior an' ah'll say hi ta your pop. He's doin' really great – he's still workin' at the drug rehab center in downtown Lexington."

Four minutes thirty five seconds. By the time Jack came back on their time together would be over. Literally over, Peggy Sue thought. Her stomach started churning and she fought back the tears. She felt a terrible wave of guilt. Poor Jack, she thought, he did not really deserve this. He had always been such a good husband and father. But he had never given her the one thing that she had always craved for - his love. Now she had Justin who did love her. She thought, it's all over Jack.

"Peggy Sue, honey, tell my pop ah truly love him. An' darlin' ah got somethin' important to tell ya too –"

Five minutes. Jack's face disappeared from the monitor and an electronic voice came over the speakers.

"Your session has now come to an end. You are requested to vacate the booth immediately in order for the next family member to make use of it. Thank you for your co-operation and goodbye."

Peggy Sue stumbled blindly out of the booth. Irene was close by and she crumpled into her open arms and she bawled loudly.

*

Gary crossed Edinburgh's old cobbled High Street and looked up at the name emblazoned above the blue painted pub on the corner - ***World's End.*** Ewan would be finishing his shift in five minutes and they would hopefully both soon be enjoying a couple of pints of Edinburgh's finest beers. Gary pushed his way into the busy bar, full of students from the universities getting their weekends off to a drunken start. The interior was one of dark-panelled wood, ancient stone walls and low raftered ceilings. Gary could see Ewan behind the crowded noisy bar, obviously handing over his shift to quite a good-looking guy that Gary had not seen before. He wondered if he could try a chat-up line on him. Ewan spotted him and Gary signalled with his tilting cupped hand to signal for a pint. Ewan shook his head in the negative and indicated with his fingers that he would be two minutes. Jesus, thought Gary, are we not getting a pint? A couple of minutes later Ewan came out from the bar and led Gary out of the hubbub in the World's End and back out on to the High Street. Gary looked at his friend in puzzlement.

"Fuck sake, Ewan, are we no getting' a drink at all?"

Ewan shook his head while he looked about surreptitiously.

"No, Gary, it's too noisy in there. Look, Jill's been on the phone. We need to talk urgently – so let's go to Chuck's iCafé. It'll be quieter there –"

It took less than five minutes for them to walk briskly to Chuck's. It was a bit like déjà-vu when they walked in. Michelle was behind the counter reading another gossip magazine and she hardly even acknowledged their entrance. Old Buster, the local drunk, was slumped in the corner near a radiator blissfully sleeping. Ewan noticed that he had an old tattered medal pinned on his grubby jacket. Ewan pointed to Gary to take a seat at one of the tables.

"I'll get the coffees, Gaz."

Ewan walked over to the counter and Michelle stood up to serve him with an expression that showed that she was totally fed up.

"Hi Michelle – can I have two Grande lattes please? It's dead in here again, especially for a Friday night?"

Michelle started preparing the coffees as she replied.

"You're right there, Ewan – ah think there was some sort of military parade up tae the Castle earlier on, ken. So ah think everyone has hit the pubs except old Buster over there –"

Ewan had heard in the World's End that it had been the 50th Anniversary of the end of the Second Afghan Conflict which effectively was the start of the long peace between the UN and the LOIN. Michelle placed the lattes on the counter and continued speaking as Ewan handed over the money.

"Ach, this place has been dying for months, Ewan. Ah reckon Chuck'll end up closing it down in a year or two."

Ewan flashed a wicked smile at Michelle as he walked back towards Gary with the coffees.

"Well, I can guarantee you'll definitely be closed for good in three years' time!"

Michelle gave Ewan a puzzled look, shrugged her shoulders indifferently and went back to reading her gossip magazine. Gary took a sip from his frothy latte with a furrowed brow.

"Is your coffee okay, Gary?"

"Aye, except it's no a fuckin' pint is it, Ewan?"

Ewan put down his coffee and prepared to give Gary an explanation for dragging him away from the World's End pub.

"Look, Gaz, I'm really worried. Jill phoned me from London this morning. The government are still putting heavy pressure on the Times and the Leaks sites to keep the lid on the Schenkler story –"

"An' ah take it that means we'll be unlikely to ever see any cash for all our efforts?"

"For God's sake, Gary – the money's no longer important. Who the hell needs money now when we are all going to be blown to smithereens in three years time?"

"Ah still plan to do a lot of things in those three years, Ewan - so ah still want ma payout from Jill!"

Ewan shook his head. Gary was still chasing the wrong God.

"Forget the money for a minute, Gary! The bottom line is that Jill has heard on the grapevine that the National Security Services are on to us. Buckley even asked her to name her sources for the Schenkler story, which is apparently as unprofessional as a senior editor can get with a journalist –"

"Jesus, Ewan, did she tell him about us?"

"No way, Gaz. But Buckley did let it slip that MI5 and the cops are crawling all over Scotland looking for us!"

Gary drained the last of his coffee and banged the coffee cup down on the saucer. Michelle raised an eyebrow and one of Buster's eyes opened sleepily.

"Right, Ewan, let's go – we've got to get back to my place and wipe everything on Schenkler from my computer –"

Before Ewan could answer Gary, the door of Chuck's iCafè crashed open and the place flooded with plain-clothes and uniformed police, some carrying sub-machine guns.

"POLICE! ARMED RESPONSE UNIT – NOBODY MOVE A MUSCLE!!"

Michelle screamed in panic dropping her magazine. Gary and Ewan sat frozen with astonishment in their seats. Old Buster was aroused from his slumber by all the commotion. A senior police officer presented himself in front of the two young men.

"Are you gentlemen Ewan Sinclair and Gary Mackintosh?"

They both nodded numbly.

"Ewan Sinclair – Gary Mackintosh – I am asking you to voluntarily come down to Metropolitan Police HQ in London for questioning on suspicion of internet sabotage on a secure network belonging to the United States of America. Are you agreeable to this?"

Before they could say anything Buster had stumbled across drunkenly to intervene.

"Hey, what's goin' on here? Leave these guys alone –"

The officer glowered fiercely at Buster.

"Excuse me, sir – you are interfering with police business."

The old drunk had experienced many a run in with the police and he did not have much respect for them. Buster volleyed an angry outburst towards the officer.

"Police business – ah've served ma country at the sharp end, sonny! Ah was up tae ma oxters in muck an' bullets before you were even born, ken. If ye had aw been here earlier ye wid hae seen me an' ma comrades marching up the Royal Mile tae the Castle –"

The senior officer held up his hand to stop Buster.

"Sir, if you don't sit down and be quiet I will have you arrested for obstruction of justice and being drunk and disorderly –"

Ewan spoke to placate Buster.

"It is okay, Buster. Tell Michelle to make you a coffee and I'll square her up next time I'm in here."

Buster raised his fists mockingly like a boxer to the group of policemen then, mumbling oaths under his breath, he staggered over to see Michelle, who was standing agog behind the counter. The senior officer turned to Ewan and Gary.

"Okay, gentlemen, are you ready to come with us?"

Gary answered back huffily.

"What is aw this about? You would think we were terrorists or somethin' with all those guns trained on us. Do ye think we killed Prince Eddie or what?"

The officer was beginning to get frustrated with all the backchat.

"You are both needed for questioning on a matter of national security. This is not the time or the place to conduct that questioning. So we can either do this the easy way or we can do it the hard way. What is it to be?"

Ewan stood up and waved Gary on to his feet.

"Come on Gary. Look, sir, we are both happy to do it the easy way."

As they all piled out to the waiting police cars Michelle put down a small cup of Americano in front of Buster.

"Ah could a told ye Buster that they two were gonna come a cropper one day, ken."

*

It was almost 10.30pm and Jill was thinking about getting to her bed. She was exhausted by the day's events. Jill had argued vehemently with Buckley about his demands to reveal her sources for the Schenkler comet story. He had argued back that there were matters of national and international security interests that outweighed the public interest and the fact one of his journalists was not obliged to reveal her sources. In the end Buckley had to accept that he could not force Jill to name those sources. She had then urgently phoned Ewan to warn him that the National Security Services and probably the CIA were hot on their trail. Jill had spent the rest of the day worrying about what would happen to Ewan and Gary. She knew that it was only a matter of time before they were caught and taken in for questioning. They would probably get the book thrown at them. She went in to the bathroom to brush her teeth when suddenly the doorbell rang. Maybe the cops are here for me too, she thought. Jill opened the door and he stood there on her landing looking beaten and cowed.

"Khan – ah wasn't expecting you at this time of night? Ah've been trying to get you on the phone for weeks –"

It had been raining heavily across Berkshire all evening and Khan stood there soaked to the skin.

"Can I come in, Jill - it is rather wet outside tonight?"

Jill waved Khan in and she made him get his wet clothes off and get into his bathrobe, which had still been in the bedroom wardrobe. Jill made some hot tea and they sat facing each other as they drank.

"Where have you been, Khan?"

Khan bowed his head.

"I know you have, Jill, but I have been very tied up with some heavy stuff lately."

"That big property deal up in Manchester -?"

Khan did not answer. He put his forehead in his right hand and he ran his fingers nervously through his thick black hair. Jill thought he looked worried and exhausted. His black eyes seemed sunken and hollow with lack of sleep.

"Khan, you look terrible – what the hell's the matter with you?"

He looked up into Jill's eyes like a caged tiger looking for some means of escape.

"I'll tell you in a minute – but you were looking for me. Did you want to tell *me* something, Jill?"

Now it was Jill's turn to feel a bit nervous. They had not been getting on for weeks and now she had some important news for Khan. Jill was not sure how he would react, but she thought that she might as well just get it out in the open.

"Khan ah'm about eight weeks pregnant. You are going to be a father –"

Khan looked at her with his eyes bulging wide in disbelief. He broke down sobbing pitifully.

"Oh god, oh Allah – wh-what have I done, Jill? What have I done?"

Jill sat beside him and took him into her arms as he continued sobbing.

"Don't you want to be a daddy, Khan?"

Khan looked deep into Jill's eyes.

"I-it's not that, Jill. I have betrayed you – I have betrayed my child –"

Jill listened completely aghast as Khan got all the months of guilt off his chest. He told her that his affair with Jill had just been a front for his operation with the Group. He admitted he had always been in love with Aisha al-Gazari. Aisha was the 'A' on the errant text message. He also said that it was the Group who had been bugging her home. Khan had ripped out the tiny bug from its hiding place. Jill could not believe what Khan was telling her. She should have been angry and shocked at what he was relating, but the investigative journalist mode switched on inside her and she was taking in every detail of his incredible story. He went on to tell her that he was the money man for the jihadists and he and the others had planned the assassination of the Prince of Wales. Jill felt her stomach churn at hearing that the man that she had been sleeping with, the father of her unborn child, was a murderer and a terrorist. But she kept her nerve.

"Khan, why are you telling me all this now?"

He looked at her with black dead eyes.

"Aisha was not meant to be in that air-car. I'm sorry, Jill, but I loved Aisha from the bottom of my heart and now she is dead. They had her killed because she knew too much. He did it and I am going to make the bastard pay!"

"Who did it, Khan?"

Khan shook his head.

"I cannot tell you. I can't get you too involved. These are dangerous men that I work with. And they are planning something so terrible that I can't go on living with all this guilt and living without my Aisha. I want you to take me to the nearest police station and I will tell them everything. Right now, Jill!"

Jill drove the air-bike with Khan riding pillion as fast as she could, heading for the police station at Richmond. Suddenly, a beam from a single headlight came up from behind them. Khan looked back and saw another air-bike closing in on them fast and he knew right away that they were in big trouble. He yelled into his helmet mic with urgency in his voice.

"JILL – go as fast as you can! It's the Palestinian behind us – he must have followed me!"

They could both feel and hear a gunshot whoosh past them and Jill knew then how dangerous things had become. She started to bob and weave the air-bike and to try to get as much speed out of the machine as she could muster. The Palestinian kept firing shots at them, each one closer than the one before. Jill saw Richmond High Street below her and dipped the bike in a dangerously steep dive. She could see the police station about three hundred yards ahead. Another shot winged past them and she heard Khan screaming in pain on his mic.

"Aaargh – I've been hit Jill!"

"Hold on, Khan!"

Suddenly, a police air-car going out on a routine patrol started taking off from the police-station and it was heading towards the two oncoming air-bikes. The Palestinian saw the car and veered his bike back into the air and began heading back in the direction of Kew. Jill whizzed past the police car which instantly put on its sirens and flashing lights. She was going too fast coming in to land by the station and the bike hit the ground too hard. She and Khan were thrown off the bike. The police car had done a U-turn in mid-air at the top off the High Street. It flew back to land beside the crashed air-bike lying at the bottom of the entranceway into the station. Two startled looking coppers jumped out of the car as a bruised and battered Jill was trying to tend to the injured Khan. Jill cried out.

"Please help me – he's been shot!"

Khan groaned up at Jill. She could see he was in terrible pain.

"It is okay, Jill, I th-think it's only a flesh wound –"

Then Khan passed out.

It was almost one o'clock on the Saturday morning and Jill had been sitting for hours in the waiting room of the Berkshire Royal General Hospital. The waiting had been punctuated with a couple of interviews with CID and field officers from MI5. Jill could detect their excitement at having made a major breakthrough in the Windsor terrorist attack investigation and there was a lot of coming and going between her and, she suspected, with Khan. She had also seen Chief Superintendent Mike Hollingsworth arriving with a cavalcade of other officers. He had not spoken with Jill but she could see he was exultant. She had also managed to get a call through to Buckley. He was not exactly thrilled at being woken up at that early hour. However, once Jill had told him that there had been a major breakthrough on the Prince of Wales story he was soon wide awake and full of excitement.

"Okay, Jill, I'm on my way to the Times office right now. I need your exclusive on this ASAP! The Bloid home page is all yours – and Jill, I don't know how you managed to be first on scene again and I don't care - bloody fantastic work, Jill!"

The two CID officers, Adams and Evans that had interviewed Jill earlier came back into the waiting room. Detective Adams looked grimly at Jill.

"Miss Geeson, we have been informed by the doctors working on Khan al Ahmed that we can no longer interview him tonight. Mr Al Ahmed has been extremely helpful to our investigation and we are currently in the process of making further fruitful enquiries, although I am not at liberty to say anything further at this stage, Miss Geeson."

Jill stood up and looked at the two detectives pleadingly.

"How is Khan? He said that he had only taken a flesh wound –"

Adams looked at Detective Evans then back at Jill.

"You will really need to talk with the doctors, Miss Geeson…look, Jill, he's in a bad way, but I can't tell you any more."

Jill felt an awful feeling in the pit of her stomach and she forced tears back. Evans changed the subject.

"Miss Geeson, based on Mr Al Ahmed's statement, and we have no reason to disbelieve it, he states that you had no idea of his involvement in the

Windsor attack. Is that correct?"

"Yes, th-that is correct officer."

"We will still require you to come to Scotland Yard in the morning - in order to make a formal statement. Do you have any objections to that, Miss Geeson?"

Jill agreed to appear at the Metropolitan Police HQ at eleven o'clock on Saturday morning and Detectives Adams and Evans left her alone in the waiting room. She watched through the glass doors at the MI5 and police entourage making their way out of the hospital. Hollingsworth passed by and he smiled his recognition of Jill from her attendance at his many press briefings. He stuck his head in the door.

"Hello, Miss Geeson, first off I have to say to you that I cannot make any comments at this crucial point in the investigation. But off the record, Jill, you have done your country and the world a great service tonight and I would personally like to thank you for that."

Jill mumbled her thanks and as Hollingsworth departed with his other senior officers, she thought, and I've done your career a great service tonight too! She had only sat down for about another two minutes when a doctor in his blues came in to the waiting room. Jill could tell from his face that the news was grim.

"Miss Geeson, I am Doctor McKendrick – I was the surgeon who operated on your partner Mr Al Ahmed. I am very sorry to say that Mr Al Ahmed passed away about five minutes ago –"

Jill was ashen.

"Oh please God no –"

"I am afraid to say that the bullet went through one of his aortic arteries and he has died from internal bleeding. There was very little that we could do for him – but he did die peacefully and without pain."

Jill began to cry.

"But ah'm carrying his baby!"

Doctor McKendrick bowed his head.

"I am very sorry, Miss Geeson. Do you want me to get someone that you can speak with?"

Jill shook her head again forcing back the tears.

"No, Doctor McKendrick, ah have work to do – ah have Khan al Ahmed's epitaph to write on tomorrow's headline story!"

BOOK 2 - EXODUS

CHAPTER 15

Earthdate: 19:15 Monday February 24, 2081 GMT

The weekend had passed in a blur. After they had been picked up by the police in Chuck's iCafè, Ewan and Gary had been whisked in an army helijet down to the Metropolitan Police HQ at Scotland Yard. They had been subjected to intense questioning over their ability to hack into NASA's E2MSN system and what they knew about the Schenkler HMM2 comet. However, the National Security Services officers from MI5 who were in charge of the interrogation made it clear to the two Scotsmen that they were not under arrest at that point in time. This was on the basis that Ewan and Gary had actually conducted 'important research', which under normal circumstances would have been deemed illegal. However, it was recognised that their discovery at this early stage was vital knowledge to the survival of the human race. Although they were not under arrest, the MI5 officers told Ewan and Gary that they had to remain, at least until Monday, in confinement at Scotland Yard for their own protection. Everyone else in the UK that they had contacted about the comet had been agreeable to withhold all information on Schenkler HMM2. In effect this meant Jill, William Buckley and all the online Leak sites. They were all effectively being monitored and kept under surveillance. On Monday evening Ewan and Gary were led into the small office at the rear of Scotland Yard. The two of them could not believe they were to actually meet the Prime Minister. They were introduced to John Ralston and then, apart from an MI5 case officer sitting near the door, the two young men and the PM sat alone around the small conference table with a monitor hibernating on top of it. Ralston playfully chided the two young Scots.

"Under different circumstances lads, I would have had the two of you hung, drawn and quartered for what you did –"

Gary, ever the joker, quipped back with a broad cheeky grin.

"Aye, typical Englishman, you guys did the same thing tae William Wallace!"

Ralston smiled and then grew more solemn.

"Indeed, Gary, but now we must get down to this evening's serious business. In a few minutes we will be connecting to a conference call with US President Trueman, UN Sec-Gen Gupta-Chaudry, Israeli PM Shalomon and I believe you will also be meeting for the first time Mr Ari Schenkler of INSACC in Tel Aviv."

The two scientists were agog at what they had just heard and were almost speechless. Ewan mustered the courage to speak.

"P-Prime Minister, you have just mentioned some of the most powerful men on the planet, including yourself. Why are we here tonight in such exalted company?"

"Well young men, we may be what you call the most powerful men on the planet. However, what the human race is facing in three years time requires some of the greatest brains on the planet. By your own sterling actions – and that of Ari and the guys at NASA too – you have both elevated yourselves into the exalted company that you speak of."

Gary was flabbergasted.

"Jeez, Prime Minister, ah think you want tae have a wee word with ma father!"

Just then the monitor in front of them came alive and they were connected through the secure lines to the White House in Washington, UN HQ in New York and Beit Aghion in Jerusalem. President Trueman introduced himself to the conference call and asked all those taking part to do likewise. Beside him in the Oval Office were Aaron Eckler and Beth O'Donnell. Ravinder Gupta-Chaudry was alone in his UN HQ office in New York. In the house of the Prime Minister in Jerusalem sat Moshi Shalomon, Yosep Goldenheim and Ari Schenkler and in 10 Downing Street John Ralston, Ewan Sinclair and Gary Mackintosh. Trueman began the meeting.

"Guys, and Beth, of course - we are part of a very select elite band of human beings who are aware of the existence of the comet we now call Schenkler HMM2 and of the terrible wrath it is about to unleash on planet Earth. Ari ah hope that you don't mind yore name being associated with this comet?"

Ari bent towards his mic and spoke nervously.

"W-well, Mr President, it is a bit of a burden to carry – and really the credit should go to Mr Sinclair for its discovery –"

Ewan spoke surprising himself with his confidence.

"If it had not been for your infamous footage, Ari, it might not have been discovered for another good few months. Anyhow, Gary and I had been jokingly calling it Schenkler from the outset."

Trueman continued.

"Okay, we are all agreed on Schenkler HMM2 – the HMM2 bit should not be overtly explained to the press, media or other outside agencies in any detail. In fact, at this stage I am proposing that today we agree a tri-partite approach to announcing this to our peoples basically in three stages. Stage one is a simultaneous broadcast of the text previously discussed and agreed between myself, the UN Sec-Gen and the two Prime Ministers present. The tenor of that announcement is basically to let the world know of the arrival of Schenkler HMM2 into the solar system. That it is heading towards our part of the solar system and that our projections are that it will be a near miss from the comet - but that Earth will suffer serious collateral damage from meteor showers from the tail. Is everyone agreed on Stage one?"

Gupta-Chaudry, Ralston and Shalomon all indicated their agreement. Ewan was baffled and he had to ask a question.

"Mr President, at first I thought the comet was going to be a near miss, but I have been over my calculations a hundred times hoping that I was wrong. Mr President, this thing is going to smash right into Earth. I'm sure Ari will back me up here?"

Ari came over on the monitor.

"Mr President, I have to completely concur with Ewan's research. Unfortunately, the gravitational pull of Jupiter will draw the trajectory of, um, Schenkler directly on a terrible collision course with our planet."

Trueman guided Aaron Eckler to speak.

"Look, guys, we ain't really disputing your research. But the way we are lookin' at it is that, until Schenkler makes that pass on Jupiter, we reckon that there is still a chance of a near miss –"

Ewan was getting irritated, forgetting the company he was keeping.

"Now just wait a minute! I know my own research and the probability of a near miss is as low as 1 in 10,000. We will be deceiving the human race by giving them false hope –"

Josh Trueman came back on using mediatory tones.

"Look, Ewan, we know exactly what your research says. But here is the problem. If we announce right away that the Earth is going to be destroyed and everyone and everything is going to be blown into oblivion – then what's going to happen? Ah'll tell you what - there will be chaos, anarchy and disorder. All human systems, such as industry, production and economies, will just totally disintegrate. Guys, what we need right now is to buy some time in order to put a plan in motion that'll give the human race a fighting chance of survival. As a result, ah propose that the next part of that plan is Stage two. That is how we get as many people off Earth before 2084 and colonise Mars. It is our only hope of survival and, in hindsight - we should have pushed it harder and faster in the late 20th century. So for now we need those industries and economies to carry on as normal. So again ah ask – are we all agreed on Stage one?"

This time everyone realising the enormity of the situation agreed with Trueman.

"Okay, so just to confirm - ah will speak to the American people at 5pm Washington time, that'll be 10pm with you John and midnight for you Moshi? Ravinder – you'll need to be ready to have a press briefing in NY following our televised statements?"

Ralston, Shalomon and Gupta-Chaudry all agreed. Trueman carried on.

"Ah will also call key heads of state personally before the announcement to let them know what is going on. For instance, Presidents Lechnikov in Russia, Jeng-Li Pan in China and ah'll also speak with Mullah Suleiman of the LOIN. Right, guys, Stage two – there is a helluva lot of planning going to be required. It is going to need a lot of international co-operation, but ah'm suggesting the key planning decisions are centered with NASA at Houston and Cape Canaveral. Is everyone agreed on that?"

No-one disputed what Trueman was saying and he carried on speaking.

"Good – now look here, we are going to have to bring all the top guys from around the world in on this. Mr Sinclair and Mr Schenkler – ah want you to come over and join a new astrophysics team to be headed up by Aaron Eckler. Mr Mackintosh – ah hear that you are the joker in the pack – but ah'm asking you to join the E2MSN computing redevelopment team to be headed up by Beth O'Donnell. What say you guys?"

Gary was first to reply in his usual comedic style.

"You're a guy who knows how to lay his cards on the table, Mr President – ye can deal me in!"

Ewan and Ari could hardly believe they had been elevated to the ranks of astrophysics superstardom but they had both only slightly hesitated before agreeing and Trueman carried on talking.

"Okay, ah have also agreed in advance with Prime Ministers Ralston and Shalomon that the – what d'ya call them, Aaron.....oh yeah, the CORSAIR observatory in Scotland and the Nimrod SH2 telescope under the auspices of the INSACC in Tel Aviv will be put at the disposal of Mr Sinclair and Mr Schenkler. Mr Goldenheim will continue to be INSACC Project Director for the newly revised Nimrod program. Again – is everyone still in accord?"

Once again the conference concurred with President Trueman.

"Right, guys, we need to start wrapping this up as we have all got a lotta work to do. Stage three then – once we have agreed plans and put into motion the attempt to mass-colonise Mars and basically at the point when Schenkler makes its pass by Jupiter – when is that again guys?"

Ewan jumped in.

"Mr President, my calculations show that Schenkler passes Jupiter at the end of September next year in 2082."

Trueman looked at Eckler who nodded.

"Yeah, that's correct, Ewan – okay, at that point we are gonna to have to announce to the world that the Day of Judgment is on its way. Jeez, guys, ah tell ya all ah ain't looking forward to that day – and ah mean the day we gotta announce it! We will also be setting up an international UN team headed up by Ravinder to plan for the likelihood that there could be a complete breakdown of law and order. In fact, ah'm actually hoping for a joint UN / LOIN task force but ah gotta speak with Suleiman about that. Okay, that's Stage three – is everyone on board?"

There was agreement by all at the meeting and Trueman began winding the conference up.

"Right, all you guys, that's the three stages that we need to put in motion at present. So before ah tell ya all ta knuckle down and get ta work on this thing – are there any last questions?"

There was a moment's hesitation between Washington, London and Tel Aviv, which was broken by Gary with uncharacteristic solemnity.

"Mr President, Gary Mackintosh here – ye talked about the attempt to mass-colonise Mars, yeah? Well there are seven and a half billion human beings on this planet. Realistically, how many humans are we going to be able to transport to Mars by 2084?"

Trueman gulped and realised that the elephant in the room had just revealed itself.

"Gary, that is one helluva question, son. Ah'm gonna put Aaron Eckler on to answer that one – Aaron?"

Eckler came over the monitors with some hesitation in his voice.

"A-a-ah, w-well we are still at the very early stages on this one. But given the timescales and the logistics – ah mean to say this is the most complex undertaking that mankind has ever taken on – ah –eh –"

Trueman barked an order.

"Jesus Christ, Aaron, give them the damn figure!"

Aaron Eckler swallowed hard.

"Realistically, we have estimated a maximum of forty five to fifty thousand humans –"

There was complete silence.

*

Josh Trueman sat at his desk in the Oval Office running over his speech for the final time as the TV crew also made their final preparations for his broadcast. The TV director bent over towards Trueman.

"Ten minutes, Mr President!"

Trueman nodded and he thought back on the last few hours since the conference call and he felt that they had probably been some of the fastest in his lifetime. Following the agenda item on Schenkler and after all the astrophysics / computer guys had departed the meeting, Trueman had another issue to discuss. The US President had turned to a separate agenda item with only himself, Ralston, Gupta-Chaudry and Shalomon present. Trueman again took the lead.

"John that was fuckin' good work your guys did on bringing in the terrorists that assassinated poor Prince Eddie and the others. Not only that but also identifying that Suleiman and the LOIN were the paymasters."

"Thank you, Josh, based on the info that Al Ahmed gave us before he died we have all but smashed the UK ring which called itself the Group. Unfortunately, two of them still elude our police and security forces for the moment. The ringleader named Mahmoud El Kharroubi and the one who killed Al Ahmed, who the Group only knew as the Palestinian. It means, Josh, that the operation to attack the planned centres for the super-storage of DNA may still be live."

Shalomon growled angrily over the monitors.

"Gentlemen, let me send a crack Mossad team into Tehran and I promise you I will take that bastard Suleiman down!"

Gupta-Chaudry intervened in more conciliatory tones.

"Moshi, what Suleiman has put in motion are certainly terrible acts of aggression. But given what is going to happen to this planet in 2084 what we can ill afford at this time is to reply with more aggression."

Trueman came back on.

"Moshi, what Ravinder says is very true. Ah have already said that ah would be speaking to Suleiman later today about 2084. Ah am going to be up front with him on Schenkler. Ah am also going to tell him that on the basis of what we know about the comet that ah will be cutting through all the crap. That we know exactly what he had planned and what he *is* planning – an' that he had better get it called off immediately. Ah think even Suleiman will realise that the collection and storage of human DNA to be transported to Mars before 2084 may be a major building block in the reconstruction - and ultimately - the continued survival of the human race!"

Gupta-Chaudry agreed.

"I completely concur with you, Josh. This is now the time for the peoples of the world to pull together in unity. Perhaps it has taken Judgment Day to finally bring about the hope of world peace."

One hour later Trueman managed to get Suleiman on his monitor. The Iranian President was his usual congenial viper-like self.

"Mr President, it is so good of you to call me again so soon. What can I do for you this evening, my brother?"

Trueman was in no mood for pleasantries.

"Abdullah, ah'm gonna cut straight to the chase here. In a minute ah'm gonna talk to you about the Group that you have been fundin' in the UK –"

Suleiman barked back angrily.

"Trueman, I hope by Allah that you are not going to start accusing the LOIN of acts of terrorism –"

The American President raised his voice in controlled anger.

"Abdullah shut the fuck up! We'll get to the Group later - but first ah have to tell you that ah'm announcing some terrible news tonight to the American people. News about an event so grave that will affect the whole fuckin' world!"

Suleiman listened, at first sceptically, at Trueman's account of the devastating comet heading towards Earth. But as Trueman detailed the data that had been researched and the three stage plan that he had already agreed with the UN, Britain and Israel, Suleiman had that growing feeling of dread in his stomach that told him that the US President was telling the truth. Trueman agreed to provide all the data to the LOIN to back up his statements about Schenkler HMM2 and Suleiman agreed to follow the three stage plan in principle. Suleiman agreed that he would make his own announcement to the LOIN states.

"Abdullah – what the world is gonna need in the next three years is full co-operation of all the nations. An' that means that the UN and the LOIN need to truly co-operate – truly have peace. What do ya say, President Suleiman?"

Suleiman was punch drunk with all the information from Trueman and he sat like a beaten fighter boxed in the corner of the ring. He was almost in tears as he spoke.

"Josh, my friend and my brother, I-I can hardly take in all that you have said – but it is indeed written in Allah's own words in the Qu'ran. The **Yawm ad-Din** – the Day of Judgment – which brings about the annihilation of all creatures on Earth followed by the Resurrection and the last judgment of God. It h-has finally come. We are all subject to that same judgment. Of course, Josh, I agree to a peace accord of all the nations. I will come to Washington and stand by your side on the steps of your White House and sign a treaty between the UN and the LOIN."

Trueman breathed a sigh of relief.

"That's great, Abdullah, that's just great. Now look, Mr President, ah don't have time for all the whys and wherefores regarding the Prince of Wales assassination and the current plot to blow up targeted Western hospitals –"

Suleiman interrupted.

"President Trueman, I have made a grave error in my own judgment and I have been ill-advised by certain partners within the LOIN. I now see that Allah has chosen a different path of martyrdom for all Muslims and I am sure that you will have similar beliefs within your own Christian faith. Please accept that I will do everything in my power to ensure that the attempt to bomb any Western hospitals is immediately called off."

Josh glanced down again at his speech as the TV director brought him back from his reflective thoughts.

"Ten seconds, Mr President."

Trueman looked up at the camera facing him and as he watched the countdown his last thoughts before speaking were – my Fellow Americans, it's only a little white lie. The 'On Air' red light flicked alive and the auto-cue began to roll before him.

"My fellow Americans – I have come before you tonight to advise you all that a new astral body has been recently discovered on the outer edges of our own solar system. It is a large comet, probably a fragment of an exploded planet, hurled towards the Sun from another nearby star system. It has been named Schenkler HMM2 after the Israeli astrophysicist who first photographed it as it passed through the Kuiper Belt in the same quadrant as Pluto. The reason I am talking

to you tonight is to tell you all that the expectation is the Schenkler comet is on a trajectory which will bring it on a near by-pass of planet Earth – current estimates are that it will pass within half a million miles of our planet in May 2084. The comet has a very large tail of rock, ice and debris. International scientists estimate that Earth will suffer multiple meteor showers in late 2083 and possibly right through to May 2084. Our planet will sustain severe collateral damage. We are still working to determine those locations on Earth which will be most affected - and we will be working with the governments of all nations to minimise that damage. However, my key message to you all is not to panic. Government and production and economies and public order should carry on in a stable and responsible manner. You should all carry on with your own lives in the sure knowledge that I and my Government will be working night and day to plan for all eventualities as the comet nears planet Earth. I can assure you I will personally keep you informed of any and all developments as they are reported to me by the teams that I have today set up under the auspices of NASA. The world is facing a great challenge – possibly its greatest challenge - and it requires all nations and all peoples to pull together in the same direction. To this end I have invited President Mullah Abdullah Suleiman to come to Washington in April to discuss a peace accord between the UN and the LOIN. I can advise you all that President Suleiman has agreed to this historic meeting and I believe this to be a major step forward in world peace. It is not the first time in human history that an astral body has heralded peace for all mankind. It is my greatest hope that this comet may also bring that same promise. I thank you all for listening and I wish you all a peaceful good evening."

"Cut!"

Trueman heard the young TV broadcast director Tony Coccio call the broadcast to an end.

"That's a wrap, Mr President. Can I congratulate you on a superb speech?"

Trueman picked up the typed sheets of his speech, looked at them momentarily, and then scattered them all over the Seal of the President of the United States of America on the floor in front of his desk.

"Son - that was one steamin' pile of bullshit!"

*

Jill sat at her workstation in the Times office. Buckley was in his own office awaiting her copy. They had both just finished listening to Prime Minister Ralston giving the pre-arranged announcement on the Schenkler comet. In fact, Jill had also tried to listen simultaneously to President Trueman's speech from the White House and she had concurred that the two speeches were remarkably similar. The London Times and the Leak sites that Ewan and Gary had contacted had all been given the go-ahead to release the information they had been given. They could all publish material on Schenkler at 23:30 GMT as long as it did not go beyond Stage one of the Trueman plan. Buckley impressed upon Jill not to cross the Stage one boundary as Ralston had threatened to make life difficult for the Times if they went too far. Jill looked at her monitor and asked herself if she had the will to carry on with the job at the Times. She had gone home to Glasgow on the Saturday night after Khan's death and just cried for hours in her mother's arms.

"Oh God mum – ah don't know if ah can do all this any more?"

Her mother Jean hugged her tight and wiped away her tears. Her father Jock kept bringing in steaming hot mugs of strong tea. Jean looked into her daughter's weeping eyes.

"Of course ye can, Jill. Ah know you have been through a heck of an ordeal lately – what with the baby coming. Then with Khan and you separating and now with Khan getting killed in this terrible stooshie that he got himself involved in –"

Jean wiped Jill's running nose with a tissue then she continued to console her daughter.

"But you're one hell of a journalist, Jill. There are goin' to be some really big stories ahead and you've still got the guts to tell them. So you get a good night's sleep in you're old comfy bed and tomorrow you'll be ready to take on the world again."

Jill kissed her mother hard on the cheek.

"Thanks mum."

With her new steely resolve Jill started to rattle together her article as she sat at her workstation, keeping one eye on the post-announcement media furore on the news.

TIMES EXCLUSIVE:

SCOTS SCIENTISTS DISCOVER NEW COMET:

METEOR SHOWERS AND MASS DEVASTATION PREDICTED

By Jill Geeson, Senior Investigative Reporter, London Times, Feb 24

Tonight the world has been dramatically informed by many of the nations' leaders that a startling new comet has been discovered entering the solar system. Prime Minister John Ralston, US President Josh Trueman and Israeli Premier Moshi Shalomon have led the way in releasing details of the new astral discovery, which is predicted to cause devastation across the globe. Russian President Lechnikov and Chinese President Jeng-Li Pan are also expected to make similar announcements tomorrow morning. It is believed that the President of the LOIN states, Mullah Abdullah Suleiman, will quickly follow suit. The world's leaders have revealed the comet will come startlingly close to Earth in May 2084, possibly as close as to within half a million miles. The leaders are reassuring the peoples of our tiny vulnerable planet that concerted plans will be put in place to deal with every eventuality concerning the bypass of the comet. It is fully expected that rock and debris being carried along in the tail of the comet will cause severe collateral damage to the planet some time between January and May of 2084 and contingency plans will be put in place by the various world agencies to deal with the outcome of this.

Prime Minister John Ralston sought to reassure the British people that he "would personally give them a full and frank update on any developments regarding the comet and its effects on planet Earth".

The comet, which is currently passing through the Kuiper Belt on the outer edge of our solar system, has been named Schenkler HMM2 after Israeli astrophysicist Ari Schenkler of the Israeli National Space and Cosmology Centre in Tel Aviv. However, the Times can exclusively reveal that the comet was initially discovered by two young Scots who had conducted in-depth research on the photographs taken by Mr Schenkler. They also followed this up with back-up research conducted at the CORSAIR observatory on the Mull of Oa on the island of Islay in western Scotland. They can be named for the first time as Islay-born Ewan Sinclair, 27, a PhD graduate in astrophysics and cosmic sciences from Oxford University, and Glasgow-born Gary Mackintosh, also 27, a PhD graduate in computer sciences from Glasgow University. At present neither Dr Sinclair nor Dr Mackintosh have been able to give any comment nor able to be contacted by the Times as they have been assisting the British and American governments with the dramatic details of their stupendous discovery. It is also believed by the Times that Dr Sinclair and Dr Mackintosh have been recruited to work on two major planning teams to be based at NASA HQ in Houston, Texas. They are both expected to fly out to the US within the next few days to begin their important planning work to deal with the effects of the Schenkler comet on planet Earth.

A spokesman for 10 Downing Street was able to give an exclusive comment to the Times about Sinclair and Mackintosh stating that "the Prime Minister has met today with Drs Sinclair and Mackintosh to express his gratitude from the British people at the very important scientific research carried out by the two Scottish scientists leading to the discovery of the comet Schenkler HMM2. PM Ralston also wished them both God speed to take up the vitally important roles ahead of them and thanked them both personally in 10 Downing Street for agreeing to join the planning teams at NASA HQ."

Jill quickly reread her article before sending it in to Buckley to do final editing. It tickled her pink to think she was writing about the monumental deeds of her old schoolmates. She thought, God, Ewan and Gary will both die laughing when they read this – Doctors, they'll say – who is it that you are actually talking about? She laughed aloud uproariously for the first time in a long time. Tears of laughter ran down her aching cheeks. Buckley stuck his head out of his office and shouted down the empty office.

"Are you okay, Jill?"

Jill laughed back.

"Ah'm fine, Buck, just fine."

CHAPTER 16

<u>Earthdate: 15:30 Monday March 3, 2081 EST</u>

Air Force One, the President's supersonic Boeing 797, had departed from Andrews Air Force Base in Maryland heading for the mid-West States. Trueman, who had been elected in November 2080, was on a two-day whistle-stop tour of Democratic Party offices to thank all his electioneering staffs for their hard work in helping him win the Presidential election. As he sat discussing his orations for the day with his speech advisor, he thought to himself, the planet may be heading for total destruction but the business of politics has to go on as normal. The thought also struck him that he was now effectively the very last President of the United States of America and it made him feel a little queasy. At that moment Secretary of State Arlene Kingstone popped her head into the President's suite.

"Mr President, Suleiman's on the red line looking for you? He says it's important – are you available –?"

Trueman smiled at her and nodded. Kingstone and the speech advisor left the 797's Presidential suite and Trueman opened the red line on his monitor and Suleiman's face appeared looking pretty glum.

"Abdullah, my friend, ah hope that it's a good evening over there in Tehran? How're ya doin' this evening?"

The Iranian did not smile back.

"Josh, my brother, I have extremely bad news for you about Mahmoud El Kharroubi and Mosab Ali Youssef – the one you knew only as the Palestinian -"

Trueman's face turned grim.

"What about them, Abdullah?"

"They have both gone deep underground – what you would call AWOL. I have been unable through all my various agencies to contact them. Josh, my friend, I fear that they are now acting out of their own volition – I think you call it a lone wolf - and I fear they will still try to hit their original targets – probably very soon."

Trueman felt that he could do without this latest crisis.

"Okay, Abdullah - thanks for the heads up. We already have terrorist threat levels in London, Boston and Toronto set at critical. Ah will pass on your information to all concerned and we must all keep close tabs on the situation."

President Suleiman responded.

"I will also keep trying to contact the two men on their secure cell phones – but they have had them off for weeks now. I have given your Secretary of State Miss Kingstone the numbers in order that your Western secret services can try and track them if they come back online. Please accept my sincere apologies and a very good night to you, Mr President."

"Sure, Abdullah, no problem – we will do everything in our power to stop them. Ah wish you a good night also, President Suleiman."

*

Earthdate: 20:45 Monday March 3, 2081 GMT

The MI5 CCTV controller operating the BB2 system picked the target up on the concourse at Kings Cross Station. She radioed out to get ground operatives on him as quickly as possible.

"Target MEK spotted leaving front exit of Kings Cross onto Euston Road at 20:45. Agents please advise when on him - over?"

Mahmoud El Kharroubi had been holed up in a safe house in Leeds for the last two weeks. Today he had travelled down on various slow inconspicuous trains via York and Peterborough to try and avoid detection. He knew that the UK police and national security services would be carrying out surveillance operations looking for him, particularly in central London and around the St Bart's area. He also knew that President Suleiman had been trying repeatedly to call him and to email him but he had not responded for fear of being tracked on his mobile or on his eTab. Based on the various current media reports Mahmoud guessed Suleiman was trying to call off the attacks on the Western hospitals. But he and the Palestinian were not going to allow a little thing like world peace to come between them and their plans. Mahmoud now saw Suleiman as a traitor to Allah's holy jihad. After Mahmoud exited Kings Cross he was lucky enough to immediately catch a London Red electribus heading down the Farringdon Road. At that point in time the MI5 controller had not had any ground agents confirm contact and in the darkness she momentarily lost sight of El Kharroubi.

"All agents please note target gone AWOL. Possibly aboard a No.27 London Red heading for Holborn - agents in West Smithfield area to hold position pending further advice - over."

Chief Superintendent Mike Hollingsworth stood nervously beside the Director of MI5 as they watched the events on the controller's monitors. Hollingsworth inwardly thought with dread that the terrorist bastard is likely to be on a crowded bus with a chest strapped full of crude explosives and we badly need him back on the ground. Suddenly, a call came in from one of the ground agents.

"Agent Four-Five responding - target MEK spotted on stated No.27 bus at junction of Roseberry Avenue and travelling on down Farringdon Road. He is likely to get off before Holborn Viaduct. Have agents and police in position and I will continue on foot towards St Bart's - over."

The controller responded with urgency as she zoomed all available BB2 CCTVs in on the No.27.

"Roger Four-Five. All units are advised that target is continuing by bus towards attack zone - over!"

El Kharroubi looked out of the bus into the cold dark night as it ambled slowly in heavy traffic down the busy Farringdon Road and he noticed it had started to rain quite heavily, streaking down the windows. It was a far cry from the dusty heat of the Maskobiyeh Detention Center in West Jerusalem. As a young student in journalism over 35 years ago at Al-Quds University in Jerusalem, Mahmoud spent months trying to make contact with his father Ibrahim El Kharroubi who was being detained in that Israeli prison known as the *Slaughterhouse.* His father was a political leader in the old Hamas organisation and he had been in and out of Israeli prisons throughout Mahmoud's formative years. When Ibrahim was eventually released from Maskobiyeh for that last time he came out an old and broken man. Hamas was also dissolved as a now defunct political and militia organisation shortly after. It was at that point that Mahmoud developed his deep hatred for the Jews and the West. He offered his services to the newly emerging LOIN organisation and he was secretly trained as a **sleeper,** becoming a respected journalist with Al Jazirah and eventually being posted to work in the UK. Mahmoud's hatred of the infidels was now so ingrained and deep-seated within his psyche. Nothing, not even Suleiman, was going to stop him from striking at the Jew doctor's hospital and, in particular, her developing DNA unit at St Bart's. If Venters was to also to die in the attack then it would be an even greater victory for the cause of the great God Allah. The No.27 jolted to a halt at a bus-stop and El Kharroubi realised that this was his stop and he jumped up abruptly and jostled himself very carefully through some standing passengers.

"Excuse me please – but I must get off here."

He jumped off the electribus into the pouring rain and as it quietly pulled away the MI5 controller quickly picked him up on a monitor in front of her.

"All agents are advised target MEK is now on foot. He is walking east on Snow Hill. It is likely that he will take Cock Lane – repeat Cock Lane. Target is to be intercepted at Cock Lane. Agents respond immediately - over!"

As El Kharroubi walked briskly down Snow Hill he noticed that the evening pedestrians had thinned out with only one or two couples huddled under umbrellas strolling in either direction. He turned into the narrow street of Cock Lane, which was empty, and he saw the well-lit buildings of St Batholomew's Hospital at the other end of the lane. He became nervous at the thought that he was now so near yet so far to his target. He was emboldened by the belief that he would soon be sitting by the side of his beloved Allah. Suddenly strong bright arc lights lit on him from both ends of the lane.

"MAHMOUD EL KHARROUBI – THIS IS THE POLICE! LIE FACE DOWN ON THE GROUND IMMEDIATELY –"

El Kharroubi froze for a second and looked through the pouring rain at the hospital which was now impossibly out of reach. Lines of armoured police had cut him off at either end of the lane. He thought about lying down as he had been instructed but then he was overcome by a great rage welling up inside him. He raised the cheap untraceable mobile high into the sodden air and screamed from the bottom of his lungs.

"Allahu akbar!"

At the same split second a hail of police marksmen's bullets ripped into his body. Mahmoud fell flat on his face on the soaking ground. With his last breath he pressed on the mobile and his body exploded with a terrible muffled crump. Hollingsworth who had watched the whole scene on BB2 yelled into the mic.

"This is Hollingsworth here! Are there any casualties – respond!"

There was a momentary silence. Hollingsworth watched on the monitors as armoured police officers move in slowly and gingerly towards El Kharroubi's smouldering and destroyed remains. Then an officer called back on the radio.

"Inspector Carrington here, sir – there is some slight collateral damage to surrounding buildings. The only casualty is target MEK. No other casualties, sir – over and out."

Chief Superintendent Mike Hollingsworth smiled to himself. He slowly exhaled a small sigh of relief and satisfaction. He allowed himself the pleasing vision of receiving his Knighthood from Her Majesty Queen Elizabeth III for his recent services to the security of his country and to the world.

*

Earthdate: 16:19 Monday March 3, 2081 EST

It had turned out to be a lovely warm bright early spring afternoon and Ruthie had decided to sit out in the manicured gardens. She had taken a few days off from the London Times, for which she was long overdue. She and her father Rolf had flown in this morning to Boston from New York's La Guardia airport. Rolf had earlier attended an international gynaecological conference in midtown Manhattan. Ruthie had shopped excitedly on 5th Avenue while her father had attended his conference. When they had later arrived by electri-cab from Boston Airport at the Harvard Medical Center in Cambridge, Massachusetts, Ruthie had been happy to let her father go in to pick up her mother Marcie. Ruthie had bought an ice cold Coke and a spicy hot dog and she now sat in the gardens in front of the impressive Harvard hospital. Marcie had been working in Boston for the last three days, stuck in planning meetings for the new human DNA super-storage facility to be sited at Harvard. The three of them were booked on an overnight supersonic flight from Boston to London. Ruthie subconsciously checked her wristwatch, she expected her parents to come out into the sunny gardens any minute now. She crumpled up the hot dog wrapper and went to stroll over to a nearby trashcan. However, she had to step back hastily as a dark-skinned and heavily perspiring Middle Eastern man rushed past her, almost crashing into her. They each made direct eye contact momentarily and Ruthie felt that she had never seen as much venomous evil in such as this man's eyes. A cold shiver ran down her spine but she was not quite sure of the reason. She gave a half-hearted shout after the impolite rushing man.

"Excuse *me!*"

The Palestinian Mosab Ali Youssef was over half an hour late arriving at the Harvard Medical Center, which he knew could compromise his mission. He and Mahmoud had synchronised their attacks for the same moment, even though they were continents apart. Mosab's element of surprise would be diminished in its effect. In fact, he suspected the infidels would already be on to him. He had arrived in Boston that morning from O'Hare after a circuitous route over the past five days via Quebec, Vancouver, Seattle and Chicago. Everything had been going to plan up until two hours ago when he discovered that the old untraceable cell phone that was to be used as his detonator had developed a fault. He could not get any power into it and he could not tell if it was the lithium battery or a faulty circuit board. The Palestinian thought about standing down from his mission, but he knew within his dark hate-filled heart that now was to be the moment of his martyrdom. He had decided to take a chance and he rigged the nail-bomb strapped around his torso to his own Group cell phone. He had to hope Mahmoud or Suleiman or anyone else for that matter did not try to contact him. Now here he was sweating profusely and rushing in the warm spring day through the gardens at Harvard. There was hardly a soul to be seen in the gardens. Just a hot dog vendor and a young woman he had almost crashed blindly into. Mosab knew with growing suspicion that it was way too quiet. He looked up at the second floor of the hospital and he began to visualise his route to the DNA Center up there. He prayed to Allah. Just give me five more minutes. Mosab then hurried towards the automated doors into the atrium of the hospital's main entrance. He was about to go through the doors when a middle-aged couple, who were trying to exit, barred his way. Rolf looked at the heavily perspiring man with a puzzled expression. Rolf thought fleetingly that he must be ill or something. He stepped back behind Marcie to allow the dark-skinned man to pass. Rolf put his hands lightly on Marcie's shoulders and gently began to guide her out of the automated doors.

"Look, Marcie, there's Ruthie over there by the hot dog stand –"

The Palestinian had just stepped inside a few yards past Rolf and Marcie when a black security guard pointing a gun at Mosab screamed at the top of his voice.

"FREEZE – don't ya fuckin' move a muscle or ah'll blow yore brains out!"

Mosab instinctively shot his hands up into the air. Rolf froze in shock with his hands still on Marcie's shoulders. No-one moved momentarily. No-one quite knew what to do. Ruthie, about a hundred yards away, was puzzled at why her parents were just standing looking at her. She began to wave and walk towards them. The hot dog vendor, a CIA agent, had pulled a gun and was radioing urgently for backup. Mosab thought about moving. The security guard was now perspiring just as much as the Palestinian. He yelled again.

"Ah'm tellin' ya – don't even fuckin' think about it!"

Time froze for just a second.

Thousands of miles away in Tehran, Suleiman had received an urgent call from PM John Ralston that El Kharroubi had been taken down in London without reaching his target.

"Abdullah, I have not yet heard from President Trueman, but the Palestinian is still on the loose. He is probably heading for Boston or Toronto –"

"Prime Minister, leave it with me!"

The black security guard had only taken one faltering step towards Mosab Ali Youssef, who still had his hands upraised, when the cell phone rang. Ruthie saw the violent flash from behind her parents followed by a great whoosh from the explosion. She never heard the massive bang or saw the millions of shards of glass and debris which exploded out of the atrium towards her. She was blown violently backwards towards the flimsy hot dog stand which disintegrated in the blast. Everything went quiet. A few moments later the hospital area was flooded with armed CIA and Boston police SWAT teams, followed quickly by ambulance and fire crews. Wailing sirens shattered the air of the quiet gardens as black smoke billowed out of the burning atrium.

*

Earthdate: 10:00 Monday April 14, 2081 GMT

Jill was mad at herself. She felt that she should not be allowing this. As they walked into St Bart's she looked at Ruthie, her left arm in a blue medical sling and her face still showing signs of healing lacerations from the tiny glass shards.

"For God's sake, Ruthie, this is madness. Why don't ah just go and see the consultant that ah went to last week?"

Ruthie put her right arm around Jill's shoulders and pulled a funny face.

"Stop worrying about my mother, Jill. She wants to be back at work and she is fine enough to see you about your amnio today –"

Jill still looked concerned.

"But, for God's sake, Ruthie – look at the state of you – you've just lost you're dad *and* your mum's just lost her husband –"

"We Jews are far more philosophical about death than you Christians – both historically and religiously. My father is now with our beloved Jehovah and he is at peace. My mother also needs her work – it is the one thing that she can cling to which makes her believe that Rolf did not die in vain."

As they took the lift up to the Human Fertilisation and Embryology Department the two girls stood musing in silence. Jill now started to feel a little concerned, more about her amniocentesis results. She felt that little niggling fear of the unknown that creeps into the subconscious. Ruthie felt a small wince of pain in her left shoulder. She had damaged it against the smashed up hot dog stand when she was thrown backwards by the bomb blast. It made her think back to that warm afternoon in Cambridge. In some ways she could be thankful that only two people were killed in the blast. Mosab Ali Youssef was blown to bits by the powerful nail bomb when the fateful call came through from President Suleiman, ironically trying to get the Palestinian to call off his terrorist attack. Rolf Venters had taken a murderous impact of nails, glass and debris. Although, he actually fought to live for two hours after the blast. Surgeons at the Harvard Medical Center battled valiantly, but in vain, to save Rolf's life. The black security guard was critically injured. He lost his right gun-toting arm and the lower part of his left leg, but he was now out of intensive care and expected to recover well in a couple of months. The CIA agent on the hot dog stand suffered severe injuries to his face and chest but he had recently been discharged from hospital. Ironically, Marcie had only suffered severe concussion, shock and a few cuts and bruises. Rolf's body had shielded her from the blast and she was able to be discharged from Harvard after only four days. That was even before her daughter Ruthie, who had been about a hundred yards away from the explosion. Ruthie thanked God that no other person had been killed or injured, although CIA planning also had a big say in the small number of casualties. Ping! Ruthie snapped back to the present as the lift came to a halt.

"Here we are, Jill."

The pair walked along to the reception area and they sat waiting for Jill to be called. Dr Marcie Venters walked out five minutes later and Ruthie introduced her mother to her colleague. Jill was astonished at how little evidence of any injuries showed on Marcie's body. She had attended the scene of the bomb blast at Windsor and had seen the devastation that could be wreaked on a human body. Jehovah obviously had other work still in mind for Dr Marcie Venters.

"Ah'm so sorry for your terrible loss, Dr Venters – but ah can't believe how well that you look after what you've been through."

"I believe that through my dear husband Rolf, God has spared me for my important work, Jill. But he did allow the blast to impair my hearing. My left ear drum was shattered by the noise of the explosion. So when God's clarion call finally comes I may not actually hear it!"

Marcie gave an amused smile at her little joke but Jill paled at the thought.

"Ah can assure you, Dr Venters - we are *all* going to hear His clarion call."

As Marcie waved Jill towards her office she looked at her daughter. They both gave each other a quizzical look and shrugged their shoulders in bemusement. Marcie asked Ruthie to wait outside and she took Jill into her office. As they both sat facing each other Marcie started looking through Jill's notes.

"Jill, of course you know why you are here today? We are going to talk over the results of your 15 week mandatory ultrasound scan and amniocentesis test. Yes?"

Jill nodded and her stomach flipped. Marcie spoke slowly and deliberately.

"Jill, I am afraid the results are not ideal –"

Jill tightened her stomach muscles to stem the rising swell of nausea.

"Just give it to me then, doctor."

Marcie looked unnecessarily down at the notes to give herself a moment to prepare herself. She breathed in deeply and then looked directly into Jill's moistening eyes.

"Jill, the ultrasound shows your baby developing normally in the physical sense, but unfortunately, the amnio shows that your baby has signs of two genetic defects – Downs Syndrome and, ahem, I'm right in saying that the father was of Middle Eastern descent – a Kuwaiti -?"

Jill's heart sank.

"Y-yes."

"You see, Jill, studies have shown there are a very significant number of new genetic defects – syndromes and variants which have been delineated in the Kuwaiti population. Many of these variants are the result of homozygosity for autosomal recessive genes –"

"Homo what for auto what – can you give it to me straight, Doctor?"

"Jill, along with the Downs Syndrome your baby is also suffering from the effects of inbreeding – something that has become increasingly prevalent in Kuwait's close-knit family culture."

Jill felt nauseous again.

"What does this mean?"

Marcie spoke calmly and unblinkingly.

"Jill, I regret to say that my professional advice to you would be for a termination. For your own sake and the baby's sake. Your baby, if born, would have a very poor quality of life indeed. However, the law does not compel you to have an abortion – it is only there to give you an informed choice."

Jill sobbed quietly.

"Doctor, ah have lost the man who was the father of my baby. Ah man that in the end ah did not really know. Now ah stand to lose his baby – my baby - that now ah may never know."

"I am truly sorry, Jill. However, you must take the time to consider all the facts. I will give you some information for you to take away and consider. Ultimately, the final decision will be yours."

Ten days later Jill, believing her world had come to an end, went to a clinic in Harley Street and had the abortion performed privately.

*

Earthdate: 13:00 Thursday April 25, 2081 EST

The three men strolled out calmly and seemingly confident to face the huge barrage of the world's press crammed onto the White House lawn. There was a spontaneous round of loud and excited applause from the crowded media. Josh Trueman placed President Suleiman to his right and UN Secretary General Gupta-Chaudry on his left. Trueman stepped forward to the podium arrayed with microphones.

"Ladies and gentlemen, my fellow Americans and to all peoples of the world – ah am proud to announce that this is truly a momentous day in the history of our planet. A few minutes ago ah was able to sit down with my friends President Suleiman of the LOIN states and Secretary-General Gupta-Chaudry of the UN. Ah am delighted to say that we have today signed the ground-breaking World Peace Accord which effectively consigns the differences between the UN and the LOIN to the dustbin of history."

The White House lawn rippled with another loud round of applause and the incessant flashlights of the myriad of photographers. Trueman egged Suleiman forward onto the podium and the smiling bearded Mullah did not take much encouragement. He spoke crisply and clearly with his Oxford-educated accent.

"Mr President – Secretary-General – I would like to thank you both for extending your cordial invite to me in order that we could fully discuss and alleviate our past differences. I too am delighted that the UN and the LOIN have been able to finally resolve these differences and indeed we have today affixed our seal to the World Peace Accord. I am also truly pleased to announce to you all that by June this year the LOIN states will again be able to take our seats again in New York and to be a worthy part of the world family of the United Nations."

The three men shook each others hands vigorously as the shots were beamed all around the world. They all smiled broadly for the cameras but deep down they all knew in their hearts that the peace of the world that they had just signed would be shattered soon enough. It had been agreed in advance with the press that there would be no questions following the leaders' announcements. However, an eager young cub reporter on her first White House briefing from the Washington Post got carried away with her self and cried out vigorously above the hubbub.

"Mr President – Mr President – do you see this as a lasting peace for the world?"

The noisy media became silent, fully expecting an answer. Trueman thought for a moment. Then he put his conciliatory arms around Suleiman and Gupta-Chaudry and spoke slowly and clearly.

"Ah think that ah can safely say on behalf of the American people and my two good friends here today that this peace will last until the end of days!"

The photos of the three world leaders cordially clinching on the White House steps would be on the lead webpage of every major bloid proclaiming inflated headlines such as *"World Peace to End all War"*. Of course, most editors were putting Trueman's vastly over-optimistic statement down to his lack of Presidential experience. On the other hand, William 'Buck' Buckley of the London Times, watching a televised broadcast while attending a press dinner, knew exactly what Trueman was hinting at. The usually tough hard-hitting editor baulked at the knowledge that he and only a few other people in the world were still keeping secret. He called his wife on his mobile.

"Darling, I just want to say how much that I have always loved you – and I will do so forever."

"Oh, Bill, darling, for goodness sake, have you been drinking too much Scotch. Go back and enjoy your dinner you silly old fool!"

CHAPTER 17

<u>Earthdate: 10:30 Monday September 22, 2081 GMT</u>

Jack watched blankly out of the window as the train pulled away from the beautiful historic Georgian English city of Bath and he was soon zipping through the rolling hills of the Somerset countryside. Jack was attired in the full dress uniform of a NASA Space Commander. He was due to fly up to Alpha Base in four days time and then take the newly commissioned Oceanus II on its maiden voyage to Mars. He had not actually been scheduled to return to Mars until late November with Oceanus. However, Top Brass had requested that he take the Oceanus II trip as he was the best and most experienced Commander in the Fleet. NASA seemed to be churning out production on the huge Oceanus-type transporters - big style. Jack had asked Irene DuPré what the hell was going on. Irene had told him that all she knew was budgetary provision had been found to start expanding the Mars bases as a consequence of collateral damage during the fly-pass of the Schenkler comet. Jack had not pushed it, although he had thought it was all a bit strange. However, his astronaut buddies all seemed to be getting much the same explanation and he thought that if the US Government had decided to start reinvesting in space exploration then it could only auger well for their future careers. Since Jack returned to Earth in late July he had not yet been able to see Peggy Sue or his two sons. When he had arrived back at his Lexington farm Jack found that his two farmhands Paddy Maguire and Ricky Esposito had been left by Peggy Sue to run the business and they had been looking after the farm without any major problems. All that Paddy and Ricky had been told by Peggy Sue was that she was moving with an RAF fighter pilot called Justin to the south of England. Paddy Maguire was apologetic about their lack of information.

"Sorry, boss, but that's all she told us – she jest up an' took off!"

It took Jack a good few weeks digging with the help of a Private Investigator in England to track Peggy Sue and his sons down. He learned that she was living with a guy called Justin Smythe, an English fighter pilot based at RAF

Lyneham in Wiltshire. The PI discovered that they were actually staying in the nearby tiny village of Cucklington in Somerset at Justin's family home at Bainley Lane Farm. Jack had managed to phone a surprised Peggy Sue a couple of days ago and said he was flying over to see his sons and to talk things out with his wife. At first she was reluctant but after saying that Justin was abroad for a few days on a Ministry of Defence sales mission in Saudi Arabia, she agreed that Jack could see the boys at Bainley Lane Farm, but only for a short time.

"But ah've made up my mind, Jack, ah ain't comin' back to ya –"

Jack was determined he was not going to give Peggy Sue Milner up that easily. During the train journey, through the glorious and golden early autumnal rolling landscape of the Somerset Downs, Jack opened his travel bag and felt inside underneath his packed clothing. The gun that he had bought on the black market in Bristol felt cold to touch and he shivered. He asked himself why had he bought it - what did he need it for? He did not really know the answer to that, but he had felt compelled to have a gun with him. The electronic train announcement startled Jack and he quickly zipped up the bag.

"The next stop for this train will be Gillingham. Please remember to take all luggage and belongings with you. Gillingham next stop."

The small market town of Gillingham in Somerset had the closest station to the village of Cucklington and Jack prepared to alight as the train pulled up to a stop at the platform. It was going to be a warm afternoon, he thought, as he stood in the autumn sun on the platform looking around for an air-taxi. A voice attracted Jack's attention.

"Want a taxi, sir?"

Jack nodded politely at the taxi driver with a thick West Country accent and he was guided over to a thirty year old Hyundai hybrid car, which was still in pretty good condition. Jack commented on it as he got in the back seat.

"Very quaint – ya don't see much ah these back in the States –"

"Oh yar, still goes like a dream. Now – where be thee going to, sir?"

Jack asked to be taken to Bainley Lane Farm and the driver, knowing it well, set off in a northerly direction out of Gillingham. The journey took less than ten minutes and Jack quickly found himself standing in front of a quaint little farmhouse with a small, tidy and attractive English garden fronted by a dry stone wall. He entered the gate and rang the front door bell. Momentarily Peggy Sue opened the door and she had obviously been expecting his arrival.

"Hi, Jack, ya better come in."

They both looked grimly at each other and the tension was thick and palpable. Jack looked around the front room of the small low-ceilinged cottage.

"Where are the boys, Peggy Sue?"

"They're still at school, Jack. They won't be home till a half after four."

Jack quickly computed that was still nearly four hours away. There was a pregnant pause and neither quite knew what to say.

"Can I get you some English tea, Jack?"

Jack ignored the question and cut straight to the chase.

"Jeez, Peggy Sue, what in hell happened? What did ah do to drive ya away from me -?"

Her eyes dropped to the floor.

"You didn't do anything. Ah just couldn't take being a Black Widow – the wife of a long-haul astronaut – anymore. I'm sorry, Jack, but ah feel happy and loved again with Justin. Ah never felt that way with you."

Jack quickly grabbed her shoulders, forcing Peggy to make eye contact.

"You're right, Peggy Sue. In some ways this is ma fault. Ah never told ya that ah loved you. But ah was comin' back from Mars to tell ya just that. That ah truly love you, Peggy Sue Milner Crossan!"

Jack moved his head forward to kiss her but she quickly spun out of his grasp.

"No, Jack! It's too late for all that. All these years and now ya try an' tell me ya love me. Ah'm sorry Jack but ah've found happiness here with Justin. He's also a man who isn't away from me for four an' five months of the year. Ah'm a woman with woman's needs an' you weren't there for me!"

Peggy Sue's rising voice shocked Jack. Something told him that maybe he really had lost her love. But now all he could think of was that he was also about to lose his two sons too.

"So that's it then. We're finished, washed up? So, what about ma boys, you takin' them away from me too? Just like I lost Isabella and Xavier?"

Jack felt an unexpected temper begin to rise in him and an old stranger from his past crept into his subconscious. The man in the room with the gun.

"No, Jack, we can arrange visitations. You can see them some when you are back here on 3R. But they like it here and they are staying here with me in England an' ah am prepared to fight you on that one!"

"No way, Peggy Sue! I want ma boys back in Lexington –"

Jack's anger grew and he felt his hand slip into his bag and touch the cold steel. My God, he thought, am I the man in the room with the gun? Peggy Sue taunted Jack.

"Over ma dead body, Jack! Ah have taken legal advice an' with you up on Mars five months at a stretch your chances of keepin' the boys are zip!"

Jack slipped the gun out and pointed it straight at Peggy Sue, whose eyes almost popped out of their sockets with fear.

"For God's sake, Jack, what the hell are you doin'. Have you gone crazy?"

Jack could not speak and a tremor began in his gun hand. The thought kept thumping away in his head. Am I really the man with the gun? Am I really him? Peggy screeched wildly at him with her arm shielding her face from the impending shot.

"JACK!"

Jack stared at her and then at the gun shaking in his hand. Without a word he spun on his heels and he ran out of the farmhouse into Bainley Lane, tears blinding him. Peggy Sue stood transfixed as he ran off. He kept running along the farm lane between tall beech hedges until he came to a large gap in the hedgerow which led into the recently harvested wheat field. He slumped down in a rough furrow leaning against the beech hedge and he stared blindly across the rough stubbly field. The rising sun caught a reflection of something which glinted in his eye. He looked down and saw that he was still clenching the steel gun. My God, he thought, was I really going to kill the woman that I loved. How could I have even thought about doing that? A great wave of loss, helplessness and desperation flooded his senses. Then a terrible thought crossed his mind. Could this be what that boyhood dream had meant all these years ago? Is this what the man with the gun was to come down to in the end? Slowly, inexorably, Jack raised the gun to his temple.

*

Earthdate: 06:00 Monday September 22, 2081 CST

Around the same time as Jack Crossan had set out on the train from Bath to Gillingham over in the south of England, Lex Crossan had just signed himself on for his first shift back at Houston Control after completing his extended sick leave and passing through the mandatory Alcohol Recovery Program. He had been fully exonerated of the murder of his wife Marna by the Houston PD and the DA's office and his Shift Commander Irene DuPré had been incredibly supportive throughout the whole period. While preparing himself for his first shift back in the Men's Locker Room, Lex reflected on the sad loss of his wife Marna and the terrible night that her Uncle Lennart Nilstrom had come to his home at Robindale Drive. It turned out the Dallas PD had flagged up Nilstrom as a possible suspect in Marna's killing on the basis of multiple unproven allegations that had been made against him for sexual offences with underage girls stretching back almost 30 years. What struck the investigating detectives was that in many of the allegations quite a few of the girls stated that the offences were committed in or around Fair Park, Dallas where Marna had apparently been shot dead by Lex. Around about the same time the New Orleans PD had fortuitously arrested the black hooker named Cupola Dome trying to pass off Lex Kosloff's credit card in a bar in the French Quarter. Cupola Dome was taken back to Houston where she started singing like a baby on the basis that she was considered for some leniency. She admitted she had been hired by Lennart Nilstrom to hook up with Lex, to show him a good time for a couple of days. She was to get Lex so drunk and stoned on drugs supplied by Nilstrom that Lex would not know when and where he had been for those lost days spent with the hooker. Cupola stated that Nilstrom told her it was just a prank that he was playing on Kosloff in return for upsetting his beloved niece and that she had no idea that any murder was involved. The detectives up in Dallas had asked Marna's parents Lars and Freda Nilstrom if they would agree to a search of Marna's things at their home, based on new leads arising in the case. Lars and Freda had no objections if it helped find their daughter's killer. The investigators quickly turned up a secret journal which had been kept by Marna since she was around ten years old, which detailed that she was a victim of a campaign of sexual abuse by her Uncle Lennart. Lennart's abuses on Marna had stopped when she reached fifteen. In the journal she had detailed all the various alleged sexual assaults which had taken place in Fair Park, particularly where Lennart Nilstrom was the suspect. She wrote many times that she hoped that maybe this time that her Uncle Lenny would go to prison but her hopes were always dashed. Her last and most recent entry, dated a week before she had left Lex, read:

> *I can't take it anymore. I have made up my mind that I am going to confront Uncle Lenny. If he does not go voluntarily to the cops and confess then I am going to go to them and spill the beans on what he did to me!*

On showing the journal to Marna's shocked parents, Lars and Freda told the Dallas detectives that Lennart Nilstrom had flown up to get some documents and jewellery from Lex Kosloff in Houston. Lars and Freda had been in a state of shock and grief. They were not even thinking of getting these things but Lennart insisted that it should be dealt with sooner rather than later. Dallas PD immediately contacted Houston and fortunately for Lex the Houston boys in blue arrived just in the nick of time. After his arrest and release from hospital Nilstrom confessed that Marna had confronted him and that he had asked her for just a few days grace to think things out before he went to the cops. However, he used those few days to fly up from Dallas to Houston to steal Lex's gun in order to implicate Kosloff. Nilstrom also discovered Kosloff had been on a bender and frequenting the red light district down at Hyde Park and Crocker and Nilstrom sought out a gullible hooker looking for an easy couple of thousand bucks. He found Cupola Dome very amenable to taking his easy money just to get Kosloff smashed out of his face for a couple of days. Nilstrom refused to confess to any of the alleged sexual misdemeanours and stated that Marna had been threatening to blackmail him for abusing her as a girl, which he denied ever doing. He alleged that he had not meant to kill Marna at Fair Park but that she had asked to meet him there where he was to pay her for keeping her mouth shut. He stated that the gun had gone off accidentally during an argument about the agreed amount of money. Nilstrom was charged with first degree murder and he was now awaiting trial in Dallas. Detectives Magruder and Madsen had come to speak to Lex. They told him the whole blackmail deal was a crock of bullshit concocted by Nilstrom to try and lessen his sentence but that Lex would still have to listen to it all come out at the trial.

Lex's recovery from the alcohol and grief was a long and tortuous road, but with each passing week he felt himself getting stronger and stronger within himself. During his recovery Lex came to know who his real friends were, including his boss Irene DuPré. Lars and Freda Nilstrom flew up from Dallas to say how sorry that they were that they could have ever thought that Lex would murder their daughter. They told him that he would always be welcome at their home in Dallas. Jimmy Soderline came by a few times and kept Lex updated with all the office politics and goings on at Houston Control and Jimmy let Lex know that the old place was Dullsville without him. Jack Crossan also came down one time from his farm in Lexington while he was on leave after getting back from Mars. Jack hinted to Lex that he was having his own problems with Peggy Sue and that she had run off with some English flyboy. Irene DuPré had to visit him regularly on official appraisals, usually with one of the HR guys, to check on his progress.

However, sometimes she popped round to Robindale Drive unofficially to bolster Lex's confidence and gradually Lex saw a friendship developing between them. It turned out that Irene had been a recovering alcoholic herself and that she had started to see the signs in Lex too. She had planned to offer him as much help as she could muster when they were supposed to meet for Lex's regular performance appraisal, but, of course, Marna's murder changed everything. When Lex's doctor signed him clear to return to work he became a little anxious, but it was Irene who convinced him he was ready to go for it. Lex sighed deeply and pushed himself off the changing bench in the locker room and headed towards the Control Room. It was now time for a fresh start, Lex thought, as he walked along the corridor. As he marched briskly along the brightly lit glass panelled corridor a familiar smiling face beamed back at him with his arms open wide.

"Well look what the cat dragged in – if it ain't ma big bro'!"

"Soderline! God, you don't know how good it is to see a friendly face."

Lex hugged Jimmy Soderline and tears welled up in the two men's eyes. They quickly shared pleasantries but it soon became clear that Jimmy was a messenger.

"Lex, a message from Irene. She needs a quick word before you go on station. Nothing for you to worry about she said, but sounds pretty damn urgent. On you go in then, ah gotta go pee!"

"Uh, Jimmy, you coulda given me better news than that –"

Jimmy shouted back as he sprinted towards the men's restroom.

"Don't shoot the messenger!"

Lex left Jimmy and headed straight to Irene's station overlooking the main Houston Control Room. Irene ushered him to sit down beside her and she gave him the briefest friendly wink. It signalled to Lex that Irene was acknowledging their growing friendship but in here at Houston Control she was still boss and it was business only.

"Lex, you don't know how good it is to have ma best controller back on the panels."

"Gee, thanks, Irene, it's good to be back – I think. Ya wanted to have a word before ah went on shift?"

Irene leaned forward towards Lex and lowered her voice in an almost conspiratorial manner. She was almost whispering.

"Lex, ah need a favour from ya. We've been trying to contact Jack Crossan as a matter of national importance but we've been unable to reach him. Ah know that you and Jack have been friends for years -"

Lex nodded.

"Pretty good friends, although we don't see each other much, what with Jack up on Mars most ah the time. However, he did come to visit me down in Robindale about three weeks ago. See how ah was doin', ya know?"

"Well, Lex, the thing is this, Jack's not actually due to be back on duty for another two days. He's due to launch for Alpha in four to take the new Oceanus II on its maiden voyage to the Big Red. But Brass have asked me to get him back right away. Apparently the White House want to see him – Trueman himself!"

Lex's eyebrows arched up and his face showed surprise, but also that he was impressed.

"Wow, Irene! The President wants to see Jack? Maybe he just wants to pin another medal on the big guy's chest?"

Irene's brows furrowed deeply.

"No, it's not that. There's something big brewin' Lex. Ah don't rightly know what yet, but Brass are running round with real tight asses at the moment. We've had Aaron Eckler and Beth O'Donnell crawling all over us for the past two weeks, making sure that Control's running smoothly, do we need any new investment and all that kinda stuff – "

"Eckler and O'Donnell – ah thought they were involved with the Nimrod SH2 program?"

Irene shrugged her shoulders.

"They are - but at the moment they have been given carte blanche to look across the whole organisation. They've also pulled some Israeli astrophysicist over from INSACC and two young hot-shot Scottish kids onto their team. While you have been away the NASA production budget passed through Congress has gone through the roof. The build budget on the Oceanus program makes the old Apollo program look like peanuts in comparison. Contracts have been let out here in the States, but also in Russia, China, Japan, Europe and India. You name it, Lex, everyone is getting' a slice of the pie. Christ, even the Israelis and Iranians have got involved in a joint construction partnership contract. Ah ain't never seen anythin' like it!"

Lex looked at Irene in confusion.

"An' you think that's why the President wants to see Jack?"

"Probably. Aw, Christ, ah don't know. All I know is that Eckler has been crawling up ma ass constantly for the past coupla days askin' why the hell Jack ain't in DC yet! Thing is - we just can't get in touch with him."

"He's in England, Irene. Jack told me he was goin' over to try and patch things up with Peggy Sue. He probably didn't take his NASA cell with him."

"Aw, Jeezus, that's all ah need!"

"He's probably got his personal cell with him. Ah know he doesn't give that number out much, but ah've got it on mine."

Irene leaned even closer to Lex and beamed a huge smile with relief written all over her face.

"Lex Kosloff, ah could jest kiss ya! Can you get down on your station an' see if ya can get Jack to report directly to the White House Chief of Staff. A-S-A-P!"

A few minutes later Lex had set himself up on his controller's station and after checking all his systems were operative he took out his cell phone and called Jack Crossan's personal number. However, it just kept on ringing out and it did not even go to voicemail. Lex swivelled around on his chair and looked up at Irene. He shrugged to let her know that he was getting no joy. Lex saw a look of panic cross Irene's face. He swivelled back to his panel and just as he was about to hang up the cell clicked.

"H-hello?"

It was Jack. He sounded cautious and his voice sort of echoed tinnily.

"Jack, thank God it's you. It's Lex Kosloff here!"

Lex stretched his free arm back towards Irene and signalled a thumbs up. He thought he might actually have heard a muted squeal of delight coming down from Irene's station.

"Lex? Is everythin' okay buddy?"

"Everythin's cool, Jack. Ah'm back at work on station just in the last few minutes and Irene DuPré had me call you ASAP. Brass has been trying to get a hold of you in the last coupla days – apparently the President wants to see you?"

"Trueman? You gotta be kiddin' Lex? God, ah'm still here in England tryin' to sort ma life out!"

"Well, you better get your ass on the first flight to Washington or your life won't be worth livin' Jack."

There was a moment's silence then Lex heard Jack laughing loudly but again with that tinny echoing sound.

"Jack, what in hell's name's funny?"

"Irony, Lex, pure irony. Ah'll maybe tell ya about it one day. Look, email me the details about DC an' ah'll get outta here and get back Stateside as fast as ah can."

"Roger that Jack. Mind me askin' Jack, but ya sound kinda funny. Where in hell exactly are ya?"

Jack laughed again.

"Lex, believe it or not, but ah am in a little ole empty church!"

Jack flipped his cell off and stuck it back in his pocket. He had literally just entered the church a few seconds before Lex rang. Twenty or so minutes before, as he sat in the stubbled field with the black market gun at his head, something inside screamed at him not to pull that trigger. Somehow he felt that it was just not his time to go. He got up and walked back towards the village and Bainley Lane Farm. Before he reached the farm he noticed the little church up the rise to his right and he felt drawn towards it. He walked up to the large board in front proclaiming that it was Cucklington Parish Church of England and continued up the stone-flagged path. The vicar and his wife were hoeing weeds as Jack walked past and they both looked agog at the uniformed American astronaut as he strolled past, still unconsciously carrying the gun in his hand. Now Jack was standing in the entrance way of the little old and musty smelling church with its rows of cracked wooden pews and ancient Bibles mulling over what Lex had just told him. He happened to cast his eyes up on to the wall of the church facing the doors that he had just entered. Jack looked at a large carved marble plaque on the wall which read:

SAMUEL CROSSAN

2ⁿᵈ BATTALION ROYAL REGIMENT OF SCOTLAND

AGE 26

KILLED IN ACTION

NAD E-ALI, 2ⁿᵈ AFGHAN CONFLICT

25 FEBRUARY 2031

DULCE ET DECORUM EST PRO PATRIA MORI

A wry smile cracked Jack's lips and he thought again, irony, Lex, pure irony. That was one poor Crossan who did not make it through that terrible day, but Jack decided that he was another one who was going to make it through on this particular day. He spun around on his heels and headed out the church doors and down the stone path. Half way down the path the vicar stood motionless leaning on his hoeing tool with his wife half-cowering behind him. Jack stopped at the couple with their jaws dropping. He unclipped the magazine from the gun and handed the gun and clip to the vicar.

"Parson, could you lose that thing for me? Where ah'm goin' ah won't be needing it!"

CHAPTER 18

Space Commander Jack Crossan was shown into the Oval Office and after being personally greeted and introduced by President Josh Trueman, a select band of attendees all introduced themselves too. To Jack's amazement the meeting comprised of various world leaders, including some of whom Jack could never have envisaged in the same room together. In the centre at the Oval Office desk sat President Josh Trueman flanked by British Prime Minister John Ralston representing the European Union, UN Secretary-General Ravinder Gupta-Chaudry, Israeli Prime Minister Moshi Shalomon and sitting next to Shalomon was the Secretary-General of the LOIN, Mullah Abdullah Suleiman. Facing the President on the other side of the desk in a semi-circle sat Aaron Eckler, Beth O'Donnell, Ari Schenkler, Ewan Sinclair, Gary Mackintosh and lastly Jack too. Trueman quickly called the meeting to order.

"Okay, guys, apart from Commander Crossan here, ya all know why this top secret meeting has been called - right?"

Everyone apart from Jack nodded assent. Jack quickly realised that this meeting was more than just a commendation and bon voyage from the President on the upcoming maiden voyage of the Oceanus II in a few days' time and there was more to this meeting than he had envisaged. Trueman continued.

"Jack, in two days you're a passenger on the Jupiter Galaxy V shuttle up to Alpha Base, is that correct?"

"Yes sir, Mister President."

Trueman hated the formality of being called Mister President but with all the great and the good surrounding him he could not tell Jack just to call him Josh.

"And, uh, a week later you launch the new Oceanus II on its maiden voyage to Mars?"

"Yes sir, she'll be carrying the regular supplies and the changeover teams for the MGals, Mars bases, ice miners, that kinda thing –"

President Trueman cut in.

"Ah here those ice miners can be a real handful, Jack?"

"They can be, sir, what with a 15 week trip in a tin can with nothing much to do. Ice miners tend to drink a lot on these voyages. To dull the senses, so to speak. Although, one thing they never put in their drinks is ice – just waters down their booze an' they don't like that!"

Everyone had a good laugh at Jack's reply, which lightened the heavy atmosphere in the room. Jack thought, maybe you could call that an ice-breaker. Trueman started to get down to the nitty-gritty.

"Well, Jack, the thing is this - the ice-miners and regular stuff won't be going with you on the Oceanus II. They have been shifted back and will be going out three weeks later on the Oceanus I."

Forgetting where he was, Jack interrupted the President.

"Oceanus I? Ah thought she was at Delta Base for a refit -?"

Trueman wagged a finger at Aaron Eckler to explain, who promptly obliged.

"Commander Crossan, you probably are aware that a lot of new projects have been progressing even before you arrived back from your last Mars trip. As part of the new-build budget approved jointly by Congress / UN / LOIN for a fleet of new Oceanus space-liners, we were able to set aside some money to fast track the refit on Oceanus I. We need her back operational ASAP to do the regular Mars run. Admittedly, a three week delay on the schedule is going to piss off a lot of staff – and ice-miners – on Mars waiting to get home."

Jack looked puzzled.

"So am ah taking the Oceanus II out empty? Ah thought she had done all her proving trials?"

Eckler got Trueman's nod to continue.

"That is correct. Oh Two has passed all her space trials and she is the most advanced spacecraft ever built by humankind. On top of that Ari and Ewan's calculations show that the solar winds, plus the 3R / Mars alignment, projects a less than 14 week trip for you and your special cargo, Jack. That's why the regular shipment has been put back by three weeks."

"Ah'm takin' some sorta special cargo?"

Trueman indicated to Eckler that he would take over the explanation.

"Jack, before we detail what you are carrying to Mars, which is of the utmost importance, ah need to tell ya somethin' truly awful, which only the people sittin' in this room are privileged to. Oh and just a handful of others around the world who are sworn to absolute secrecy. At some point we are going to have to divulge this info, but now is not yet the right time as we are still at the forward plannin' stage. Therefore, we need to know that you can keep this knowledge under your hat until such time when we can reasonably announce this to the world at large. Can you, Jack?"

"Ah guess so. Yes sir!"

Jack tried to sound confident but he shifted nervously in his seat. Trueman looked around at Ralston, Gupta-Chaudry, Shalomon and Suleiman and they all nodded for the President to continue.

"Jack, you already know that we have announced that this Schenkler HMM2 comet thing – incidentally named after Ari here – is on a near-miss collision with Earth an' that the tail of this thing is going to cause quite a bit of collateral damage?"

"Ah did hear, sir, that we might be shiftin' some vital equipment to Mars to avoid possible damage –"

"Yes, Jack, we did sorta put out that story. But that is not it. You see, Jack, the comet is not goin' to be a near-miss after all. It is goin' to hit Earth!"

"Jee - zus – sorry, Mister President! It's goin' to hit 3R – what sort of damage are we talkin' about?"

"Mr Sinclair – can you explain please?"

Ewan gulped nervously. Never in his wildest dreams did he ever envisage that he would have to explain his theories in front of the most powerful men in the world.

"W-well, Jack, ah, Commander Crossan, you see at this very moment the Schenkler comet is not actually on a direct collision course with Earth and if it remained on its current trajectory through the solar system it would indeed fly by and miss us by a whisker and we would only suffer collateral damage from tail debris. However, when the comet passes Jupiter in almost exactly a year from now, our predictions show the pull of the gas giant's gravitational force will ever so slightly adjust the comet's path and put it on a direct collision course with our planet. Would you concur, Ari?"

"Absolutely, we have gone over these calculations a million times and we are 99.9 per cent certain – we will be 100 per cent certain after the Jupiter pass."

There was a slight impasse in the meeting as all this started to sink into Jack's brain. It was Crossan who spoke first.

"So, what kinda damage are we lookin' at? Billions dead, nuclear winter, what?"

It was Aaron Eckler who replied.

"Jack, have you ever seen a dum-dum bullet hit a watermelon?"

Jack gulped visibly and his mouth went dry. All he could think of at that moment was Peggy Sue, his boys Milner and Jack Junior and his dad Andy. He did not even nod or reply. Trueman came in with almost a soft whisper.

"It is total, Jack – oblivion! After May 2084 there will be no Earth. But that has to stay between us all until the Jupiter pass to give us time to plan an evacuation to Mars. By that time even amateur astronomers will have worked out we are going to be totalled!"

Jack nodded dumbly and he tried to suppress the rising bile in his throat. He wanted to run out of the Oval Office, run to his family, but he knew that he was called here to carry out a mission for his country, for his world and he shook himself back into the here and now.

"S-so where do ah come in, Mister President?"

Trueman indicated to Beth O'Donnell to carry on with the details.

"Your cargo on the Oh Two will be made up of three main component projects, Jack, with the variously trained specialist staff for each individual project. The first project involves the installation and eventual deployment of newly designed interspacial ballistic missiles with the most powerful nuclear warheads ever devised –"

Mullah Abdullah Suleiman interjected with a pleased smile on his face.

"We came up with that – or should I say it was a joint Iranian / Israeli venture. Apologies for my intrusion, Mister President, please carry on Miss O'Donnell."

"The plan is to deploy the nukes from the Martian space stations when Schenkler – sorry Ari – when the Schenkler comet comes at its closest point to Mars."

Jack look puzzled.

"So we can destroy this thing – or shift its trajectory?"

Ewan Sinclair answered.

"This astral body is just over one and a half times the size of Pluto, Jack. It will be like hitting it with a peashooter!"

"Jeezus – sorry again Mister President – but what the hell is the point?"

Trueman indicated for Beth O'Donnel to continue with the explanation.

"Carry on, Beth."

"The point is that we need to give the world some sort of hope, Jack. After the Jupiter pass we have to announce to the world that we are facing oblivion. We have to announce that we are trying the nuclear strike from Mars to give us breathing space, to, uh, to –"

Trueman finished Beth's trailing sentence.

"To try and stop the breakdown of world order, Jack. By the time the nuclear strike fails and the comet passes Mars then anybody who ain't on the Big Red or well on his way there won't be going anywhere but to meet his Maker!"

Beth got the okay to continue her presentation.

"The second project is the first delivery of materiel and construction workers to begin the expansion of the super-glass pods which will hold all the new immigrants, livestock and crop production plants. Based on the small-scale tests of cattle and crops already on Mars we believe that we can successfully expand on those tests to provide a reasonably reliable food source to meet the needs of the immigration program. Pod materiel will continue to be transported from 3R for as long as deemed possible – probably until late into 2083."

Jack was trying to do impossible sums in his head. All he could think of was that Oceanus I could only carry a maximum of 350 passengers per trip and he tried to fit seven and a half billion humans into his computations. His head was spinning.

"How many immigrants are we talking about?"

"Realistically, twenty five thousand tops."

Trueman interrupted, raising his voice somewhat and making all heads turn towards him.

"Whoa there just a minute! Twenty five thousand? Eckler – when you briefed us before you estimated we were talkin' between forty five an' fifty thousand?"

Eckler and O'Donnell looked at each other, then down at their notes and Eckler spoke.

"S-sorry, Mister President, but once we reviewed all the factors, the timescales, the construction project and the limitations put on us by the amount of livestock and crop seed that we could realistically shift, w-we had to review the numbers down. We are not even a 100 per cent sure we can even hit twenty five –"

Trueman thumped the Oval Office desk hard.

"Aw, Jesus Christ, this whole fuckin' thing just gets worse every time ah hear about it!"

The meeting collapsed in on itself as each started murmuring with their neighbour about the implications of the drop in numbers and how it might affect their own backyard. Trueman thumped the desk again to bring everyone back to order.

"Okay! Okay, let's say twenty five thou tops. We might have to live with that. But Eckler – I want you and O'Donnell to look again at those numbers and if there is any way of getting them up – then find it! Right, Beth, let's start wrappin' this up for Jack – and no more surprises –"

"Yes, Mister President. Okay Jack, the third and final project to be delivered by Oh Two relates to the E2MSN. This is where Gary Mackintosh comes in and I'll let Gary explain. Gary?"

Gary thought along similar lines to Ewan's nervous thoughts earlier in the meeting but he swallowed hard and threw himself into his spiel.

"The problem we face Commander Crossan is that if and when our wee planet is destroyed we effectively lose overall control of the Earth to Mars Satellite Network. Ah have been workin' with the team in Houston to develop new supercomputer equipment to transfer the control of the E2MSN from Earth over to Martian control. If we lost computer control on Mars after Earth is destroyed then mankind would be thrown back into the dark ages. You will be transporting the equipment and computer boffins who are goin' to set up the transitional transfer of the network over to Big Red control. The NASA guys have given it just the worst possible acronym – NOAHSARK!"

Someone mumbled Noah's Ark as a question and Gary continued with an explanation.

"NOAHSARK – Network of all Human Specific Archives Records and Knowledge. Basically, once the network is fully functional on Mars we intend to digitally transfer just about anything that we humans have learned, written down or spoken about in the last one million years. The feelin' is that our continued survival depends on retaining all our combined knowledge. The bottom line is that we are the only living organism on this planet that knows we are getting' blown to Kingdom Come. Using all that knowledge might teach our Martian survivors that one day they will also have to move on out of the solar system to ensure the survival of the human race."

That sobering thought made everyone pause for horrified reflection. Beth broke the silence.

"That's it in a nutshell, Jack – Mister President?"

Trueman began winding up the meeting.

"Well, Jack, you look as terrified as the rest of us feel. Are you prepared to take the Oceanus II on its maiden voyage now knowin' what we all know an' keep it under wraps?"

"You gonna shoot me if ah don't, Mister President?"

Everyone in the room burst out laughing with relief from the tension. Jack nodded his assent.

"Sure, ah'll take the Big Baby to Mars for ya, sir."

*

Earthdate: 20:30 Wednesday September 24, 2081 EST

That same evening, following the debriefing meeting with Jack Crossan in the Oval Office, Ewan and Gary caught an air-taxi out to Washington Dulles Airport. As the Scots pair stood in the arrivals lounge for the incoming Virgin Galactic supersonic from London Heathrow, Gary noticed Ewan was on edge.

"Ye look a wee bit nervous, Ewan?"

"I'm just looking forward to seeing her. She's been through a lot this year and I'm just hoping she'll be happy to see me – eh, I mean us, Gary –"

Gary slipped his arm around Ewan's shoulder and hugged him tightly.

"Och, stop worryin' yerself silly, Sinclair. Tell ye what? If she does na want ye, then ye know ye can always have me – free gratis!"

Ewan laughed half-heartedly.

"Gaz, you know I love you, mate. But just not like that."

Gary felt a small pang of unrequited love shoot through his heart. Then they spotted that the arrival passengers had started to file out past the US Customs declaration areas and there, looking thoroughly professional and, at least to Ewan, drop-dead gorgeous was Jill Geeson. Ewan blurted out.

"JILL!"

She waved excitedly and the three school friends threw themselves into each other's arms and hugged and cried. Gary brought them all back down to Earth.

"Right, you two. Stop yer blubberin' an' let's get an air-taxi to the hotel. We've booked intae the nearby Candlewood Suites for the night an' then we fly down to Houston tomorrow afternoon. We've got two rooms – an' dinnae worry Jill – Ewan and me are sleepin' together tonight!"

Jill pushed Gary teasingly on the chest.

"Och, Gary Mackintosh, you've not changed a bit this side of the Pond!"

After settling in to their rooms at the Candlewood Suites Dulles the three Scots all met down in the bar for a quick couple of night caps before retiring for the evening. Jill went into detail on her exciting new post. Her role at the London Times had effectively been scaled back by Bill Buckley. She was now to become their Houston-based correspondent dealing directly with all the emerging and reportable issues relative to the Schenkler HMM2 comet. This meant that Jill had to provide two columns per week on any new developments to the Times bloid and for that she still reported to Buckley. Jill told Ewan and Gary that Ruthie Venters had been promoted to Jill's old job as Investigative Reporter. Ruthie was now such a deep friend to her and Jill said how much Ruthie had supported her through and after the abortion. In fact, they had supported each other as Ruthie also needed a shoulder to cry on after witnessing the terrible death of her father Rolf at the Harvard Medical Center bombing. However, the exciting part of Jill's new role was as the newly created post of Houston Correspondent for Sky News, part of News Corps International, as was the London Times. It had always been Jill's ambition to become a specialist correspondent on television. Ewan and Gary told Jill about their meeting at the Oval Office, although, of course, they did not divulge any details on the top secret aspects of the meeting. They did give Jill a heads up on Jack Crossan taking the new Oceanus II on its maiden voyage and Jill agreed that she could do an interesting feature on that development. Ewan and Gary also agreed to introduce Jill to their bosses Aaron Eckler and Beth O'Donnell. They assured Jill that if anything on Schenkler was going to be released through official channels then she would hear it first through Eckler or O'Donnell. Jill asked them all about Houston where amazingly the three friends were all now going to be working.

"So, Ewan, you said that you've found a place for us all to stay in Houston?"

"We have, Jill. For the first three or four months when Gary and I started on our respective projects we stayed in hotels. By that time we were both bouncing off the walls and Beth O'Donnell suggested one of the Houston Controllers was looking to take in boarders. It's a great place in the south-west suburb of Robindale with a big room for Gary and me and a separate one for you. And it has a swimming pool too."

"Wow, sounds great!"

"There is only one small problem, Jill –"

"What's that?"

"Well, the guy – he's a nice guy – name's Lex Kosloff – well, he's a recovering alcoholic. Lost his wife recently, nearly lost his job too. So that means no drink allowed in his home."

"Ah think we can all cope with that, eh boys?"

Gary threw in his usual joke.

"Speak for yersel', Jill. Ah like a wee drink now and then. Ach, it is no' too bad. There's a wee Irish bar just two blocks down. You'll like it as it's very apt for you. It's called the Craic Pot!"

"Ha, ha! Very funny Gary Mackintosh."

Gary felt it was time to skip out and leave Ewan and Jill and let them have a quiet moment together.

"We-ell, guys, ah'm knackered. If you two guys don't mind ah think ah'll call it a day."

After Gary went upstairs to the room that he and Ewan were sharing, Jill and Ewan nervously sipped their drinks, neither knowing what to say. Ewan broke the ice.

"God, Jill, you don't know how good it was to see you arrive tonight. You look so beautiful –"

"Ewan, ah was so happy to see you too. Ah really need your friendship –"

"Friendship – and hopefully – something more? Jill, I still have strong feelings for you."

"Ah know you do, Ewan. Ah don't think you ever lost them. But ah need to ask you to take it slow. My own feelings about Khan and the baby are still all over the place. Ah'm still carrying a lot of hurt and rejection in my heart and ah need time to heal."

Ewan took Jill's hand gently in his. His eyes told Jill that he would give her all the time she needed and that he would be there for her when she felt ready.

CHAPTER 19

The big yellow New York air-taxi arrived in front of the United Nations HQ building on FDR Drive. Marcie Venters paid the driver and made her way quickly into the main building in good time for her scheduled 10.30am meeting. A good deal of progress had been made on the Super-storage of Human Procreative DNA programme and most of the planned medical centres were now fully operational, including an additional centre in Tehran as agreed and sponsored by Mullah Abdullah Suleiman.

Marcie thought back to the official opening ceremony in Tehran only three months ago, which she had attended as Programme Director of the super-storage roll-out, and Suleiman had been invited along to cut the ceremonial ribbon. Suleiman had also arranged a private meeting at the Presidential Palace between himself and Marcie two hours before the opening ceremony. Marcie was very apprehensive as she was led into the Mullah's opulently decorated private office. Suleiman was extremely courteous and magnanimous in his reception.

"Doctor Venters, please accept my most humble greetings and to express how gratified that you have been so kind in coming to meet with me. I realise that meeting here must be very difficult for you?"

Marcie swallowed hard, but spoke slowly and with conviction.

"Your Excellency, you of all people will fully appreciate that the long painful history of the Jewish race – and, of course, the Arab race – has taught us that we must face adversity without hatred and that final judgment will be left in the hand of our shared and one true God – Jehovah and Allah. In my heart I grieve daily for my beloved Rolf, but truly I blame no man for his untimely death. I certainly hold no grudge against you personally, Your Excellency."

"I would be pleased if you would call me Abdullah – at least in private? May I call you Marcie?"

"Of course, Your Ex– I mean, Abdullah."

"Marcie, please accept my deepest and most humble apologies. If I could turn back time and do more than I did to stop the dreadful and unnecessary bombing in Harvard, which I erroneously sanctioned, I promise you I would do so. I can only hope that Allah will forgive this old Mullah for a sin that deeply burdens my soul."

"I believe in destiny, Abdullah, and with Rolf dying and me surviving, it was fated to happen. Our true destiny – God has written in the stars for us."

Marcie was puzzled by Suleiman's response, which he did not elaborate on as he shook his head slowly and Marcie thought that he looked a little teary-eyed.

"Marcie, more than you know – more than you know."

Marcie had brought a full and detailed report to the UN HQ for the senior members of the World Health Organisation and she was sure that they would be very impressed with her programme's progress. Marcie presented herself at reception.

"Dr Marcie Venters to meet the board members of the WHO at 10:30."

The receptionist searched for the meeting on her computer and looked puzzled. She looked up at Marcie.

"Sorry, Dr Venters, did you say WHO?"

Marcie fumbled with her mobile phone to try and call up her diary.

"Yes, the WHO. Don't tell me that I've got the wrong day?"

"No, it's not that at all. But I've got you down for a 10:30 with the Secretary General."

"The Secretary General! There must be some mistake?"

The receptionist made an internal call to double check the meeting. As she spoke she waved over a UN security guard.

"No mistake, Dr Venters. Karl could you please take Dr Venters up to the Sec-Gen's conference room. She is expected. Doctor if you follow Karl he will take you up to your meeting."

Marcie blindly followed the security guard named Karl and he took her up on the private lift to the top floor of the UN building. As they stepped out into the corridor the glass windows afforded them a great view out over Brooklyn, where Marcie was born. However, Marcie was in too much of a daze to admire the view over the Hudson. Her mind was racing too much trying to think why the meeting plan might have changed. Maybe Gupta-Chaudry was interested in hearing her report and he was chairing the meeting with the WHO Board? Yes, that must be it, she thought.

"Here ya are, Doctor Venters."

Karl ushered Marcie into the conference room. Marcie looked around the table scanning for any WHO faces that she might recognise. There were none. Some of the faces she did recognise - but mainly from their TV appearances, because she had never met any of them bar one before in a personal or professional capacity. Secretary-General Ravinder Gupta-Chaudry ushered Marcie towards an empty seat.

"Dr Venters. Thank you for joining us today for this meeting. First of all may I apologise most profusely for bringing you to New York on the expectation that you were going to provide your update report to the board of the World Health Organisation."

"Well, Mr Secretary General, to say that I'm confused would be an understatement."

"I'm afraid Doctor that you had to be brought here with a measure of subterfuge on the basis that this meeting had to be kept secret. But, please, Dr Venters let me introduce you to the other attendees."

As Gupta-Chaudry introduced the others around the table Marcie tried desperately to work out why she needed to be at some secret meeting in the UN HQ building. Then the thought occurred to her that maybe the authorities had uncovered some new bombing plot against her super-storage programme by another extremist cell. Quickly she scribbled the names of the attendees as the Secretary-General spoke. The ones she knew from TV were John Ralston and Moshi Shalomon and, of course, Mullah Abdullah Suleiman, who she had met recently. The others all from NASA were introduced as Aaron Eckler, Beth O'Donnell, Ari Schenkler, Ewan Sinclair and Gary Mackintosh, none of whom Marcie knew. She looked down at the word 'NASA' that she had written on her notepad and thought, why NASA?

"I also extend apologies from President Josh Trueman who would have been here but he is otherwise engaged in Washington."

"P-President Trueman is apologising to m-me?"

Gupta-Chaudry smiled at Marcie's incredulous façade before calling the meeting to order.

"Dr Venters, you have been summoned here today in relation to your innovative work on human DNA and human procreation. However, before we get to that part we need to fill you in on a few blanks and it was for that reason that this meeting was convened in secret. However, very soon the secretive nature of this meeting will be quickly superseded by events."

"I am sorry, Mr Secretary-General, but I am completely in the dark here."

"Again I apologise most sincerely, Dr Venters. I am going to hand you over to the NASA team to give you the background details. Aaron?"

Eckler introduced himself but quickly handed the presentation into Ari and Ewan's hands. Ari started.

"Dr Venters, have you been watching on the news about the new comet Schenkler HMM2?"

"Hmm, only a little. I have been so tied up with my super-storage programme that I don't have much time for TV. I believe it is due to come close by Earth in a couple of years' time. Is that correct?"

"Certainly that is what has been reported, Doctor. The comet was first discovered entering our solar system by my colleague Ewan Sinclair here, however, I was the first person to inadvertently catch it on film, so somehow the name Schenkler got appended, of which I am not that particularly proud of. The HMM2 part came from the fact that the INSACC in Israel and NASA in Houston had separately given it acronyms. Dr Venters, I believe that you are Jewish like myself?"

"Yes, I'm Jewish."

"Well the HMM2 is a sort of Jewish / Christian conglomeration. HM is Har Meggido and M2 stands for Messiah 2."

Marcie's eyes widened based on an unknown fear rising within her.

"A-Armageddon!"

"If I explain further we will get to that. Ewan and I have been monitoring the progress of the comet practically on a minute by minute basis as it orbits around the Sun. A key point in its trajectory took place in the last few days as it passed within a 100 million miles of Jupiter and it was our calculation that it would be influenced by Jupiter's enormous gravitational pull. The trajectory of the comet would only be altered slightly, but that slight adjustment put it on a direct collision course with Earth. The comet is of a magnitude that when it impacts in about a year and a half, Earth will be totally destroyed. Doctor, after May 2084 there will be no Earth."

Marcie stared wildly around the table, her hand nervously rubbing at her mouth and chin. She was close to tears as she spoke.

"My God, this is terrible, awful. In God's name, why were we not told about this?"

Aaron Eckler answered.

"The scientists needed to be 100 per cent sure about this, Dr Venters. If we had told the world this awful thing and chaos and anarchy ensued. Had we found out we were wrong the consequences would have been unimaginable.

Unfortunately Ari and Ewan confirmed their findings in the last two days and we are now 100 per cent sure of a total impact. Is that correct guys?"

"100 per cent."

"Totally."

Marcie remained perplexed and rubbed her head agitatedly in her hand.

"But why bring me here to tell me this? I thought that I was coming to report my work to the WHO. But now it appears that all my work will be destroyed in what – Ari said a year and a half?"

John Ralston, the British Prime Minister, spoke for the first time.

"Dr Venters, unbeknown to you I have been to see some of your ground-breaking work at St Bart's and also at Harvard. I have been extremely impressed by what I saw. The point of you being here is that our hope is that not all of your work *will* be destroyed. Please allow Beth O'Donnell to explain."

Beth looked down at her notes and then addressed Marcie.

"Dr Venters, since NASA first became aware of the Schenkler comet we have been planning for all contingencies concerning the survival of the human race –"

Marcie blurted out in confusion.

"Survival! But I thought we were talking about the total destruction of Earth -?"

Gupta-Chaudry raised his hand gently.

"We are indeed, Dr Venters. But please allow Beth to explain our plans in some detail."

Beth carried on speaking.

"As I stated, Doctor, NASA has been planning for all contingencies regarding the survival of the human race. The key plank of our plan is the mass transportation of as many humans, livestock and food crops as humanly possible to new bases being constructed on Mars as we speak. However, as you are probably aware, Doctor, Mars is an extremely hostile environment and our best outside estimate is for the emigration of only twenty five thousand men and women at best to Mars. We don't even know for sure what the long-term survivability probability of those twenty five thousand souls on Mars will be. History tells us that human colonisation in hostile environments even here on Earth have ended disastrously –"

Gary Mackintosh interjected light-heartedly.

"We Scots'll vouch for that! The Darien Project was a tragedy for Scotland. Worst of all - we ended up having to join with England!"

Beth smiled politely and continued.

"Indeed, Gary, therefore, we need a supplementary plan to back up the colonisation of Mars. Simply put, we need you to come up with a plan for the transportation of as much human DNA, in terms of, male sperm, female eggs and human embryos as we can possibly ship to Mars to a single super-storage fertility unit to be constructed there. Obviously, the hope is that the twenty five thousand will procreate and increase in population naturally on Mars, but if there is a catastrophic failure then we need the backup of the fertility unit to increase the chances of survival."

Beth paused to let this sink in with Marcie. During the impasse Gupta-Chaudry took the lead.

"Doctor Venters, I realise that this is terribly difficult for you to comprehend. I can assure you that each and every one of us around this table finds that trying to make sense of all this is mind-boggling and *we* have been working on this for many months now. Knowledge over time does not make it any easier to deal with it. However, for the survival of our species, deal with it we must. Doctor, on that basis, are you willing to head up the planning side for the selection and transportation of fertile human DNA components to be shipped to Mars."

Marcie wrestled with her conscience and her gaze rested with Suleiman, who proffered her a kindly nod. Her thoughts returned to her recent meeting with the Mullah, where she had told him: Our true Destiny – God has written in the stars for us. She remembered Suleiman's reply, 'more than you know – more than you know'. She now knew that he had known at that time what Marcie and the world's destiny was to be.

"Mister Secretary-General, it is indeed mind-boggling. However, I have to believe that God spared my life at Harvard in order to take on this onerous task. I can say nothing else, but that I will do what is asked of me."

Beth O'Donnell spoke next.

"Doctor, we thank you for your co-operation with this awful mission. There are two further components to the planning process that we would require you to lead –"

"Two more components?"

"Yes, Doctor. Firstly, and on a much smaller scale and where scientifically viable, we also want to collect, select and transport as much frozen non-human DNA from flora and fauna to Mars in order that they may be procreated at some point in the future –"

"But, Miss O'Donnell, my specialisation is in human DNA, this is not my field of science?"

"We realise that, Doctor Venters, however, you are the recognised world expert in super-storage techniques and processes. We will put you in touch with all the leading genetic experts in the field of flora and fauna and all we ask is that you lead this team from the point of view that you are the lead expert and also that human DNA takes precedent when it comes down to limited resources as it is bound to do."

"Well, it is a big ask, but I'll do my best. I feel as if I'm treading water with two fingers in the air. I hope the third component doesn't swamp me entirely."

Beth looked across to Gupta-Chaudry and he felt as Chair that he should continue.

"Doctor Venters – Marcie – the third stage is, as you call it, a really big ask. You see, there are multiple criterion that we have had to lay down concerning the selection of the twenty five thousand, supplemented by first and second reserve lists, the details of which will be supplied to you. The key criterion are that men and women will be selected in equal measure between the ages of 16 and 45 and that they have also been screened for fertility. Some of the – can we call them applicants – will already have their DNA results on your super-storage database, but not all of them. We need you to lead the programme to select the most fertile and healthy humans on the planet. All electronic data required to be kept on all three stages will be co-ordinated by Gary Mackintosh who is leading the team to transfer computerised data to Mars –"

Gary raised his hand.

"It's called NOAHSARK, Marcie, but I can see by the look on your face that it's no' the time to explain that acronym!"

Marcie forced herself to speak.

"Mister Secretary-General, genetics is not some kind of a game. What you are asking me to do is play some kind of experiment akin to what the Nazis did during World War Two in the death camps. I don't know if I can do what you are asking."

"Marcie, we know it is a terrible responsibility. However, unlike the Nazis, the selection process will, as far as possible, ensure the survival of every race, colour and creed on the planet on a proportional basis with no fear or favour of political interference. This is purely down to one thing, Doctor Venters – giving the human race its best chance of survival. Will you do it on that basis?"

In her minds' eye Marcie saw herself raising that dreaded third finger as her head sunk beneath the waves of confusion and consternation metaphorically drowning her.

*

Earthdate: 18:45 Monday November 2, 2082 EST

In the en-suite washroom he was as sick as a dog. In fifteen minutes President Josh Trueman had to address his nation and the world nations on 3DTV and to make the most dreadful announcement that any world leader has ever had to give. He thought to himself that due to the secrecy surrounding the impending event, that even his wife Dalia and his two grown up children Jak and Karolina would also be hearing it for the first time. Boy, was he going to hear it tonight from Dalia, his greatest confidante, for keeping this one from her! He looked at his watch and thought it was time that he made his way through and after a quick mouthwash to get rid of the bilious taste, Trueman stepped through into the Oval Office, where he was immediately greeted by the White House broadcast director Tony Coccio.

"Are you feeling okay, Mister President? You look a little pale?"

"Ah'm feelin' fine."

"Maybe I'll get make-up to put a little colour back in your cheeks, Mister President?"

"Just you tell make-up to go take a hike. Trust me - this speech won't need any special effects!"

The speech indeed worried the broadcast director, mainly because he had not seen it and because it would not be played on the normal autocue. It was being transmitted to a specially constructed autocue on the President's desk from a secret CIA office in Langley, Virginia.

"But you see Mister President, the lack of autocue on our side of the camera presents a problem, regarding panning in and out on your face at appropriate moments."

"Look Tony, ah am stuck behind the Oval Office desk. Ah aint gonna be jumpin' about the room. Just play it by ear an' everthin' will be fine."

Trueman took his seat at the Presidential desk and fiddled about with the dummy notes on the desk in front of him, straightening them up to compose himself. They were only there for effect and he would be using the transparent autocue sitting at the front of the desk, which would be out of the camera shot. He thought about all the other world leaders around the planet who would be making similar simultaneous speeches and tried to think how they were feeling. A few minutes passed and then Trueman saw the red 'On Air' light flicker on and he watched Tony Coccio count down the last few seconds with his fingers and then point at the President to go.

"My Fellow Americans – and my fellow citizens of the world – in February last year I announced to you all the news that scientists had discovered a new comet named Schenkler HMM2, which had passed through the Kuiper Belt and had entered our own solar system. Calculations at that time suggested that the comet would come spectacularly close – about half a million miles – to our planet and that the Earth would suffer significant collateral damage from the comet's passing tail. Our key scientists have been employed on a 24/7 basis in tracking the comet's trajectory and only in the last few days Schenkler passed about 100 million miles from the surface of the gas giant Jupiter. I have been informed by NASA that the gravitational pull of Jupiter was strong enough to deflect the trajectory of the comet by the smallest degree. I now have the gravest duty of announcing to the world that the trajectory of the comet has been put onto a direct collision course with Earth. The outcome for the planet and everything living upon it is almost certainly one of complete annihilation, predicted to be on 26 May 2084. I can assure you that it is with a heavy heart that I have to deliver this news to the world. However, I can assure everyone that world leaders have been planning ahead of this worst possible outcome. We have recently launched a joint mission aboard Oceanus II carrying the most powerful interspacial nuclear missiles. These will be launched from platforms orbiting Mars as soon as the Schenkler comet comes within striking distance of the Red Planet. Our fervent hope is that we can deliver enough nuclear blast to deflect the comet just enough to bypass Earth. But, realistically the joint world leaders have agreed that we need a Plan B and that is for the survival of the human species in the event of the expected total impact. The plan is to take as many men and women along with selected livestock and food crops on a mass immigration to new settlements being constructed on Mars even as I speak with you. Our limited resource capabilities plus the hostile environment of Mars puts a heavy constraint on our ability to send as many humans as we would like and thus there will have to be a stringent selection process. Tonight is not the time to discuss this and the details of the process will be provided by every nation's government, in conjunction with the UN and the LOIN, very shortly

to you all. Tonight is, however, a time for prayer and reflection. Most religions have predicted such a terrible event, whether it be the Day of Judgment, Armageddon or the Yawm ad-Din. It would appear that such a day is now upon us, but I can assure you that we will work night and day to stave off such a calamity occurring, and especially to do everything in our power to ensure the survival of the human race. It is my belief that God gave us the brains and the know-how to comprehend our Universe and that ultimately one day we knew we would need to venture out into our solar system and beyond in order to ensure our survival. That day has now come! What we need to do is to keep a clear vision, not to panic and for us all to pull together for the survival of our species. My thoughts and my prayers extend to you all on this fateful evening."

The autocue finished with 'Good night and God bless you all' but Josh Trueman did not have the heart to say it as he felt there was nothing good about it. He sat staring at the camera until Tony Coccio indicated they were 'Off Air'. Trueman quickly pushed himself out of the Presidential chair and his intention was to find his wife and two children as fast as he could. As he brushed past the young TV director who was standing dumbly and looking a ghastly colour of grey, he joked darkly.

"Ya look a little pale, Tony. Want me to get make-up to put a little colour back in your cheeks?"

*

Minutes later standing in front of another camera in the NASA press room in Houston, Jill Geeson prepared to announce the breaking news to viewers on the Sky News channel. Her heart was thumping with the surge of adrenalin, even though she was one of the few people who knew that this day would come. She heard the anchor in Sky's London studio announce her.

"And for more on this breaking news it is over to our Houston correspondent, Jill Geeson. Jill?"

"Tonight in Washington the President of the United States has just announced to the world, news of the greatest calamity to ever face mankind, which will befall us in less than a year and a half. In short, barring a miracle, our tiny blue planet Earth is about to be destroyed by a freak comet which has inadvertently stumbled into the solar system. I have with me the Scots scientist who first discovered this comet and who has been working closely with the NASA team to follow the comet's path, Doctor Ewan Sinclair. Dr Sinclair, am I right in stating that you were the first man to discover the Schenkler HMM2?"

Ewan, standing a little awkwardly with mic attached, quickly glanced at Aaron Eckler and Beth O'Donnell, a few feet away out of camera. He had been warned to be as guarded as possible with his answers.

"W-well, I would not like to be overly credited with the discovery on my own. It was really joint team work between myself and others in the UK, along with the Israelis at INSACC, such as Ari Schenkler, who captured the first images, and also the team working at NASA here in Houston."

"Would you accept that it was your original theory that predicted that the comet was going to fully impact with Earth rather than the original near miss theory?"

"Well, again, although I may have made some early predictions, it required months of detailed work by myself and Ari Schenkler to plot out the trajectory of the HMM2. We had to await the recent bypass of Jupiter and the effect of the Jupiter pull before we could state categorically that the comet was on a direct collision course."

Jill caught her director state into her earpiece: 30 seconds, Jill, one last question.

"Dr Sinclair, do you believe that anything can stop the onslaught of this comet from destroying the Earth?"

"We have got to hope that we can. You have just heard the President announce an interspacial nuclear strike to try and deflect the path of the comet –"

"And are you an expert on nuclear missile technology, Dr Sinclair?"

"Umm, no –"

"We'll have to leave the discussion there for the moment. This is Jill Geeson in Houston. Back to the studio in London –"

Before the cameraman could even announce they were 'Off Air', Ewan blazed at Jill.

"Christ's sake, Jill. You made me look a bit silly there with that nuclear missile question –"

"Ah was just doing my job as a reporter, Ewan. Ah've been holding all this back for a long time now and it just, sort of, came out."

Beth O'Donnell pounced in on the scene.

"Jill, you were a bit out of order there. The bottom line is that somehow we have gotta let mankind cling on to some kinda hope. Otherwise we risk total anarchy."

"Hope! Christ, Beth, we are all kidding ourselves on here. If we are lucky, only 99.9% of the human race is goin' to be obliterated, including you, me, Ewan and Eckler over there. Where is the hope in that?"

That same evening Marcie Venters had arranged to stay a couple of nights with her unmarried sister Ruth Esther Bloom, who still lived in the Bloom family home in downtown Brooklyn. After listening to Trueman's speech with Ruth on the 3DTV and after they had hugged and cried together, Marcie walked the few blocks down to the new B'nai Jeshurun Synagogue next to the cemetery where her father was buried. She entered thinking that many distraught Jews would be dragging themselves here to pray for deliverance, but it turned out that the synagogue was empty. Marcie had not brought herself here for deliverance, but to try and seek guidance on what she perceived as an awful and impossible task. A door creaked noisily and an old wizened rabbi entered into the main hall of the synagogue. He spotted Marcie, head bent in prayer, and he walked quietly over to her.

"My name is Rabbi Israel Moss. Have you heard the news?"

"Yes, Rabbi, I do believe the Messiah is definitely on his way this time!"

"You sound a little cynical about it all?"

Marcie gave a short false laugh.

"Rabbi, what have we Jews got to be cynical for? We've had it cushy for the last three thousand years and then God tops it off by wiping us all out."

"But surely there is hope that this is not the end of the human race. The best people on the planet will be working to ensure the future survival of mankind –"

"Rabbi Moss, is it? Well Rabbi, you're looking at one of them and I'm not sure that I want the job!"

"What do you mean, my daughter?"

"I mean that today I have been chosen as one of those best people to select who lives and who dies. Rabbi, did you lose any ancestors in the death camps?"

"I believe so. It was such a long time ago."

"Well, my father Ezra etched every ancestor we lost into my brain. I became a doctor like my father before me and our ethos was to perform our duty to our fellow man diametrically opposed to the creed of those Nazi butchers. But taking on the responsibility of saving the so very few at the expense of so many is such a terrible burden, that it makes me feel like one of those Nazi camp doctors."

"Daughter, this has been such a horribly confusing evening for me that I do not quite comprehend what you are talking about. However, from what I have read the Nazis systematically planned to wipe out the Jewish race. This they failed to do so and you and I are testimony to that. From the little you have said, I seem to understand that you will be working to help with the survival of the human race. However little that you save, one thing is for sure. If you fail then maybe there will be *no* human race. Surely that puts your task still diametrically opposed to the Nazis and something your father and your God would agree on?"

Marcie looked up at the old preacher with moistening eyes.

"Thank you, Rabbi."

CHAPTER 20

<u>Earthdate: 10:35 Thursday August 5, 2083 EST</u>

Jill stood in front of camera on the White House lawn. Although it was just after half ten in the morning it was already shaking up to be a scorching summer's day and the heat was adding to her feeling weak and shaky. She had just come out of the Press Briefing Room and she could feel her legs wobbling slightly, waiting for the anchorman in London to give her the go-ahead. She could hear him cueing her in on her headset.

"- And it's straight over to our Houston correspondent Jill Geeson at the White House for important breaking news. Jill?"

Jill sucked in a deep lungful of warm air and looked straight into the camera, knowing many millions would be taking in her every word.

"As some of you may have already watched a few minutes ago, the White House has just issued a press statement regarding the deployment of the interspacial nuclear missiles from platforms on MGals Two and Three orbiting the Red Planet. Ten missiles in total were launched carrying the most powerful warheads ever devised by man. All ten missiles hit the target of the Schenkler HMM2 comet at a range of thirty five million miles out from Mars. Unfortunately, the briefing had to report that the missiles have failed to alter the trajectory of the comet and that it will still impact with planet Earth as predicted on 26 May 2084. The White House statement also reaffirmed that the comet's collision with Earth will result in a total impact. Our planet and everything and everyone on it will be totally and irrevocably destroyed -"

Jill gulped hard and she could not stop an involuntary tear from running down her flushing cheek.

"- And we now have to prepare ourselves for the worst possible scenario to ever face humankind. US President Josh Trueman will be making a Presidential statement this evening and he is fully expected to urge people around the world to remain calm, to continue to live their lives as normally as possible and that all efforts should be redoubled to ensure the completion of the immigration programme to Mars. This now represents the only certain way to ensure the survival of the human race. With this, the gravest of news for all mankind, this is Jill Geeson at the White House, for Sky News, handing you back to the studio in London."

*

<u>Earthdate: 07:30 Saturday August 7, 2083 CST</u>

Two days after the apocalyptic announcement from the White House, Lex Kosloff arranged an 'End of Days' dinner party at his home in Robindale Drive. He and Irene DuPré had prepared a huge buffet spread, including many exotic foods and delicacies that their guests might never have the chance to eat again. Invited to the party was Lex's old friend Jack Crossan, on extended space leave after returning from the Oh Two mission. Jack had been working at Houston as part of the team overseeing the build of the huge Oceanus fleet and the training of the new astronaut teams which would be required to begin transporting the selected emigrants to Mars. Truth be told, and unbeknown to the masses, there was already almost five thousand essential men and women working and living on Mars. They were mainly technicians, construction engineers, ice miners and various scientists who were busily employed in ensuring that the expansion of the super-glass pods to house the human, flora and fauna were going to be ready for the mass arrivals. The fast expanding glass covered township being constructed on Mars lying about halfway between Mount Olympus and the Martian North Pole was called Capitol Base. The first Oceanus fleet of 25 spaceships carrying around 10,000 men, women, animals and plant stock would ship out from Earth orbit in little more than five weeks' time and the second and final fleet of similar size would ship out to Mars scheduled for 28 February 2084. This was deemed to be the ultimate safest date for the emigrant fleet to sail in order to ensure that they were beyond the massive blast zone which would be created by the Earth's destruction. Jack was scheduled to command one of the Oceanus fleet ships blasting off for Mars on that final date. Lex had also invited his three Scots lodgers, Jill Geeson, Ewan Sinclair and Gary Mackintosh to the party. Also invited along was Ari Schenkler, Ewan's colleague at NASA HQ, who Lex and Irene had met in passing at Houston Control. Jill had also asked if her friend Dr Marcie Venters could join them and Lex was delighted to have Marcie along. Marcie had been working and attending meetings in New York but she had a couple of free days before flying on the Virgin Galactic service back to London. Marcie had invited herself down to Houston to catch up with Jill and pass on news and regards from her daughter Ruthie, who was still working at the London Times. Marcie was staying at the nearby Robindale Ramada.

Interestingly, following the terrible proclamations by the various world leaders, world order had not broken down into a state of anarchy and chaos. In fact, quite the opposite seemed to have taken place. Areas of conflicts in Africa, the Middle East and Asia, in particular, had actually found the opposing sides falling into a state of non-negotiated peace. Violence and crime became negligible around the globe and estranged families and friends were making a serious point of getting back together. People continued to get on with their daily lives and they were tending to fall in two main philosophical camps - the Optimists and the Fatalists. The Optimists still stuck to the view that mankind would find a way to divert the catastrophe even though the interspacial nuclear missiles deployed from Mars were wholly unsuccessful. However, the team at NASA including Ari, Ewan and Gary had looked at all sorts of crackpot ideas and they had reported back to the UN and LOIN that computer models showed that they were all futile. This had included trying to fire powerful lasers at Schenkler to shift the axis of the meteor - landing teams of astronauts onto the surface of Schenkler to deploy more nuclear fission and / or fusion bombs - or trying to erect giant solar wind sails to deflect the comet. They had also considered the impossibility of destroying the Moon in order to shift the Earth's axis around the Sun. The NASA team concluded that wasting precious time and resources on these futile ideas which was better needed for the construction of Capitol Base on Mars and the Oceanus fleet was reluctantly accepted by the UN / LOIN alliance. The Fatalists tended more towards the viewpoint that the future of mankind was now in the hands of a higher authority in the universe, whether it be God or Nature, and that they were prepared to accept their fate. Churches, synagogues, mosques and temples were packed out with every passing week. Of course, the eight friends who were sitting around the dinner table that evening were very much more towards the latter camp of Fatalists. They all knew the dreadful truth of Earth's fate. Everyone had gotten on famously around the dinner table and they all had eaten far too much and probably had drank too much. Even Lex and Irene had allowed themselves one small glass of wine each for the toast at the end of the meal. Lex stood up before his guests and raised his glass.

"Here's ta sharing good food with good friends and great people. It's not exactly the Last Supper, but maybe not far off it. So ah give y'all a toast - to the End of Days!"

The guests all stood and raised their glasses in salutation.

"THE END OF DAYS!"

As they all took their seats there was a momentary pause for reflection which, after a few seconds of silence, Irene broke.

"Well, y'all, have ya all thought about your situations? For instance, will you be applying to get a place on the Mars immigration lottery? Afraid poor ole Lex and me are too old to apply. Ah guess we'll be too busy shippin' out the lucky twenty five thou' anyhow, izzat right Lex, honey?"

"Fraid so, baby. But ah couldn't pick a better gal to end ma time with."

"Shucks Lexie sweetie pie - you keep saying those sweet thangs an' ya ain't gonna go far wrong with me."

Everyone laughed loudly and then Marcie spoke out next.

"I'm also afraid Irene that I fail to qualify by being on the wrong side of forty five."

Irene raised her palms outwards towards Marcie and put on a look of mock incredulity as she compared her own rather bulky frame to Marcie's slim figure and smooth youthful-like complexion..

"You gotta give me the number of your dietician. Ah need me some of his elixir of youth!"

"Elixir or no elixir, Irene, I am happy to end my time on the same planet as my late dear beloved Rolf. I do hope that my daughter Ruthie might apply, but, of course, as we all know the chances of being selected are many millions to one."

Jack Crossan spoke up next lowering his voice in a more sombre tone.

"Actually, ah too fail the forty five test, but ah suppose ah win a 'get outta jail free' card on the basis of bein' a Space Commander. We are a scarce commodity at present an' we gotta do our duty whether we want to or not. Tell the truth, ah would rather stay here on 3R with ma two boys. They are both too young to be selected."

There was a general shaking of heads and Marcie spoke up for the rest of the group.

"Jack, we all understand what you are saying but these missions to Mars are vital for the survival of mankind. I have wrestled with my own conscience as to whether my work in DNA selection is right or wrong and I have reconciled myself that it is. But, without survivors on Mars to carry on and progress my work, then there is no point to it. You, however, have the task of ensuring those survivors make it for all our sakes."

Jack nodded sullenly and looked around the group of friends and answered with little conviction in his voice.

"Ah guess you're right, Marcie."

Ari spoke next.

"Well, the Americans have had their say, so as the one Israeli here, I shall state my piece and leave it to our Scottish friends to wind it up. My position is slightly different from Jack's. Ewan and I also receive that 'get out of jail' card on the basis that astrophysicists will be needed on Mars, but in our case it is not compulsory to go. I fully intend to return to Tel Aviv ASAP and to be with my beautiful wife and daughter so that we can all be together at the end."

The mood was getting more sombre by the minute and Gary butted in on a lighter note.

"Well guys, ah'm definitely no goin' tae apply for Mars. Ma sexual proclivity is no very conducive to the survival of the species!"

Marcie tut-tutted in a maternalistic manner.

"Now Gary, the selection process does not exclude applicants on the basis of race, creed, colour, gender or sexual orientation. So long as your sexual production, so to speak, passes the test, then there's nothing to stop you applying."

"Ah suppose so, Marcie, but ma jokes are so bad that they'll probably exclude me from Mars on that basis alone. Seriously though, ah've made up ma mind not to apply."

Ewan looked around the table a little sheepishly and then took his turn.

"I know that Ari let you all know that we both get the option to take a place as astrophysicists on the trip to Mars. But I too will not be going. Jill - I'm not leaving Earth without you! I want to be with you until the end."

Irene threw up her hands in exasperation and laughed loudly.

"Lord Almighty! Ain't nobody on this God-forsaken planet want to go to Mars? Way things is goin' we'll be putting people onto those Oceanus spaceships at gunpoint! Jill, please tell me you want to go to Mars, honey, please cheer me up?"

Jill looked around the table then her eyes fixed on Ewan's before she spoke her piece.

"Ah guess ah am the odd one out here tonight, Irene. Ah will certainly be applying for the immigration programme. My job as a journalist means recording human history on a day to day basis and my belief is that mankind will still have a future – maybe not here - but certainly on Mars. Ah still hope to be there recording that future. On a more personal level and as Marcie also knows - ah unfortunately had to abort my precious wee - b-baby. But ma hope is that in time ah can have another baby and a healthy baby. An' if you want to be a part of that - Ewan Sinclair - then indeed you will take your place on that flight to Mars!"

They all laughed and Gary threw in one last quip on the discussion.

"Well, Ewan, ah guess ah'm no longer sharing the bedroom wi' you from now on!"

*

Jill listened on her cell phone as it rang Ewan's number. Jill had just arrived back at her hot-desk in the Sky News office in downtown Washington on Philadelphia Avenue. She knew Ewan would still be in the office at NASA in Houston and he would probably be up to his eyeballs in work, but she needed to call him. She now knew her feelings for Ewan. They had both made passionate and sensual love the night of the dinner party at Lex's home and they both knew they were deeply in love with each other. Reuniting with Ewan after all these years that had passed, had a cathartic effect on Jill. The hurt she had carried inside her over Khan al Ahmed's deception and the loss of her aborted baby now felt as though it had been thoroughly cleansed from her soul. Even though she might only have nine months left she had been feeling happier now than she had been in years. Well, until today and that is why she was desperate to hear Ewan's voice. However, lately she seemed to be spending more time up in Washington than down in the Sky office in Houston. The political ramifications of the impending Armageddon always seemed to be currently outweighing the scientific and cosmic ramifications. She was feeling a bit down on her luck because she had not seen Ewan for nearly two weeks and Jill longed to hear his soft Islay intonations as she mused aloud to herself through the eternally continuous ringing on her cell.

"God, it sure is appropriate that it's a Black Friday!"

Then he answered.

"Hello? Jill?"

"Ewan, thank God. Ah was hoping that ah would catch you."

"No probs. But I've got to go into a meeting to give my latest progress report on the Schenkler comet, Jill, so is it a fast one?"

Jill felt her voice start to break.

"We-ell, ah-h – och, Ewan it can wait till ah see you –"

Ewan detected that Jill was close to tears and he felt that it was better if she got the problem off her chest now.

"It's okay Jill – whatever it is, you can tell me."

"It's just that – um – ah got ma email result on ma application for the emigration programme today. Ewan – ah've only made the second tier reserve list, which puts tens and tens of thousands of people in front of me. My chances of going to Mars are pretty slim. Oh God, Ewan, ah'm going to lose y-you!"

Jill burst into tears and Ewan attempted to console her.

"Look Jill, if you're not going to Mars, then I'm not going either. Do you think I would leave you behind?"

Jill took a deep breath and composed herself.

"No way, Ewan. You fully deserve to go. It was you who identified Schenkler in the first place. From that knowledge mankind at least hopes to save twenty five thousand and you deserve to be one of them. Anyway – we need your kind on Mars to identify the next rogue comet and help work towards pushing man further out into deep space. Ultimately, if we don't eventually get out of this solar system then we are all doomed!"

In Houston Ewan was shaking his head and he spoke through an emotionally constricting throat.

"Okay, Jill, I'll think about it and we'll talk more when you fly back to Houston. Looking on the bright side, at least you are on one of the reserve lists. There are billions of men and women who are not on any of the immigration lists for Mars. So let's not completely write off your chances just yet."

*

Earthdate: 12:00 Monday September 20, 2083 CST

It was the start of a new working week but all normal work around the globe was suspended as billions of people were glued to their 3DTVs. Everyone gathered together to watch the televised feeds coming down from Alpha Base showing the Oceanus fleet of twenty five spaceships pushing off slowly at first, one by one, until they were far enough out of Earth's gravitational pull to fire up their fusion drives. Jack Crossan had detailed fleet command to his old second-in-command Xi Xhu Pan. Jack would command the second fleet departing in February 2084. The ships carried the first wave of 10,000 young men and women and with their departure also went the hopes and dreams of the billions left behind. Each ship was cheered off enthusiastically by the billions of viewers as it was filmed passing close by Alpha Base. Jill reported the momentous event in human history from the

Sky News office in Houston and she was hoarse and exhausted by the time the twenty fifth and last Oceanus had blasted off and disappeared from the screenshots heading out towards Mars. She stoically finished her report as viewers looked into the empty blackness of space still on their screens.

"Today the hostile Red Planet somehow feels a more hospitable place to be."

Immediately after finishing reporting at around three in the afternoon Jill grabbed an air-taxi and headed for the nearby City Hall a few blocks away in downtown Houston. On the way there she tried to fix up her make-up and take the tired look out of her eyes with fresh mascara and a helping of bronzer. As she stumbled up the steps of City Hall she saw Jack Crossan in full Space Commander's uniform waiting there for her in the atrium. He looked slightly disheveled and unshaven as he gave her a weary wave.

"God's sake, Jack. You look about as bad as ah feel."

"Ah am done in, Jill. Ah have been training the crews for those twenty five ships up there without hardly a break for the last few months. Ah only have a coupla days off then it is back onto training for the final fleet. By the time ah'm finished ah will hardly be fit to command a paper boat never mind an Oceanus spaceship."

Jill laughed.

"Ah'm knackered too, Jack. Ah feel that ah've been reporting non-stop for weeks. Is everybody here?"

"Ah think so –"

Jill tried to straighten out Jack's tie and brushed off his uniform.

"My God, Jack. We don't exactly look like the best man and the best maid, do we?"

They pressed on into City Hall which was packed full of various wedding parties all keen to tie the knot before that fateful date with Armageddon. As they entered the Function Hall Lex and Irene ushered Jack and Jill to join them quickly in front with the impatiently waiting Registrar. Seated behind the happy couple were many of Lex and Irene's family, friends and colleagues from NASA. They included Jimmy Soderline, Aaron Eckler, Beth O'Donnell, Ari Schenkler, Ewan Sinclair and Gary Mackintosh. Even Lars and Freda Nilstrom, Lex's former in-laws, had flown in from Dallas to celebrate the wedding. Later at the intimate reception Jill and Ewan sat hand in hand listening to the various wedding speeches. Ewan lent across and whispered in Jill's ear.

"Jill, you know I love you so much. Why don't you and I get married too, before everything comes crashing to an end?"

"Ewan, ah love you too. But ah will only marry you under one condition."

"What condition, Jill?"

"Ah will only marry you if and when we both get safely to Mars."

Ewan gazed at Jill, perplexed.

"But you made me promise to take my place on the Oceanus fleet even if you don't make it out the reserve list. That might mean that you may never be my wife –"

Jill brushed Ewan's cheek with the softest of touches.

"Well then, ah don't propose to tie you down as a would-be widower here on Earth, when you might have to find a new wife on Mars. We can only hope for some divine intervention which will see us both walk down the aisle in Capitol Base."

"But, Jill –"

"No buts, that's the way it's got to be!"

They were then raised to their feet along with the other guests as Lars Nilstrom raised his glass.

"Ah give you a toast – the bride and groom."

"THE BRIDE AND GROOM!"

CHAPTER 21

Earthdate: 09:30 Wednesday January 5, 2084 GMT

Gary Mackintosh groaned aloud with the pounding pain in his head. The whole world had been celebrating this New Year like there was no tomorrow, mainly because there *was* literally no tomorrow. Gary had been drinking hard since Hogmanay but it was more to drown his sorrows than to celebrate and he had awakened in the fog of a deep black depression. He had made a lot of money through his work on the computing projects to transfer the E2MSN to Mars Control and the NOAHSARK database. Both of these projects were now almost complete. He only had some peripheral work to see them to final stage sign off, which had left him feeling a bit redundant. There was also some strange information that he had stumbled on that left him feeling confused and depressed. It was something he had meant to speak to Ewan about but had not found the right moment. Virtually all his money and the stock portfolio that he had built since his school days had been transferred into Martian commodity stocks on the NYSE. His intention had been to transfer his stock holdings to Ewan, the lost love of his life, shortly before Ewan was to set off for Mars next month. He felt that if he left his stock transfer until the last possible minute, probably a few days before 28 February, when Ewan was scheduled to blast off with the last Oceanus fleet, then he would make an absolute killing. However, on 30 December, following some devastating meteor showers from the tip of Schenkler's tail, there was a stock market crash. Martian stocks crashed spectacularly, along with most other Earth-bound commodities. Gary had urgently called his stockbroker in order to sell his stocks. However, when he eventually got a hold of him, Gary was told that his stocks had been wiped out and that he was now virtually broke. All he had left was about $14,700 in the bank and an open return ticket from Houston to London Heathrow. He had bought the flight ticket to fly home and celebrate the New Year with his family and friends in Glasgow for the last time. His last few days in Glasgow had been spent in an almost drunken stupor, which had not helped his depression one bit. Last night his old Glasgow University mates poured him on to the Glasgow Central to London Euston train to head for his return flight to Houston from Heathrow. Gary held his thumping head in his hands and tried to focus his eyes when he began to realise he was in a first-class sleeper compartment. He noticed that the train was stationary. He looked at his watch, 09:32. Must be in Euston by now, he thought. Gary drew up the closed blind on the window and looked out onto a chilly frost-covered platform. However, he was perplexed when the station signs did not read Euston but instead read Carlisle, still 300 miles north of London! He noticed that there were quite a few cold-looking passengers milling around on the platform. Still dressed in his clothes from the previous evening, Gary grabbed his travel bag and staggered out onto the platform, immediately noticing a railwayman in uniform.

"Hey, mate, what the hell's goin' on? How're we no' in London yet?"

"Sorry, sir, but there's been a meteor strike on the main line at Penrith. They say it's practically wiped out the whole town."

The news momentarily snapped Gary out of his hangover.

"Bloody hell! Does that mean we're stuck here?"

"They're looking at sending the train back up to Edinburgh and diverting it down the East Coast, but at the moment there is no timescale for this happening."

The black wave of depression again clouded Gary's brain.

"Aw, fuck this! Are there no any trains runnin' out of this God forsaken place, man?"

The railwayman, who was a Carlisle local, looked scathingly at Gary and with a slight sarcastic sneer in his voice, he spoke back.

"There is a train on Platform 1 leaving for Grange-over-Sands in two minutes. It's over there – maybe the sea air will do you some good, sonny!"

Gary had no time or inclination to pick a fight with the man, so he just took off across the concourse and jumped onto the small local train. As the train began to wind its way around the Cumbrian coast in increasingly sleety conditions, with the snow-covered mountains of the Lake District on his left and the icy-grey Irish Sea on his right, he began to wonder what in God's name he was doing. Grange-over-Sands? He had never even heard of the place. Oh well, it will have to do, he thought, who will miss me anyway? About half an hour later he alighted at the small old-fashioned and slightly dilapidated seaside town to be met by a biting sleet-laden wind coming off the freezing sea. He quickly checked in to the first B&B which had a vacancy sign showing, situated close by the railway station. After grabbing a tasteless greasy breakfast which did not sit well in his ailing stomach, he decided to go for a walk. The sleet had gone off but the biting westerly wind caused him to head inland in an easterly direction away from the sea and he found himself walking along a deserted country road with tall pine woods lining either side. Looking to the north-east he could see a pall of blackish smoke rising into the sky and he guessed that it was from the town of Penrith still burning after the meteor strike. Gary had been walking for about an hour when he came into a small hamlet, which consisted of a few cottages, a café and a small rundown church. Gary was freezing by this time and he stepped into the warm café and ordered some tea and scones. He must have been sitting morosely for some time as the waitress sidled over and absently wiped his table.

"Something got you down, lad?"

"What-t?"

"Is it all to do with this comet thing?"

"Ah don't know, aye well, sort of –"

The waitress put a gentle hand on Gary's shoulder.

"Don't you worry, lad, the man upstairs will sort it all out in the end."

"Och, ah was brought up a Catholic but ah don't really believe in God."

"In the end we'll all believe, mark my words."

Gary sat for a few more minutes finishing off his pot of tea, then he paid and tipped the waitress, who gave him a knowing smile as he stepped back out into the village street. Across the road he spotted the little old and slightly decrepit church. He was about to turn around for the walk back to Grange-over-Sands when he somehow felt compelled to walk over to the church. The door creaked loudly when he pushed it open. Gary had not been to church since he was a wee boy in the Sunday school at St Margaret Mary's. The church was empty and hollow-sounding as he walked down the aisle towards the altar. He sat in one of the pews near the front and he quickly glanced around. He was completely alone in the musty old church and he felt cut off from the rest of the world. Involuntarily, Gary felt his body to begin spasmodically trembling, not from the cold, but from raw fear. Subconsciously, his hands came together and he looked upwards to the rafters and for the first time in his life he really began praying to God.

"You there Big Man?"

Gary's voice echoed and bounced around the bare walls of the empty church.

"Maybe not. Ah probably don't merit your attention anyway. You've got bigger fish to fry than me at present, haven't you? There's billions of us wanting answers from you an' that's a pretty tall order to meet, even for you God."

The church remained silent and Gary's head sunk onto his clasped hands resting on the pew in front of him. He listened quietly for a few moments, waiting for something to happen. Nothing did. Then he spoke again, raising his voice a notch or two.

"Ah don't know what you want me to do God! Do you want me to finish it now? Ah've lost everything that ah worked for anyway, so what's the point of goin' on? Do you want me to walk up that mountain out there an' throw myself off, or walk back to the sea an' throw myself in or just fling myself under a train? Maybe you'll be saying that ah'll be with you in less than five months anyhow. But why don't we both just finish it here and now? Eh, God, what do you say?"

Gary peered around seeing only emptiness and cold. Silence. He jumped to his feet and raised his arms aloft, in a cruciform position.

"FUCK SAKE, GOD! Just one word. Yes? No? Just one sign. That's all ah'm askin' for –"

He slumped back onto the seat of the pew and unconsciously back into the prayer position. He wept profusely. Tears blinded him and mucus streamed out of his nose and mouth.

"Ah'm sorry, God, ah am so sorry. Ah have no right to ask you for anything. Please can you forgive me?"

There was no crack of thunder. There was no blinding light from heaven. There was no heavenly choir of angels, nor any booming voice from above. However, as Gary wiped the tears and snot away he slowly felt a distinct change come over him. He felt the black heavy fog in his brain lift away and a warm calming feeling spread throughout his body. When the warmth had spread from his head down to his toes he was left with a feeling of peace. All his inner demons had been exorcised and he never felt better in his life. He looked to the rafters and mouthed, thank you God. Coming out the church gate he looked across at the café and the waitress was standing outside having an e-cig break. Gary shouted across to her with a broad smile on his face, pointing skyward as he walked briskly back towards Grange-over-Sands and back to finishing off his projects in Houston.

"The man upstairs has sorted it out for me."

The broadly smiling waitress waved him enthusiastically off down the road.

"Told you he would, lad!"

When he got back to the B&B he quickly checked out and when he went to the train station he found that there was a diversionary train to Lancaster leaving in half an hour which would get him back on to the main line to London. He had been unable to get a signal on his cell in Grange-over-Sands. It had probably been disrupted by the meteor strike at Penrith. However, his cell was fully functioning when he arrived in the old fortified town of Lancaster and he put a call through to Ewan in Houston. It was still early morning in Houston but Ewan's face appeared on screen almost immediately. Before he could speak Ewan was blurting at him excitedly.

"Jesus, Gary – you don't know how good it is to hear from you. Thank God you are alright."

"Alright? Well ah sure ah'm alright now. Why?"

"We've all seen the meteor strike hitting Penrith on the news over here and we thought the worst because we hadn't heard from you. There was a sleeper train from Scotland going through Penrith at the time and it has been obliterated. You're dad Frank has been bombarding me with calls all morning to see if I had heard from you."

Gary looked at his cell. Twenty six missed calls.

"Jeez, Ewan, ah'm sorry. My life kinda got diverted for a while in more ways than one. Ah guess ah must have been on the sleeper behind the one that got hit. But it's just to say ah'm okay now. Back on track so to speak an' ah'm heading back to Houston ASAP. Ah'll get off the line an' call my family right now."

"Okay, Gary. Look forward to seeing you back, mate."

"Oh, by the way Ewan – there's something ah've found in NOAHSARK that I need to speak to you about – *one day*. But it'll keep for now."

*

<u>Earthdate: 11:20 Saturday January 8, 2084 EST</u>

It was a bitingly sharp frosty Virginian morning with a crystal clear blue sky as the three cowboys rode across the stubbled bare fields, a-whoopin' and a-hollerin'. Jack Crossan was happier than he had been in years as he and his two young sons Milner and Jack Junior galloped over the top fields of his Lexington ranch. The State of Virginia had never looked so beautiful. Even the sight of the half-moon high in the pale blue winter sky with the now clearly visible Schenkler comet lower on the moon's left seemed somehow strangely beautiful. Jack thought, how paradoxically magnificent in its cosmic beauty but catastrophic in its final outcome. What the Big Bang can create the Big Bang can destroy. However, today was not about destructive thoughts but about the joy of being alive. Jack had recently come to a sort of reconciliation with Peggy Sue and like most countries around the world, schools had been shut down since Christmas, for good in most cases. Peggy Sue's partner Justin Smythe had also been given a month's leave from the RAF, part of the peace dividend brought about by the onset of Armageddon. Jack had invited his two sons, Peggy Sue and Justin out to spend the holiday on the ranch. Jack had managed to engineer two weeks off from his gruelling schedule of training for the new astronaut teams and also preparing himself for his own upcoming flight of the last Oceanus scheduled for 28 February, just eight short weeks away. It was likely that when he went back to the programme at Houston, Jack would never see his two boys alive again. But for now Jack was determined to enjoy his last few days with Milner and Junior. They pulled up their panting horses next to the woods on the western edge of the ranch, which was verged with frost rimed rye grass. They let the horses rest and feed on the grass and Jack put his arms lovingly around his sons shoulders.

"Wow, guys, that was fun, huh?"

His youngest son Jack Junior excitedly agreed with a slightly English accent which made Jack wince a little.

"That was really great dad – we've not had much chance to ride in Cucklington. Too much going to school and loads of homework."

Milner quipped boyishly, still retaining his Virginian accent.

"Yeah, pop, it's great we don't need to go back to school again, ain't it!"

"No it ain't Milner – education is one of the greatest gifts that we can ever get –"

Jack pointed up to the comet.

"- without education and knowledge we would never have known what we do about Schenkler and –"

Jack let his sentence hang unfinished. Milner sort of finished it for his father.

"Are we gonna die, pop? Mom says that we are all gonna die."

Jack pulled the three horses closer together. He pushed back the boys' cowboy hats and ruffled their hair.

"We're all gonna die one day."

Milner and Junior's eyes filled up and they bravely fought back tears. Jack lifted their chins up.

"Look boys, it's a big deal, but it's nothing to be afraid of –"

Jack Junior snapped at his father.

"Yes, dad, but you're getting to go to Mars. We're too young to get that chance. So you'll live and we'll die here on Earth."

They all looked at each other with pursed lips in momentary silence. Jack thought for a few second before responding. He put his arms around the boys' shoulders and drew them in close.

"Boys – ah sorely don't want to leave you here. But ah've gotta do my duty and take those guys out to a new life on Mars. But ah promise ya both this – that one day we will all be together again. We'll meet again in the sweet bye and bye. Promise?"

The boys spoke in unison.

"Okay, pop, it's a promise."

"C'mon then, guys, let's ride back to the ranch. Mom and Justin are makin' good ole fashioned burgers an' fries – yeah?"

They all fist pumped into the air and turned the horses around and galloped home yelling and cheering, scattering cattle left and right. Jack reined his horse back slightly to let Milner and Jack Junior gleefully charge ahead as they rode back to the ranch. He did not want them to see the tears which were freely rolling down his cheeks and blinding him. The thought went through his mind that this would be the last of these happy days with his beautiful sons. In fact, Jack was soon to find out how quickly those happy days were to come to an end. As the three of them all crashed cheerily into the big ranch kitchen with the meaty smell of burgers salivating them, Jack immediately saw the worry in Peggy Sue's eyes.

"Jack, Beth O'Donnell called. You've to get up to the White House this afternoon for a meeting with Trueman. They are sending down an air-limo in the next hour to take you back to DC."

"Did Beth say what was going on?"

"No, but it sounds bad, Jack."

Milner grabbed his arms around Jack's torso and cried out. Jack could also see Jack Junior's lips quivering and restraining tears.

"No, daddy, you can't go – you're still on holiday with us. Please don't go!"

"Sorry, guys, I gotta go. But ah'll probably be back in the morning –"

Justin, who was standing by the big Aga stove as acting cook, defused the tense situation.

"Hey, c'mon you guys, we've still got time for those famous American burgers that you all rave about. Let's eat!"

*

By four thirty in the afternoon Jack was sitting in the Oval Office with Aaron Eckler, Beth O'Donnell, Ari Schenkler, Ewan Sinclair and Ravi Gupta-Chaudry. Abdullah Suleiman and John Ralston were patched in on the White House conference system. Jack, who had only arrived in Washington half an hour ago in the executive air-limo, had been quickly briefed by Eckler a few minutes ago and the group sat tensely awaiting the arrival of the President. Trueman immediately marched into his office with his private secretary Jimmy Swarbrick. He stood in front of his big comfy executive armchair, looked at the assembled group, then he slammed down his briefing papers with a resounding thump. He then seemed to slump into his chair and opened the meeting with a resigned groan.

"Aw, fuck it all! Can we take any more of this bad news stuff? Ah'm getting' sick and tired of sitting in front of a camera an' bein' the harbinger of doom to the peoples of the world."

What the assembled group knew and had been briefed on was that at 9:36am that morning, communication had come into NASA HQ, relaying that one of the fleet of twenty five Oceanus spaceships had apparently disappeared without trace. It had five hundred passengers and crew on board. Oceanus XIII appeared to have been destroyed, however, none of the other fleet ships were close enough to Oh XIII to see what had happened. There had just been an immediate cessation of communication from Oh XIII to the fleet and NASA HQ. The boffins at NASA had been poring over all the available data and Eckler's team had brought the results to this executive briefing. Aaron Eckler nodded at Ewan to begin.

"Mr President, I'm afraid that it is bad news. All data points to X-triple-I being instantaneously destroyed in a catastrophic incident. Although the flight path of the Oceanus fleet is well away from Schenkler's trajectory, we believe that it is likely that rogue debris has been thrown out of the comet's tail which has collided with the ship. Indications are that the impact was a direct hit on the fusion drive engine resulting in the ship being instantaneously destroyed in a nuclear explosion."

Trueman laid his elbows on his desk and covered his etched face with his big hands. He squeezed his eyes shut tightly as his fingers threaded worryingly through his thinning wiry hair. Eckler spoke.

"Mr President, they wouldn't have felt a thing –"

Trueman looked up.

"Who was the commander of X-triple-I?"

Jack replied solemnly.

"Commander Bethan Jones, sir, only twenty six. Ah trained her personally. She was one of ma best students and a sad loss."

Trueman nodded a thanks at Jack.

"She got family?"

"A dad Andrew and a younger sister Megan, sir."

"Ah'll speak personally to them before, um – Bethan – gets plastered all over the news. She is indeed a sad loss, but more than that we have lost five hundred souls an' we can ill afford that kind of collateral damage. These guys were part of our salvation!"

The group looked towards Eckler who quickly scanned his brief before speaking.

"It is indeed a terrible loss, Mister President. However, we unfortunately had to factor into our risk assessments that out of the fifty Oceanus that we planned to fly to Mars, there was the possibility of losing at least two ships to catastrophic events such as this morning's with X-triple-I."

"Jeez, Aaron, we're only managing to send twenty five thousand to Mars. Surely we cannot afford to lose a thousand?"

"Mr President, we have built in contingency plans for such an event. We have two reserve lists, primary and secondary, and that means that five hundred new immigrants will be selected from the primary reserve list to go on the final launch on 28 February. Jack, your job will be to ensure that you pick the best new crew from your reserve astronauts already in flight training, okay?"

"Ah'll get down to Houston ASAP and get right on it?"

Trueman responded quizzically.

"Okay, Aaron, so we got the people and the crew ready to go, but ah thought we were only building fifty Oceanus for the job?"

"Admittedly, it's a tight call, Mr President, but we had already factored in the build of another two Oceanus ships in case they were needed – one in Europe and the other in Iran. I am hoping that PM Ralston and Mullah Suleiman will be able to confirm that they can complete the build and transfer to Alpha Base for pre-launch trials by the end of January?"

Trueman leaned towards the conference screens.

"John? Suleiman? Are you guys able to deliver at least one of these two ships on time?"

London came through first.

"Josh, I've spoken with my scientific advisors and although they say there are some technical issues, we are confident that we can deliver you another

Oceanus to Alpha Base by the thirty first of this month. The key funding and resources have been provided by Ranulf Olafsen's ROMANCE organisation in Sweden."

Suleiman in Tehran followed up Ralston's call.

"Josh, my honourable friend. I too have spoken in the last hour with my scientists. They say that the thirty first is a very difficult target, but by stripping the build down to the barest minimums, we believe we can achieve delivery. It will not be a very pleasant trip for the five hundred but we'll get them to Mars, by Allah we will!"

Trueman turned back to Eckler.

"So does that mean we are going to send another thousand not originally in the plan?"

"Well, Mr President, yes, on the basis that a) Jack's team passes the two ships fit for purpose after some pretty quick space trialling – Jack?"

"Ah'm on it, Aaron."

"- and b) it is still on the basis that we unfortunately expect to lose one more ship in our calculations. If they both make it then good and well, although it will mean some overcrowding at Mars Capitol Base. But we will just need to deal with that."

Josh Trueman was feeling a bit better than when he first entered the Oval Office some minutes ago.

"Well, thank the Lord that there is some good news –"

Ewan interjected slightly nervously.

"Um, Mr President, we may have a little more on the good news front. I'll let Ari tell you – after all, it is his comet!"

Trueman looked over at the young Israeli astrophysicist.

"Well, Mr President, as you know the Earth has been continually bombarded with debris from the comet's tail over the last few weeks and months – large meteor showers, which have caused considerable collateral damage and loss of life –"

"Yep."

"Obviously over those few weeks the Earth has continued on its orbit around the Sun and the Schenkler comet has now effectively passed inside Mars' orbit and its trajectory places it smack bang on course to collide with Earth on May 26 as predicted –"

"That's *good* news!"

"Well, no, obviously not, Mr President. However, the comet's tail is no longer on the same path as Earth, so for the next few months we should be spared the damaging meteor storms that we have been suffering."

The President looked at his private secretary Jimmy Swarbrick busily scribbling notes on his eTab writer.

"Jimmy, ah've got to address the nations on the six o'clock newscast. Write me up a draft speech. Ah think we can demonstrate that out of adversity we still have some hope left to give!"

CHAPTER 22

Earthdate: 16:05 Friday January 14, 2084 EST

Six days after she had broadcast the news report on the loss of Oceanus XIII, Jill was on a welcome break from the stresses of pre-apocalyptic TV journalism. She was attending a 2-day course on space flight acclimatisation at the Kennedy Space Centre in Cape Canaveral, Florida as part of her selection to the secondary reserve list. Although, in the end, she had found that the two days were no less stressful than the day job. Yesterday she had a full day on lift off training and procedures and she was subjected to all sorts of G-force manoeuvres which left her absolutely drained. Today she was on zero gravity training, which included working underwater in full space gear and also taken on a supersonic sub-space flight which performed zero gravity manoeuvres. There was also a simulated spacewalk training session in full space flight gear which was designed to cater for the possibility of transfer from one spaceship to another in case of emergency. Jill found the training very stimulating and enjoyable and she was even going to propose doing a future feature on the training programme for Sky News. However, by four in the afternoon on the Friday she was utterly exhausted and she could not wait to fly back to Ewan in Houston later that night. She was getting her stuff together in the ladies' locker room when a female flight training assistant popped her head in the door and all the girls getting ready to leave looked up.

"Is there a Jill Geeson in here?"

"Ah'm Jill –"

"Can you give the Senior Flight Training Instructor five minutes of your time?"

Jill finished getting ready and hauled herself and all her bags along to the instructor's office where she found two male trainees who had been on the two day course also sitting there. Captain Carswell asked her to sit beside the other two trainees and then addressed them all cordially harking back to an old movie from the late 20th century.

"Well, how was survival training?"

The three trainees all laughed and in unison answered.

"We survived!"

Captain Carswell then addressed them in a more solemn tone.

"As you are all aware we lost one of our immigrant ships last Saturday – the Oh-X-triple-I –and all on board perished. A terrible thing, awful. In fact, Jill, ah saw your report on Sky – you did a terrific job there – very humbling."

"Thank you, sir."

"Well, guys, the thing is this. It appears that the boffins are gonna manage to scramble up two more Ohs than had been originally planned. This means we gotta shuffle the reserves around. So you three guys have been selected to move up from secondary tier to primary tier reserves."

Jill and the other two trainees gasped audibly.

"Now, don't get your goddam hopes up too high. Still means you're one step away from an actual seat goin' to Mars. Hell though, it's a heckuva lot better than the place ah've got – ah ain't goin' nowhere!"

Jill could not wait to call Ewan. Somehow, inexorably, she felt their destinies were being slowly drawn together by some higher force. Although, she knew that Ewan would be more pragmatic and view it more from the glass half empty perspective. He would say that she was still not definitely seated beside him on the Mars trip. Bloody scientist!

*

Earthdate: 16:45 Friday January 14, 2084 EST

That same afternoon Jack Crossan, dressed in his full formal space commander's dress uniform, flew up in his hired Chevy air-car to the small town of Gettysburg, Pennsylvania, quaintly preserved since the terrible battle of 1863. As his air-car dropped down into Gettysburg the whole landscape was covered in fresh snow. Eerily the scene from above looked so preserved and out of time that it could easily have been from an old black and white photograph taken back during the American Civil War. Jack arrived at the home of Andrew Jones, father of the ill-fated Space Commander Bethan Jones, and he stepped out of his parked air-car. He hesitated nervously before the house, which sported one of the prized preservation plaques on the red bricked wall. "Civil War Building – July 1863". Jack was not looking forward to meeting Andrew Jones. However, it appeared that Andrew had been expecting Jack's arrival and he opened the small door and ushered Jack in to the tiny living room. A young girl stood in the middle of the room and Andrew, ashen-faced and red-eyed, introduced his younger daughter Megan Jones. They all sat down and Jack drew out a blue velvet covered box from his briefcase, which he opened and turned towards the father and daughter. Megan sobbed softly.

"Mr Jones, may ah call you Andrew?"

Andrew nodded solemnly with his head slightly bowed.

"Andrew – Megan – ah have been sent by order of the President of the United States – Josh Trueman – to, ah, to present you with this posthumous US Air Force Medal of Honor in recognition of the bravery and valour shown by your, ah, your daughter Space Commander Bethan Jones USAF. Bethan gave her life freely and honourably in the pursuit of the survival of the human race. Ah personally knew and trained Bethan and she was a fine student and a skilled astronaut. Andrew – she was a very brave girl – one of the best."

Andrew leaned over and lightly touched the shining medal, tears rolling freely down his cheeks.

"Andrew, ah would ask you to accept this medal on behalf of a grateful nation – indeed, a grateful world."

A sort of ironic snort was exhaled from Andrew's mouth and his voice began to rise in ire not specifically directed at Jack.

"Commander Crossan, c'mon now, what use is this bullshit token to me or Megan?"

"Well, it's for –"

"Ah know what it's for, Jack! But what use is such a bauble now? I lost my wife a few years ago to cancer. I've now lost my oldest daughter. And in four months' time I'm gonna lose my only surviving daughter –"

Megan began sobbing a little more loudly and Andrew put his arm around her shoulder protectively.

"– and also my own life. Bethan's medal will be obliterated along with us. So what use is that?"

Jack bowed his head looking at the glinting medal and his lips quivered as he spoke softly.

"Ah'm also gonna lose the woman ah still love dearly and two young sons too –"

Andrew's voice softened apologetically and he replied through blinding tears.

"Ah'm so sorry, Jack. Our hearts are just broken over the loss of our beautiful sweet Bethan. We had taken solace in the hope that Bethan was going to survive on Mars. But that has been taken away from us."

They all lapsed into a momentary silence and the old Civil War house seemed to creak and groan as if joining in with their collective grief. Then Jack, after a flashing thought, looked up and directly into Andrew's tear-filled eyes.

"Here's the thing, Andrew. In six weeks' time ah'm Fleet Commander for the last flights to Mars of the Big-Oh fleet. It would be ma honour to take an' wear Bethan's Medal of Honor an' ah promise you and Megan that your daughter's medal will find a special place of honour in Capitol Base. How would ya feel about that?"

Andrew's eyes lit up and Megan gripped her father's arm excitedly.

"You would do that for ma Bethan? Then she would be remembered forever?"

"It would be ma honour an' privilege to do that for you, Andrew."

Andrew was too choked to speak, but Megan cried out happily.

"Oh, daddy, it would be like Bethan made it to Mars for us after all."

*

Earthdate: 14:10 Monday February 21, 2084 CST

Thunder clouds were massing to the north of the Johnson Space Center but the onset of a massive electric storm had not deterred the crowd of almost one million from converging on the perimeters of the Shuttle Launch Pad. All the major 3DTV networks were also in prime position. It was estimated that the 15:00 hours launch of the last Jupiter Galaxy V shuttle carrying the final 100 immigrants up to Alpha Base for transfer to Oceanus LII would command the largest single TV audience in history. They would be watching the final chosen few carrying all the hopes and dreams of the whole of mankind. However, what the watching humanity was unaware of, was that the storm rolling in was seriously jeopardising the chance of a successful take-off for the mighty shuttle. Man's future seemed to be being dogged by the forces of nature at every turn. Back at Houston Control nerves were frayed to breaking point. This launch represented the final window of opportunity to transfer these immigrants before the last Oceanus fleet sailed in one week's time on 28 February for Mars. Any delay to the fleet's departure after that date would seriously jeopardise any of the Oceanus craft still within the predicted blast zone caused by Schenkler's devastating and total impact with Earth on 26 May. This would mean that Aaron Eckler's risk assessment of the loss of one more Oceanus could turn out to be a grave underestimation. Eckler knew that the bottom line was that the shuttle had to take off today or it was not going anywhere. Eckler also knew that he had another major problem. On board Oh LII the ship was carrying Jack Crossan and Ewan Sinclair. Both Jack and Ewan had been held back to the last because their work on the programme back here on Earth had been crucial to the success of the Mars mission. However, Eckler now knew that if they did not take off today the Oceanus fleet was losing its appointed Fleet Commander and its best astronaut and Mars would undoubtedly be without its best astrophysicist. As the time check boomed around the Johnson Space Center and Houston Control - "T-minus-49 and counting" - Eckler snapped at Director of Control Irene Dupré standing beside him.

"Christ, Irene, what's the latest weather check on that storm?"

Irene tapped through to the weather controllers' latest update and turned to Eckler.

"It's lookin' pretty bad, Aaron. Weather guys say it will be right on top of us in about 40 minutes – right before launch."

"Aw shit, that's all we need. These shuttles are pretty sturdy beasts, but you and I know they are really designed for fair weather launches."

Irene nodded in agreement.

"What ah'm also worried about is the condition of the shuttle crew. They've been up and down to Alpha Base delivering the immigrants, the flora, fauna, DNA stockpiles and all the other stuff needed for the trip. They're just about at breaking point, Aaron."

"Well, Irene, looks like we are all in the lap of the Gods – as per usual."

On the launch deck area Jill was having her own problems. She was the only TV reporter in the world who had made it on to the flight selection lists, albeit, only on to the primary reserve list. This meant that she had been given the requisite space flight and launch training. For that reason Jill had been selected as the only reporter to be able to report via a static camera link attached to the corridor deck leading directly on to the huge Jupiter Galaxy V. No other TV crew were authorised to be on the launch deck, only ground crew. Jill stood pensively in front of the camera in full space flight gear with her helmet tucked awkwardly under her arm. Half an hour ago before she went on air she had had an emotional farewell with an equally tearful Ewan. He begged Jill to be allowed to stay.

"Jill, I'm sick to my stomach. I don't want to leave you. I love you too much to go."

Before Jill answered she bit hard on her lip to stop herself from crying. She watched the other immigrants filing past on the covered derricked corridor leading on to the shuttle. She turned to Ewan dry-eyed and almost hissed at him.

"Ewan Sinclair – get your arse on that ship right now! Those people there are going to need your expertise up there on Mars!"

Jill pulled Ewan in towards her and kissed him hard on the mouth. Then she immediately pushed him away towards the shuttle entrance door. She turned her back on him as if concentrating on the static camera that she was going to give her worldwide report to. She did not want Ewan to see the tears rolling freely down her face in case he failed to leave her. When she glanced around a moment later he had gone on board.

"T-minus-45 and counting."

The booming announcement over the tannoys snapped Jill back into her present predicament. The impending lightning storm had been playing havoc with the 3DTV electronics and the anchorman at Sky News had been trying unsuccessfully in the last five minutes to cue Jill in. She had to be off the derrick by T-minus-20, so if she did not get a report in by then it would be too late. Jill's director was screaming frantically down into her headpiece.

"Fucking hell, Jill. We're still not getting any feed from the camera and we weren't hearing you until a coupla minutes ago."

"What should ah do then? Just go on sound report only?"

"Aw fuck it, Jill, I don't know. Give the fucking camera a good bloody shaking and see what happens."

Jill gave the static camera a thud and immediately her director screamed back that she was now in full view on TV and he directed the anchorman to bring her on air in five seconds.

"And now we can go over to our reporter at the shuttle launch – Jill?"

A large rumble of thunder and the start of a heavy downpour introduced Jill's report. As she began, she wondered if anyone was hearing or seeing her, but she soldiered on anyway. Jill could not be sure, but indeed the world was watching.

"This is Jill Geeson reporting for Sky News. I am standing on the gangway just yards from the last of the momentous launches into space from planet Earth of the mighty Jupiter Galaxy V shuttles. On board are 100 men and women who represent the last surviving hopes of mankind. In just over 30 minutes they will take off to join the other twenty odd thousand men and women who will blast off from Alpha Base in a week's time on route to mankind's new planet of hope – Mars!"

"T-minus-29 and counting."

A large bolt of lightning snaked its way down from the heavens and struck the nose cone of the shuttle. The big Jupiter was fully earthed and the electricity dissipated harmlessly, but the near strike badly rattled the already frayed nerves of Canadian pilot Captain John Alexander and German co-pilot Flight Lieutenant Vibka Liebherr. The radio crackled and Lex Kosloff in Houston Control came on.

"Control to Eagle One. We saw you take a lightning strike head on there. Can you give us a status report? Over."

Captain Alexander reported back.

"E-Eagle One to C-Control. All systems still go here but ah'm p-pretty shook up. If this gets any worse ah think we might n-need to delay the launch a few hours. Over."

Lex looked back up to Irene DuPré and Aaron Eckler who both slowly shook their heads in unison.

"Control to Eagle One. Sorry guys, but no delay. Launch must go in T-minus-28 and counting. Report your status. Good to go? Over."

There was a long pregnant pause and Lex again pressed the crew for an answer.

"Control to Eagle One. Repeat. Are you good to go? Over."

The German Flight Lieutenant crackled a response.

"Eagle One to Control. Vibka here – I am good to go. Over."

"T-minus-26 and counting."

Jill was still on the derrick reporting although she had been pretty shaken by the near lightning strike a few minutes ago. She carried on bravely, now shouting at the top of her voice, as the huge Lockheed-Rolls Royce rocket engines began to thunder into life and compete with the fierce oncoming storm.

"We are now just twenty six minutes to lift off and it as if a great battle between man, machine and nature has begun. In less than six minutes I will need to get clear of the gangway along with all remaining ground crew as the huge engines rev up to full lift off power. The gangway will be drawn clear of the Jupiter shuttle, in effect, cutting the last umbilical lifeline between we billions left on Earth and the few humans destined to become our surviving descendants on the hostile Red Planet. At this point we can only wish them all - bon voyage."

At that very split second Jill let out a scream live on 3DTV to the watching billions, who would all have seen the lightning strike the hull of the Jupiter shuttle just yards behind her for the second time. A startled Jill kept on reporting.

"Who says lightning doesn't strike twice?"

Lex saw the second lightning strike on the shuttle as he was still trying to communicate with the crew.

"Control to Eagle One. Got Vibka's okay to go. John need your good to go. Over."

Again there was a momentary pause, then Captain John Alexander's frighteningly high-pitched tones came across the airwaves, but he was garbled and incoherent. Irene DuPré came on to Lex's headset.

"Jeezus, Lex, what the hell's goin' on in that cockpit? Over."

"Control to Eagle One. Vibka! Vibka! Please respond? Over."

In the cockpit Vibka was struggling to control John Alexander and she did not know if he was having a heart attack, a seizure or a nervous breakdown. She yelled at a cabin crew member to find a doctor on board. While she fought to calm the captain down she called back on her headset.

"Eagle One to Control. Captain Alexander currently unwell. Seeking medical advice on board. Please advise situation? Over."

Lex swivelled in his seat and looked back up at Irene and Aaron then he spread his arms out questioningly seeking an answer. He watched them have a quick conflab and then he saw Eckler put on a headset.

"Control to Eagle One. Mission Director Aaron Eckler here Vibka. We are delaying lift off by one-five minutes, repeat one-five, until situation stabilises. New lift off now T-minus-40. If Eagle One unable to lift off in T-minus-40 and counting then mission abort will be announced. Please acknowledge compliance. Over."

"Eagle One to Control. Vibka acknowledging and Wilco. Doctor now attending Captain Alexander in cockpit. Will update ASAP. Over."

The booming time check was recalibrated and announced to the watching world.

"Mission delay. Launch in T-minus-39 and counting."

A huge gasp arose from the crowd of a million watchers who were now being utterly drenched in the increasing downpour. It did not take a technical genius to know that this storm would play a part in whether the launch would happen or not. The rest of the watching world held its collective breath. Jill had called in to her director and asked what was going on and he screamed back at her.

"Jill, how the fuck would I know! Just wing it, kiddo, the whole fucking world is watching you!"

The static camera light signified she was back on air.

"This is Jill Geeson still reporting from the gangway of the Jupiter Galaxy V shuttle awaiting the launch of the last immigrants to join the Oceanus fleet up in Alpha Base. In the last minute or so Houston Control has just announced a fifteen minute delay to the actual launch. At present we do not have any details as to what has caused this delay. It may be the atrocious weather conditions or that a technical fault has been found or – or – hold on – hold on – the door of the shuttle is being reopened and –"

Jill was momentarily interrupted as two fully suited medics hurried along the gangway past her.

"- and it now appears that there may be a medical emergency on board the shuttle. When we get further details we will get these to you all when we have more on this developing story."

"T-minus-35 and counting."

Lieutenant Vibka Liebherr called in to Lex.

"Eagle One to Control. Sit Rep on Captain Alexander. Doctor on board has diagnosed a small but significant stroke. Medics now on board will take Captain Alexander off for hospital treatment. Over."

Aaron Eckler ripped off his headset and slammed it down on the desk beside Irene. Well, he thought, that is it all fucking over now. He was about to suggest aborting the mission when an instantly recognisable voice came on the tannoy.

"Eagle One to Control. Commander Jack Crossan here. You there Lex ya old fart? Copy?"

"Control to Eagle One. Lex here Jack. Over."

Crossan threw communications convention to the wind.

"Here's the deal Lex. I've basically never flown one of these babies except in simulators, but Vibka here has some flying experience on the Jupiters. What say we Vibka pilots an' ah'll be her co and let's get this thing to fuck outta here?"

"Jack. Eckler here. Vibka has only got ten hours flight under her belt! You're really a Big Oh pilot. Even John Alexander with all his experience would struggle to get the Jupiter safely through that storm out there. It's too big a risk –"

"Well, Aaron, it's an even bigger fuckin' risk if we abort an' end up stayin' down here on a doomed fuckin' planet!"

Lex looked up pleadingly and he received thumbs up from Aaron and Irene. Houston Control broke into loud cheering and hollering.

"Control to Eagle One. Lex here Jack, old buddy. You are cleared for lift off in T-minus-32 and counting. Copy?"

"Eagle One to Control. Lex, ah just need five minutes to do somethin' an' then we'll do final checks and countdown. Over."

Back out on the gangway Jill was reporting the dramatic news of the sick captain. She was still shrieking above the roar of the engines and the storm, both of which seemed to be coming to a climactic crescendo.

"It appears that the male taken off the Jupiter shuttle by medical staff was indeed the pilot Captain John Alexander. It would also appear that this must put the actual launch in serious jeopardy –"

A member of ground crew approached Jill as she was still reporting.

"Please Miss Geeson, ah have been asked to request that you vacate the gangway immediately."

"Fuck off! You've given the shuttle an extra fifteen so ah'm staying for an extra fifteen too. It's not T-minus-20 yet?"

She heard the director in her ear screaming at his controllers to keep the camera rolling. Prime time 3DTV!

"Yes, Miss Geeson, but there is a serious risk of you bein' harmed by the storm. You must leave now –"

"Hey, buddy, will you take your fuckin' hands off me! Ah'm not going anywhere and by the looks of it, without a captain, ah don't think your fuckin' shuttle is goin' anywhere either!"

Jill tried to squirm out of the ground crewman's tight grip on her arm as he slowly moved her out of camera shot and tried to pull her along the gangway away from the shuttle. Suddenly they were both stopped in their tracks by a shout from the door of the shuttle. Jill turned around and saw a widely grinning Jack Crossan standing in the open doorway. He shouted above the din.

"Jill! We've now got an empty passenger seat – you up for a trip to Mars?"

"B-but ah'm only in first reserve?"

"You're the only one here ah see that's suited an' booted. So get your ass in here an' let's get the hell outta here!"

Jack organised a quick seat reshuffle before final countdown and he managed to place a tearful Jill beside a totally gobsmacked Ewan. Jill was completely speechless too. She had lost her voice temporarily as a result of having to shout above the din of the engines and the storm. The shuttle take-off through the storm was pretty hairy but Vibka and Jack pulled the

Jupiter through all the thunder and lightning into the calm of the Earth's upper atmosphere and they glided safely towards the docking station on Alpha Base.

CHAPTER 23

The following evening President Trueman was the host of a gala dinner in the White House State Dining Room to celebrate the success of the immigration programme. Twenty four ships of the first Oceanus fleet commanded by Xi Xhu Pan had successfully arrived in Mars orbit. For the past few weeks they had been shuttling the immigrants, livestock, flora and fauna, DNA stockpile and other freight in a huge operation down to Capitol Base. So far the transfer had gone smoothly enough. There had been only two major downsides to the project so far. Firstly, the tragic loss of the five hundred immigrants on the Oh XIII commanded by Bethan Jones. Secondly, Dr Marcie Venters had been horrified to hear that a small percentage of the human DNA stock had been compromised and had to be destroyed. The core temperature of one of the liquid nitrogen containers had accidentally risen due to a fault in the cooling system on the Oh IX. Marcie was distraught, however, Aaron Eckler assured her that the loss was much less than had been included for in the project risk assessment. Eckler even cajoled Marcie with black humour stating that she was fortunate that the losses had not been greater. Due to her own superstitious nature Marcie had demanded that no human or animal DNA materials be carried on board Oh XIII. Eckler had Beth O'Donnell reengineer the freighting plan to comply with Marcie's wish. O'Donnell even managed to find some space on Jack Crossan's Oh LII for some additional DNA stock to be shipped that Marcie did not have in her original programme. In six days' time the second Oceanus fleet of a further twenty seven spaceships would set off on the fifteen week trip to Mars. By the end of March Gary Mackintosh's team would hand over fully functioning control of the E2MSN to Mars Control. One by one the network satellites orbiting in Earth's critical blast zone region would be destroyed by the comet's impact. Those satellites and the space station Midway Island, which had been evacuated, would be taken out of the E2MSN system. Basically, everything that could be achieved on Earth had been effectively completed. Trueman had gathered a great number of the men and women who had worked towards the survival of mankind to tonight's gala dinner. The great and the good were all there in full formal attire. Amongst the many world leaders were Ravinder Gupta-Chaudry, PM John Ralston, Mullah Abdullah Suleiman, PM Moshi Shalomon, the Chinese, French and German Presidents and the Russian Premier. Royalty was represented by Queen Elizabeth III and the Prince Regent David of Great Britain, the Kings of Belgium, Netherlands, Denmark, Saudi Arabia, Queen Sofia of Spain and the Sultan of Brunei amongst others. Representing the NASA team were Aaron Eckler, Beth O'Donnell, Ari Schenkler, Marcie Venters and Gary Mackintosh. Marcie had been seated at one of the long tables beside Suleiman on her right and they were enjoying themselves enormously. Through the project they had become great personal friends. On Marcie's left hand side she had been privileged enough to get an invitation for her daughter Ruthie. Ruthie was also getting on famously with the US President's handsome young son Jak Trueman. Jak Trueman had been seen as a potential rising talent in politics but his career in the Democratic Party was destined to be cut short. Josh Trueman solemnly realised that this would be the last time that he would have to address such a formal state occasion. He indicated to the Master of Ceremonies that he was ready. The MC rose his voice above the amiable hubbub.

"Your Royal Highnesses, Excellencies, Ministers, My Lords, Ladies and Gentlemen – I give you the President of the United States of America!"

Trueman arose from his seat at the top table and quickly surveyed his last big audience. He had no notes or autocues.

"Ah ain't gonna be speechifying to you all tonight. Tonight we are just goin' to eat an' drink an' party till dawn an' just have ourselves a real good time. Suffice to say, however, that the world owes a big debt of gratitude to the many men an' women who have sacrificed their time, their talents and effort to bring this Mars project to a conclusion an' to give the survival of the human race a fighting chance. It would be remiss of me not to add my own personal thanks. All of you here tonight have played your part. Ah salute you an' to your valiant teams - the whole world salutes you all. It was Mother Teresa of Calcutta who said, 'not all of us can do great things, but we can do small things with great love'. It is my belief that it was through our love for each other, that in the end, we have pulled this mission together. We have found a way to send our descendants out into the uncharted waters of the solar system to explore the next step in human history. Hopefully, they will have learned that for mankind to survive they need to set aside the old hatreds an' the old prejudices an' work together for the whole of humanity. So, before ah do end up speechifying – ah propose a toast to you an' all mankind – great love!"

The assembled guests all rose in unison and raised their glasses, cheering as one.

"GREAT LOVE!"

The doors of the State Dining Room were swung open and in marched the United States Marine Corps Band accompanied by the Field Marshall Montgomery Pipe Band playing Robert Burns' Auld Lang Syne. The assembled guests were still standing and they linked arms and sang their bursting hearts out. When they all sat down to eat there was hardly a dry eye to be seen.

*

Earthdate: 19:30 Monday February 28, 2084 CST

The second Oceanus fleet of twenty seven spaceships had been taking off from Alpha Base space station at half hourly intervals since early this morning. So far everything had gone without a hitch. The time had now come for Fleet Commander Jack Crossan to fire up the conventional rocket engines designed to pull Oceanus LII away from Alpha Base and out of Earth's gravitational pull. In thirty minutes he would fire up the fusion drive engines on the Iranian-built craft and bring his ship into fleet formation. He clicked on the tannoy and spoke directly to the passengers back in the huge cabin area.

"Okay folks, this is Commander Crossan speaking. We are about to be given the all clear from Houston Control to depart Alpha Base. So make sure that you are firmly strapped in and helmets locked on and let's all say goodbye to Mother Earth."

Jack flicked the switch off and he gulped hard and bit down on his lower lip. He thought of Peggy Sue, Milner and Jack Junior watching on 3DTV down in Cucklington and he fought back the tears.

"Ell-Eye-Eye to Houston Control. Clear for launch from Alpha Base. Copy?"

Jimmy Soderline was on shift, but Lex and Irene both stood behind him teary eyed and clinging on to each other.

"Houston Control to Ell-Eye-Eye. Copy - clear for launch from Alpha Base. God speed Jack. Over."

Jack turned to his Indian co-pilot Rajeev Subhinder and his Brazilian navigator Joanna Cespao and they both indicated with a thumbs up. Jack powered up the rocket boosters to full thrust and the Oh LII glided away from the space station, which had anxious faces crammed against every porthole. They knew they were watching the last flight to Mars from Earth's orbit and all they could do now was return back down to their homes and await the end. In their flight seats Jill and Ewan tried to hold hands awkwardly through their thick spacesuit gloves and they tapped their helmets together lovingly. The tears streamed as they both thought of their loved ones being left behind down in Glasgow and Islay. They had a private mic connection which allowed them to communicate until they got the all clear to remove their helmets. As they felt the forward thrust begin on the big Oceanus, Ewan checked how Jill was feeling.

"Well, Jilly, here we go. No turning back now. How are you feeling?"

"Ah'm feeling pretty awful. The thought of leaving all our family and friends behind. Ah'm feeling sick to ma stomach, Ewan –"

"Me too, baby. The thought of never seeing my beautiful Islay again. God, it all doesn't bear thinking about it. Hey, that's a couple of times that you've been feeling sick today?"

Jill looked away from Ewan, paused for thought, then she turned back.

"Ah'm four weeks pregnant, Ewan. Ah hadn't told you 'cos ah wasn't supposed to be here an' then our baby would never have been born."

"My God, Jill, does that mean - ?"

"Yes it does, Ewan –"

"No, what I was going to say, Jill, does that mean that we are going to give birth to the first Martian?"

Jill banged her helmet against Ewan's in pretend annoyance, as they both grinned broadly at each other. Fifteen minutes later they saw Jack Crossan come half floating towards them in the zero gravity of the cabin. He patched his mic into their loop system.

"Had to take a leak, so ah've left Rajeev in charge for five. You guys look happy? Jill, you look like the cat that got the cream"

"We're going to have a baby."

"Jeez, guys, does that mean - ?"

"Duh, yes, Jack we're goin' to have the first Martian!"

Back on the flight deck Jack took the controls back from Rajeev and they all made their preparations for the switch over to nuclear fusion drive. Five minutes later after Jack had called through all the final checks he set about turning on the fusion engines. Jack hit the switch and the green light came on and the fusion engines fired into life. Seconds later the big Oh gave a violent shudder and a red warning light came on and a klaxon sounded in the cockpit indicating that the fusion engines had not fired up properly. He switched off the fusion drive, continuing to burn the rocket boosters, and they went about going through their check lists again. Jack hit the switch a second time and again the ship shuddered followed by the red light and klaxon. He could hear some screams coming through from the passenger cabin. Rajeev looked at Jack with worry etched on his brow.

"What do you reckon, Jack?"

"No idea at present, Raj. Let's continue to burn on rockets. The slingshot we got from Earth still has us heading for Mars, but without the fusion drive it will take us six months to get there. Six months we don't have. At this velocity we will still be well within the blast zone perimeter."

Jack called back through the E2MSN to Houston and he caught Jimmy Soderline just about to come off his shift. He reported the failure to fire up the fusion drive. He said there was no imminent danger to the ship, but as the LII was now falling behind the fleet, Jack's command should be delegated to Commander Mohmed Malik in charge of Oceanus XXVI. Jack then asked Jimmy Soderline to get through to the Iranian nuclear tech boys ASAP and to quickly come back with a solution. Jack let Jimmy know that the solution had to come sooner rather than later or else it would be too late for the Oh LII to get clear of the blast zone. There was enough rocket fuel on board to propel the ship at rocket thrust speed for another 24 hours or so. Thereafter, without the fusion drive the spaceship would be free-falling towards Mars. However, Jack ordered Rajeev to keep the rocket burn at full thrust to try and eke out as much forward momentum as possible, even though they both ultimately knew it would not be enough. Back in Houston Jimmy handed the problem over to Lex Kosloff, who had just come on shift. Lex passed the problem up the chain of command. This meant pulling Josh Trueman back along to the Oval Office from a quiet family supper. Trueman made the call to Tehran getting the President of the LOIN out of his bed in the middle of the night.

"Suley, sorry to wake you at this late hour."

"Josh, my esteemed friend, please do not worry about it. Not too many sleeps to go anyway as your American kids would say."

Josh laughed then fell serious again.

"Suleiman, we still have one last fight on our hands. Your last Iranian built ship the Ell-Eye-Eye has failed to engage its fusion drive."

"Alluha akbar! Josh, I am so sorry. I know we had to cut corners to get it ready on time. Sounds like we cut one too many."

"Look, Suley, we don't have a lot of time. Can you get your best tech guys over to Houston an' maybe they can work somethin' out?"

"Josh, I will bring them personally on my private supersonic jet."

"Okay, ah'll meet you down there an' we'll knock a few heads together!"

*

Earthdate: 05:45 Tuesday February 29, 2084 CST

The Iranian technical team had arrived in Houston Control just after five in the wee small hours of the last Leap Year in Earth's history and they had now been debriefed. Trueman and Suleiman stood up beside Irene DuPré's station, alongside Eckler and O'Donnell. Alongside Lex sat the two Iranian fusion drive experts and Gary Mackintosh was called in for his computer expertise. The worry was that over nine hours of fusion drive thrust had been lost by the Oh LII. Every minute lost meant the ship might not make it beyond the blast zone perimeter. However, the aim was to get the fusion engines firing and give Jack and his ship a fighting chance. The two Iranians, Saeed Mohammed and Hossein Tehrani, had Lex submit instructions for Jack to transmit a diagnostic report. The two experts had pored over it for hours and it seemed to Lex that no enlightenment was forthcoming. Gary also tried to make sense of it, however, he was no nuclear physicist and most of it was gobbledegook to him. At eight in the morning, with nothing seeming to be happening, Trueman called for a conference in one of the meeting rooms.

"Okay, guys, we are badly losing time for those guys up there. What is the bottom line?"

The senior Iranian expert Saeed spoke in his own Persian language and Suleiman translated.

"Josh, the diagnostic reports seem to indicate that there is no intrinsic fault with the nuclear fusion cells nor does there seem to be any fault with the engines."

"Well where does that leave us? Are we to just let them sink or swim!"

Saeed spoke again through Suleiman.

"If we could get the Oh LII to try and fire up the fusion drive again and find some way of transmitting all the available data from the ship's computer live then it may show up the problem."

"Okay, can we do that anybody?"

Gary spoke up. He did not even use Mister President as they were all equals now.

"Ah could hook up a live feed with the Oh LII through the E2MSN. Jack could then transmit all the ship's live data back to Houston."

"Let's do it."

Half an hour later Gary had patched into the on board computer's main server via the E2MSN and Jack was told to give the fusion engines another go. After going through the standard check list he set the switch again. For a third time the Oh LII shuddered and the warning light and klaxon issued forth once more. Jack radioed back to Houston.

"No go, Lex. Will continue to run on rocket boosters meantime. Over."

"Houston to Ell-Eye-Eye. The data is streaming in Jack. Tech boys are on it. Over and out."

Saeed, Hossein and Gary pored over the engine fire up procedural data with Suleiman acting as an interpreter when needed. By ten o'clock they were all becoming exhausted and exasperated and Hossein, who had been the main project engineer for the fusion engines, spoke agitatedly in Persian, which Suleiman translated.

"I'm adamant Saeed, there is no major fault showing in the engines. The data shows that they are firing up okay."

Saeed replied, again through Suleiman.

"Yes, Hossein, but it is as if they are not being maintained. Almost as if they are being switched off again."

A light illuminated in Gary's head and he held up his hand as he quickly pored through data sets on his screen.

"That's it boys, ye've cracked it. It's not an engine problem, it's a computer glitch!"

The puzzled Iranians asked for a translation and Suleiman continued to speak as Gary elaborated. Gary had identified that the fault was in the ship's on-board server, which was causing the fusion drive switch to be turned off automatically every time it was engaged. He also outlined that finding the faulty circuit or chip which was causing the problem was nigh on impossible. In fact, even if it could be found it would be unlikely that the hastily built ship was carrying a valid replacement. Suleiman's head bowed and his hand went to his forehead in resignation.

"Then the Ell-Eye-Eye is doomed?"

Gary had a twinkle in his eye.

"Well, maybe not quite, Suleiman."

"What do you mean, my friend?"

"Gary's ma name – hacking's ma game. What we do is use the E2MSN an' hack in to the Ell-Eye-Eye's computer. We by-pass the main server an' remotely fire up the fusion drive from here."

"Allah be praised. You can do this?"

"Well with Saeed and Hossein's tech help ah can give it a bloody good try!"

Just after ten in the morning after a quick conference, Gary, Saeed and Hossein reported back that they had been able to hack past the LII's main server and they had loaded the engine start up programme on to Houston's main server for transmission to the crippled spaceship. Lex called Jack and explained what they were going to try and Jack agreed that it was their only shot remaining. After clearance from Houston, Jack and Rajeev went once again through all the start-up checks and Jack gave Lex the all clear. Gary nodded to Hossein who then transmitted the engine start up programme through Gary's hack up to the Oh LII. There was radio silence for that awful moment as they all held bated breaths, then Jack's voice crackled down the airwaves.

"Ell-Eye-Eye reports fusion drive on and functioning!"

He was interrupted by the resounding cheering from Houston Control.

"It must have sustained some damage in previous start-ups. Only getting ninety per cent fusion thrust. But at this moment in time ah'll take that. Over."

Trueman shook Eckler's hand vigorously.

"Good job, Aaron!"

"Thanks, Mister President. But with a fourteen hour delay and only ninety per cent thrust it will be nip and tuck whether they make it."

"Well, truth is, Aaron, none of us will be around to find out!"

CHAPTER 24

Schenkler HMM2 was now so close to Earth that it shone brighter in the sky than even the brightest Moon. Like most things in the cosmos it commanded that immense beauty that most humans could appreciate. However, it was difficult to appreciate the beauty of something so omnipotent, a glorious celestial body that was just about to wipe out everything in its path. Impact with the comet was expected within the next hour and predicted to be in the mid-Pacific basin close to the Marianas Trench. Geophysicists had calculated that as this was a particularly weak point in the Earth's crust. Schenkler would easily smash its way through the crust and then on through the mantle and finally into the molten iron core of the planet. Following the initial impact, huge tsunamis hundreds of feet high would rip across the continents destroying everything and everyone in their paths. Volcanic eruptions would spew out at all points across the globe followed by huge pyroclastic flows. Once the core had been breached the Earth's tectonic plates would become highly unstable and the planet would crack open like an egg and end in an awesome apocalyptic nuclear explosion measured in the billions of Hiroshimas. Over the last few weeks everyone left behind on Earth were in their own unique way preparing to meet their Maker. There had been some minor anarchic outbreaks at various flashpoints across the planet, but, in general, most people had resigned themselves calmly to their fate. There had been a sort of holiday atmosphere which had prevailed for weeks. In the main men and women had resolved to stay in their hometowns or travel to their birthplaces. Many had even arranged to go to significant locations salient to their lives or their faiths. Somewhere that they would be most happy to end their days. Holy places like Rome, Lourdes, Jerusalem, Bethlehem, Mecca, Medina and sacred sites along the Ganges River were filling up to bursting with pilgrims of all faiths - including those who previously had no faith. Like many Hindus, Jains and Buddhists, Ravinder Gupta-Chaudry had travelled home to India to the sacred city of Varanasi, also known as Benares. The UN Gen-Sec had drifted away from the Hindu faith which had been fervently practised by his family for generations. However, as Ravinder bathed in the warm Ganges waters he felt that it was more than a mere coincidence that it was the Hindu festival of avatarana. To soak in the Ganges at this time was said to rid the bather of the ten sins or the dasha hara. No place along its banks is more longed for at the moment of death by Hindus than Varanasi, the Great Cremation Ground, or Mahashmshana. Those who are lucky enough to die in Varanasi, are cremated on the banks of the Ganges, and are granted instant salvation. Ravinder thought as he bathed with the massed chanting throngs just how lucky he was. The little town of Megiddo in Israel had filled up with hundreds of thousands of pilgrims, Jewish and Christian, who wanted to feel like they were fulfilling the biblical prophecy of Armageddon. A few hours ago on the edge of Megiddo National Park they had received a short address by President Moshi Shalomon, who had come with his own family from his nearby birthplace of Haifa. He spoke in Hebrew and in English to the massive crowd.

"….and it is written in the scriptures – *'then they gathered the kings together to the place that in Hebrew is called Armageddon'.* In the Jewish religion it is believed that the Messiah was still to come and in the Christian faith that one day he would return on Judgement Day. One way or another I think today we have been given God's answer and soon we will all sit at Jehovah's right hand for eternity."

Ari Schenkler was not to get sight of his very own comet today as it was coming in from the east well below the Israeli horizon. He had gone up to use the main telescope at the INSACC last night to marvel at how close HMM2 was and he looked back with a great deal of pride in the work that he and Ewan Sinclair had carried out. To have predicted that a lump of rock from beyond the solar system would impact with his little blue planet and to have gotten that spot on was a testimony to man's knowledge, intellect and ingenuity. He had taken comfort in the fact that at least Ewan was continuing to carry those special human talents onwards to Mars. Ari had thought about flying his air-car this morning the ninety kilometres north to Megiddo. In the end he and Ava decided to take their daughter Sarah to Gordon Beach beside the Lahat Promenade in Tel Aviv. They spent the morning playing with Sarah on the beach, making sandcastles, paddling in the Mediterranean and eating far too much falafel and ice cream. Ari even bumped into his old INSACC boss Yosep Goldenheim. Yosep was also enjoying a last day at the seaside with his new young wife Rebecca Menachim, Ari's old colleague, and some of his grown up children from his first marriage. In the afternoon Ari and Ava relaxed in deck chairs holding hands tightly as they watched their last views of the beautiful glorious Sun starting to lower in the clear blue western sky. Sarah slept obliviously in Ava's lap. In Tehran Mullah Abdullah Suleiman was spending his final afternoon leading Friday prayers in the packed Shah Mosque in the city of his birth in Isfahan. So many people had turned up that the adjacent Naqsh-e Jahan Square was packed solid and Suleiman and the Imams had to address the multitudinous crowd through loudspeakers. The great cry of Allahu Akbar resounded time and again around the packed square. In England PM John Ralston decided to spend his last day at the Prime Ministerial retreat of Chequers near Aylesbury in Buckinghamshire. He had invited family and friends, both political, religious and social, to join him in a brunch-style barbecue. The weather was pleasantly warm with just a hint of the onset of the summer that was never to be hanging in the sweet-scented blossom-filled air. After the barbecue the PM had organised a short service led by the Archbishops of Canterbury and Westminster. This was followed by a bounce cricket match, Ralston's favourite sport and pastime. The intention was that the match would not be able to come to a final conclusion for obvious reasons. The PM gave the scorekeeper strict instructions that every player was to be recorded as 'Not Out' on the big scoreboard that he had brought in for the occasion. Further towards the West Country Peggy Sue Milner and Justin Smythe decided to take Milner, Jack Junior and their two golden retrievers for a long walk in the sunshine from Bainley Lane Farm to a favourite picnic spot looking across the valley from Cucklington to Wincanton. Peggy Sue regaled the boys with stories about their father Jack when he was a small boy in Virginia and growing up and meeting Maria Conchita and then later marrying Peggy Sue. They were fascinated to hear about the time that Jack held on tightly to Uncle Jimmy Reid's picket fence and found that he was 'flying' and also the time that their father thought that there was a man with a gun in his bedroom. After she had finished the stories about Jack, young Jack Junior cast his eyes past Peggy Sue and he seemed to be sitting entranced.

"Junior, are ya okay, son?"

The boy pointed back to an old rickety fence standing behind them on the edge of a wooded area.

"When the big comet comes maybe we could all hold on to that fence and then maybe we could fly too? Like poppa."

Tears rimmed Peggy Sue's eyes.

"Oh my baby, that is so the best idea an' ah think that is jest what we're all gonna do."

*

Further up north in Glasgow, Scotland Gary Mackintosh had flown home from Houston a couple of weeks ago and he was staying with his parents Frank and Annie. They now lived in a swanky new home in Kelvinside which Gary had bought them well before his stocks and shares had crashed. They had decided to spend their last day together going around the art exhibitions of Kelvingrove Art Gallery and Museum. They had agreed that it was such a terrible loss to the human cultural experience that all the great works of art around the world would be destroyed. Gary's NOAHSARK project had preserved virtually of the great artworks digitally, but as he and his parents stood admiring Salvador Dali's immense opus Christ of St John of the Cross, they knew that in the end there was nothing to beat the real thing. They finished their day by walking across to Garnethill and took a final Mass in St Aloysius RC Church. Across the Atlantic the sun had only risen about an hour ago on Galveston Bay. Lex had been raised in Galveston, Texas as a boy and he and Irene had come here to face the end. They were joined by many tens of thousands who had decided to enjoy their last day by the warm waters of the Gulf of Mexico. Everyone there could not help but notice that the bird life of the estuarial nature reserve was acting like crazy and the sky was filled with confused swirling flocks of many species. It was like a scene from the Hitchcock horror film 'The Birds'. Lex commented to Irene that the birds obviously knew something big was on its way. Irene said that Schenkler was obviously playing havoc with the Earth's magnetic fields. Lex's maternal grandmother used to tell him blood-curdling stories of how she lost an ancestor in the Great Storm of 1900. At least 8,000 people lost their lives in Galveston when the unpredicted hurricane brought in a devastating flood, causing the greatest natural disaster to hit the United States. Lex and Irene knew that within an hour or so the 1900 Galveston Flood was about to be totally eclipsed on the scale of human disasters. It was just after 8am when Josh Trueman's air-limo arrived at Crestwood Park in Birmingham, Alabama. Josh had been raised in the tough Crestwood neighbourhood and he felt like a returning prodigal son. A moderately sized crowd had turned out to politely applaud Josh and his family as they made their way up the white-painted wooden steps. The modest building was made of wood and stucco, which had been hastily constructed, but it still made Trueman feel immensely proud. He thought to himself that every other US President had one and his supporters in Alabama had ensured that he was going to have one too. His heart was bursting with pride as he stepped up to the mic holding a pair of ceremonial scissors with which to cut the red, white and blue tape behind him.

"Ladies an' gentlemen, boys an' girls, it gives me the greatest of pleasures to inaugurate the President Joshua Spengler Trueman Library. However, ah muss say - if you want to read anythin' in it you had better be quick!"

Just about the same time, Dr Marcie Venters and her daughter Ruthie arrived at the B'nai Jeshurun Jewish Cemetery in Brooklyn, New York. They had walked from the nearby Holiday Inn Brooklyn where they had been staying these last few days. Marcie's sister Ruth Esther Bloom had already had a full house as she had invited many Bloom family members to a last reunion and Marcie and Ruth had gone to the farewell party last night in Marcie's old home. Marcie and Ruth were both carrying flowers as they walked smartly over to the Bloom family grave. They both laid their bouquets at the graveside and a tearful Marcie ran her fingers over the carved Hebrew inscriptions. She thought to herself that soon she would be with her beloved husband Rolf and her esteemed father Dr Ezra Bloom. Marcie recited the Talmudic benediction of the Ḳibbuẓ Galuyot.

"Blow the great trumpet for our liberation, and lift a banner to gather our exiles, and gather us into one body from the four corners of the Earth. Blessed be Thou, O Lord, who gatherest the dispersed of Thy people Israel."

Ruthie whispered a much shorter prayer as the mother and daughter hugged each other tightly.

"Our Father, our King! Disclose the glory of Thy Kingdom unto us speedily."

*

Earthdate: 13:55 Friday May 26, 2084 GMT

The Red Planet was now much larger on Commander Mohmed Malik's main monitor and he was feeling much happier and certainly more secure. He had successfully brought the second fleet of twenty six ships well beyond the blast zone perimeter and there was now only three weeks left to go until they were all safely in Mars orbit. His key concern now was that Jack Crossan's ship was still limping along well behind the fleet. The last that Mohmed had heard from Mars Control was that the Oh LII was still struggling within the danger zone. On the bridge of the LII Jack, Rajeev and Joanna were more than just concerned. They were extremely fearful of their chances. In the last seven days the fusion drive performance had dropped down to 85 per cent. If anything, the ship was slowing down rather than speeding up. On the screens in front of Jack the key concerns he was monitoring were threefold. Firstly, there was the Red Planet sitting in the screen's cross-hairs, but to Jack, it still looked too small, too distant and too unattainable at this juncture. Secondly, there was the schematic view of the ship as an audible blip moving inexorably to the left away from Earth with a line indicating the boundary of the blast zone perimeter. To the left the screen had a green 'safe zone'. Just inside the perimeter line was an amber 'critical zone' and the right side of the screen was the red 'danger zone'. The ship's blip had only just crossed from the red zone to the amber zone in the last hour. Navigator Joanna Cespao's calculations showed the vessel was highly unlikely to reach the safe green zone in time. Thirdly, there was the monitor sending pictures back from the little shining blue dot that was Planet Earth, which was about to collide with the Schenkler comet within the next few minutes. It would take about another forty eight hours for the shock waves from the massive explosion to reach this far out into the solar system and Jack knew that the waves would be dissipating rapidly by then. His problem was that NASA's calculations still forecast that the shock waves could still do a heck of a lot of damage to even the sturdiest Oceanus this far out. Jack knew the ship he had got was cobbled together at the last minute with every corner in the book cut. He feared that the LII could easily be destroyed and he and Rajeev worked furiously to find a way to eke out just a little more power from the fusion drive. Try as they might they could not get it above the 85 per cent mark. They also did not want to tinker too much in case the fusion drive cut out completely and they ended up with the startup problem again. Jack felt that it was time to make the awful announcement to the expectant and fear-filled passengers.

"This is Commander Crossan speaking. Ah have to announce that total impact is now imminent. Ah know many of you would like to watch and ah will put a view from the E2MSN up on the seat-back monitors. For those of you who do not want to see it ah would advise you to look away now."

Jill just mouthed to Ewan, oh my God! Moments later everyone watched the immense flash as their beautiful blue planet exploded in a massive nuclear fireball. Huge concentric rings of gas and debris rapidly expanded outwards with the explosion carrying the shock waves rippling out into deep space. Earth was no more.

*

Everything and everyone that the passengers and crew on the Oh LII had loved and cherished, and also those of the survivors on Mars and those still travelling there in the second fleet, had been completely and utterly obliterated. Blown into eternity. Billions of years of the evolution of life on Earth had been snuffed out in an instant. In human history this certainly ranked as the most significant of events, but the random thought occurred to Jack that life was probably being extinguished and reborn on millions, even billions, of Earth-like planets throughout the universe. Probably even throughout the multiverse if indeed it did exist. However, the enormity of this apocalyptic catastrophe was too much for most of the passengers. There was a great deal of hysterical screaming and wailing. Jack, who had to fight to control his own nerve, now had a ship full of grieving souls to steady.

"Uh, this is Commander Crossan again…"

His voice had a partial calming effect on most of the passengers, although many still sobbed bitterly.

"What we have just witnessed is truly such a terrible event that none of us could ever have imagined happening in our wildest dreams. But now we have a fight on our own hands. In about forty eight hours it is likely that we will have to face being hit by the shock waves of the blast. When ah give the command everyone has to be fully strapped in an' everything has to be completely battened down. Anything that cannot be fixed or is deemed superfluous will have to be jettisoned into space. Everyone on board needs to follow my commands to a T or else they could seriously jeopardise the safety of this ship and everyone on board. Ah trust that ah have made myself crystal clear?"

Jack's old colleague Xi Xhu Pan had been languishing in 'rest and recoup' on Magellan, the old 'Rust Bucket', which had been pressed back into service. MGals 2, 3 and 4 had been overstretched, being utilized to process the incoming immigrants on the first fleet and there was no room left at the inn for Xi Xhu and his crew. Xi Xhu had also watched his beloved planet being vapourised, blown into oblivion. Almost immediately after the terrible event Xi Xhu and his crew were ordered to take a space tender and transfer over to the empty Oceanus II and await further orders. Xi Xhu guessed that Jack Crossan must be in trouble. About two hours after the demise of Planet Earth, Oceanus II was given clearance to leave Mars orbit. Commander Xi Xhu Pan had obtained permission from Mars Control to take the empty ship along with his skeleton crew on what was effectively now deemed a rescue mission. With any luck Xi Xhu would be turning back in less than 48 hours when Jack radioed through that the LII had made it safely beyond the blast zone perimeter. However, the signs did not look good and Mars Control felt that the Oh Two should set sail immediately as it could take up to four weeks to reach Jack's ship. God only knew what Xi Xhu would find if and when he got there.

*

Marsdate: 14:10 Sunday May 28, 2084 CBT

About ten hours ago Jack had recorded in his log that they were no longer receiving any further transmissions showing the destruction of Earth and the evolving resultant gas cloud that was all that remained of the planet. Joanna Cespao was able to calculate and report that this was almost certainly due to the destruction of Midway Island, which had been left deserted but operating on minimal autopilot. The shock waves were on their way. Jack had noted about half an hour ago the first signs that the shock waves from the Armageddon blast were rippling out towards them and he estimated that they were still about three hundred thousand miles short of the blast zone perimeter. The Oh LII had started to demonstrate a slow bobbing pitch as if a once calm ocean now had low rhythmic waves beginning to rise and fall beneath its hull. Over the last 24 hours he had ensured that everything deemed crucial to the survival of his passengers had been tightly screwed down, such as oxygen supplies, medicines, food and drink. If it was not critical Jack had it jettisoned. This included all flora, fauna and the small amount of livestock and animal feed the ship was carrying in its hold. Jack even had to make the decision to ditch Marcie Venter's last despatch of human DNA, which had been designed to make up for the losses incurred when the Oh XIII exploded. Jack felt bad about it, having known how much work Marcie had put into her project. To appease Marcie's memory he had the refrigerated DNA containers jettisoned away from the Sun on a bearing heading out towards the Kuiper Belt and on beyond the solar system. Maybe, he thought more in hope, that in the eons of time the DNA might land on some life-supporting planet somewhere out there in the Milky Way and that evolution may once again take its course. It was the best he could do for Marcie. The bobbing motion was now beginning to pitch the ship quite vigorously and he ordered Rajeev and Joanna to strap in as tightly as possible. The passengers had been strapped in with full space gear on for the last two hours. Jack had Rajeev personally inspected all five hundred. Jack found the sight of all of those fear-laden eyes totally gut-wrenching. When he had come to check on Ewan and Jill he had given them a less than confident thumbs up. Jill's hands were lain protectively across her womb and a single tear rolled down her cheek as Jack had carried on with the check. Back in the cockpit Jack sealed on his space helmet and double-checked that he was fully strapped in. He switched on his mic for a final announcement.

"Okay, everyone. This is it. Get ready for the Big Dipper ride of your life. Good luck and God speed!"

A few minutes later and the ship was caught in the first big shock wave and it began to pitch and toss violently. Jack looked across at Rajeev and he could see that they were both straining every sinew in their bodies trying to handle the controls. Many of the passengers were screaming wildly but there was nothing Jack could do for them. Initially, Jack had fought hard to keep the ship on a direct course for Mars. However, he felt that this was putting too great a strain on the ship and it was almost impossible for him and his co-pilot to control. He shouted an order through his mic to Rajeev.

"Ride the waves, Raj! We can't fight them!"

Initially, riding along with the waves seemed to Jack to be helping, but then the next big shock wave came slamming into the ship. If the first wave was huge then this one was a veritable tsunami. The G-force pressures were painfully severe and Jack clenched his teeth tightly. The ship creaked and groaned under the enormous pressure and she bobbed out of control in space like a tin can in a hurricane ravaged ocean. Lights and circuits were exploding and popping in the cockpit and also out in the passenger cabin. A small fire had started in the hold but it was quickly controlled by the automatic fire safety system. The monitors, indicators and controls were going haywire and Jack had no idea which way the ship was heading. It almost felt to him as if the LII was rolling down the side of a near vertical wave like an out of control surfer. Then it seemed as if the wave had momentarily passed over them and Jack and Rajeev fought hard to stabilise the ship.

"No – idea – which – way – headed – Raj!?"

Before his Indian co-pilot could even venture a response an even bigger tsunami-like shock wave crashed into them. The pain from the G-forces was incredible and Jack could no longer bear it as he cried out.

"AAAAARGH!!"

Jack heard Joanna Cespao screaming behind him. He turned round with great difficulty to see that Joanna's helmet had cracked open under the pressure and blood was spurting out into the zero gravity cockpit in crazily floating red globules. Joanna slumped over. She was dead. Jack looked across and saw that Rajeev was also slumped in his seat. He was either dead or unconscious. Jack thought, this is looking bad. Smoke from the burning circuits mixed with Joanna's floating blood made visibility in the cockpit increasingly difficult for Jack. Another catastrophic crash collided into the groaning ship and which caused the fusion drive engines to cut out completely. The ship went into freefall and it felt to Jack as if it must be spinning like a top. His head felt as if it was ready to burst. He tried to look around, but it was as if he was moving in slow motion. A dark shadowy figure appeared to be floating towards him as if in some sort of terrifying flashback.

"Mom - Mom! Pop! Come quick! There's a man in ma room with a gun."

Then, blackness.

CHAPTER 25

<u>Marsdate: 18:30 Sunday May 28, 2084 CBT</u>

Over four hours had now passed since either Mars Control or Xi Xhu Pan on the Oh Two had heard anything from the Oh LII. What did not help was that the shock waves from the Schenkler-Earth collision were much stronger than Ewan and Ari's NASA team had predicted in their computer modelling forecasts. This had caused an extra two of the satellites, which had been transferred by Gary Mackintosh's team at NASA to the new Mars Network (MNET) from the now defunct E2MSN, to either have been destroyed or taken out of commission. This had also been causing serious disruption to the MNET and the best technicians were working hard at Capitol Base to reconfigure the system. Radio communication between Mars Control and Xi Xhu was patchy at best but still functioning. The Control Director was trying to decide whether to recall the Oh Two back to Mars. The view in Mars Control was that time was now passing and there had been no radio signals from the Oh LII, no distress signals, not even a blip. Xi Xhu was not keen to give up so easily on his old commander Jack Crossan and the five hundred souls who might still be alive out there somewhere in space.

"Oh Two to Mars Control. Request forty eight hours to continue search towards last bearing of Ell-Eye-Eye. Over."

Xi Xhu waited the few suspenseful moments of radio silence then the Shift Controller replied through a badly crackling and hissing reception.

"Mars Control - to Oh – Two. Further – search – for forty eight – hours – sssshhhhh - !"

The radio message cut out unfinished in a hiss of radio static followed by silence. Xi Xhu turned to his co-pilot Verne Andriessen and told him with a wry smile that he would assume that meant that they were good to go. Xi Xhu set his ship on a bearing towards the last known location within the amber zone for the Oceanus LII. He could not help but notice with a lump in his throat the bright speck on his monitor on the same bearing almost thirty million miles further away. It was the gas cloud swirling and transforming in space that was once his beloved Planet Earth. Xi Xhu boosted the fusion drive on the Oh Two to full power and he set sail on a rescue mission more in hope than expectation. Even if the seemingly crippled LII was still intact it was still almost four weeks away. If it was in a bad way then it might not have enough oxygen and supplies left to last four weeks. Given that there had been no signals at all from the LII, Xi Xhu assumed that it must have lost its main fusion drive, power supplies and main computer systems. He guessed that it would be in freefall through the solar system, not necessarily heading for Mars, and therefore, it could be hundreds of thousands of miles off the course that he was currently heading for. However, he was determined to give Jack Crossan and the LII a chance. At least to give Jack forty eight hours' grace - if he could just keep Mars Control off his back.

*

<u>Marsdate: 10:10 Tuesday May 30, 2084 CBT</u>

Jack's eyes slowly rolled open and his head lolled about for a few minutes. From the dim blue lighting he guessed the Oh LII was running on emergency power only and as he slowly focussed his eyes he could see that most of his monitors were either smashed beyond repair or in idle mode. He wondered how long that he had been unconscious and strapped in to his pilot's seat. He looked at the small monitor on his sleeve, which he noticed was miraculously still operating and looked at the time. It was still in Earthdate mode but still functioning. My God, he thought, I've been out for nearly two days. He looked across at Rajeev Subhinder and he was still in the slumped position that Jack had last remembered his co-pilot being in before blacking out. His navigator Joanna Cespao's dead body was in a terrible state. Most of her visor had been ripped away and her skull had cracked open like a ripe melon, exposing dried blood, bone and brain matter. The ship seemed to Jack to be continuing through space in freefall but at least everything appeared to have calmed down outside the ship. The shock waves from the blast of Earth's death throes appeared to have passed. Jack looked again at his sleeve monitor and it indicated that there was still an oxygen-helium mix atmosphere present in the cabin, although he could see that it was only being detected around fifty per cent levels to normal. We must be leaking oxygen badly, Jack thought with mounting concern. Gingerly he removed his helmet. He gulped in a breath and found that he could breathe normally. His body was aching badly so he unstrapped himself slowly from his pilot's seat. He floated himself across to Rajeev and looked at his co-pilot's sleeve monitor. It showed that his co-pilot still had vital signs. He was still alive. Jack thought it would be better not to try and move Rajeev. It would be better to see if he could find a doctor alive in the passenger cabin, although he dreaded opening the air lock from the cockpit. Would anyone still be alive out there? Jack pulled back the thick heavy door onto a horror scene from Hell. A few of the seats had been sheared from their moorings just from the great pressures exerted on them by the shock waves. With their dead passengers still strapped in they had crashed about the passenger cabin, causing tremendous damage and death. In the same way that Joanna Cespao had died, Jack could see that quite a few passenger's helmets had exploded under the G-forces exerted on them and their dead faces were in a horrific mess to witness. It seemed to Jack on first sight that possibly all of the passengers had been killed outright as nothing or no-one seemed to be stirring. He cried out.

"Is there anyone alive?"

At first no-one moved and then slowly one by one Jack watched stiff aching arms being raised throughout the length of the passenger cabin. He shouted that if possible to do so they could safely remove their helmets, which some of them started to do. He slowly floated from one survivor to the next, gauging their levels of consciousness and those who needed urgent medical attention. Within a few minutes he had identified two doctors and two nurses all of whom had either none or only minor injuries. He directed them to where he hoped they would find the medical supplies and commanded them to start triaging the injured and to set up a sort of temporary field hospital. He continued on floating between dead and injured passengers, reassuring those badly injured that doctors would attend them as soon as possible. Jack knew from sight that some of the critically injured would not make it and he tried to give them a last word or two of comfort. His stomach was churning at the horror he was witnessing, the crying and groaning and suffering. At least, he thought to himself, that it had been quick for Milner, Jack Junior and Peggy Sue. They would not have suffered. Moving towards the back of the passenger cabin he slowly floated towards Ewan and Jill's seats. He could hardly bear to look. Ewan seemed to be in a similar situation to Rajeev. He was still unconscious with his helmet intact, but his sleeve monitor showed that he still had vital signs. Ewan was still alive. Jack shouted back to the medics.

"Doc, this one up here is bad! Have a look when you gotta minute?"

One of the doctors signalled a thumbs up and went back to treating his current patient. Jack moved over to Jill. She was alive and conscious. Jill had taken her helmet off but she looked groggy and she was sobbing quietly. Jack took her gloved hand and looked at her sleeve monitor. Jack was encouraged as her signs did not look too bad.

"Jill, how ya feelin'? Are you injured?"

"Ah don't think so, Jack. B-but – what about – what about ma baby? What about Ewan!?"

"Look – try not to worry, Jill. Ewan's out cold, but he's alive. An' when the doctor gets around to you an' Ewan – well, he'll check out your baby too. Ah've gotta go check everyone else, so try not to get too stressed an' ah'll get back to ya later. Okay?"

Jack carried on checking throughout the passenger cabin. By the time that he had gotten around everyone he guesstimated that out of five hundred cabin crew and passengers there was around a hundred and fifty dead and probably around another fifty or sixty injured to various degrees between critical, serious, severe and minor. He was assisted by some of the uninjured passengers to shift the floating separated chairs with their dead passengers. They moved them into the hold and strapped them down as they were likely to cause more damage and injury in the passenger cabin. When Jack floated back to the field hospital area he found that there were now four doctors of varying experience and six nurses in attendance. He was assured that they would do their best to get the medical emergencies dealt with as best as they could and he headed back to the cockpit. Jack knew that with the spaceship flying God knows where in the solar system and the likelihood that the oxygen supply was dwindling that his job was to somehow try and get some power and communications back up and running. As he entered the cockpit he was greeted with a welcome sight. His Indian co-pilot had come around and was sitting recovering in his seat with his helmet off. Rajeev grimaced a pain-ridden white flashing smile at Jack.

"Thank God, Raj, you're alive. How're ya feelin'?"

"I've felt better but I think I'll make it. Poor Joanna didn't though, Jack?"

"Ah know, Raj. It's God awful out there in the passenger cabin too!"

Jack placed a blue plastic cover over Joanna's upper body for the moment until her body could be taken to the hold. She would have to be moved later. He and Rajeev set about checking what power, instruments and systems were working, which were damaged and what was irreparable. After a couple of hours of checking and testing they had made some conclusions and calculations. The fusion drive engines and drive system was beyond repair or at least in their view beyond firing up again. There was still some rocket fuel in the boosters although they would need to get vital parts of the system powered up again in order to be able to fire up the rockets. Jack also decided that they should hold the rockets in abeyance for the moment until they had established their position, direction of travel and distance from Mars. They had both roughly guesstimated that they had been probably blown about two hundred thousand miles off course by the shock waves and as far as they could establish they were continuing to travel further away from the Red Planet with each passing minute. At present they had no vital monitors or functioning computer systems and no functioning radio. Worst of all was the perilous state of the oxygen supply, which on their sleeve monitors indicated it was down to about forty nine per cent. This confirmed to Jack that there was a definite leak, which they would have to try to find and plug it. Even then Jack guessed that there was only enough oxygen for the survivors to last three, maybe four weeks. With the fusion drive out of action and the small amount of rocket fuel left there was no way of turning the LII around and getting to Mars in three or four weeks. Jack had to hope that Mars Control would have had the presence of mind to send out a rescue mission. Even if they had, Jack knew that he needed to find a way of getting a communication out on their position. With the LII being so wildly off course any rescue ship from Mars would be looking for a needle in a haystack. Rajeev could see the worry etched on Jack's brow.

"What do you reckon our chances are, Jack?"

"Slim, Raj, pretty damn slim!"

About half an hour later the doctor who had signalled a thumbs up to Jack reached Ewan and Jill to assess them. He was the nominated lead surgeon and he introduced himself to Jill as Doctor Abdul Maqbara. He dealt with Ewan first but reassured Jill that he would check her and her baby in a few minutes. Ewan was still unconscious, however, Dr Maqbara was encouraged by the fact that Ewan's vital signs were still reasonably strong and stable. He told Jill that he intended to move Ewan down to the field hospital for further assessment. The young Saudi doctor explained that they may need to keep Ewan in an induced coma for a day or two until they could determine any brain or internal injuries. Jill blurted out in a flood of tears.

"Please doctor – ah don't want to lose Ewan!"

Dr Maqbara tried to reassure her that Ewan was in no immediate danger and that for her own sake and the sake of her baby she needed to stay as calm as possible. He then began to attend to Jill and looked at her quizzically.

"How did you manage to get onto the Oceanus programme when you are well into a term of pregnancy?"

"It's a long story doctor. Don't ask. Ah wasn't even supposed to be here."

"You shouldn't have been. NASA even decided that under-16 year olds were not robust enough to make this trip never mind a foetus in the womb."

"D-does that m-mean ma baby - ?"

"It doesn't mean anything yet. Stay calm and let's have a look at the little fellow?"

Maqbara gently unzipped her from her spacesuit and thoroughly examined Jill for any signs of external or internal injury. He then concentrated on her womb and cervix and listened for the baby's heartbeat. He then helped Jill back into her spacesuit and looked her straight in the eye.

"Well, Jill, looks like you got through the space storm injury free. You're a very lucky girl."

He looked around at the dead bodies all around strapped in their seats to reaffirm to himself just how lucky Jill and he himself was in surviving the shock wave impacts. It all seemed down to a matter of sheer luck. The doctor guessed that Ewan was probably hit on the head by one of the seats which had ripped free, but that Jill sitting beside him had been totally untouched. Jill impatiently tugged at Maqbara's spacesuit sleeve to bring his concentration back onto her.

"B-but ma baby – is the baby alright?"

"Y'know Jill, it's a small miracle. But your baby seems to be in pretty good shape considering what we all went through. A good strong healthy heartbeat. About four months along I would wager?"

Jill nodded in agreement feeling tears of relief welling up inside her.

"Jill, I would prefer to have been able to conduct an MRI or even just an ultrasound scan, but I'm afraid we don't have that equipment available on board. You'll need to wait until we get you down on Mars for a full assessment. But that doesn't mean that you need to be worried. Meantime, we'll keep a good eye on you and the baby until we get there. Okay?"

"Thanks, doc. Please look after Ewan for me too?"

The doctor smiled and nodded then floated off to get help to move Ewan into the field hospital area. Back in the cockpit Rajeev had worked minor miracles and he had restored some power functions. He had also managed to get some of the computer systems up and running. However, he and Jack had not been able to restore any radio communications and they had still been unable to make any contact with Mars Control. They had now been able to ascertain their position in the solar system with a fair degree of accuracy and also where Mars was in relation to them. They could also tell that their current trajectory was continuing outwards in the solar system away from the Sun and away from Mars. Jack took the decision to try and fire up the rocket engines as he felt that he needed to reverse the Oh LII's direction of travel and start heading back towards Mars. Even if it was going to be painfully slow without the fusion drive. Jack thought, better going towards the Big Red than away from it. They tried firing the retro rockets to bring the ship around and with luck the rockets fired up first time. Jack brought the Oh LII around on a bearing of 170 degrees to bring the ship on a trajectory towards Mars. He then tried to fire up the main rocket engines. Unfortunately, they sort of coughed and died.

"Damn, Raj, it is one step forward and two steps back."

Jack tried again and to his relief this time the rockets fired up. The LII started heading back towards the Red Planet. Jack took the boosters up to full power. The monitors indicated that the ship was only giving him around 5,000 miles an hour. Jack and Rajeev both knew this was far too slow to get the survivors safely to Mars with the dwindling oxygen supplies. The monitors indicated the oxygen level had dropped to 45 per cent. Jack ordered Rajeev to go and investigate the source or sources of the leaking oxygen and see if anything could be done to plug the gaps and minimise the losses. Rajeev floated out of the cockpit on his mission and Jack turned his attention back to attempting to restore communications. Jack worked furiously through the systems and checklists for about forty minutes but he felt he was getting nowhere. Then suddenly he had a bit of a brainwave. He fiddled around with a few programmes and then suddenly a message popped up on his communications monitor.

LOCATOR BEACON ACTIVE. PRESS F13 TO ACTIVATE DISTRESS SIGNAL.

Hallelujah, Jack thought, it is better than nothing. Jack pressed the F13 button and activated the locator beacon distress signal and it immediately began sending out a slow PING. He was able to play around with the ping sequencing and this allowed him to send out a bespoke ping which made him smile wryly to himself. All he could do now was to keep heading slowly towards Mars and hope that someone out there in that direction was picking up his distress signal.

*

<u>Marsdate: 14:40 Tuesday May 30, 2084 CBT</u>

The Control Director at Mars Control down in Capitol Base had been ranting and raving over the radio waves at Xi Xhu Pan for the last few minutes. The MNET system had been fully restored and radio communication was now crystal clear. Xi Xhu was adamant that he thought that he had had been given full authority by the Shift Controller to conduct a forty eight hour search for Jack Crossan's missing Oceanus. The Director insisted that he had not been given any such instruction and Xi Xhu stated that he must have misunderstood as a result of the comms glitches two days ago. The Director ordered Xi Xhu to turn his ship around immediately and head back for Mars orbit. The Director's view was that he had already lost the Oh LII and he was not about to lose the Oh Two on his watch as well. Xi Xhu pleaded over his radio.

"Oh-Two to Mars Control. Only have about four hours left of the forty eight. Request permission to complete search then return Mars. Over."

As they waited in radio silence in the cockpit of the Oh Two for the Director's answer an unusual sound suddenly came through their comms link. Ping-ping-ping-PING-PING-PING-ping-ping-ping.

Xi Xhu looked at his co-pilot Verne Andriessen and both their jaws dropped simultaneously. The Director's voice cut through their shocked expressions.

"Mars Control to Oh-Two. Request denied. Orders are to return to Mars immediately. Repeat immediately! Confirm. Over."

Xi Xhu and Verne ignored Mars Control for the present as the signal came through again, loud and clear. Ping-ping-ping-PING-PING-PING-ping-ping-ping.

"That must be the Ell-Eye-Eye, Xi! But what kinda signal is that?"

"It's an old 20th century distress signal. Morse code. SOS. Save our Souls. My God, Verne, they're still alive!"

Xi Xhu replied in the negative to the Control Director about returning to Mars and that they had now picked up a distress signal from the Oh LII. Mars Control were soon able to confirm that they too were receiving the locator beacon ping. Xi Xhu and Mars Control did not take too long to triangulate the LII's position, which was worryingly further out than they would have hoped for. They could also quickly compute that the LII was travelling back towards Xi Xhu and Mars but it would take about twenty six days to reach them. Xi Xhu requested authority to embark on the rescue mission and after a few moments left hanging in anticipation, the Control Director ordered him to proceed post haste to intercept with the distressed Oh LII. Xi Xhu took the fusion drive engines up to the max, but he still wondered if it would be enough. Hang on, Jack, hang on, buddy.

CHAPTER 26

<u>Marsdate: 23:20 Monday June 26, 2084 CBT</u>

Twenty six days had now passed since Jack managed to send out the locator beacon distress signal from the Oh LII and unfortunately the ship had not heard a peep or come into contact with any rescue mission from Mars. Jack was also well aware that he was unlikely to hear anything from Mars Control. The Oh LII had no viable incoming communications functioning. Only the outgoing ping. The Oh LII had only managed to sail just over three and a half million miles towards the Red Planet in that time. Jack reckoned they were still at least seven million miles away from their goal and safe haven. Rajeev had identified some of the oxygen leaks and a small engineering team under his command had been cobbled together to try and minimise the leakages. The team was only partially successful and oxygen supplies were now sitting dangerously at just over three per cent and the atmospheric levels on the cockpit monitors were flashing up 'CRITICAL'. Even with strict rationing Jack and Rajeev knew the oxygen would run out in less than a day. In fact, Jack had been unable to allow the doctors to give any additional or enriched oxygen supplies to the injured patients in the field hospital. Partly as a result of that decision there had been seven more deaths in the last three weeks. Jack felt awful, however, Dr Maqbara assured him that the deaths would have inevitably occurred anyway. It felt to Jack that his main duty these last three weeks had been on conducting the funerals of nearly one hundred and sixty of his passengers. The loss of so many burdened Jack deeply. As each vacuum-sealed wrapped body was jettisoned out into space it felt like a dagger in the heart to Jack. Rajeev could see that everything was really taking its toll on his commander. Rajeev had volunteered to take on the duty of conducting half of the funerals but Jack had barked back at him that as Space Commander it was his solemn duty to perform them. Rajeev backed off. Jack knew within himself that he was beginning to crack under the strain but he felt that he must try to protect Rajeev from the stress of this most awful duty. If Jack was to lose the plot he felt that he needed his co-pilot to be in a better place than he was mentally at present. The only good news story in the last three weeks was that Dr Maqbara had brought Ewan Sinclair out of the medically induced coma after seven days of unconsciousness. Ewan had been slowly responding well to treatment. He was still confined to bed or sometimes allowed to sit in a seat. Ewan's his legs were temporarily paralysed. Gradually he was showing signs of feeling returning to his lower limbs. Ewan's speech was slurred and his thought processes were impaired, but again as each day had passed he showed signs of improvement. Maqbara had diagnosed a likely minor blood clot on Ewan's brain, although without a CAT or MRI scanner he could not be conclusive. His prognosis was that Ewan should make a full recovery given time and healing. Jill was now just short of five months pregnant and again the doctors were happy that the baby was still developing normally. The doctors did not want to risk an amniocentesis test in space as it was an unknown or unrecorded procedure. There had never been a pregnancy in space before. However, blood tests did not show up any abnormalities. The doctors were fairly certain that her baby did not have Downs Syndrome or the homozygosis which had caused Jill to terminate Khan al Ahmed's baby. Jill and Ewan were elated at the news.

"Let's get married Ewan – now."

Jill felt the need to marry Ewan imminently. Jack Crossan had not spelled out to the passengers the critical situation that the ship was currently in. However, Jill's newshound nose had been able to sniff out that the oxygen supply was now at dangerously low levels and ultimately all on board the Oh LII might not survive to see Mars. She did not let on to Ewan that they were in danger as she did not want to cause any set back to his recovery. Ewan slurred his loving response.

"Yes – let's – get - married, Jill. Ah - love you - so - much."

Ewan and Jill were married at noon on Thursday 22 June 2084 on board the spaceship Oceanus LII. The wedding was legally performed by Space Commander Jack Crossan. All the passengers were invited to celebrate the wedding with the happy couple, apart from those patients still in the field hospital, tended by one doctor and one nurse. Now four days after the wedding Jack and Rajeev sat idly in the cockpit. There was nothing more that could be done to speed up the Oh LII or repair any of her crippled systems. In fact, Jack had ordered everyone on board not to conduct anything of a strenuous nature in order to conserve every last ounce of oxygen. Jack looked at the 'CRITICAL' message continually flashing on his monitor and thought that things were beginning to look futile for everybody on board. Rajeev seemed to be reading Jack's thoughts.

"What do you reckon Jack? It's not looking too good?"

"Ya know what ah'd like to do, Raj?"

"No, but I'm not sure I'm going to like it."

"Ah'd like to turn my ship around an' just head for home."

"But Jack, we are heading for home. Mars *is* home now!"

"Nah, Raj, Mars will never be a real home to me. Earth is ma home. Ah wanna go back to ma boys an' ma lovely Peggy Sue –"

Rajeev Subhinder was now getting increasingly concerned about Jack's state of mind. He thought that the stress and lack of oxygen was beginning to play tricks with Jack and Raj was not quite sure how to deal with it. So the two of them fell back into silence. The Oh LII slipped on silently through space inching ever so slowly towards Mars, with just the intermittent ping-ping of the locator beacon breaking the silence. Too slowly to save them all. Jack seemed to have slipped into a sort of trance and the worry of it made Rajeev find it difficult to concentrate. He looked across at Jack who seemed to have fallen into a deep sleep. Rajeev's eyes also started to feel heavy and he urged himself not to fall asleep, but he could not help himself. He slipped into unconsciousness.

Dong-dong-dong-DONG-DONG-DONG-dong-dong-dong.

Rajeev's eyes half opened but they rolled shut again.

Dong-dong-dong-DONG-DONG-DONG-dong-dong-dong.

This time Rajeev came to with the metallic knock-knocking ringing in his head and he scanned his functioning monitors for any developing fault message. He shouted across to Jack to try and waken him.

"Jack! Jack! I think we might have something going wrong, JACK!"

Slowly Jack started to come around.

"Whassup?"

"We've developed some sort of a knock. Maybe the ship's starting to break up?"

Dong-dong-dong-DONG-DONG-DONG-dong-dong-dong.

Jack's head shot bolt upright and he started to unstrap himself from his seat.

"That's not a knock inside the ship, Raj. That's a knock **outside** the ship. It's SOS – my God, Raj, there's someone out there!"

Jack craned his neck to peer out the small porthole on his side of the cockpit and then he turned around and smiled broadly at Raj.

"Fuck me, Raj, if the Oh Two isn't sittin' on our starboard bow."

An astronaut outside with a jetpack on and attached to a long white umbilical cable had hauled himself around to Jack's porthole and he tapped the SOS on the thick glass. Jack and Rajeev waved wildly back to indicate that they had seen him. Raj floated over and began hugging Jack with relief.

"HALLELUJAH! We're saved!"

Jack gave the thumbs up to the astronaut and then quickly announced to the passengers that a rescue ship had arrived just in the nick of time. Raj smiled broadly at Jack as they listened to the raucous cheering and rapturous applause coming from the passenger cabin. The relief on board was palpable, although Raj thought that he could still detect a glimpse of sadness in the back of Jack's eyes. Out in the passenger cabin Jill hugged Ewan and swore that she loved him to bits.

"Oh, Ewan, ah love you - ah love you - ah love you!"

Ewan joked that the feeling in his foot must be getting better as Jill seemed to be standing on it. Jill joked back that it must be something else because how could Ewan feel her weight on his foot in zero gravity. They both laughed and cried at the same time with utter relief. Jack floated past them on the way to the main air lock and he gave them both a thumbs up which they gladly reciprocated. Ten minutes later Jack returned through the passenger cabin with the spacewalking astronaut, who turned out to be the Oh Two's co-pilot Verne Andriessen. Verne and Jack were mobbed by cheering passengers floating around them, welcoming them like returning heroes. Jack had to firmly remind everyone that the oxygen supply was critically low and that at present everyone needed to conserve their energies. Jack and Verne joined Rajeev in the cockpit and after much back slapping they sat down to listen to Verne's account of the tale of Xi Xhu Pan ignoring orders from Mars Control to give up the search. Then Verne related that they had received Jack's SOS just as they were about to be forced back to Mars. Jack nodded sagely.

"Ma ole pal Xi Xhu. Ah trained him well."

Jack detailed that it was critical that they started transferring the passengers as soon as possible to the empty Oh Two as there was now only two per cent oxygen left on the Oh LII. Verne outlined that the two ships were cruising parallel to each other at five thousand miles an hour on the same course for Mars, sitting four hundred metres apart. Xi Xhu was arranging a space tender on the Oh Two to shuttle between the two ships and it could carry twenty five passengers on each trip. The whole transfer would take a good few hours to complete, which should leave more than enough oxygen on the Oh LII in order to complete the rescue mission. Verne would stay on board the Oh LII to co-ordinate the transfer. Once they had finished discussing the plan in detail Jack announced to the passengers to get fully suited up for their imminent transfer to Xi Xhu's ship. Initially, the able-bodied women would be transferred in batches of twenty five, then the men would follow and finally the injured, the medical staff and crew members would be last to transfer. Rajeev was assigned to select the groups for transfer. Jack would continue to maintain the ship on a parallel course with the Oh Two and Verne would organise the transfers through the air lock on to the space tender. Jack looked purposefully at Raj and Verne.

"Okay, let's get the job done."

About half an hour later Jill was selected to go in the first group of women on the space tender which had docked safely and was connected to the main air lock. She protested to Rajeev that she wanted to transfer with Ewan who would be in the last group of injured passengers. However, Ewan with his quiet Highland manner insisted that his new wife and baby must go on without him and Jill tearfully relented. Jack also assured her that Ewan would soon be joining her. Reluctantly Jill disappeared through the air lock and stepped onto the small cramped space tender. Once Raj and Verne had initiated the transfer process the space tender was able to do a round trip in about fifteen minutes. In about three and a half hours most of the passengers had been safely transferred. Verne had switched back to steer the Oh Two and Xi Xhu had come over to oversee the last transfer from Jack's ship. When Xi Xhu had stepped on board he and Jack hugged each other like long lost brothers. Jack could not thank him enough for saving his ship and especially his passengers.

"You would've done the same for me, Jack Crossan!"

The final transfer would consist of about ten of the most seriously injured passengers, including Ewan. Followed by Dr Maqbara, three nurses, four of the remaining cabin crew, Rajeev, Xi Xhu and lastly Jack. As Ewan was passed carefully through to the space tender Jack offered him a handshake.

"You look after Jill for me, Ewan. You've a great wife there."

Ewan looked at Jack quizzically as he entered the air lock.

"Hey – Jack – you can – help me – look after – Jill too. See you – in few minutes?"

"Yeah, yeah, sure Ewan."

When Ewan was placed safely into his seat in the space tender a strange thought occurred to him. Ewan slowly thought back to the night of the friends' End of Days last supper at Lex Kosloff's house in Robindale Drive in Houston. A dawning thought struck him about something that Jack had said. Jack had said he would rather stay on 3R with his two boys. An involuntary tear ran down Ewan's cheek. As the last of the injured patients were being transferred on board the space tender Dr Maqbara quietly pulled Jack aside. One of the injured patients had taken a turn for the worse with certain fatally rupturing internal injuries. Maqbara told Jack that the man was unlikely to survive more than an hour or so and certainly not the four week trip to Mars. The dying man had asked to speak to Jack. Jack went over to the field hospital area where the young man, obviously in agonising pain, still lay strapped on a bed.

"Hey there young fella – an' what's your name?"

"Jorge Mendoza, Commander –"

"Jorge, just call me Jack. So ya wanted to speak to me, Jorge?"

Jorge squirmed and grimaced in pain and a trickle of blood came out the side of his mouth, which Dr Maqbara wiped clean.

"Y-yeah, Jack. You see - I'm not going to – to make it – to Mars –"

"Whoa there Jorge, don't talk like that. Sure ya are – issat right doc?"

Maqbara surreptitiously shook his head almost imperceptibly from side to side to indicate that it was in the negative. Jorge carried on speaking through the pain barrier.

"No need - to kid me, Jack – I know – I'm – dying. I – want to – stay here – and – you just – send me – home – Havana –"

Maqbara shrugged his shoulders at Jack. Xi Xhu was floating across towards the air lock gesticulating his hand in a circular motion to indicate that it was time to hurry things up. Jack indicated silently for the doctor to go on ahead. After Maqbara reluctantly moved off towards Xi Xhu and the air lock, Jack turned his attention back to Jorge. Jorge was fading fast.

"Jack – promise – me – send – home –"

"Ah promise you, Jorge, you'll see the sun rise on Havana again."

Jorge smiled weakly and lapsed into unconsciousness. Jack stood for a moment with a great lump in his throat. A great wave of fear and anxiety swept over him. He turned and floated slowly over to Xi Xhu who was furiously beckoning Jack to get a move on.

"C'mon, Jack, let's go. We can't waste any more time."

"Poor guy over there – he ain't got long to go, Xi."

"Yeah, the doc told me. You going to leave him here on the Ell-Eye-Eye?"

Jack stood silent for a moment, head slightly bowed in thought.

"Jack?"

"Ah'm not goin' with you Xi. Ah'm takin' Jorge back –"

"Back? Back where, Jack? There is no back!"

"Back to Earth, Xi, that's where. Ah've just realised that Jorge an' me, we want the same thing in a way. He wants to go back to Havana an' ah want to go back to ma boys an' – an' ma Peggy Sue."

"Jack, you're talking crazy talk. There is no Earth. You don't even have enough oxygen or fuel to get you there and back safely to Mars."

"Ah know that Xi. But me an' poor Jorge over there – we are just gonna point ourselves at that gas cloud back there an' we'll just take what we find. That's the way it's gotta be, Xi."

"But – Jack -?"

"Time for you to get your butt off ma ship, ole buddy. You've got the future of mankind to think of. You need to get your passengers back to Mars or you've wasted your time comin' out to save them. So go on – get the hell outta here!"

The two old friends just stared into each other's moistening eyes and then they hugged each other tightly for the last time. Jack unzipped his breast pocket and took something out. Jack handed Xi Xhu the Medal of Honor which had been awarded to Commander Bethan Jones saying that he had promised her father it would make it to Mars. Xi Xhu Pan took the medal and then he passed on through the air lock, which Jack engaged in the locked position. A moment later he felt his Oh LII rock slightly as the little space tender pushed gently away towards the Oh Two for the last time. He walked back over to Jorge on the hospital bed. Poor Jorge was dead. Jack wept silently over the young dead Cuban. He wept for the eight billion humans wiped out in an instant by what in cosmic terms was an insignificant mass of rock and ice - Schenkler HMM2. He pulled himself together and went back into the cockpit and strapped himself into his pilot's seat. He squinted a look out of the porthole. Jack watched the Oh Two slowly boost up its fusion drive and begin to pull away rapidly from his own battered ship. He could tell from his long experience as an astronaut the point at which Xi Xhu had deemed to be safely away from the Oh LII. Jack could see the fusion drive power up to the maximum. The Oh Two zoomed away from him towards Mars at a speed in excess of around twelve thousand miles per hour. He saluted and wished them bon voyage. Jack stared at the glow of the engines for quite some time until the Oh Two disappeared into the black void of space.

EPILOGUE

Jack had lost track of time, although he was aware that a few days had certainly passed by. After the Oh Two had disappeared out of sight he had managed to use the retro rockets and turn the Oh LII on a bearing for what was once his beloved Planet Earth. There was just about enough rocket fuel left in the tanks to boost up to a fraction under four thousand miles per hour. He burned the remaining rocket fuel within a few hours and for days the ship had just been freefalling through space on a trajectory towards the Earth gas cloud, but Jack was more hopeful than expectant that the ship would remain on the correct course. Anyway, he thought, he would not be around to see it. The oxygen indicator was now sitting virtually on the empty mark and he knew that it would not be long before he and Jorge would be making the same final journey. His breathing was getting shallower and he was gulping hard to find good breathable air. His thoughts were becoming wilder and more frantic as he was being slowly starved of the life giving oxygen.

"Well, Mother Earth, ah wonder what you look like now? Just a swirling mass of gas an' molten debris. Yeah, but to Jorge an' me you're still home."

Jack was never actually going to see the gas cloud. There were no telescopes or satellites left to transmit any images from the destroyed E2MSN within what had been the blast zone perimeter. However, he began to imagine wild shapes in his mind as if he was looking through a set of psychologist's Rorshach inkblot test cards. His imaginings kept drawing him back to an old familiar shape and which he kept trying to shake out of his befuddled brain. Try as he might the shape became more and more vivid and fixed until he felt that he had become reconciled to this shape. In his mind's eye he was certain that this was *indeed* the shape of the gas cloud.

"Mighta known, Earth, that you would be the man with the gun."

All of a sudden Jack felt a calmness within himself. He no longer feared the old vision from his childhood. In fact, he embraced it almost joyfully. Jack laughed a little too high-pitched, a little bit too crazily. He knew it was not long now. He could see Milner and Jack Junior running towards him through his lush ripening wheat field back on the Crossan ranch in Lexington, Virginia. The boys were waving and laughing and beckoning for Jack to join them. Peggy Sue was running towards him too. She was young again, like when they first met, so beautiful and so full of love for him. Peggy Sue was calling to Jack and he strained hard to hear her last lovely words. He stretched out his arms to embrace the one true love of his life. Peggy Sue called out.

"We'll meet again in the sweet bye and bye!"

The Oh LII glided silently towards the newly formed gas cloud within the inner solar system and beyond the cloud shone the beautiful bright shining Sun.